Praise for Linda Winfree's *Fall Into Me*

"'Hearts of the South' continues to be a series I look forward to, and one I can recommend without reservation... For this reader, *Fall Into Me* is a solid Grade A."

~ *The Good, The Bad, the Unread*

"...a five star masterpiece...the reader is sucked in and not released until the very last page...I can't wait to read more of the "Hearts of the South" series."

~ *Ecataromance*

"...a book I could just not put down..."

~ *The Romance Studio*

Look for these titles by
Linda Winfree

Now Available:

What Mattered Most
Uncovered

Hearts of the South Series
Truth and Consequences (Book 1)
His Ordinary Life (Book 2)
Hold On to Me (Book 3)
Anything But Mine (Book 4)
Memories of Us (Book 5)
Hearts Awakened (Book 6)
Fall Into Me (Book 7)
Facing It (Book 8)

Fall Into Me

Linda Winfree

A Samhain Publishing, Ltd. publication.

Samhain Publishing, Ltd.
577 Mulberry Street, Suite 1520
Macon, GA 31201
www.samhainpublishing.com

Fall Into Me

Print ISBN: 978-1-60504-432-3
Digital ISBN: 978-1-60504-366-1

Editing by Anne Scott
Cover by Anne Cain

First Samhain Publishing, Ltd. electronic publication: January 2009
First Samhain Publishing, Ltd. print publication: November 2009

Dedication

For Connie, because math, music, and their connection are cool. Without you, Troy Lee wouldn't be such a math genius. Thank you for being so willing to check my numbers.

Special acknowledgement to Jamie Sullivan of the Georgia State Patrol for providing me with the proper formulas for accident reconstruction.

Finally, much thanks to Anne for being willing to take a chance on a book I hadn't finished yet and for her infinite patience with my being timeline-challenged.

Chapter One

She'd stepped into *Steel Magnolias* hell.

Trust her sister Hope to have scheduled her for a cut and color on the same afternoon their mama was getting the ladies' mission circle ready for Wednesday-night church. The caustic odor of perm lotion hanging in the busy salon attached to her parents' home assaulted Angel's nose. She set her bag on the shelf by the door and waved at her sister before crossing to plop a kiss on her mother's cheek.

"Hey, Mama."

Her mother landed an answering kiss somewhere in the vicinity of Angel's cheek but never paused in backcombing Ella Sutter's silver curls. "Hey, baby."

"Miss Maureen, Miss Ella." Pasting on her best pageant smile, Angel nodded at the ladies, each occupying one of the beauty stations. Their sister Lenora sat under the dryer and Angel gave her a wave.

Bestowing her own sister with a pointed look, she picked up a magazine and settled onto the loveseat under the picture window. Over her shoulder, Hope stuck out her tongue. Taking the high road, Angel brushed aside the leggy vine hanging in the window and insisting on attacking her. No question where her own green thumb came from—the salon overflowed with vigorous plants in all varieties, sharing space with shampoos, hairstyle books and photos of Hope's girls at various ages.

"How have you been, Angel?"

Angel stilled, the tapping of her turquoise cowboy boot coming to a complete halt. Miss Maureen met Angel's eyes in the mirror. Angel swallowed a groan. Like she hadn't known that one was coming. She'd managed to avoid being in here on a Wednesday afternoon since Jim's defection, just so she wouldn't have to face the old biddy's questions. Maureen watched her with an avid gaze, the salon's bright lights glinting off her large gold knot earrings and matching necklace.

"I'm fine, Miss Maureen, thanks for asking."

"Are you still running that bar?" Maureen's voice dropped to a shocked whisper on the last word and Hope rolled her eyes, working the pick through Maureen's thick hair.

"The Cue Club? Yes, ma'am, I am." Angel leaned forward with her best devilish wink. "But I'm thinking of changing the name to the Den of Iniquity and getting some exotic dancers. You know, strippers."

Miss Maureen's eyes widened, pencil-thin brows nearly reaching the salt and pepper curls falling onto her forehead.

"She's just teasing, Maureen." Mama waved a dismissive hand.

Lifting her magazine again, Angel caught Lenora's brown gaze and the glint of appreciative laughter there. Hard to believe the two women were sisters, but people probably said the same thing about her and Hope. Her sister, younger by a year, had never done anything to get herself on the gossip radar. Angel stayed there enough she probably had her own no-fly zone, closed to other transgressors.

"I guess you were surprised by Jimmy's getting married like that." The eagerness was back in Maureen's voice.

Angel tried to act like the question hadn't punched her in the chest. Darn it, she was supposed to be over that. Aware of her mama's sudden attention, she shook her head, her best "who cares" laugh tinkling through the ammonia-laden air. "Yes, ma'am, I was, but he's so happy I can't hold it against him. She's a real sweet girl too, and smart. She handles my accounts down at the bank."

Again, she picked up a hint of admiration in Lenora's gaze. Hope gave her a silent thumbs-up behind the chair. Angel subsided into her magazine. She hadn't suffered through four years of Mrs. Louella Hatcher's drama classes for nothing, then. She'd managed to control her voice and sound normal, almost cheerful. Let Miss Maureen take *that* to prayer meeting.

Hope made short work of finishing Miss Maureen's curls. She layered on a protective shield of hairspray and spun the avocado monstrosity of a chair around. "All right, Miss

Maureen, you're done. Angel, hop in the chair while I check Miss Lenora for Mama."

While Hope turned off the dryer and lifted the helmet, Angel settled in the seat and released the clip holding her mass of blonde hair, letting it fall past her shoulders. She fingered the ends. Maybe she should listen to Hope and lose a couple of inches.

Hope returned and ran a brush through Angel's hair, pulling harder than strictly necessary. "I wish you'd let me give you a darker blonde. That new Sunlit Wheat would be gorgeous on you. This is too light."

Angel blew out a breath. They had this conversation every six weeks when she had her ends trimmed and roots touched up. What would it hurt to entertain her sister's enthusiasm, just a little? "Show me the color."

Hope gave a little squeal of delight, bouncing on her toes and clapping silently. "You'll love it."

She handed Angel the color card. Angel studied the sandy tone then gave her California bleached blonde a critical stare. The darker blonde was a pretty color, a few shades lighter than her natural dark, dark almost-brown blonde.

Hope sifted her fingers through Angel's hair. "It would be really pretty with some highlights and a shorter, layered cut. Something up to date, a little more sophisticated."

They had this discussion every six weeks or so as well and Hope tried to convince her to give up the one-length cut with big bangs, the style Angel had kept because Jim had always liked it.

She touched the dry ends once more. What did it matter what Jim liked any longer? The years she'd spent wearing his engagement ring intermittently meant nothing, especially since he'd brought a new wife home from Biloxi little more than three weeks ago.

Rat bastard.

Maybe she should thank him. His sudden switch in affections had pushed her out of her routine, made her examine other possibilities in her life, in other men, like what could come from her on-again, off-again flirtation with Cookie.

She shivered in remembered pleasure. She liked him, always had, liked his sense of humor beneath the gruff exterior, liked the quiet way he seemed to take in everything around him.

She wasn't crazy about his habit of not returning phone calls, but she'd had extensive experience with that during her long on-off relationship with Jim. She absolutely loved the way he made her feel physically—the man was hell on wheels in bed. Besides, he was busy, she was busy, so if they hadn't reconnected yet, no big deal. She had no doubt they would, soon.

"What do you say, Angel? Let me give you a brand-new look."

Angel narrowed her eyes at her reflection. A fresh look. Wonder what Cookie might think of that? She could swing by the sheriff's department before she opened the bar, see him in person.

"Angel?"

"I'm thinking. Give me a minute." Sheesh, Hope was pushy when she got on a tear about something.

"Ella tells me Tori has a new beau," Maureen tittered.

A pleased smile tipped the corners of Lenora's mouth. "She does. I couldn't be happier. Mark's a good man."

Angel's mama gave Ella's curls a final fluff and reached for the hairspray. "Mark Hatcher?"

"No." Lenora shook her head. "Mark Cook."

Mark Cook? A too-familiar icy shock slithered through Angel's veins, the same sensation she'd experienced when Jim appeared on her doorstop and stammered through his explanation about returning from a week-long gambling expedition with a new wife and needing Angel to return the diamond ring she'd worn erratically since their early twenties.

Ah, darn it, not again. Surely not.

In response to Maureen's and Mama's questions, Lenora chattered about her daughter's blooming relationship with sheriff's investigator Mark Cook. The same Mark Cook Angel had finally gone to bed with not quite three weeks before, the one she'd pinned her brand-new hopes on.

She released a breath she hadn't known she was holding and met her sister's sympathetic gaze in the mirror. She let go of her hair. "Do what you want with it."

An hour later, her new blonde color and highlights were done. The ladies had departed and Mama had disappeared into the main part of the house to start supper as Daddy would soon be ambling in from a long day at the factory. Angel was glad for the silence. She felt...raw. Stupid. Naïve.

She hurt.

Hope removed the damp towel from beneath the neckline of the plastic cape Angel wore. Angel squinted at the mirror, rubbing a fingertip over her forehead. It had to be there, even if she couldn't see it.

"What are you doing?" Indulgent laughter vibrated in Hope's voice, mingling with lingering concern.

"Looking for the invisible tattoo."

Hope sprayed water over Angel's hair. "What?"

"You know, the one only men can see that says 'Brainless bimbo, use as directed'."

Hope popped her arm and reached for the scissors. "Stop that."

"What is wrong with me, Hope?" She rubbed at the slight sting left by her sister's love pat. The tangible hurt was preferable to the emotional one holding her chest in a death grip.

"There's nothing wrong with you, Angel. It's your approach. Daddy's old saying about why buy the cow if you can get milk for free is true." Hope waggled her ring finger, thin wedding band gleaming.

Angel pushed her sister's hand away. "I don't necessarily need one of those. But I'd like to be something more than the wrong guy's good-enough-to-fuck."

"Oh, Angel." Hope wrapped her arms around Angel's shoulders and squeezed. "I'm sorry, honey."

"Don't be sorry." Angel shrugged away from the easy embrace. "Just give me a cut that'll make me brand new."

ꟽ

She was late. Angel popped another MickyD's fry in her mouth and pressed harder on the accelerator. If the drive-through line hadn't been so long...but darn it, she'd needed a dose of hot, crispy therapy after the day's revelation. She reached down to turn up the radio, letting Carrie Underwood blast through the small interior. She also needed a dose of loud music with attitude.

She swooped around the curve and noticed too late the

sheriff's unit parked under a pecan tree off to the right. The white car pulled out behind her and blue lights flared, headlights sparking.

Damn, damn, *damn*.

She didn't need this, not today.

Slowing, she pulled to the side of the road, the low-slung Mustang bouncing a little over the rutted shoulder. The patrol car slid to a stop behind her.

A tall familiar figure unfolded from the car and pique twisted through her. She killed her engine and pushed the door open. Arms crossed over her chest, she met the deputy at the rear of her vehicle.

"Anyone ever mention you drive too fast?" His rich voice rumbled over her, the timbre and rhythm of it hinting at the raw power he could belt into a microphone.

"Just write me a ticket, Troy Lee. I'm not in the mood to go through the whole 'Do you know why I stopped you?' scenario."

"Hey, you cut your hair. I like it." A wide grin creased his handsome face and crinkled the tanned skin around his vivid blue eyes, fringed by long dark lashes she knew most women would kill for. Good thing he had a ruggedly square jaw or he'd be too pretty.

She rested her elbow on her hip and waved a hand. "Did you not hear me? I'm not in the mood. So just get out your little ticket book and start writing."

With one finger, he tipped the rim of his campaign hat up. "Actually, I wanted to see if you had a couple of Saturday nights open on the club's band schedule."

Tension gathered in a knot at the base of her neck. "Then stop by the bar when you get off duty and check. I'm late."

He hooked his thumbs in his gun belt. "Which would explain why you were going seventy-two in a fifty-five."

Her French fries were getting cold and the clock was ticking. And again, there was that not-in-the-mood angle. "Troy Lee."

His easy smile reappeared. "Okay, okay. I'll check in later. But slow down. Better to get there late than not get there at all."

Jesus help her, he sounded like her daddy. Another engine hummed in the distance and moments later a steel-silver unmarked unit appeared around the curve and slowed to a stop behind Troy Lee's unit.

He cast one glance at the car and tensed. "Shit."

Her thought exactly. She knew that car, knew who the driver would be—the last man she wanted to see. Sure enough, the driver's door swung open and Mark Cook emerged. Tick Calvert climbed from the passenger seat with slow, cautious movements.

She wouldn't have thought it possible, but Troy Lee's entire body went even tighter. "Wonder what I did wrong now?"

"Am I free to go?" Angel rubbed at her arms and tapped a toe against the grass as the two men approached. Darn it, the wind was cold against her bare legs and she really didn't want to stand here and indulge in a "hey, how are you" conversation with Mark Cook, aka Rat Bastard #2. No surprise he hadn't returned her calls, if he'd been busy getting involved with Tori Calvert.

Wonder if that had been before or after they'd run into Tori the night of that single date? Oh, God. Her face burned and she somehow kept from pressing her palms to her cheeks. She'd been the one to bring Tori up that night, right after... Darn it, he could have said something then, if he'd not been interested in anything further than a roll in the sheets.

She sighed. Conferring rat-bastard status on him wasn't fair. Flirting with her forever, taking her out once for a hamburger and following that with pretty damn good sex didn't exactly constitute swearing an undying commitment. He could, however, have returned one of five flippin' phone calls and told her he was seeing someone else now.

Obviously, she didn't rate common courtesy from either of the men who'd found someone better. Good heavens, she needed a French fry.

Tick glanced through the driver's side window as they passed Troy Lee's car and his eyebrows lifted. He tagged Cookie's chest and pointed at something on the dash. Troy Lee closed his eyes on a muttered oath.

"Troy Lee." She really wanted to get out of here. There'd be people standing in the parking lot, her fries would be a cold, gummy mess and then there was the whole never-wanting-to-look-Cookie-in-the-eye-again thing. "I asked if I could go."

His lashes snapped up and color touched his prominent cheekbones. "Yeah."

He flipped open his ticket book, scribbled across the top page and tore a sheet free. Incredulity shot through her. He was writing her a ticket. Damn it. Dumped via the gossip grapevine and now a speeding ticket. Could it get any worse?

"Here." He extended the yellow copy in her direction. She fixed him with her best glare, the one that could shut down a brewing bar scuffle in less than two seconds, and took it without snatching or crumpling. "And slow down. I mean it."

"Thanks." She spun away as Tick and Cookie reached them, but not before noting that Cookie looked everywhere but at her. Even his obvious discomfort didn't lighten the squeezing around her heart or the constriction at her throat. She slung the car door open and sank behind the wheel. She fired the engine and shifted into gear, glancing in the rearview to see if the road was clear. In doing so, she caught a perfect glimpse of Cookie's face. Her eyes burned and she blinked hard. Oh hell, no. She wasn't going to cry over him, any more than she'd let herself cry over Jim and those ruined hopes.

She eased onto the road at a sedate speed. As of today, she was brand new. No more speeding. No more pinning her hopes on any man. She lifted a fry and bit into it, cringing at the soggy texture.

And definitely no more cold fries.

"Let me see that." As Angel's Mustang purred away, Calvert indicated the ticket book and Troy Lee passed over the stainless steel cover. He straightened his shoulders and waited, a blend of anger and anxiety churning low in his gut, sending a wave of heartburn into his chest.

Calvert raised his eyes, disbelief all over his features. "Seventeen over the limit and you wrote her a warning?"

Troy Lee lifted his hands. How to explain he'd never had any intention of writing Angel a ticket? Stopping her had been primarily a way to slow her down and secondarily an opportunity just to see her, with the excuse of checking on band slots at the Cue Club. Once he'd glimpsed the hurt tension on her face, no way was he writing a ticket. The woman seriously looked like she'd lost her last friend in the world. He wasn't used to witnessing that expression on Angel Henderson, natural-born optimist.

Calvert was still giving him the look. Troy Lee shrugged.

"She was...having a bad day."

Wrong thing to say. He knew it as soon as the words left his mouth and aggravated disgust bloomed on Calvert's face. Troy Lee bristled under that too-familiar look. Damn it, he wrote more tickets than any deputy in the county. Hell, he probably wrote more tickets than any state trooper who worked Chandler County. So what if he'd let Angel off with a warning?

"At least you didn't trade her out for it." Calvert snapped the book closed and shoved it back at him.

This time the anger sent a flood of heat up his nape and into his face. He bit down hard on the inside of his cheek. Opening his mouth always seemed to make things worse with Calvert. He'd damn well keep any comment to himself. God knew he was tired of the "at least" statements.

He balanced the metal book on his palm and hooked his other thumb in his belt, forcing a relaxed posture. "So were you looking for me?"

"Yeah." The way Calvert bit off the single syllable didn't bode well. Troy Lee cast about for anything he'd done recently that would fall under the umbrella of Calvert's definition of dumbass.

Nothing. He had nothing. The last few weeks had gone well, probably because Calvert, out on sick leave, hadn't been around to push him into the cycle of being nervous, trying too hard and then fucking up accordingly.

So what was he in deep shit for now?

He sighed. "What did I do?"

Again, the wrong thing to say or maybe the way he said it came off wrong. Regardless, the wall of disapproval grew at least another foot. He glanced sideways at Cookie, who'd been watching the interplay with folded arms and a bored expression. Now, the investigator shook his head, a pained grimace twisting his brow.

Calvert rested his hands at his waist and leaned forward slightly, emanating the air of a pissed-off drill sergeant. "Let me tell you about the phone call I just fielded from Bubba Bostick. You know, the cochairman of the county commission."

Oh, shit. Shitshitshit. This was going to be about that ticket he'd written...damn. He braced himself, chewing the inside of his cheek again. He wouldn't launch into an explanation that would only set Calvert off further.

Would. Not.

Blood flowed against his tongue. The sizzling knot of heartburn moved higher in his chest.

"Your little method for coding your tickets?" Calvert circled a finger over his palm. "Seems Judge Barlow shared that information with Mr. Bostick. It also seems you wrote Mr. Bostick's son a couple of tickets last week and he's taking offense to how you coded his kid."

Yeah? Well, Troy Lee had taken offense to the little prick's attitude.

With Calvert's color high, he'd keep that observation to himself. Actually, even flushed with annoyance, Calvert was still pretty pale. Was it too much to hope that the guy would have sudden complications from his surgery and have to go home for a few more weeks?

Or maybe a year.

"Troy Lee?" Cookie's quiet voice broke between them. "Explain the system to me. I didn't take the phone call so I'm lost."

"And maybe why the hell you need one," Calvert snapped.

"Maybe because I write at least twice as many tickets as anyone else on the department and I lose track of who's who when I go to court." The words were out, brimming with attitude, before he could call them back. He shifted his attention to Cookie. At least he could breathe when he had to talk to Cook. He straightened his shoulders. "All I do is code the corner of the ticket according to the driver's attitude so I can refer to it in court. A smiley face for positive, a blank circle for neutral and a—"

"A circle with a dot in it for the negative, right?" Calvert crossed his arms over his chest and scowled.

"A circle with a dot..." Awareness dawned in Cookie's gray eyes and he guffawed. "You drew an asshole on Paul Bostick's ticket?"

"He smashed his radar detector at my feet and called me a son of a bitch. Hell yeah, I drew an asshole on his ticket, after I wrote him a second citation for littering. He's lucky I didn't run him in."

"Good Lord help us." Calvert rolled his eyes heavenward.

"Does Bostick want me to drop the ticket?" Troy Lee tapped his ticket book against his thigh. If so, he'd fight that, politics or not. The kid had deserved the speeding citation. Maybe writing the littering one had been vindictive, but still...

"No." Some of the agitated aggression fell away from Calvert's posture. "But he seemed to think it might be inappropriate to have assholes drawn all over the copies going through Judge Barlow's office."

Actually, Scott Barlow thought it was the funniest damn thing he'd ever seen. Or so the young judge had told Troy Lee after a pick-up game of hoops one Saturday morning.

Cookie heaved a sigh and shook his head. "Troy Lee, couldn't you use a numerical system instead? One for positive, two for neutral, three for negative?" He quirked an eyebrow at Calvert. "Don't you think that would satisfy Bubba?"

"Probably." Calvert passed a hand over his jaw. "Just no more assholes, all right, Troy Lee?"

No more other than the one standing in front of him. "Yes, sir."

"Then get back to work." Calvert swept a hand in the direction of Troy Lee's unit. "And if someone is doing seventeen over, write 'em a ticket, whether they're having a bad day or not. Got that?"

"Yes, sir." He rubbed his palm over the burning in his chest and tried to remember that Calvert was fifty percent of the reason he'd wanted this damn job in the first place. Definitely a hundred percent why he stayed. Before it was all over, he'd find a way to show the son of a bitch he had what it took.

Chapter Two

"You really have to lay off that kid." Mark Cook eyed Troy Lee's unit as the deputy pulled onto the blacktop and headed toward the county line. Mark swung the unmarked unit in the opposite direction, toward town. "You're going to break him."

"Someone needs to break him," Tick muttered from the passenger seat. He grimaced and passed a hand over his side. "He's going to be the freakin' death of me."

"You know what the problem is, don't you?"

"Other than the fact he has the common sense of a fence post?"

Mark ignored the smart-ass rejoinder. "You're just alike."

Tick's head whipped in his direction. "What?"

"He's just like you when you were a rookie."

"Yeah, I doubt it." Tick snorted. "I was never that damn...stupid."

"No, you were worse. Trust me. I remember."

"You're—" The sudden jangling of a Gary Allan song cut him off. He lifted his cell, glanced at the display and groaned before lifting it to his ear. "Hey, Aunt Maureen."

Mark smothered a chuckle. Tick rested an elbow on the door, shading his eyes while he listened.

"Aunt Maureen, I really don't think—"

Even Mark could hear Maureen's agitated squawking as Tick tried to get a word in.

"Aunt Maureen...Aunt *Maureen*. You're getting all worked up over nothing. I'm sure there are going to be no strippers out at the Cue Club."

Mark choked on a laugh. Tick looked sideways at him and

shrugged, eyebrows lifted in his where-does-she-get-this-stuff expression.

"Yes, ma'am, I'm sure. The county has an ordinance against exotic dancing... She said what? A den of iniquity?" Tick sighed. "Aunt Maureen, that's just Angel's sense of humor. I'm sure she was teasing you. Yes, ma'am... Yes, ma'am. Goodbye. Yes, I love you too. Bye now." He snapped the phone closed and laid it on his lap. Laughing, he dragged both hands down his face. "Sweet Jesus."

"Strippers at the Cue Club?" Mark slowed to take the turn onto 112. "That's hilarious."

Tick shook his head. "Obviously, Angel Henderson was teasing about hiring strippers and changing the name of the place to the Den of Iniquity and Aunt Maureen took her seriously."

"The Den of Iniquity?" He could just imagine those words coming out of Angel's mouth, accompanied by one of her wicked winks. He shifted in the seat, little pitchforks of guilt stabbing at him. Something about the way she'd looked at him when he'd stepped out of the patrol car earlier said his not returning her messages had been a bad thing. Actually, taking her to bed when he didn't intend to pursue a relationship had been a bad idea too, but he'd been so wrapped up in falling the rest of the way in love with Tori Calvert that it had taken days for that reality to sink in. He'd been a bastard all the way around with Angel.

"That's what your badge bunny said."

Mark slanted a swift glare in Tick's direction. "Don't call her that. She's not a cop groupie and you know it."

Genuine contrition flashed over Tick's features. "Yeah, I know."

Silence descended, broken only by the whir of tires on blacktop and the occasional crackle of radio traffic. Mark watched the road, pine trees and the lime mine flashing by, and waited. He could almost *feel* the thoughts running through Tick's head and no way was the conversational minefield over that easy.

Tick was too damn stubborn to let it go and Mark knew it.

He tapped his thumb against the steering wheel. Wonder if they'd make the Delta Pines crossroads before Tick—

"You slept with her, though, didn't you." The quiet

comment was more a statement of fact than a question and the underlying condemnation set Mark's nerves on edge.

"Really none of your business, Tick." He flexed his fingers around the wheel. "I never asked you about the string of blondes, remember?"

"You're dating my little sister. That makes it my business." Tick fidgeted against the seat with the movements of someone who'd given up on finding a comfortable position. "And the blondes were different. I wasn't sleeping with any of them."

"Your little sister is twenty-seven and old enough to make her own decisions without your approval."

"You're thirty-nine and less than a month ago you were still indulging in one-night stands with women you didn't bother to call again." Tick drummed his thumb against his knee. "And I'm supposed to be okay with this whole thing between you and Tori?"

"The horse is dead, Calvert. Quit beating it." Mark rolled his neck, trying to relieve the sudden tension sitting there. Hell, he wasn't proud of his past, but he didn't need his partner throwing it in his face every time he turned around either.

"So explain to me how I'm supposed to believe you're going to treat Tori differently than Angel or your other playmates."

Goddamn, he was like a dog with a worn-out bone. Mark tightened his fingers and loosened them once more. Stopping the car and whipping Tick's ass was out of the question. The guy was recuperating from major surgery. Not to mention the fact it would make Tori mad and really solve nothing. When Tick got like this, the only thing that really made a difference was time.

"Because." Mark relaxed his jaw with an effort. "The difference between Tori and Angel or the others is the same one between Falconetti and Cicely St. John or Lynne Harris or any of the other blondes you went through when you came back from Mississippi and Falconetti had dumped your ass."

Let him argue with that.

Tick fixed him with one long glare and turned away to stare out the window, still tapping his thumb against his knee. Fine. Let him stew.

"Chandler, C-3." The radio crackled, doing little to break the tension hovering in the car.

Mark lifted the mike. "Go ahead, Chandler."

"10-50, 10-52 at the intersection of Stage Coach and Jackson Dairy. All other units are busy. Can you respond?"

"10-4, Chandler. 10-76." Mark replaced the mike and flipped on the light bar. He pressed down on the accelerator, and the police package Crown Victoria responded instantaneously with a muted roar and a rush of power. They were only a couple of miles from the reported accident and obviously an ambulance was on the way as well. Man, he hated that intersection, the site of two fatal wrecks in the last year.

Pine woods flashed by, interspersed with fields recently stripped of cotton and peanuts. A heavy scent of cow manure and damp feed hung in the air and permeated the car's interior via the air vents.

The crossroads loomed, a late-model Ford pickup and a little red sports car jammed together. Steam rose from the crumpled hoods. Mark brought the unit to a halt just inside the intersection and grabbed the mike, calling them in as arrived at the scene and requesting dispatch of a wrecker. He released his seat belt and popped the trunk, sparing Tick a rapid glance. "Can you secure the intersection while I check the vics?"

"I think I can handle that." Heavy sarcasm laced Tick's words, but Mark didn't reply. Tick wasn't supposed to be in a patrol car at all, just sitting behind a desk part-time until his six-week post-operative checkup, which was nearly four weeks away. When Falconetti learned Tick had worked a wreck, she'd have his ass.

Mark couldn't wait to tell her.

He jogged to the Ford. The teenage driver was on his feet, already yapping into his cell phone. Recognition slammed Mark with a wave of irony. Paul Bostick.

"You all right?" Mark looked him over—no obvious injuries other than a scratch to his forehead and a small cut on his wrist.

"Yeah, I'm good." The boy's voice shook and he pointed at the cell. "I called Daddy. He's on his way."

Mark directed him to the embankment behind his unit, a safe distance from both vehicles and any oncoming traffic. "Sit down for me over here until the ambulance arrives so the EMTs can take a look at you."

He returned to the wreck and went to the driver's side of the red car, which at one time had been a Mazda, the same make and model as Tori's. The entire front end was demolished. Hell, soon as he could, he was putting her in something safer, like a Sherman tank. She was a horrible driver, an accident waiting to happen.

The car door stood open, the driver, also a teen, sitting sideways and sobbing into her cell phone, big tears running down her face. Why did he just know those phones had had something to do with this wreck?

The girl cried so hard she was incoherent. He hunched before her, visually assessing her for injuries. Like Paul, she seemed to have only minor cuts and contusions, an angry red streak cutting across her collarbone, most likely from the seatbelt.

"Kaydee? Kaydee, are you all right?" The panicked female voice coming from the phone was audible even over the girl's smothered wails.

Mark gestured at the phone. "Your mom?"

She nodded, fresh tears spilling over. He held out a hand for the cell. "Want me to talk to her?"

She passed him the phone.

"Do you hurt anywhere?" he asked before lifting the baby-pink rectangle to his ear. She shook her head, folding her arms around her knees as she wept. "Hello, this is Mark Cook with the Chandler County Sheriff's Department. Who's speaking, please?"

"Oh my God." The female voice broke. "This is Sara Davis, Kaydee's mother. Is she all right?"

"She appears to be okay." He slanted a reassuring smile in Kaydee's direction. "However, she has been involved in a traffic accident at the intersection of Stage Coach Road and Jackson Dairy. Do you know where that is?"

"Yes, thank you. I'm on my way. Are you sure she's all right?"

"I don't see any visible injuries other than minor cuts and bruises, but an ambulance is en route." Actually, the approaching siren told him it was just around the curve. "The paramedics will check her out, but she seems to be fine. Would you like to talk to Kaydee again?"

"Please."

He handed off the phone to the slightly calmer teenager. The ambulance appeared, coming to a stop at the shoulder. One

EMT jogged over to where Tick was talking with Paul. The second joined Mark at the car.

"Hey, sweetheart, I'm Jim. Let's check you out, okay? Hey, Cookie." Jim Tyre opened his medical kit.

"Jim." Mark nodded. He let the medic take over and stepped back. Catching Tick's eye, he mimed sketching the scene. Tick shook his head.

Mark pulled his notebook and made quick work of drawing a rough outline of vehicle positions and skid marks. A pair of wreckers arrived moments later from Lawson Automotive, followed quickly by Bubba Bostick and both of Kaydee's parents. For the next twenty minutes, Mark found himself taking statements while Tick handled worried parents. Finally, Mark issued Paul a citation for failure to control his vehicle. The kid trailed his father to the family SUV, an unhappy bent to his head and shoulders as Bubba read him the riot act for garnering a third ticket, as well as causing an accident, in less than two weeks.

As Kaydee and her parents departed, Jim and the second paramedic, Clark Dempsey, approached.

"Kids were lucky." Jim jerked his chin at the skid marks on the other side of the intersection. "If he'd been a little farther the other way, she'd be dead."

"Yeah." Tick glanced at Bubba's departing vehicle. "Maybe his daddy can slow him down some."

"You look good, man." Jim clapped a cautious hand on Tick's shoulder. "But are you supposed to be back on active duty yet?"

"Hell no, he's not." Mark hid a smirk behind his hand. He wouldn't have to tell Falconetti. News of Tick's on-the-road adventures would be back to her by nightfall.

"Congratulations on the baby too." Jim grinned, and when he rested his hands at his waist, sunlight glinted off his shiny new wedding band. "Rhonda's already wanting us to start trying."

The devilish darts of guilt took aim at Mark once more. Angel Henderson had dated Jim off and on forever. Probably part of the reason she'd gone to bed with him on that first and only date had been her rebound situation with Jim's sudden marriage.

Shit, he really was a bastard.

A bastard who needed to apologize, badly. In person.

Oh, hell yeah, Tori was going to love that idea.

A white sheriff's unit topped the hill, slowed and angled in behind the unmarked car. Troy Lee emerged, tipped his campaign hat at the EMTs on scene and stopped at Mark's side. "What's up?"

Mark shrugged and gave him a brief rundown. "I cited him for failure to control."

Troy Lee squinted at the skid marks, the area where the kid's truck had left the roadway and the second set of rubber lines where he'd entered the intersection and slammed Kaydee Davis's car.

"How fast did he say he was going?"

"Fifty, maybe fifty-five."

Troy Lee snorted. "More like seventy. He's lucky he didn't roll the truck."

Frowning, Tick studied the marks. "How do you figure that?"

"Geometry and trig. You know, high school math."

"Troy Lee." Warning hovered in Tick's voice and his brows lowered in a scowl.

"I'm serious." Troy Lee spread his hands. "It's basic geometry and trigonometry. Simple angles and drag coefficient. He left the road at what looks like a thirty-degree angle, re-entered more on a forty-five. When you enter that and the drag coefficient for dry pavement into the formula, you get approximately seventy miles per hour."

Tick stared at him. "You just did that in your head?"

"Well, yeah." Troy Lee shrugged, but Mark didn't miss the small flash of smug satisfaction in his eyes. The kid liked knowing something Tick didn't. Mark could relate, and hell, Troy Lee probably needed that. The younger man cast another glance at the skid marks and shook his head. "Damn kid is going to kill somebody one day."

ထ

Angel poured a couple of shots of whiskey for two regulars, shimmying her shoulders to the rhythm of Miranda Lambert's "Kerosene" blaring from the jukebox. She'd fed dollar after dollar into the machine earlier, ensuring a steady stream of getting-even-with-the-man-who-done-you-wrong songs. The female patrons appreciated it, the small dance floor packed with girls hooting, hollering and hoofing it up.

Actually, programming a few more wouldn't be a bad idea. Lord only knew that if Donna Martin got half a chance, there'd be nothing but Patsy Cline love songs, and that was the last thing Angel needed tonight. She tugged a five from her pocket and waved it at her full-time bartender. "Hey, Julie. Got five ones?"

"Only if you play at least one Blake Shelton number for me."

Angel flashed the too-skinny brunette a big smile. "Just for you."

Julie took the five and unfolded it. A square of yellow paper fell to the floor. Julie retrieved it and held it out, along with the ones. "Hey, you might need this."

Oh, yeah. She needed that ticket like she needed a man in her life. With a sigh, she unfurled the paper, looking to see what the fine was this time. Sure enough, her name and information was filled in—Lord help her, she'd gotten enough tickets that he knew it by heart?—but he'd checked the warning box and across the bottom, he'd scrawled *slow down*. With a Kilroy-style smiley face wearing a campaign hat.

Her eyes prickled. What a sweetheart. And she'd been short with him. She'd have to make sure he had an extra Saturday slot on the band schedule to make up for that and maybe she'd toss in one of the house burgers he liked so much. Slipping the ticket into her pocket again, she headed for the jukebox.

Singing along with Miranda's lyrics about giving up on fickle love, she slid another bill into the slot and surveyed the selection. Nothing slow, nothing romantic and definitely nothing that qualified as crying-in-your-beer music. Ten selections later, she wandered back to the bar.

Only to find herself face-to-face with Mark Cook.

Her stomach clenched, then fell, leaving a hollow space behind. He was out of uniform, dressed casually in jeans and a black polo shirt that made his eyes gleam more silver than gray. *Damn* it, what was he doing here?

"Hey, can I talk to you a minute?" Awkwardness tightened his features, drawing his mouth into a taut line.

She pointed at the door, glad to see her hand was steady. "Get out."

"Angel—"

"I said get out. I don't want to talk to you, Cookie. You had your chance to have a conversation with me. No, not one chance. That was *five* chances."

"I know. I'm sorry."

She jerked her chin toward the exit sign. "Go on. Go. Before I decide to get all *Coyote Ugly* on you and auction your ass off to the lowest, trashiest whore I can find. Oh, wait." She tapped her forehead with two fingers. "I forgot. That would be me."

He scowled. "Don't say that. Hear me out, would you?"

"The only out you're getting from me involves that door and you on the other side of it."

"I'm sorry." Genuine regret coated his words. "I was a bastard all the way around."

"Well, I'm not going to argue with you there." She folded her arms over her chest and tapped the toe of her boot on the scuffed wood floor. "So does your new girlfriend know you're here?"

Brows raised, he grimaced. "Not yet."

"I'm sure she'll be thrilled." Needing something to do with her hands since he obviously wasn't going to leave and strangling him would result in her having to wear a really ugly orange jumpsuit, she picked up a bar towel and began polishing a highball glass. "What do you want from me, Cookie? Absolution?"

"No." He shook his head. "I just couldn't leave things the way they were."

"You left them that way for more than two weeks."

His shoulders lifted and fell with a deep breath. "I don't have an excuse for that, except I—"

"Except you were a bastard. We covered that." She set the glass aside, picked up another. Darn it, he actually seemed sorry, more than Jim had been when he'd showed up to retrieve his ring. Shoot, she'd known this one was decent. "So do you love her? Are you happy with her?"

"Yes. And yes." Even so, the tight set of his jaw spoke of his true remorse for the way he'd treated her.

Angel ran the towel around the inside rim of the glass.

"Well, I hope she appreciates it. You know, that you love her."

The first hint of a smile lifted one corner of his mouth. "I think she does."

With a less than ladylike snort, Angel swapped glasses. "Bet Tick doesn't."

"You have no idea."

A remnant of feminine pique enjoyed that thought. Maybe that evened things out. She nodded. "So we're good then—"

"Hey, Angel." Troy Lee's low tenor voice vibrated between them. He leaned on the bar next to Cookie and grinned at her. "Tell me I left my new pack of guitar strings here."

My God, the boy had a great smile, all dimples and white teeth against tanned skin and a little touch of stubble. No wonder he set hearts aflutter everywhere he went, with that grin and those bright blues. She gestured toward her office. "You did. Didn't your mama teach you to keep up with your stuff?"

He made an amused grunt in his throat. "Christine? You should see her studio. She can't keep up with anything."

Cookie rolled his eyes. "Hey, math genius. We were having a conversation."

Math genius? She cast a speculative glance at Troy Lee then turned her best "whatever" look on Cookie. "Our conversation was over. You were a bastard, I'm grudgingly forgiving you, and now it's time for you to go home to the girlfriend." She bestowed a winning smile on Troy Lee. "Deputy Farr here and I have to schedule some band dates."

"Right. Thanks, Angel. Good night." Cookie saluted her with his index finger and disappeared into the smoky air and chattering crowd.

Angel pulled a Corona, popped the top and placed it before Troy Lee along with the small bowl of lime wedges. "You call your mother Christine?"

"Stepmother. Long story." He flashed that grin again and jerked a thumb in the direction of Cookie's retreat. "What was that all about?"

"One-night stand. Long story."

"We'll have to trade later." He stuffed a lime into the bottle. "Although your story is probably more interesting than mine."

"Doubtful." No way she was giving him that anecdote. Food, maybe. "Have you eaten?"

He squinted at the ceiling in simulated concentration before his teeth gleamed in a smile. "Not since lunch."

"Burger or a Big Cheesy?"

"Burger." Beer in hand, he came around the bar and followed her into the kitchen. He rested his hips on the prep table and lifted the bottle to his lips. My, he was a long drink of water, tall and toned with lean muscles rippling under that faded Dave Matthews T-shirt. Too bad she wasn't ten years younger and totally off men for life. His gaze lingered on her like a palpable touch while she slapped a patty on the grill. He cleared his throat. "Bad day, huh?"

Did he really think it would be that easy? She laid out a bun and spread mayo and mustard on it, leaving off the ketchup because she knew he detested the stuff. "Math genius, huh?"

"Something like that." He angled his bottle in her direction, a speculative light in his eyes. "Know what you need, Angel?"

"What's that, Troy Lee?" She couldn't keep the exasperated indulgence out of her voice.

"A guy who'll show you a good time. I mean, someone to hang with, without all the sex and expectations."

She stilled in the middle of layering pickles, lettuce and tomato on his burger. Lord, that sounded good. Of course she didn't know any men interested in that scenario. No sex or expectations. Right. Ironic humor washed through her like a wave of acid. Shoot, Jim had brought his laundry by her house the Thursday before he left for Biloxi. His tighty-whities had been tumbling around in her dryer while he'd tumbled her. Before the week was up, he'd been back with a new wife. Obviously, too, Cookie had been looking for sex with no expectations of a follow-up.

Okay, enough of the self-pity. She stilled the shaky desire to bawl. Smile, flirt, pretend nothing was wrong. That was the way to go.

Cocking one hip to the side, she rested her hand on it and looked at him, dead in those baby blues. "Why, Troy Lee Farr, is that an offer?"

Chapter Three

"Maybe." Troy Lee smiled around the mouth of the bottle. She was relaxing, the visible strain draining out of her body as she busied herself with assembling the hamburger. "Do you want it to be?"

She slanted a mock-flirtatious look at him from beneath thick lashes. "Maybe."

He laughed. Yeah, she would be okay. Probably he should have left well enough alone earlier, but something about the sheer unhappiness on her face when she'd been talking to Cookie had drawn him closer as soon as he'd walked into the club, propelled him to interrupt. The weird impulse didn't make sense. Rescuing distressed damsels had never been his thing, badge or not. Besides, Angel Henderson didn't seem like anybody's idea of a damsel in need of rescuing. This was one lady who could hold her own.

She slid the plate, hamburger cut in two, in his direction. One glance at the half-pound monstrosity dripping with fat red tomato and glistening green lettuce, and his taste buds sat up to beg in anticipation. The woman could make a serious burger.

He lifted half for a bite. "Hey, about band dates..."

Tomato juice, in cahoots with the mayonnaise, spurted at him and trickled down the side of his mouth. He glanced about for a napkin.

"You have atrocious manners." Laughing, Angel swiped at the corner of his lips with her thumb just as he darted his tongue out to catch the spicy dribble. Instead he captured a taste of smooth female skin along the tender side of her palm. Heated reaction slammed into his lower belly.

Her lips—man, she had the most beautiful, kissable mouth

he'd ever seen—parted on a gasp and she dropped her hand, stepping back so fast she caught a boot heel on the padded floor covering in front of the food-prep area and lost her balance.

Her hands flailed and panic sparked in her eyes. Tossing the burger toward the plate, he grabbed her waist to steady her.

Their combined momentum—his pulling and her leaning forward to overcompensate for the lost equilibrium—brought them torso to torso. The reality of her, soft breasts, flat stomach, lean thighs, combined with his too-long-to-think-about state of celibacy. Heated reaction speared lower than his belly this time around and provided his dick with a mind of its own.

Her big blue eyes widened and he jerked back, making sure she was secure on her feet before he released her. He yanked a hand through his hair, his neck blazing. "I'm sorry. I'm a guy, it's been a while and licking you..."

If anything, her eyes went wider. His face burned Habanera-hot.

"Holy shit, I didn't mean... Angel, I swear I wasn't..." He fumbled for words. Damn, this was worse than screwing up with Calvert.

She laughed, clapping a hand over her mouth to muffle the pretty sound. He closed his eyes. F-uck. This ranked right up there with committing a warrant error that almost let a serial murderer walk. Jesus, he was a goober.

"Why, Deputy Farr, I do believe I'm flattered." Easy banter tinged her voice and he opened his eyes to find her leaning against the table, one turquoise boot crossed over the other. Friendly teasing sparkled in her eyes and amusement bowed that gorgeous bottom lip. All the tension was gone from her body and for that reason alone he dredged up a grin. For some things it was worth making an ass of himself.

She patted the center of his chest. "Eat your burger before I forget I'm too old for you and toss you on the prep table for a quickie."

Holy shit. Images kicked off in his brain, of those slender hands with pink-polished nails dragging his T-shirt up and over his head, scraping down his abs and going for his belt while he ran his palms under the skirt of that flirty little brown dress she wore. He cleared his throat, trying to ignore the parts of his anatomy, other than his face, now chili-pepper hot. God, he really had been celibate too long. No, make that he'd been waiting for her too long.

"You're not too old for me." Glad to hear his voice coming out in a properly scoffing tone rather than a strangled squeak, he took a more cautious mouthful of his hamburger.

"Sure, hon, whatever you say." She made short work of clearing the vegetables from the worktable. She rinsed her knife, eyeing him. "How old are you again? Twenty-four?"

"Twenty-six." Why did people always drop two or three years off his age?

"Ten years." She slapped the knife against the magnetic strip on the wall. "Almost eleven. That's definitely too old for you."

He snorted. "Whatever. My dad was thirteen years older than Christine and they were married almost twenty years."

"*Were* married."

"He died."

"Oh." She smacked a hand over her mouth. "I'm sorry. I assumed—"

"It's okay." He chuckled, watching her while he took another chomp out of the thick sandwich. "You got something against dating younger men?"

"Honey, right now, I have something against dating all men." She bit her lip, considering. "Although, I've never dated anyone younger."

"Maybe you should." He wrapped his hands around the edge of the counter and tried to appear nonchalant. Hell, her reaction meant too much and that wasn't good, but the feel of her still reverberated through him, bringing with it a sense of opportunity he didn't want to let slip by. He'd already let one missed chance with her kick him in the teeth. "Someone who'd show you a good time—"

"I know, without all the sex and expectations." She twirled a finger in the air. "And where, pray tell, am I supposed to find such a paragon of manly virtue, Troy Lee?"

He swallowed. "You asked if I was offering."

She stared at him a moment, opened her mouth, closed it again and shook her head. "Troy Lee."

"What?" He managed to get a lungful of air in and out. At

least she hadn't outright laughed. If she blew him off, well, he'd deal. Play it light and easy, like it didn't matter that he'd screwed up something else, that she didn't want him.

"Be serious."

"I am. Give me one reason why not." He lifted his hand as her lips parted. "Other than the age difference."

"I...you..." She firmed her lips, tapping one toe on the floor.

He laughed, too-strong relief making his stomach jittery. "You can't do it. You can't find one reason why we shouldn't go out."

"It's crazy."

"So?" He shrugged. "Galileo's theory that the sun was the center of the universe was pretty insane for his time and I'm sure somebody thought Einstein's theory of relativity was crazy when he first proposed it."

"That is hardly the same thing."

"But you can't give me a better reason why not." He leaned forward and winked. "Come on. I'm a fun date."

She rolled her eyes, then narrowed them as she studied him. "Just for a good time."

"Exactly."

"No sex."

"Nope." He looked down at his feet, pretending to consider a major point before lifting his gaze to hers. "Kissing has to be okay, though. I like kissing and supposedly I'm pretty good at it."

"I like kissing too." Wistfulness darted over her face but disappeared so fast he thought maybe he'd imagined it. Good, because he sure as hell wanted to kiss her. Now would be good, but moving that fast didn't fit the equation.

He rolled his shoulders in an easy shrug. "So I'm off Saturday."

She did that exasperated eyes-lifted-heavenward thing he'd witnessed at least a dozen times when some drunk was trying to get his keys back. "I have to open the bar Saturday, remember?"

"Not until five." He spread his hands in an expansive gesture. "Saturday morning. Pick the time. We'll go for breakfast or something."

Hands at her hips, she looked away for a moment and

puffed her bangs from her face. He thought he heard her mutter something about being crazy, but then she turned those crystal blue eyes on him and he didn't care how damn crazy any of it was.

"Fine," she said, shaking her head. "Saturday morning. Nine o'clock. Don't be late."

Exotic tinkling music greeted Mark as soon as he opened the door. Finding Tori in his apartment at the end of the day wasn't a surprise. Finding her in flowy low-slung pants and a tiny camisole, shimmying in front of the television was a different story. He closed the door and eyed the seductive sway of her hips.

"Belly dancing?"

She nodded, barely glancing in his direction, biting her bottom lip in concentration while mimicking the movements of the trio of women dancing on the television.

"Exercise video." Her voice emerged a little breathy and a whole lot sexy. "Works the core."

"It definitely works something." He leaned his shoulders against the door and watched. She had the hips for this, sweet and curvy.

She jerked her chin at him. "Get over here and kiss me, and maybe I'll forget you're late."

Pushing away from the door, he crossed to brush his mouth over hers. With a saucy wink, she gave an extra wiggle and bumped her hip against his. "You're going to have to do better than that if you don't want me to fuss about you being late."

He grinned. Every day they were together, she grew more secure, more comfortable in their physical interactions. He loved that, loved watching her bloom into the warm, confident woman she'd been destined to be. Hell, he just loved *her*.

"Well, come here then." He wrapped an arm about her waist and tugged her against him. Turning her face up to his, she wound her arms about his neck, and their lips met. With an approving murmur, she curled closer and opened her mouth beneath his.

"Mmm, that's better." Eyes sparkling, she leaned back in the circle of his arms. "So why are you late?"

"Yeah, about that." He released her and stepped back. She

wasn't going to like this, but he didn't intend to have secrets or lies between them. Rubbing a hand over his nape, he cleared his throat. "I went by the Cue Club to see Angel Henderson."

Her face closed, her entire posture stiffening. "Really."

"Tori—"

"Any particular reason why?" Her chin lifted in silent challenge, but he didn't miss the flash of uncertainty in her dark eyes. Damn it, he hated seeing that insecurity when she'd become the single most important element in his life.

"I owed her an apology." He kept his voice calm and quiet.

"And you had to go see her? Email or a phone call wouldn't work?"

"No, it wouldn't. I was a complete ass and she deserved to hear that in person."

"An ass how?" Glancing away, she brushed her hair behind her ear. "You're going to have to explain it to me."

He resisted the need to pull her to him and smooth away the doubt clouding her features. He settled for cradling her chin in his palm and tilting her gaze back to his. "First, you need to understand that Angel is not a threat to you where I'm concerned, in any way, shape or form. Okay?"

She lifted a hand, palm up. "Well, it's hard to—"

"Tor, I love you." He leaned in to kiss her. "Do you believe that?"

She curved her fingers along his jaw. "You know I do."

"I haven't said that to a woman in almost twenty years. I don't treat it lightly and you have to believe that nothing is going to change the way I feel about you." He turned his head, rubbing his mouth across the soft inside of her thumb. "Do you believe that?"

"Yes." She tapped his chest, sharp enough to sting. "But that doesn't mean I'm happy you went to see her. Now explain."

"All right." He chafed a hand down his nape. "That night you saw us together at the ER?"

"You slept with her." The miserable resignation in the words was hard to miss.

"I did. While it didn't mean anything to me beyond the moment, she was on the rebound and I think she read more into it than I ever intended." He met Tori's troubled gaze. "I'm not proud of it, Tori, you know that. Anyway, she left me a handful of messages in the last couple of weeks."

"And you didn't call her back." A pained frown twisted her brow. "Oh, Mark, that was really not smart."

"Yeah. It wasn't decent of me, either. Anyway, Tick and I ran across her today while Troy Lee had her stopped for speeding—"

"Wait. Tick was *working*?"

"Um, kinda."

"Lord, he has no sense. Cait will kill him when she finds out." Tori's shoulders hunched. "Go ahead."

"It was pretty obvious she'd heard about you and me, and just as obvious that she was hurt. I couldn't just not apologize and I couldn't do it standing by the side of the road with Tick and Troy Lee there."

"You're right." Sounding slightly mollified, Tori leaned into him and wrapped her arms around his waist. "She deserved an apology and I wouldn't expect less of you than to give it to her in person."

He stroked his thumb across the strip of waist bared between her camisole and pants. Damn, she had the silkiest skin. "So we're good."

"Yes, we're good." She pressed a kiss to the corner of his mouth. "It's done, it's over, it has nothing more to do with us. Right?"

"Right." He caught her chin between his other thumb and forefinger and kissed her. With a pleased murmur, she turned her face into his neck. He smiled and nuzzled her ear. "So about that belly dancing...do I get a private showing?"

Her giggle flushed him with pleasure and warmth. "Maybe. Are you going to play private chef? I ate a candy bar for lunch."

"So that's how it is." Why wasn't he surprised? With a soft swat on her butt, he released her. "You only want me because I can cook."

"Well, someone has to do it." An impish expression wrinkled her nose. "And you don't want it to be me."

"This is true." He wrapped an arm around her neck and pulled her with him toward the kitchen, completely secure that all was right with them and feeling better that things were straight with him and Angel. "So I cook, you dance...sounds like a good trade to me."

ꟹ

She had lost her mind.

Angel flicked her new layers into place around her face. The haircut had been a great idea. Agreeing to go out with Troy Lee? Maybe not so great. In the two days since Wednesday night, she'd picked up her cell more than once with the intention of canceling, but each time she'd put the phone away without doing so. Last night she'd even found herself unable to sleep, like when she'd been a little girl and it had been the night before a trip to Six Flags in Atlanta.

She was making way more of this than it was. He'd said just for fun, just for a good time. He was the epitome of "not serious", so why was she so keyed up?

"Oh, you know why." She addressed her reflection, finger-combing the long layers once more. "You just don't want to admit it."

She was wound up over what it had felt like to be pressed close to that tall, muscular body. Muscular being the key word, since he definitely had muscles in all the right places, from a hard chest to firm biceps and nicely toned forearms. She sighed and lifted her arm, flexing her own biceps. Yep, a good thing they weren't getting naked together. She wasn't flabby, thanks to the lifting she did to stock the bar and working in her yard, but she wasn't Ms. Universe by any stretch of the imagination.

But she would like to know if his abs were as tight and hard as the rest of him.

A solid rap at the front door set off a ripple of blended apprehension and anticipation. With one last fluff of the still unfamiliar hair, she scooted out of the tiny bathroom and hurried to the front door. Smoothing her skirt, she pulled up a bright smile and swung it open. "Hey."

"Morning." His dimples deepened as he talked, and oh Lord, her knees actually tried to go weak as she looked at him. He was casually dressed, all good-looking and yummy in a long-sleeved sage green T-shirt and khaki cargo shorts that revealed calf muscles as perfect as his biceps. His short dark hair was adorably mussed, in a way several local men paid her sister big bucks to maintain.

Positive she was staring and probably on the verge of drooling, she dropped her gaze and stepped back. "Come on in."

He strode inside and cast a quick glance around the living room before his attention fell on her. His lips twitched and he chuckled. "What are you wearing?"

"Um, clothes." She looked down at the white dress with its empire waist and silver sequin trim that gave it a flirty, Grecian air. Sure it was a little summery for November, but the weather forecast was calling for temperatures in the high seventies and she'd planned to add her short denim jacket. "Why?"

"It's a little dressy for hiking out to the river." He lowered his eyes to her boots. "And you're just asking to twist an ankle, wearing those on that terrain."

"Hiking? To the river?" She shook her head, really taking in for the first time his own footwear, sturdy boots made for trekking. "You said breakfast, Troy Lee. Not woods and bugs and snakes."

"Snakes aren't moving right now." He made a *pfft* sound at the idea. "I figured we'd grab breakfast to go and head for the Outpost. There's a great place about a half-mile up where we could sit and eat."

He was serious. She'd envisioned a nice leisurely breakfast at the diner or maybe even brunch at Coney Hall, and his idea of an enjoyable outing involved slogging through the woods. Oh, it was a very good thing they weren't in this for more than fun.

He passed a hand through his hair, mussing it further. "I guess I should have explained what I had in mind or asked what you wanted to do, huh?"

He looked crushed, darn it, like a little boy who'd crafted some hideous homemade valentine only to have it spurned by the cutest girl in the class.

"No, that's okay. A walk would be nice." What was she saying?

Relief chased some of the tension from his features. "How about a compromise? We pick up breakfast and take it up to Riverfront Park? The nature trail is paved if you're serious about a walk."

Pavement? Now that she could handle. "It's a deal. Let me grab my jacket."

He held the door for her, then waited, glancing around the porch while she locked up. As they went down the concrete pathway to where his green Wrangler waited outside the fence, he took her hand easily.

"You look great, by the way." He opened the door and helped her with the slight climb. "I really do like the new hairstyle. The color too. It suits you."

"Thank you." Flustered, she tucked her billowy skirt around her thighs. "I'll tell my sister you approve. It was all her idea."

"Well, it was a fantastic one." He shut the door and strode around the hood. Once behind the wheel, he grinned. "Ready?"

"Yes." Maybe. Unless she was getting in over her head, which she already feared she was. He made her feel too good, too special, with his easygoing admiration and friendly attention.

The fresh morning air, already holding a promise of the unseasonal warmth to come, rushed in through the open vehicle, tousling her hair, kissing her cheeks.

He drove easily, one hand on the wheel, the other resting atop the gearshift, at an ambling speed that said he was in no hurry to get where he was going. She was so accustomed to always being five minutes behind and hurrying to catch up that the sensation of slowness made her skin itch.

She eyed the instrument cluster. "You're not even driving the speed limit."

He slanted an ironic glance in her direction. "You mean you know what one is?"

"Oh, you're funny."

"Angel baby, I've worked here for nearly three years. Do you know how many times I've stopped you for speeding in that time?"

More than she could count. She squirmed in the seat. "I don't know."

He lifted his hand from the gearshift, flashed five fingers, made a fist, flashed all five once more, then held aloft a single digit.

"Eleven? No way you've stopped me eleven times."

"Yes way. I can pull out the logs to prove it, and that's just me, Ms. Speedy Gonzales. That doesn't count Chris or Steve or Cookie—" He bit the name off and grimaced. "Sorry. You probably don't want to talk about him."

"It's okay." She tucked her tangling hair behind her ear, only to have it tossed free by the playful wind once more. Oddly enough, it was okay. She hadn't thought about Cookie, not really, since Thursday night, as all her brain cells seemed intent on fixating on the male body in the Jeep next to her. She hadn't thought of him at all this morning, her attention captured by Troy Lee's sweet teasing. Being free of the hurt bitterness felt good and she patted Troy Lee's thigh. "Really. I mean it. It's okay."

"I'm glad." He covered her hand with his, heat traveling up her nerve endings from the dual contact of hard thigh under her palm and warm male skin atop her wrist and hand. He grinned at her but didn't let go. "So what sounds good for breakfast?"

She made a valiant effort not to flex her fingers around the tight muscles beneath them. Was wanting to touch, to explore just a little such a bad thing? "Lisa's is good and they do takeout. Or there's the diner on the courthouse square."

"Lisa's," he said with a decisive tone. Lifting his hand, he downshifted for the looming red light. "I eat enough of the diner's food during the week."

Her hand felt lonely and bare with his gone, and what was she supposed to do now? Leave it? Move it? As casually as she could, she raised both hands to smooth her hair behind her ears now that the wind rush wasn't as severe.

He made a left onto 19, heading south from town to where Lisa's Café sat in a refurbished farmhouse in the middle of a pecan grove. He parked and came to open her door. Again, he folded his fingers around hers on the short walk to the wraparound porch and the restaurant's entrance.

Lord, he was such a sweetheart. Why hadn't some smart girl snapped him up before now?

He propped the authentic screen door open with his hip and reached for the doorknob on the hundred-year-old oak slab. The door swung inward as he did so and Angel stepped closer to him to allow the departing patrons to pass.

He rested a hand on her shoulder. "What do you like here—"

"Excuse us. Oh." Jim's voice reeked of discomfort and Angel's simple pleasure in the morning evaporated. "Angel, hey."

Angel closed her eyes. Great. A nice Saturday run-in with her ex-fiancé and his new wife.

Just what she needed.

Chapter Four

She couldn't hide forever. Angel opened her eyes and pasted on a big, bright smile. "Hey, Jim, Rhonda. How are you?"

Rhonda's mouth stretched, but Angel wasn't sure the expression could be called friendly. "Good, thanks. You?"

"Fine, thank you." My, how polite they all were, as if this wasn't the single most awkward situation Angel had ever encountered.

Troy Lee rested his hand at her waist in a light nudge. "I hate to rush you, honey, but if we don't get a move on, we're going to be late."

Bless his heart, he was sweet *and* smart. She nodded and laid her hand over his, letting him direct her toward the door. "You're right. Y'all excuse us."

Jim mumbled something and ushered his bride toward the parking area. With Troy Lee's palm still warm on her waist, Angel slipped inside. The heavy door closed behind them.

"I'll be with you in a minute," Lisa called from the dining room, her voice harried.

"I could hug your neck," Angel whispered as they approached the glass case, filled with luscious desserts, which served as the ordering and checkout counter in the large foyer.

"Later." His resonant murmur, close to her ear, sent a ripple of awareness through her, creating a flutter of attraction deep in her belly. "We have that whole kissing thing to try out."

She turned her head, meeting devilish blue eyes, intensely conscious that he still hadn't dropped his hand, each finger a warm imprint through the thin cotton of her dress. "Don't push it."

With a laugh, he reached for two of the laminated menus

available for take-out customers. Against her, his fingertips moved in an absent rhythm while he perused the menu. It took her a moment to decipher the motions. Rolling her eyes, she prodded his hand aside. "I'm not a guitar, Troy Lee."

"What?" He looked up, blinking as though she'd pulled him from a daze. This time sheepishness tinged his wonderful grin. "Was I playing frets again? Sorry. It's a habit. I do it unconsciously when I'm thinking."

Sweet, smart and endearingly goofy. Dropping her gaze, she picked up her own menu. "What looks good?"

"You."

"Troy Lee. Behave."

"If you insist." His long-suffering sigh stirred the ruffled hair at her temple. "I'm getting the grilled PBJ."

"Oh, that sounds fantastic. I think I want one too."

"I'm sorry y'all had to wait." Lisa Johnson appeared from the dining area. "I'm short a waitress this morning and it's killing us. Are you ready to order? Oh my God, Angel, I love your hair. You should have cut it a long time ago."

"Thanks." She fingered the ends and glanced up at Troy Lee and his I-told-you-so eyes. "Are we ready?"

"Yeah." He laid the menus aside. "Couple of grilled PBJs. Some fruit?" He looked at Angel in inquiry and she nodded. "The fruit sampler and a large coffee for me."

"And Angel wants our strawberry tea, right?" Lisa's red lips showcased sparkly white teeth.

"Exactly."

"All right then." Lisa scribbled the order on a pad and shooed them toward a couple of plush chairs near the tall windows facing the porch. "Give me about ten minutes and we'll have you good to go."

Angel sank onto one, tucking her skirt about her legs and crossing one ankle over the other. Troy Lee took the second chair, his body half-turned toward her, his arm resting along the back and his fingers close to her arm.

"You handled that well." His voice quiet, he jerked his head toward the door.

"Yes, well, it's not like I can be ugly about it, you know?" Heat flushed her cheeks. For the second time in three days, he'd been privy to the mess she'd made with some other man. "I see her at the bank almost every day and his parents go to church with mine."

Troy Lee's gaze trailed over her face. "He's an idiot."

She blinked. "Excuse me?"

"It's the only explanation for his letting you go."

Keep it light. Keep it fun. Repeating the mantra, she tapped his knee. "You're a sweetheart. I think I like hanging out with you."

She'd expected a deep chuckle and more of his cheerful teasing. Instead, a frown brought his brows together. "I wish you wouldn't—"

"Here are your drinks anyway. Bill's putting a rush on your order, but it'll be a couple more minutes." Lisa's breezy voice shattered the sudden tension hanging around them. "Troy Lee, you want me to go ahead and ring you up?"

Troy Lee held Angel's gaze a moment longer, the intensity of his regard making it hard not to squirm. Then he pushed up and tugged his wallet free, the moment with its weird crackling awareness sliding away as he crossed to pay for their food. Whatever he'd been about to say disappeared in the busyness of collecting their breakfast once it arrived and returning to the Jeep.

Somehow, the shining promise of the morning seemed tarnished, although she wasn't sure how so. Because of Jim? Because of her own reaction to Troy Lee's disparagement of Jim's choices? Whatever it was, she stared out at the passing townscape and found herself wishing for those moments when he'd held her hand against his leg or teased about kissing her. That made absolutely no sense, because they were simply in this to spend the day together as friends, to enjoy themselves. So why this sudden urge to mourn for something lost?

Once they arrived at Riverfront Park, he jockeyed the Wrangler into a spot near the fountain, its myriad jets sending random spouts of water sparkling into the air. Determined to put them back on the same old footing, Angel pinned on a bright smile as he came around to open her door. And if he didn't take her hand this time...well, he was carrying the bag holding their breakfast. Even if he did have it hooked over his wrist, coffee in the same hand, and his right one free.

Below the sidewalk and the landscaped seating areas, a sloping bank of grass fell away toward the murmuring river, edged now with a wide concrete walkway. He gestured toward the covered gazebo next to the playground then toward the benches that lined the waterfront. "Where do you want to sit?"

Lord, why did it all feel so awkward between them now? She lifted her shoulders in an exaggerated nonchalant shrug and sipped at the warm tea, laden with strawberry sweetness. "The gazebo's fine."

He swept a hand in that direction, ushering her to precede him. There, she slid onto a bench at one of the small tables dotting the cedar floor and shivered a little, the warmth of the sunlight dissipating under the heavy roof. Silently, his face devoid of expression, he set out their food and took the seat opposite hers, his attention turned out over the sluggish brown water.

She unwrapped her sandwich, the crusty golden bread dusted with powdered sugar. The idea of choking it down tightened her throat. "So what are your plans for the rest of the day?"

His blue gaze darted in her direction. "Not much. I may go for a run with Chris. Band practice this afternoon before we play your place tonight."

Nodding, she reached for a piece of kiwi. Still seeking a way to take them back where they'd been, she wrinkled her nose in a cheeky moue. "I love when y'all play the club. The local girls hear you're on stage and show up in droves."

His brows twisted in a long-suffering grimace. "Yeah."

She nudged his foot with hers. "Oh, what's the matter, Troy Lee? Most guys would love to be in your place."

He unfolded the wax paper around his sandwich. "What place is that?"

"Being the county heartthrob." She tore off a small bite of toasty crust. "I mean, come on. We both know you have your pick of the local women."

He looked up then, a sharp gleam in his eyes. "You think?"

The heavy irony in his voice didn't make sense. She swiped her finger across the white dusting on her sandwich before licking the sweet substance from her fingertip. "What is wrong with you?"

His gaze dropped to her finger and mouth, then lifted to her eyes. "Nothing."

"That's my line, boy." She reached for her tea. "Women own

that word, remember?"

He didn't rise to her teasing, his gaze locked on hers. "Don't call me boy. I'm at least eight years beyond that, Angel."

"You"—she pointed at him—"are in a weird mood."

For a long moment, he watched her before the lingering tension drained from his features. "Yeah." He glanced away toward the water once more. "Something like that."

She eyed his profile. A muscle flicked in his jaw. She picked up her sandwich, took a bite she didn't really taste, chewed, swallowed. "So what are y'all playing tonight?"

"Probably the usual." He turned his attention back to her, or at least his food, reaching for his own PBJ. "Don't worry, we'll keep the dance floor hopping."

With the shift in topic, the awkwardness diminished somewhat and they spent the following minutes eating, sharing more silence than conversation. When they'd finished, he collected the wrappers and bag and dropped them in a nearby trashcan. Turning, he dusted his hands. "Ready for that walk?"

"Oh Mark, no."

At Tori's exaggerated groan, Mark slanted a look at her while he put the Blazer in park. "What?"

She cast a glum appraisal around the lot belonging to Uncle Robert's Used Cars. "I despise car shopping."

"We're not shopping. We're looking." The door creaked as he pushed it open and came around to open hers. She turned sideways in her seat but didn't slide from the truck.

"It's not like you're going to part with the Blazer, so this is pointless." She perked up, a smile curving her mouth, and she ran a teasing finger down the center of his chest. "There is, however, a little vintage shop just around the corner. That, my dear love, is the way to spend Saturday morning. Antiquing. Not car shopping."

"No." He kissed her. "No antiques. Not today."

"But you're going to make me look at cars you have no intention of buying." She pouted but let him pull her from the cab. "At least I purchase things when I go shopping."

He turned her to face the massive offering of vehicles. "What do you want to look at?"

"Iron bedsteads." On a sigh, he gave her a look and she

shrugged, completely unapologetic. "You asked what I wanted to look at."

"Tick's right. You can be a brat when you want to." He squinted at a gleaming Volvo SUV with low miles. "Doesn't your brother Del have one of these?"

"Yes." Complete boredom dripped from the monosyllable.

If an insurance salesman drove one, it had to be safe, right? He looked down the first row of vehicles, trying to remember what he'd read or heard about safety ratings, mentally checking off the models he'd seen crumpled and twisted with major injuries or fatalities involved.

"Tor, have you ever thought about trading in that tin can of yours?"

She groaned. "So that's what this is about. Mark, I like my car and it's only four years old. Besides, it's paid for."

"Honey, all I'm asking you to do is look at something a little bigger and maybe safer." He cupped her chin and rubbed his thumb across her jaw. "Seeing what that pickup did to Kaydee Davis's Miata the other day scared the hell out of me."

She scowled at him for a long moment. "Fine, I'll look. But no promises."

"Deal." He wrapped an arm around her shoulders and tucked her close to his side. "So, what do you want to look at?"

"Well, nothing my brother the insurance salesman would drive."

They spent fifteen minutes wandering up and down the rows, deflecting an overeager salesperson, stopping to inspect a vehicle that caught her eye or his. They agreed on little concerning the cars, but Mark could think of few things better than simply being with her, their fingers intertwined, and catching a glimpse of her beautiful smile every so often.

"Hey, this is cute." She stopped at the end of one line, peering into a lime green Beetle. He paused at the trunk and frowned, his attention captured by what was transpiring one row over. Well, didn't that just beat all?

"Mark?" She joined him, laying gentle fingers on his arm. "Isn't that Bubba Bostick?"

"Yeah." Mark's mouth firmed. Bubba stood deep in conversation with a salesman while Paul circled the performance package F-150. "And that kid does not need that truck, not the way he drives."

Tori slid her hand down to entwine their fingers. "Maybe Scott Barlow will suspend his license after this last citation."

"Maybe. Might be the best thing." Obviously, Bubba didn't intend to stop the kid driving or even slow him down, not if he was buying that vehicle for the boy. Troy Lee's insistence that Paul was a fatality waiting to happen echoed in Mark's head. Man, he hoped the kid didn't end up dead in an accident.

"Mark?" Tori pulled him from the musings. "What do you think of the Beetle?"

He eyed the nearly neon paint job. "I think I don't get why someone would want a green car."

She wrapped her arm about his waist. "Come on, then. Let's go look at more cars until I expire from boredom."

ꕥ

He'd screwed up, again. Considering his track record, that in itself wasn't surprising. Troy Lee bounced the basketball off the free throw line, set his mark and shot. The net swished and he loped to retrieve the ball.

The whole "just for a good time" angle with Angel? Massive miscalculation. The caveat, while he was pretty sure it had been what had ultimately induced her to say yes, provided her with no incentive to see him as more. However, since she obviously regarded him as too young to be seriously worth her time...well, that only exponentially compounded the problem.

He shot from the sideline, the net swishing again.

"Not bad for a white guy." The gravelly voice, only recently deepened, held equal notes of friendly mockery and admiration. Devonte Richardson stood at the opposite sideline, dribbling the ball from one hand to the other in a "V" formation.

"Yeah? Last weekend, it was not bad for an old guy." Troy Lee held up his hands for the ball. Devonte ignored him and floated the orb toward the hoop with the effortless grace and power that had college scouts crawling over themselves to sign the seventeen-year-old senior.

Troy Lee retrieved the ball, already feeling the flow of anticipation and competition. Weekend pick-up games of one-on-one had been a ritual for the pair since Troy Lee had first moved into the tiny one-bedroom apartment next door to the mirror-image unit Devonte shared with his grandmother.

"Not bad for a snot-nosed kid."

"Snot-nosed kid's going to whip your old, white po-po ass." Devonte moved in to block him, gliding, arms spread wide as his smirk.

Troy Lee quelled his own grin. "Better not let Miss Francie hear you talking like that. She'll have your hide."

"Yeah? Hide this." With a swift, practiced lunge, Devonte stole the ball in mid-dribble and took it to the goal in a beautiful lay-up.

The move set the tone for the aggressive game, and a half hour later, Troy Lee collapsed against the chain-link fence, an arm over his midriff. He bent double a moment, staring at the glittering shards of a broken beer bottle. His chest heaved, his heart trying to thud out of his ribcage and sweat dripping from his slick skin. Playing ball with this kid was almost like running hills.

"Whatsa matter, dawg?" Grinning and completely unwinded, Devonte moved the ball in the classic "V" once more. "Too old to take it?"

"Something like that." Troy Lee straightened and grabbed his discarded T-shirt to wipe his face. He looped it around his neck. "Heard FSU's assistant coach was at your last game."

"Yeah, dawg. Cool, huh?"

"Very." Damn, his abs hurt now—not that it had anything to do with Devonte's elbow slamming into them as Troy Lee had gone up for a shot. Off the high school court, with no refs around, the kid played ball by the rules of the hood. College though...college would be good for him, good for Miss Francie, would give him an opportunity a lot of the local kids never got. "What did I tell you about calling me 'dawg'?"

Devonte's only answer was a shrug and another wide smirk. Troy Lee shook his head and rubbed a hand over his chest. The heartburn was acting up again, and while he'd like to blame it on that elbow to the gut, he knew it had more to do with worrying over where he stood with Angel.

He jerked a thumb over his shoulder. "I gotta go clean up and get ready to play tonight. Say hey to your grandma for me."

Devonte performed a flawless hook shot. "Man, when you gonna learn to play some *real* music?"

Funny, his high school music teacher, the one who'd

pushed so hard for him to apply to Julliard had often asked the same thing. With a wave, Troy Lee ambled back to the long, low brick building that made up one leg of the aging low-income housing project. The heavy smell of frying chicken and simmering greens wafted from Miss Francie's open window. In his own apartment, after popping a couple of Tums, he dropped the sweat-damp shirt in the hamper and eyed his torso in the mirror over the tiny vanity. He ran a hand across the mark at the top of his belly, centered between his ribs. Yep, that was gonna bruise.

After a shower, he donned jeans and a T-shirt, grabbed his guitar and headed for the Jeep. He paused while stowing the instrument case and frowned at the sight that greeted him. On the side street, Devonte climbed into the rear passenger seat of a late-model, still-bearing-the-dealer-tags Ford F-150.

A new Ford F-150 with a hopped-up performance package engine and Paul Bostick behind the wheel. The truck rumbled off in a blast of loud music. Shaking his head, Troy Lee settled in the driver's seat. He didn't get some parents. Reward the kid for causing what could have easily been a fatal wreck by buying him a forty-thousand-dollar pickup.

He backed out of his parking space and headed in the direction of the Cue Club, trying to quell the anxiety jumping in his stomach and making the acid burn into his chest all over again. Somehow, he had to find a way to convince Angel he had what it took to be something more than her "just a good time".

A cramp stabbed at Angel's left arch and she leaned on the bar, lifting that foot behind her. Patrons packed the club and she'd been hustling all night, trying to help Julie stay caught up at the bar. Julie had hollered out last call ten minutes before and the band was winding down with their traditional final number, but no one seemed willing to straggle out yet.

A regular ambled up and passed over his credit card to settle his tab. Angel took it with a smile and returned the aching foot to the floor with ginger caution.

"Thank you. Good night!" Troy Lee's voice, amplified by the sound system, rumbled over her. He grinned, mouth close to the mike, and lifted a hand. "Y'all go home."

How many times had she heard him close a set with those words? Tonight she wasn't sure if she was glad to hear them or not. Her feet hurt and she was tired, so going home sounded good on that accord. However, closing down probably meant seeing him for a few minutes, something that made her inexplicably nervous. The morning had gone well, even with that weirdness at the beginning of breakfast, so no reason existed why she should be anxious about talking to him.

Wasn't like they were serious or anything.

"Thanks, Hugh." Angel passed the credit card and receipt over. Shoot, even her face hurt from pasting on so many smiles tonight. Not that she was complaining, mind you. She loved when business was good. She was just bone-deep tired.

Julie nudged her and tilted her chin toward the stage. "These girls are crazy-stupid over that boy."

Following the direction of Julie's gaze, Angel watched as Troy Lee and Clark Dempsey, the EMT who played drums for the small group, were waylaid by a little blonde and a willowy brunette, both in their very early twenties. The blonde giggled and held out a permanent marker in Troy Lee's direction. While he uncapped it, she tugged down the already low vee of her T-shirt, exposing the rounded curve of her upper breast and the edge of a lacy red bra.

"Oh my God." Julie laughed, a puffing, choked titter. "Did he just sign her boob?"

"He sure did." To Angel's relief, her voice came out normal after fighting its way past the tsunami of possessive pique swamping her. The blonde graced Clark with the opportunity to autograph her other breast and the brunette touched Troy Lee's arm, rubbing her palm over his biceps as she flirted. With a smile, he extricated himself from the contact.

Angel swallowed hard. Darn it, this whole scenario shouldn't kick her in the chest the way it did. They were friends and she didn't own him. Besides, she knew what it was like to be passed over in favor of a younger, more desirable woman.

The brunette snagged the marker from Clark as he finished his signature with a flourish. With a sultry flutter of her lashes, she passed it to Troy Lee and turned her back on him, hitching the waistline of her hip-riding jeans down just a bit to provide him room to sign the small of her back. The thin pink strand of a rhinestone-dusted thong rested across her hip above the faded denim. Eyebrows raised, Troy Lee exchanged a look with Clark but bent to scrawl his name across the smooth skin just the same.

Angel pulled her gaze from the tableau. As the club's patrons trickled out, she buried herself closing out tabs, tallying receipts and disbursing charged tips to servers.

Behind her, wood clattered on the polished bar. "Hey."

She tensed at Troy Lee's voice, the rich tones sliding over her like caressing fingers. She schooled her features and turned to face him. "Hey yourself."

She laid her paperwork out on the bar and tried not to look at him. His hair stood up in damp spikes and his shirt clung, a fine sheen of sweat on his skin. Lord help her, she could smell him, a blend of spicy deodorant, male sweat and musky warmth that kicked off images of hard sweaty sex and writhing bodies. Ooh, her hands wrapped around her footboard while he pumped into her from behind... Her belly clenched on a fluttering of arousal.

She clamped down on the reactions by dragging up the picture of the brunette touching him, of his hand at her hip while he autographed her skin. He swiped a wrist over his damp forehead and she reached for his customary Corona. Silence stretched while she wrapped up the day's reconciliation and he sipped at the beer.

Julie returned from supervising cleanup and patted Troy Lee's shoulder. "Starting your own fan club?"

He grimaced and took a long pull. "I guess."

Julie laughed and wandered into the kitchen. The picture of his touching the girl flashed in Angel's head again, bringing that breath-stealing wave of jealousy with it. Angel separated ones into stacks of fifty, rubber banded them and stuck them in the bank bag. "You don't have to hang around here, you know."

He stopped with the bottle halfway to his lips. "I always stay to make sure y'all get out okay."

"We're fine."

His brows lowered, eyes narrowed. "Trying to get rid of me?"

"Of course not." The small laugh she produced held sufficient scoffing. "I just wasn't sure if you had something to do or not."

More like someone to do. The mean and so-not-like-her thought darted through her head. Darn it, the last month had done a real number on her.

His eyes constricted further, to glittering blue slits. “Jealous and bitchy really doesn’t work on you, Angel baby.”

“Don’t call me that.” The unreasonable annoyance prickled beneath her skin. She didn’t want his pet names, didn’t want to fall any further into him, when all that would happen would be his leaving and her getting hurt all over again. “And I am not jealous.”

Without answer, he simply watched her. She stacked the next set of fifty bills against the bar with a sharp smack. “I am not jealous, Troy Lee. If you wanted to go out with one of those girls, it’s nothing to do with me.”

His shoulders moved in an easy shrug. “If I wanted to be with one of them, then I wouldn’t be sitting here. So what does that tell you?”

She paused and met his gaze straight on. “You should be seeing someone your own age, Troy Lee.”

“Please don’t start that bullshit again. It’s not the issue and you know it.”

“Really. What, pray tell, is the issue?”

“We’ve been out one time and already you’re looking for me to cut and run.” He shook his head. “You’re doing it again. Speeding ahead, looking for where you think you’re going, instead of seeing what’s along the way. You gotta learn to slow down and enjoy the ride, Angel.”

How was she supposed to argue with that?

They lapsed into silence once more, although some of the tension had dissipated. She finished her closing while he nursed the Corona. Her girls, including Julie, drifted out in twos and threes, until only the two of them remained. She locked the deposit in the safe, grabbed her bag and flipped through her keys to the one that secured the front door.

Outside, the sultry promise of the sunny day had dipped into a damp chill and she was glad to have his warm presence at her back, blocking the slight breeze, while she locked the door.

Guitar case in hand, he strolled across the parking lot at her side to where his Jeep waited next to her Mustang. He tossed the case into the passenger seat and she eyed the Wrangler’s bikini top. “You’re going to freeze.”

He cast a quick glance at it. “Nah. It’ll be nice to cool off after being under the lights.”

She fiddled with her keys, turning them between her fingers. “Well, good night then. Thank you for walking me out.”

“You’re welcome.” His gaze lingered on her face. With a lazy movement, he rested a hand on the roof of her car, bringing his long body into her personal space and filling her with breathless intensity.

She should speak, should laugh, should do *something.* Instead, all she could do was stare into those lash-fringed baby blues and imagine all the wicked possibilities suddenly trembling between them.

He lifted his other hand and sifted the fingers through her hair at her temple, rubbing a couple of strands together. One corner of his mouth hitched up. “About that kissing thing.”

Oh, this was so not like her...hadn’t she always been a take-charge kind of girl? And here she was, her back pressed against the driver’s side door, keys clenched in one hand, watching those beautiful eyes draw closer as he took the initiative and leaned in.

She closed her eyes before his mouth touched hers. Oh please, don’t let it be any good. It would be so much easier to walk, to let him go if—

Warm lips, a hint of lime and Corona. Pliable flesh, a bit of pressure, a suggestion of persuasive seduction, her bottom lip sucked lightly between his. Breathless, giddy desire plunging through her, swirling in an achy spin lower in her belly, pulsing to life between her thighs.

He lifted his mouth, caressed the corner of hers, then sought her lips once more. She rested her hands against his chest, over his thudding heart, and offered her mouth up to him, allowing his tongue to tease her lips apart.

Oh, this was good, playful strokes, a light tangle of tongues and lips. He moved closer, hard thighs brushing but not pressing to her own, both hands braced now on the car roof, his body holding her prisoner and providing shelter all at the same time.

She slid her hands up, over tight shoulders and into hair still damp at the edges. He growled an approval low in his throat, a deep male sound that clenched her belly with desire all over again.

He lifted his lips from hers and nuzzled her ear. “I get off at three tomorrow afternoon. Let’s do something.”

All the somethings they could do tumbled through her head. She spread her fingers across his shoulders and tried to focus on an idea other than more kisses, his hands on her naked skin, his body taking hers over and over until they lay satiated in her bed on a sunny Sunday afternoon.

"I have this rule about staying home and vegging out on Sunday afternoons after dinner at my mama's." Was that breathy voice hers? Lord, she sounded like a phone-sex operator.

He trailed his mouth down her neck and she felt him smile. "How about if I bring over a movie? About five, maybe? We can play couch potato."

The ideas she had about getting him on her couch didn't involve being couch-potato inactive, but she nodded. "Sounds good."

He straightened and pulled back, laid a caressing finger in the center of her lips. His eyes simmered with lingering passion, but his grin was as easy as always. "Five it is. I'll see you then."

Chapter Five

After four uneventful rounds of his patrol route and almost twice as many hours of teeth-clenching boredom, Troy Lee turned in the direction of the cemetery on Old Raiford Road. Just as he'd suspected, Chris Parker's K-9 unit sat on the other side of the hill, tucked under the spreading live oak. Gravel crunching under his wheels, Troy Lee slowed to a stop alongside and lowered his window.

Chris's head rested against the seat, dark sunglasses covering his eyes. Troy Lee shrugged off a wave of resentment. Weird how Chris or Steve or Cookie could catch a power nap while on duty, yet if he tried it, he was guaranteed a carpet-calling session with Calvert. Guess his dad had been right about life being neither fair nor equal.

He rested an elbow on the windowsill and studied Chris, trying to figure out if he was really asleep. Parker possessed the ultimate poker face, a trait that served him well in their shared profession.

"What's up?" Chris didn't move, but his lazy voice hinted at complete alertness.

"Absolutely nothing. This place is dead."

"Be grateful." Chris straightened but left his sunglasses in place. "We could be in the middle of another shift from hell."

"This is the shift from hell. I'm bored out of my freakin' skull." At least he only had an hour or so to go.

"Go write a ticket." A smirk played around Chris's mouth. "And draw an asshole on it."

"Shit, does everybody know?" Troy Lee slumped in his seat.

"Nah." Chris waffled a hand outside the window. "Cookie told me. He thinks it's hilarious."

"Glad somebody does," Troy Lee mumbled. "Calvert sure as hell didn't."

"He's got a lot on his mind right now."

"Yeah. That's right now. What about the last two and a half years?"

Chris harrumphed in mild amusement. "You've got a point."

Yeah, the point being that Calvert hated him and Troy Lee's goal of proving his worth to the man he'd seen as the embodiment of what he'd wanted to be as a cop was improbable. He should give up, go to another department, but something wouldn't let him, maybe the same something that had kept his dad puzzling over a seemingly unsolvable equation right up to his death.

"Hey, was I imagining things or was that Angel Henderson I saw you with yesterday?" Chris's quiet question pulled him from the futile musings.

"Yeah." Troy Lee squelched his radio as it squawked with a transmission between Steve Monroe and dispatch. "Why?"

"Just wondering." Chris shrugged and Troy Lee got the impression the K-9 officer was sizing him up behind the dark lenses. "You know, if that was awkward, with her and Cookie's past."

A one-night stand, Angel had called it. Was that a "past"? Besides, Cookie was completely wrapped up in Tori Calvert, so Troy Lee didn't really see him as either competition or an issue where Angel was concerned. Somehow he doubted she'd been thinking of his commanding officer either when he'd kissed her the night before. He could still taste her, feel her fingers buried in his hair, hear the breathless quality of her voice.

Keeping his hands off her while they watched a movie this evening was going to be a bitch.

"Earth to Troy Lee." Chris waved.

Troy Lee blinked at him. "What?"

"I asked if it was awkward."

Probably not as awkward as Chris being the center of recent speculation around the department about his sexuality, although he seemed to take it in stride, had even made offhand jokes about it during their morning runs. Troy Lee shrugged. "No. It's not awkward."

Chris nodded. “Good.”

Troy Lee twisted his arm to check his watch. Forty-five minutes. One more circle through town, checking the ins and outs, and he was done. Another two hours after that—time for a shower, maybe a run and to pick up DVDs from Video Central—and he could show up on Angel’s doorstep. He gunned the motor and reached for the gearshift. “I’m outta here. Gonna make one more round before I sign off.”

“Yeah, me too.” Chris started his unit. “Later.”

He was mere minutes away, a mile or two from town, when dispatch requested available units to respond to a disturbance at the strip mall that held the video store, a sandwich shop and an insurance office. He waited ten seconds, hoping despite his earlier desire for something to do that Chris would pick this one up. It just sounded like the kind of call that would end up making him late for his date with Angel. No reply was forthcoming from Chris and he reached for the mike with a muttered oath.

“10-4, Chandler, C-13 en route.”

He pressed harder on the accelerator, the police package responding with a low growl and a spurt of speed and power. Less than three minutes later, he pulled into the parking lot. His stomach clenched on a wave of dread and adrenaline as he spotted the ancient blue Ford parked sideways across the parking spots at the front of the video store. Oh fuck, the Stinsons. Just what he needed. Jed Stinson was a mean drunk and always wanted to do everything the hard way. Having his wife leave him and get a restraining order only made him madder and meaner.

Damn it, Troy Lee had known this was coming, ever since Maggie had taken the job working the register at the video place. Once Jed found out how to contact her, it wasn’t like the son of a bitch would leave her alone.

Troy Lee cruised to a halt just beyond the tail of Jed’s truck, called in his arrival and, as an afterthought, asked dispatch to phone Tori Calvert, who’d been walking Maggie through the delicate, dangerous process of separating herself from the abusive relationship. With a request for backup, he settled his hat on his head and exited the car.

“Mr. Stinson.” He nodded at the whipcord-lean man lounging against the hood of the Ford, arms crossed over his chest. Through the store's front glass, Troy Lee glimpsed Maggie's pale, frightened face, phone pressed to her ear. He motioned toward his unit. "Step over here with me a minute."

With one last malevolent glare at the front of the store, Jed complied, although his body language remained fidgety and angry. Troy Lee examined him—bloodshot eyes, wrinkled clothes, unshaven jaw. The untucked shirt offered concealment of a weapon, and Troy Lee knew from experience the man carried a hunting knife. "How much have you had to drink today, Mr. Stinson?"

Jed shook his head, chin lifting at a pugnacious angle. "Ain't drunk."

"I never said you were." He kept his voice steady and laced with calm authority. "At this time though, Mr. Stinson, you are under arrest for violating a restraining order. Turn around and place your hands on the vehicle, please."

Jed's expression never changed. "Ain't going to jail again."

F-uck, why did it always have to be the hard way? He was going to end up fighting the son of a bitch into the car. The last time it had taken him and Cookie both to subdue Jed, and Cookie had ended up needing stitches.

Troy Lee reached for his cuffs, keeping the other hand just above his holster, ready for multiple actions. "Turn around. Hands on the car."

A flash of white paint and silent blue lights passed on the side street at the same time a snazzy silver Miata darted into the parking lot.

"Fucking bitch." Jed stiffened all over, his hand going under the edge of his shirt. Adrenaline spiked through Troy Lee's system.

"Stop." He closed his fingers on the butt of his nine. "Hands where I can see them."

Jed ignored him, his infuriated, bleary gaze locked on Tori Calvert's car. Shit, let her be smart enough to stay put. Jed took one step forward, body tensed on a wave of fury and vengeance. *Pull his gun. Take Jed down physically.* The options shot through Troy Lee's brain. Jed was crazy, high at the moment on booze and retribution, and unlikely to respond to the gun as threat or control. One option.

Take him down.

He rasped his cuffs open and darted an assessment over

Jed's stance. Incapacitate that hand, the hidden one. Another engine purred into the lot and behind him Tori's car door opened with a quiet snick. Jed's eyes widened, narrowed, set on his prey. He coiled in preparation for a leap.

Damn it. *She opened the door.* Troy Lee grabbed Jed's arm as the hand came from under his shirt, the blade of a wicked hunting knife glinting in the dull sunlight. Hell, the fucker was strong.

"Drop it." He put all the pressure he could on Jed's wrist, twisting to get behind Jed, keeping clear of that knife and trying to get him down at the same time. "Drop it."

Under the pressure of his fingers digging into Jed's nerves, the knife finally clattered to the pavement. Now fully enraged, Jed screamed obscenities and fought his hold, kicking and flailing. Troy Lee used the nerve point in the wrist to bring him to his knees and shoved forward. Jed jerked backward, the top of his skull colliding with Troy Lee's chin.

His teeth snapped together and pain jarred through his head. He managed to get the cuff around one wrist and his knee in the small of Jed's back as Chris joined him, grabbing the other arm and bringing it around to be cuffed as well.

"About time you got here," Troy Lee panted. Blood dripped from his chin, splashing the front of his uniform.

"Looks like you had it under control." Chris laid his knee across Jed's wriggling shoulders. "Quit fighting, Jed."

Jed bellowed something that sounded like "ain't going to jail" interspersed with every foul word imaginable.

"Wanna bet?" Troy Lee clenched his teeth and regretted it as agony pounded along his jaw. "Swear to God, Jed, I'll hogtie you if I have to, but you're going to jail."

With Jed still protesting, he and Chris managed to get him searched and in the back of Troy Lee's car. The closed door muffled some of his incensed yelling. Troy Lee rested against the trunk and swiped his wrist across his chin. His hand came away smeared with blood.

Chris surveyed him with a critical eye. "Bet you need a couple of stitches."

"Nah. Butterfly bandage. It'll be all right." He went to grab his clipboard out of the front seat. The sooner he got the paperwork done, the sooner he could go 10-6, 10-42. A glance at the storefront showed Tori inside, calming Maggie.

He shook his head. "Really wished she'd stayed in the damn car."

"Who, Tori?"

"Yeah." He jotted the date and address across the top of the form. "He went crazy when he saw her."

"Probably blames her for..." Chris's voice trailed away in an uncomfortable cough and Troy Lee looked up from his clipboard. Cookie's Blazer slowed to turn into the lot. Unease slithered down his spine and coiled around his gut. Calvert was riding shotgun and even through the windshield the fury tightening his features was apparent.

Troy Lee closed his eyes. Hell, this was going to be fun.

Mark leaned on the counter and waited for a pause in Tori's quiet, intense conversation with Maggie Stinson. Jittery anxiety still jumped in him, but Tori seemed all right. Movie trailers blared from televisions in each corner of the store, the noise making his skin crawl.

Maggie pushed her thin hair behind her ears. "I'm going to wash my face."

"All right." Tori smiled. "I'll be right here."

He waited until Maggie disappeared into the backroom. "Are you okay?"

A rueful expression crossed Tori's pretty features. "Other than feeling like an idiot for not reading the situation better and almost getting Troy Lee hurt? I'm good."

He nodded, finally letting the relief have its way. He flicked a finger toward the door marked *Employees Only*. "How about Maggie?"

"She's really shaken up, and to make it worse, feels guilty for calling 911." Her troubled brown gaze darted toward the front glass and her posture slumped. "Oh, Mark. Go stop that, please."

He followed the direction of her gaze. Sure enough, Tick stood with Troy Lee in the middle of the parking lot, giving him hell. His face flushed, Tick stabbed his index finger into the palm of his other hand. The kid wasn't saying anything, his features set in a stoic mask, his gaze trained somewhere beyond Tick's shoulder. Chris had retreated to the driver's seat of his own patrol car.

A sigh shook his shoulders. Obviously, Tick didn't understand the concept of "lay off". "Let me go see if I can calm Tick down."

He pushed the door open. At least Tick wasn't yelling. Instead, he seemed to be speaking in the low, deadly tone he used in the interrogation room. Mark approached, noting the muscle flicking in Troy Lee's jaw. Ten to one, the kid was chewing the inside of his cheek.

"Do you understand how easily she could have been hurt?" Tick laid a hand across his side, where Mark knew the surgical incision ended.

Mark clapped an easy hand on his partner's shoulder. "Hey, Tick, go wait in the truck."

"What?" Tick stopped mid-harangue to stare at him.

"Go sit in the truck." Mark gestured toward the Blazer. "Now would be good."

Tick glared at him for a moment then threw his hands up and stalked toward the Blazer. Mark hooked his thumbs in his belt and studied Troy Lee. The blank mask remained in place; he continued to stare at the middle distance.

"Better get Jed to lockup." Rotating his wrist, Mark glanced at his watch. "Your shift ended twenty minutes ago."

Mouth tight, Troy Lee nodded. None of the tension drained from his stance.

Mark darted a look at Troy Lee's unit, Jed's silhouette visible through the back window. "You did good, kid. Jed's a tough arrest."

"Yeah." He rolled his shoulders, each motion tight and uncomfortable. "Can I go now?"

"Sure." Mark watched as Troy Lee walked to his patrol car and slid into the driver's seat. The young deputy wheeled around and pulled out of the lot. With a wave, Chris followed. Mark went to confer briefly with Tori before returning to his Blazer.

In the passenger seat, Tick glowered, bouncing his thumb off his knee. Strain painted a white line about his mouth. "Is there a reason I'm waiting in the truck?"

"Yeah." He fired the engine. "Because I asked you to."

"Very funny, Cookie."

"Fine. You're sitting in the truck because there's real

potential in that kid and I refuse to let you ruin him single-handed." He shifted into reverse.

"What?" Surprise vibrated in Tick's voice, raising the deep timbre almost to a yelp. "Do you realize what could have happened if Jed had—"

"Tick." He turned onto the two-lane highway. "She's fine. Feels bad for misreading the situation and leaving the car before Troy Lee had Jed cuffed and in the unit, but she's fine. And Troy Lee had it in hand. He controlled the scene, had Jed pretty much subdued when Chris got there, which you'd have known if you'd bothered to stop and ask before you jumped on him."

Tick ignored that and waved a dismissive gesture at the passing scenery. "Where are we going?"

"To get a cup of coffee and talk before I run you home."

"I'm not going to like this conversation, am I?"

A grin quirked at Mark's mouth. "Probably not."

Minutes later, they were settled into a back booth at the diner on the four-lane highway, mugs of steaming black coffee before them, and Tick looked anything but happy. "Go ahead, Cookie. Out with it."

Mark ran a fingertip around the rim of his cup. "You're not Superman, Tick, even if you think you are. You need to go home and stay there until your doctor actually clears you to return to duty."

Tick frowned over a long sip. "If this is about me helping you work that wreck—"

"It's not." Mark folded his hands around the hot pottery. "It's about you being out of your comfort zone and taking that out on Troy Lee. I'm telling you, Tick, I'm not letting you break him. If that means you go home until your head is straight, then that's what it means."

"Who the holy hell died and left you in charge?" A flush darkened Tick's cheekbones. "The last time I checked, I was the one with rank."

"You might have rank, but you're no FTO. If we're talking chasing down organized crime or murder leads or anything to deal with federal law, I'll give you that, Lamar. But taking stupid rookies and turning them into good cops? That's my field of expertise."

"You cannot send me home."

"Oh, I think I can. See, I happen to have an in with your very own version of kryptonite, Superman. She's about five-six, black hair, green eyes, owns your ass and you know it. Trust me. Not only can I send you home, I can keep you there."

"You would too." Pure disgruntlement tinged Tick's voice.

Mark didn't even try to restrain a smirk. "Damn right I would."

Tick slumped in the booth, tracing idle patterns on the faux-wood tabletop. "What do you mean, out of my comfort zone?"

A chuckle rumbled up from Mark's chest. Did Tick really not see it? "You're a total control freak, Tick. Probably worse than Falconetti is, I think. Look what's been going on in your life for the last month, stuff that you can't control—your wife's uterine rupture, your son's premature birth, your cancer diagnosis. Hell, even me and Tori. You don't think I know your issues with us go deeper than your doubts about my level of commitment to her?"

Tick lifted his mug. "You don't know what you're talking about."

"Yeah, I'm clueless. That's why I haven't figured out the reason you keep showing up at work when you're not supposed to be. You know, because it's the place you can control things when you have none over what happens with that baby in the NICU."

He was sure when Tick opened his mouth and closed it again, the words "go to hell" were being left unsaid. He leaned forward. "Shit, Tick, your whole life just changed. Y'all have waited forever for this baby and the reality of finally having him would be an adjustment even without the other stuff. Man, you've gone from being numero uno in Falconetti's life to sharing her with the one other person she loves as much as she does you. No wonder your center of gravity is off. One thing, though, is for damn sure—you're going to lay off that kid."

ꙮ

Troy Lee ran, feet nailing the track's pavement with perfect rhythm. His iPod was turned up, and Rage Against the Machine battered his eardrums so loud they should be bleeding. Fury pounded in him, hitting with every smack of his worn runners, blending with the waves of heat emanating from the asphalt.

Damn it all, he was supposed to be with Angel, drowning in her presence, forging more between them. He couldn't take this overwhelming anger to her, though. He'd given up playing the whole scenario through his head over and over. Reliving it didn't change anything. On the blackboard of his mind, he laid out the variables—Calvert's expectations, his previous screwups, the odds of reconciling the two. That kept coming up a big fat zero.

Maybe something more lurked out there, some indefinable factor he couldn't see. Maybe that something more was missing within him, a trait or strength he didn't possess. Maybe he should just quit.

The idea hurt. He let the rhythm of running, the utter familiarity of the track take him. Memory flashed in his mind, his father standing before the big chalkboard in his study, frowning over the massive, multilayered theorem he'd pursued for years. A couple of years after his death, another professor at Georgia Tech had finally solved the equation, but he'd made it clear he wouldn't have been able to succeed without Troy Farr's groundwork.

Troy Lee clenched his fingers into tighter fists, nails biting into his palms. His dad hadn't quit. Every single night of his life he'd stood before that blackboard, tossing a piece of chalk up and down, thinking. Somehow, quitting, letting Calvert's low opinion of him win, dishonored his father's perseverance.

However, he had to find a way to deal with it. Proving himself didn't seem to be working, no matter what he did. He rounded the curve, no closer to a solution than when he'd started, but the endorphins were kicking in, relieving the tension and rage. Yards in front of him, Cookie leaned on the fence and Troy Lee's body tightened all over again. He slowed the punishing pace, as much to begin taming his thundering heart as to prolong the inevitable.

Wasn't like he could avoid this conversation. He eased to a walk mere feet from where Cookie waited and tried to catch his breath. Sweat coated his skin, dripped from his hair, plastered his T-shirt to his body. Cookie extended a bottle of water covered with condensation. "Chris thought I might find you here."

"Yeah." Troy Lee seized the bottle on a burst of gratitude and bent double. "Well, you found me."

His voice emerged hoarse and shaking with exertion. Straightening, he walked out a circle and poured icy water down his throat, a hand at his side where a familiar stitch stabbed him. The too-cold liquid kicked off his heartburn and he grimaced, bending again as his lungs cramped, refusing to let him breathe fully.

When he could finally draw air in again, he uncurled and met Cookie's patient gray gaze. "Particular reason you wanted to find me?"

Cookie shrugged, his hands clasped easily, forearms resting on the fence. "Tick was pretty hard on you. Wanted to make sure you were okay."

"I'm fine." He picked out a point beyond the older man and focused on it, the way he did when he was running a race and needed to tune out the existence of competitors around him.

"Yeah. That why you're running yourself in the ground out here?"

He shrugged and took another slug of water. "I run every day. No big deal."

"I could make excuses for him, talk about what all's going on in his life right now, but I won't. He was a son of a bitch, pure and simple, and he shouldn't have jumped down your throat without reading the situation first."

Troy Lee rolled his shoulders again and looked away. "Yeah, whatever. Doubt it'll be the last time."

"I'm working on him, Troy Lee."

Working on him? Right. "Is that all you wanted? I've got somewhere to be and I'm already late."

"What are you doing in law enforcement, Troy Lee?" Cookie regarded him like a particularly difficult puzzle. The question slammed Troy Lee in the chest. Hell, now Cookie was going to start in on him. A frown twisted Cookie's heavy brows. "Or maybe I should ask what you're doing in police work down here."

"I'm in law enforcement because it was real." As he reacted to Cookie's easy, natural authority, the words spilled out before he could stop them. Troy Lee gave a short, harsh laugh and looked away. "As to what I'm doing down here...don't ask."

"Real, huh? It's definitely that." Cookie's calm voice brought

Troy Lee's attention back to him. "But real compared to what?"

"I don't know." Annoyance crawled under Troy Lee's skin. "Math, art, music."

"Makes sense." Cookie cleared his throat. "Listen, Troy Lee, don't let today set you back."

Set him back where? Into negative numbers? Didn't Cookie get it? Hell, he was at zero, he was *failing*, had been failing since day one in Chandler County. In the past, he'd skirted failure—coming in second or third in a race, making a B on a math exam—but he'd never outright failed at anything.

Until he'd put on the six-pointed star and everything had gone to hell.

"You're not a quitter." Cookie's quiet statement brought him back to reality with a jolt. Troy Lee looked up to find the investigator watching him the way Christine did a piece of clay, figuring out what to make of it. "Are you?"

"No." He straightened as much as his burning chest and cramping gut would allow. "I'm not."

"Good." Cookie's nod and slow smile of approval lightened the weight of personal disappointment somewhat. "We can work with that."

Angel tried to settle down, first with the piece of cross stitchery she'd been working on for almost two years and then with the latest *Southern Living*. Ridiculous, really, to be disappointed and completely at loose ends because Troy Lee had called to say he'd be delayed, had been edgy about whether or not he'd even show up.

A now-familiar engine rumbled to a stop outside. Anticipation fired to life and had her heading for the door. She swung it open within moments of Troy Lee's knock. At her first sight of him, hair damp and ruffled, a white T-shirt untucked over his jeans, her stomach lifted and fell with a distinctive flutter of female reaction. She lifted a nervous hand to brush her hair away from her face. "Hey. I'm glad you made it."

"Me too." Tension lingered in his voice, but he smiled as he stepped inside.

She leaned up to feather a kiss over his lips. He stilled for an almost imperceptible breath. The next, he seized her shoulders and she found herself backed to the wall. His chest warm and hard against hers, he took her mouth in a full, hot kiss filled with a hunger that bordered on desperation. Desire slammed into her and she parted her lips, allowing him full access. She wound her arms around his neck and gave into his devouring. He groaned and pressed closer, hips canted into hers. Even with heavy denim separating them, she couldn't miss the hardening ridge nestled against her belly.

"No." On a strangled sound, he pulled his mouth from hers and rested his forehead on the wall next to her temple. He gasped, his chest heaving.

She ran the tip of her tongue over her lips, tasting him still. Her entire being buzzed with passion, doing the whole singing-the-body-electric thrill. "No, what?"

He turned his head and swept his mouth across her cheek. "Not ruining this with you by going too fast because of today."

"Today?" Shifting to meet his blue gaze, she fingered the edges of his hair. She caught a glimpse of a bandage under his chin. "Did you have a bad day?"

A grimace crossed his face. "Something like that."

She nodded, still stroking the soft strands at his nape. On a shaky exhale, he released her, laid his palms against the wall and levered away. He leaned down to retrieve the small bag he'd dropped earlier. "Still interested in that movie?"

"This is nice." Two and a half hours later, the relaxation in Troy Lee's voice mirrored the boneless slump of his posture on her couch. Whatever tension he'd been carrying when he came through the door had drained away while they'd laughed through a light comedy.

"It is nice." She'd given up trying to keep a decorous distance between them halfway through the film, and now her head rested against his shoulder while they watched intrepid plumbers-turned-ghost-hunters on one of her satellite channels. She dipped a lazy hand into the almost empty popcorn bowl on his lap and pressed her thigh closer to his. "I can't remember the last time I slowed down enough to actually watch television like this."

He shifted, lifting his arm to drape it along her shoulders. "Told you…you gotta slow down and enjoy what's along the way."

They lapsed into silence, watching while sensors and

cameras were placed in a 1930's-era school building. She fanned her fingers over his knee and trailed a fingernail along the seam of his jeans in an idle up-and-down movement.

Onscreen, two of the ghost trackers walked down a dark hallway, trying to lure out any unseen spirits with questions and reacting to noises beyond their range of sight. Troy Lee coughed and set the bowl aside, removing his arm from her shoulders with the movement. Focused on the television, she settled her head against his arm once more, tracing the seam before drawing random designs with her fingertip on the top of his leg.

He coughed again and dropped his hands in his lap. She drew her leg up, knee bumping his, and traced the word *boo* on his lower thigh. "Do you believe in ghosts?"

"No." His voice emerged strangled and rough. He cleared his throat and she clued in to the shallow way his breathing had changed. Her gaze dropped to his hands, loosely draped over his zipper, then she lifted her eyes to his.

An impish grin pulled at her mouth. "Oops."

"Oops, my ass." His lazy smile set off swirls of desire low in her belly. He turned halfway and slid his arm behind her, playing with a stray tress of her hair. "So, Angel, when was the last time you made out on the couch?"

Made out? Did anyone actually do that anymore? With Jim, the goal of any kissing and petting had always been his getting her into bed with as minimal fuss as possible. The idea of wrapping up with Troy Lee Farr, kissing and touching and going no farther, sent a thrill through her.

"I can't remember." She ran a finger down his chest. "But it sounds like fun to me."

On a dark chuckle, he sifted one hand through her hair and lowered his head for a series of light, nipping kisses. She nipped back, nibbling at his lower lip before opening her mouth to allow him deeper access. With a sigh, she gripped his shoulders, let her hands slip over his biceps to the leanly sculpted muscles of his chest. He rewarded her with a low groan of pleasure.

With his fingers teasing riffs over her spine, he slanted his mouth across hers at a different angle. His taste, blended with a lingering hint of salt and butter, exploded on her tongue as the kiss deepened.

"Mm-hmm." Purring her approval, she snuggled closer, rubbing her fingertips down his chest and over the indentation of his abs, fanning them over his sides. The clean scent of him, warm and male, infiltrated her senses, saturating her, filling her.

"You taste so good," he murmured into her mouth. "Feel so good."

She wrapped her arms around his neck and pulled him down. A low laugh rumbled from his throat and he stretched them out, chest to chest, belly to belly, thighs to thighs. He stared at her, his blue eyes dark and stormy with pleased desire. His torso lifted and fell with an uneven rhythm, but his familiar easy grin curved his mouth.

She wriggled closer. "I like this."

"Me too." He traced her cheek with the back of his hand. "Being with you…it makes a lot of things better."

She ran her finger along the slight cleft in his chin, gently brushed the bandage on the underside. "What happened? Cut yourself shaving?"

"Hardly." He grimaced, but slid a hand down to rest just above her butt, snuggling her into him. "Busted my chin on a suspect's head while I was trying to subdue him."

"I'm sorry." She caressed the spot with a light finger.

"It's nothing." A hint of wickedness danced in his eyes. "But you can kiss me and make it better if you want to."

"You'd like that, huh?" On a shivery laugh, she eased in to take his mouth. With a smooth motion, he pressed her back and leaned over her, thumb caressing her ribcage while his tongue made teasing forays between her lips. Long fingers molded the side of her breast, but he didn't try to take the caress further. Something about the kissing, the soft sighs and touches, left her giddy in moments.

He ran a finger along her side, down the curve of her breast, dipping in at her waist, resting at her hip. "You're so soft."

She made a moue. "Too soft."

"Uh-uh. I like it." His hold tightened on her for a split second before he twisted his wrist to look at his watch. "I have to go."

She poked at his side, amazed at how hard he was, everywhere. "Afraid you'll miss curfew and get grounded?"

Pushing her back, he plundered her mouth in sweet retaliation for several long moments. “Working a split shift that starts at three a.m. I need to get my ass in the bed.”

Offering him her bed lay on the tip of her tongue, but she swallowed the words. This was enough for now, these sweet passion-filled moments in his arms, with nothing but kisses and hot embraces.

He buried his face against her neck. “You need to get some rest too. One night off a week isn’t enough.”

She rested her cheek atop his hair. “What time do you get off tomorrow?”

“Seven.” The word was muffled against her skin. His breathing puffed over her in a warm, tickling burst.

“Come by the bar. I’ll make you a burger.”

“Deal.” They disentangled and she walked him to the door. There, he leaned down to mold his mouth over hers. “Good night.”

“Sweet dreams.”

One corner of his lips quirked. “I’ll be dreaming of an angel. Damn straight they’ll be sweet.”

Long after he was gone, she leaned against the door, eyes closed, hugging close memories of the touch and taste of him, of the way he made her feel, and worrying, just a little, that she was already in way too deep.

Chapter Six

The rich aroma of roasting turkey saturated the hot air. Angel leaned against the sink, fanning herself and watching Mama mix up her famous cornbread dressing. The heat and aromas, usually mouthwatering, combined to leave her almost nauseous.

"Mama, there has to be something I can do." Maybe having a task to keep her hands busy would make her feel better...and steer her obsessive mind away from missing Troy Lee. Lord, he'd only been gone a day.

"I've got it, hon." Mama turned the dressing with nimble fingers one more time. "You can see if your daddy needs some tea, though."

Considering he hadn't rattled his glass, it was unlikely, but Angel trailed through to the den anyway. Her mama's waiting on Daddy hand and foot blew her mind. Let Troy Lee Farr rattle a tea glass at her, just once—

Oh, my Lord, she was full-gone on him, envisioning the two of them living together. Shaking her head, she went down the two steps to the sunken den, dark with wood paneling and blessedly cool after the kitchen. On the old console television, massive balloons and marching bands filled a New York street. Daddy was stretched out in the recliner, eyes closed.

Angel leaned down and whispered a kiss over the top of his bald head. He startled a bit and opened his eyes. "Hey, baby."

With a smile, Angel perched on the arm of his chair. "Hey, Daddy. Mama sent me to see if you needed more tea."

He lifted the tall tumbler imprinted with a whitetail buck and examined the contents. "I'm fine."

Filled with a burst of affection, she wrapped an arm about

his shoulders and hugged him. "Hope and Darryl and the girls should be here soon. Then you and Darryl can watch football all afternoon and be sorry."

He made a sound of assent in his throat, his gaze sliding sideways to the third recliner. He patted her knee in awkward comfort. "Not the same without Jimmy here, is it, sweetheart?"

For a split second, the question pricked, then she laughed. "Daddy, I haven't even thought about Jim in days."

The absolute truth of that statement sank in. For the past two weeks, all she'd been focused on was Troy Lee. Crap. For a girl who'd supposedly been in it only for fun and a good time...she'd failed miserably.

"It's all right, baby." Her daddy cleared his throat. "I understand."

"Daddy, seriously." She hugged herself, feeling freer than she had in, oh, forever. "I could care less that Jim isn't here. He made his choice, I'm glad he's happy. I'm over it and I have moved on."

"Angel!" Mama's harried voice trailed in from the kitchen. "Your cell phone is ringing."

Excitement spiked in her. She could think of only one person, really, who would be calling her cell on Thanksgiving Day. "Coming."

She hurried to snag her purse from the kitchen counter and paw through it for her cell. Yes, it was definitely Troy Lee, as Josh Turner's "Your Man", the ring tone she'd programmed for his number, continued to peal. Darn it, she had to get a smaller purse.

Triumphant at last, she pulled the metallic turquoise rectangle from underneath her change purse. She flipped it open and lifted it to her ear with a breathless "Hello."

"Hey." His dark-as-molasses voice slid over her ears. "I missed you."

"You too." She cast a look at her mother's back and slipped out the door to the deck. "Happy Thanksgiving."

"Are you having a good day?" Even over the less-than-clear connection, she could hear the wistfulness coloring his tone.

It would be better if you were here. "Yes. Mama's just now making the dressing, but we always eat a late Thanksgiving dinner. How about you? Prepared to eat too much turkey?"

"Turkey? Um, Christine's not much for the traditional meal."

"Really?" She couldn't imagine. Her mother's turkey, dressing, sweet-potato casserole and pecan pie were the highlight of every November. "What are y'all having?"

"It smells like…moo goo gai pan. And General Tso's chicken. I think."

"You're eating Chinese takeout for Thanksgiving dinner?" Even she heard the shocked horror in her words. "Oh, Troy Lee."

He laughed, the deep sound warming her all the way to her pink-tipped toes. "It's okay, babe. It's kind of a tradition and I'm with family. That's what counts, right?"

"Yes." She leaned against the wall by the door and fiddled with the ends of her hair. "So when are you coming"—she swallowed the word home—"back?"

"Probably sometime tomorrow. I have to be on duty Saturday at seven a.m." A female voice rose in the background. "That's Ellis. I'm being summoned, so I'll let you go. Happy Thanksgiving, baby. See you soon."

"Bye." She whispered the word even as the connection died. Melancholy shivered through her. Doggone it, she *was* in too deep with him.

Even worse, she didn't care.

"Ellis, I said I was coming." At his younger sister's yell, Troy Lee pushed up from the couch. For the first time ever, he wanted to be somewhere other than home for Thanksgiving.

He ambled up the stairs to the house's second level, where the kitchen and dining room shared space with Christine's studio. Weak sunlight streamed in through tall windows, highlighting the multicolor pottery dishes waiting on the rough-hewn table loaded with white cardboard takeout boxes.

"What do you want to drink?" Ellis poked him in the ribs with a set of chopsticks as she passed by to the kitchen.

"Anything's fine." He peered into a container. Yep, General Tso's chicken. He'd been right about the moo goo gai pan, and more boxes held shrimp lo mein and egg rolls. His mouth watered and he smiled, remembering Angel's shock at the idea of what he considered the ultimate Thanksgiving meal. Thinking of her sent a dart of mingled warmth and loneliness through him.

Christine folded her voluminous skirt around her legs and handed him a pair of chopsticks. “Phoning someone special?”

He paused in the act of snitching an egg roll and darted a look at her serene, knowing expression. No point in trying to prevaricate. She knew him too well. He laid the steaming wrap on his plate. “Angel.”

“Oh.” A pleased smile flirted over Christine’s mouth and she nodded. “Angel.”

What was that all about? Shrugging, he reached for the box holding the General Tso’s chicken.

“Mom.” His other sister Montgomery rested her elbow on the table and leaned toward her mother, a teasing glint in eyes the same shade of blue as his own. “She’s older than he is.”

He gave her a look. One day he’d learn not to confide in her. She couldn’t keep a secret if her life depended on it.

“Really?” Christine ladled shrimp lo mein onto her plate. “There’s nothing wrong with that.”

Ellis set a glass of iced water before him and sank onto the chair next to his. “Does that mean I can go out with David Norton?”

Christine pinned her with a look. “No.”

With a pout, Ellis subsided. Troy Lee swallowed a chuckle. Although she was only sixteen, she was already enrolled at Georgia Tech, a freshman just a year behind Montgomery, who was a sophomore at nearly twenty, attending the Atlanta campus of the Savannah School of Art and Design. Since that made Ellis think she was all grown-up, having to toe Christine’s relatively strict line grated.

“So tell us about your Angel.” Christine clicked her chopsticks at him.

His Angel. Damn, he liked the sound of that. “She’s...great. Smart, funny, owns her own business. Makes the best burgers you’ve ever tasted.”

Not to mention absolutely beautiful and a fantastic kisser. More than that, they clicked in a way he’d not experienced before. He could laugh with her, talk with her. Hell, he was beginning to think this was the woman he could live his life with.

And what had he done? Convinced her it was all about fun

and games.

He was a damn idiot. But at least he was an idiot who knew where he wanted to be.

"So." He closed the sticks around a piece of spicy chicken. "Would it bother you if I didn't spend the night and went home after dinner?"

He didn't miss the excited look his sisters exchanged, a verbal giggle of sorts. Christine smiled her serene smile, pleasure lighting her eyes. "Not at all."

Something was off. Feeling like he was trapped in one of those "how many things can you find wrong" cartoons from the Sunday paper, Mark followed Tori out to her mother's patio and settled next to her on the glider. The sense of things being out of whack niggled at him, the same way it did when somebody moved the stuff around on his desk when he was out of the office.

At first, he'd thought maybe it was being here with Tori for the first time in the official "boyfriend" role and having her other brothers Del and Chuck size him up the way Tick had been doing for weeks, but neither Chuck's open yet easy assessment nor Del's quiet observation got under his skin. Maybe it was being part of a family celebration when he'd been alone for so long.

Mentally shrugging off the unease, he relaxed and let himself enjoy simply being in Tori's presence. Full and replete, most of the adults had wandered out to take advantage of the warm afternoon. On the lawn, Chuck tossed a football with his sons. Del's teenaged daughters had gone down to the dock with iPods and cell phones. Inside, Lenora Calvert enjoyed some quiet grandmother time with Chuck's daughter while her daughter-in-law rocked the youngest to sleep. That left Mark and Tori on the patio with Del and his wife Barbara and Tick and Caitlin. Home from Georgia Tech for the first time this semester, Blake, Del and Barb's son, lounged on the steps leading to the screened porch and shared anecdotes about his freshmen induction into college life.

"Oh man, I have to tell you this one. You won't believe it." Blake tossed his long bangs away from Calvert-brown eyes and rested his elbows on the top step. "I'm enrolled in Calculus II, right? And I'm thinking, hey, I survived Ms. Francesco's AP class, I should be okay."

"Why do I hear a 'but' coming here?" Del leaned back on the chaise and draped his arm around Barbara's shoulders. "And maybe an 'F' on your grade report?"

"I'm holding on to a B." Blake's teeth flashed in a grin. "Barely. Anyway, this class is hard. So I join a study group with some other kids because midterms are coming up and I know I have to pass that exam. A couple of weeks ago, we're over at Ellis's house, studying—"

"Ellis." With a knowing expression, Barbara poked Del's ribs.

Blake rolled his eyes. "Mama, she's sixteen and she has a crush on our TA."

"Wait." Tori lifted her hands with a laugh. "Sixteen and a freshman at Georgia Tech?"

"Yeah. Wild, huh? She's wicked smart." Blake leaned forward, hands between his knees. "But you have to let me tell the story."

"Go ahead." Tori subsided, wiggling her shoulder under Mark's arm. Warmth flashed out from the contact.

"So it's late and we're stuck on derivatives and I'm so lost it's pitiful. I'm not the only one, either. So Ellis says, 'I'm calling my brother. He can explain it.' So she calls him, right? Puts him on speaker on her cell. Sure enough, he can explain it where I can understand it, and everybody is taking notes as fast as they can. The whole time I'm writing, I'm thinking, I know that voice. I've heard this guy's voice before. Then the police radio starts squawking in the background and I finally realize who it is." Blake paused for effect. "Troy Lee."

Tick chuckled. "What?"

"Swear to God, Ellis's brother is Troy Lee Farr." Blake held up both palms. "The next hour, he's explaining derivatives and integrals over the phone and he'd put us on hold when he stopped to write a ticket or whatever, although it must have been a slow night."

Tick rested his elbow on the chair arm and his mouth against his hand. "Troy Lee Farr tutored you in Calculus."

"I'm telling you, the guy is a math genius. We all made A's on the midterm."

"So Ellis's last name didn't clue you in before she called?" Tori asked, echoing Mark's thoughts.

Blake shook his head. "Ellis uses her mom's maiden name instead of Farr. Doesn't want people in the math department judging her or treating her special because of her dad."

Barbara wound her fingers through Del's. "What do you mean, because of her dad?"

"He was some bigwig math professor up there. They named an entire wing of the math building after him when he died. He was mugged leaving school late one night. The guy hit him in the head and he never came out of the coma." Blake shrugged. "According to Ellis, that's why Troy Lee became a cop. He'd been a physics major, with a minor in music, but after that he switched to criminal justice."

Tick's eyebrows lifted, a wry expression twisting his face. *Wish he'd stayed in physics.* Mark sensed the thought flashing through Tick's head as surely as if he murmured it aloud.

"Anyway," Blake went on, "I considered asking him to tutor me when I take physics next semester, but then I thought about how much he hates Uncle Tick and decided maybe not."

"Hates me?" Tick dropped his hand on a *pfft*. "Right."

Tori snorted. "If you treated me the way you do him, I'd hate you."

"Thanks a lot." Wry sarcasm laced Tick's voice. He turned irritated eyes in Mark's directions. "I suppose this is where you're going to chime in? Tell me how much the kid and I have in common?"

Mark opened his mouth, but Caitlin's quiet laugh forestalled him.

"He is a lot like you." She laid her palm on Tick's thigh in an easy contact Mark had witnessed dozens of times. The disconnect Mark had been trying to pinpoint all day coalesced in his mind. It was the two of them—

"He is not." A visible wave of tension moved through Tick's body, like watching the beginning of tsunami after an underwater quake. He shifted, Caitlin's hand falling away from his leg.

"You're right." Del's relaxed tone broke the silent vibrating strain. "You're not that good at math."

Tick's tight grin looked more like a grimace. "Just because you can do amortization schedules in your head..."

Del laughed and the conversation turned in another direction, the awkward moment seemingly forgotten. Mark stretched his arm along the back of the glider and watched. That's what had been niggling at him all day—the differences in their interactions, Caitlin's unusual reserve, the way Tick kept a certain physical distance between them.

Tori nudged him in the ribs. "I'm going to see if Mama needs help in the kitchen. Come with me."

No doubt existed in his mind that Lenora Calvert's kitchen was as spotless as always, but he followed regardless. In the sparkling clean room, Tori turned into his embrace and rested her nose against his shoulder.

"I was afraid of that," she muttered, muffled by his shirt.

He was such a sucker for her. All he wanted to do was find a way to take the sadness and worry out of her voice. With a sigh, he wrapped his arms around her waist. "Afraid of what, honey?"

"That." She waved a hand toward the patio. "He's going to pull into himself with the Captain America act—"

"Superman."

"—and shut her out in the process because he's had to face his own mortality and he can't control what happens with Lee."

He rested his cheek against her hair. "Don't worry. Falconetti's pretty good at sizing up a situation and taking control. She'll reel him in."

At least he hoped so.

"What are you doing here? You're supposed to be in Atlanta."

At Chris's surprised voice, Troy Lee looked up from the monthly traffic report he was compiling ahead of time. He shrugged as Chris fed quarters into the soda machine. "I came home early."

"So why are you here?" Chris slumped into the chair at the vacant desk fronting Cookie's.

Because he'd needed something to do and the empty squad room had offered both a distraction and quiet, with the only noise the muted squawking from the radio room downstairs. "I could ask you the same question. You're not on duty, either."

"Yeah, but I don't have family anywhere." Chris popped the soda top and swigged, grimacing.

"I wanted to come home, okay? Sheesh. I needed to kill

some time, so I figured I'd start on this." He entered another ticket number into the spreadsheet. Chris snorted a laugh and Troy Lee looked up, annoyed. "What?"

Chris's knowing gaze made his skin crawl. "You just referred to Coney as home. You've never done that."

"Slip of the tongue. Big deal."

"Yeah." Humor lurked in Chris's monosyllable and the silence that fell after it.

Aware Chris was studying him like some kind of lab specimen, he entered a couple more tickets—damn, Angel had two warnings this month—and turned his head to glower at his friend and colleague. "What?"

"She really has you hooked, doesn't she?"

He didn't even have to ask who Chris meant. He turned back to the computer. "No fishing metaphors. Makes me think of..." He jerked a thumb over his shoulder in the direction of Tick Calvert's office.

"So why are you here, if you came home to see her?"

He didn't miss the emphasis Chris placed on home. "Because she's *not* home."

"How many times did you go by?"

He held up three fingers and waited for the ribbing to begin.

Chris laughed, softly. "Dude, you're a stalker."

"I am not a stalker. I want to surprise her."

"So you're driving by her house repeatedly." Chris snickered over a swallow of soda and stretched his legs out, crossing one ankle over the other. "Sounds like stalking to me."

"Did anyone ask you?" He cast sideways glances at Chris between ticket numbers. Chris never made a big deal about being alone at the holidays, but being without family had to be a bitch. Even as aggravating as Ellis and Montgomery could be, he wouldn't trade them for anything. "What did you do today?"

"Worked with Hound. Watched the bowl game. Took a nap."

"You lead a sad life, Parker." A sad, *lonely* life from the sound of things.

"I'm not the one stalking women."

"Woman, singular. And I'm not stalking her." He laid aside a stack of officer copies and saved the file to the department server. Maybe Cookie would be the one to review the recap.

That way, maybe he'd avoid another little visit with Calvert, going over each and every fucking line. "I'm...waiting for her."

"You know it's after nine, right?" Chris tapped his watch. "When was the last time you went by?"

"Shit, after nine? You're kidding me." A twist of his wrist confirmed the fact it was closer to nine thirty. He'd immersed himself in the data entry and...damn it. "I gotta go."

Angel picked up her cell from the bedside table and put it down again for what had to be the fifteenth time. This was ridiculous. Okay, fine, she missed him. She wanted him around. However, she was nearly thirty-seven years old. Old enough not to have these girl-with-a-crush urges to call him just to hear his voice. To lie against the pillows and listen to him talk, to imagine him in that very same bed beside her.

He'd be home tomorrow. Besides, hadn't her mama always said it was bad manners to phone after nine o'clock?

"You can wait." She addressed her reflection in the mirror over her dresser with a stern voice. She'd take a long hot shower and go to bed early. Darn it all, why hadn't she opened the bar tonight?

In the shower, she soaped and loofahed and shaved, lathered, rinsed and repeated. Cleaner and smoother, but not relaxed, she pulled on a camisole and pajama pants and stared at the empty expanse of her bed. Shoot, if she went to bed, she wouldn't be able to sleep. She'd end up staring at the ceiling, thinking about his smile, his eyes, his hands, his mouth. Oh yes, she was gone on him.

What was she going to do about it? He seemed perfectly happy with what they had. She'd given one man way too much of her life already, waiting for more. She'd given another way too much too soon, hoping for more. Did she dare leave things as they were, let the relationship unfurl as it would?

Her cell phone vibrated to life and she jumped as "Your Man" filled the air. Anticipation buzzed through her. She snatched up the phone.

"Hello?" The syllables emerged breathless and damn near quivering.

"Did you know you have the sexiest phone voice, ever?" His rich tenor filled her ear, the tones lazy and satisfied, the way he sounded after thoroughly kissing her.

"Hmm, don't think so." She strove for casual and relaxed, although she wasn't sure she pulled it off. "At least no one's ever told me that before."

"Well, you do," he murmured. If she closed her eyes, she could picture him, sprawled out, phone at his ear, while he drove her crazy with the sexiest male voice ever. The insidious desire pinched at her again. "So what are you doing?"

"Talking to you," she replied with just the right note of cheekiness. Good, she didn't sound too eager. "I just got out of the shower and ready for bed. What are you doing?"

"Standing on your front porch talking to you."

Her ability to breathe stopped stone cold. "What? Troy Lee, don't tease."

"Who's teasing? Come to the door and see for yourself."

A blend of hope and annoyance swirled within her. Barefoot, she padded through the living room. "I swear, if this is some kind of a joke, I'll—"

She swung the door open and the words died in her throat. "Oh my Lord."

Under the porch light, he grinned at her and snapped his phone closed. He held aloft a cellophane package. "I brought you a fortune cookie."

She stared at him, her voice gone, swallowed up by surprise and sheer, overwhelming joy. One thumb hooked in his pocket, he appeared relaxed and almost boneless in his jeans and a T-shirt emblazoned with "26-2". Somehow, she tamped down the swamping desire to throw herself into his arms.

His eyes gleamed, burned. "Don't."

"Don't what?" She finally found her ability to talk, although the words came out shaky and small.

"Don't hold back." His blue gaze dark and serious, he didn't temper the words with a grin. "I don't want you to."

She tucked damp hair behind her ears, suddenly aware they were talking about more than the obvious. "Are you sure about that?"

One corner of his mouth hitched up. "I've always been sure."

"What happened to just for fun, no sex or expectations?"

A chuckle escaped him in a low rumble. "I had to say something to get you to go out with me."

She laughed, eating him up with her eyes, wondering what she was supposed to say or do next.

He held the cellophane packet up again. "So do you want your fortune cookie? I mean, I drove four hours—"

"I want you."

His eyes went from smoldering to blazing. "Angel baby, I'm yours. Hell, I'm so yours it isn't funny."

A hot stare trembled between them, and in one step forward, two steps backward, her back landed against the wall inside the door and his mouth covered hers, kissing, teasing, devouring. She pushed at the door with one hand and somehow got it closed.

He lifted his mouth, chest heaving. He nuzzled her ear, uneven warmth rushing over her skin with each of his breaths.

"I want to know everything about you," he murmured, hands moving over bare shoulders. His lips found hers. "What makes you moan, what turns you on, what makes you come apart."

"Yes." Her knees threatened to weaken, to leave her melted and boneless in his arms. "Oh Lord, Troy Lee, I want that."

And more, that elusive something more, that specialness she'd never been for any other man. She wanted to lose herself in him, fall into them.

"Let me." He dipped the very tip of his tongue between her lips, teasing, tantalizing, while his body pressed into hers, so she felt every hard inch of him. "Let me know you all over."

She surged up against him, wrapping her arms around his neck. In a silence punctuated by kisses, she drew him the short distance to the dimness of her bedroom. He stared at her and sifted his fingers through her hair, stroked along her throat and shoulders, hooked his forefingers beneath her camisole straps and slid them down her arms. In their wake, he danced caresses along her bare skin.

"I've dreamed about this, about you," she whispered, shivering as fingertips, callused from strumming guitar strings, feathered over her collarbone and traveled down to just touch the rise of her breasts.

"Me too." He traced the lacy edge of her camisole. "Dreamed about you, thought about you, fantasized about you."

"Fantasized?" Her breathless voice dripped with the arousal he brought to life within her. No one had ever claimed that she'd inspired his fantasies, and all sorts of wicked possibilities tumbled through her head as she pondered what he'd imagined, what he'd done while thinking of her. She flicked a glance up at him, from his burning gaze, to his fly and back again.

A slow, devilish smile revealed white teeth and he leaned in to whisper near her ear, “Yes, I did, while thinking about you, if that's what you're wondering.”

Her faced burned, even as another flush of arousal sizzled through her, ending in a wet, pulsing heat between her legs. His dark chuckle tickled her ear. “It shocks you, doesn't it, that I jacked off while thinking about being inside you. You're awful naïve, for a woman who keeps giving me hell about being older than me.”

With every word, he made teasing little forays just under her camisole. She moistened dry lips. “There haven't been that many men who would have had reason to think about me and...and...”

“You can't get it out, can you?” He laughed again, still touching her as he circled to stand behind her, fingertips rubbing maddening trails along the edge of her cami. “Have you ever done it?”

“Done what?” Now his chest pressed against her back, his arms enfolding her as he teased.

His humor rumbled through her and he pressed his lips to her shoulder. “I thought not.”

“That doesn't mean anything, Troy Lee.” She tried for a stern note, but with his mouth doing sinful things to her neck while he edged the camisole down, she couldn't pull off more than a husky protest.

“Maybe not.” The thin fabric pooled at her waist. He hooked his thumbs in it and swept it and her loose pajama pants down in one easy movement. Hot palms spread over her belly, covering, heating, enticing. “Or maybe it means Jim Tyre was too much of a dumbass to inspire you.”

“Why are we talking about Jim?” She shivered, anticipating the movement of those long-fingered hands, maybe one upward to her breasts, another down to the damp heat trembling and unfurling at the top of her thighs.

“Because I want you to get that I'm not him.” His teeth scraped at her earlobe. “It's not going to be about ten minutes in the missionary position, with a couple of quick feels as foreplay. Or maybe having you on top when the mood is adventurous."

Shock slid over her and she turned her head. "How did you—"

"He looks the type." His fingers moved in a soft fret over her skin, but his hands didn't change position. "A little too straight arrow to inspire a woman like you."

"Like me?" With her head turned toward him, she could see their shadowy reflections in the old mirror above her dresser, light glimmering over her pale nudity while he almost loomed behind her, fully clothed, his face taut with desire.

The easygoing almost-too-pretty-boy was gone. In his place was all male, all man, set on ravaging her. A visceral thrill moved over her. "What do you mean, a woman like me?"

"One who takes charge and likes to make things happen." He nipped at her ear once more. "One who knows what she wants. You do, don't you, baby? You know what you want me to do to you."

Oh Lord, did she. The picture that had repeated in her brain over and over flashed through her mind—her hands wrapped around the footboard, his tall body behind hers, having him all over her while he drove into her again and again.

"Yes." Her raw whisper tore from her throat.

"Then show me." All laughter had disappeared from his deep voice. "Make me give you what you want."

Chapter Seven

She wrapped trembling fingers around his wrists. Under her touch, his skin was hot, and crisp hair abraded her fingertips. She closed her eyes, his "make me give you what you want" beating in her head. What did she want?

Him, all over her. His hands, playing her body the way he did a guitar.

On a deep inhale, she spread his arms, moving one palm up to her breasts, sliding his other hand to the juncture of her thighs. He caught his breath, thighs brushing her butt, his fingers tightening. Roughened fingertips swept over her nipple.

"Oh yeah, baby." His murmur rushed over her ear. "Make me give it to you. Do you know how freakin' sexy that is?"

Heat flushed her face, her momentary embarrassment soon lost to the sensation sizzling out from his soft tweaking at her nipple. His other hand flexed beneath her easy hold, fingers sliding over intimate folds. "Show me how to touch you."

Eyes closed tight, she pressed his palm over her mound, urging his fingers into the moisture between her legs. Soon, he'd picked up the rhythm she set, plunging two fingers inside her while the heel of his hand ground against her clit. At her breast, he plucked at her nipple, rolling and teasing the hard flesh. Tense desire bloomed low in her belly, growing, uncurling, heating her body. A moan slipped from between her lips.

She released his wrists and clutched the sides of his thighs, afraid her knees would give out. He nipped and suckled a path from her ear, down her neck, across her shoulder. "You feel so good, Angel, so hot and soft...damn, I love how soft you are, all over..."

His gravelly voice only added to the irresistible sensation

swirling through her. She pressed her spine against his front, even the oft-washed denim of his jeans a sensual torture against her sensitized body. The exquisite pressure swelled and she dug into his legs, a hard shudder moving over her. "Troy Lee, I'm going to come."

His lips fastened on the area between her neck and shoulder for one intense second. She bowed, straining against his hand. "Troy Lee—"

"I want to taste you." He moved with an agility and speed that froze her already reluctant lungs. Using one arm about her waist, he lifted her easily to the bed, her back still to him, and on her knees, she grasped at the footboard, old and worn smooth by time, to steady herself. Her body buzzed and tingled, on the edge of climax, and she sucked in a shaky breath. He pumped his fingers inside her, a slow in-and-out slide, and his other hand spread across her stomach, tilting her to him, the soft cotton of his T-shirt rubbing against her thigh. The next second his mouth was on her, his tongue a hot, wet rasp over her clit, slipping, gliding, skimming. Every muscle she possessed went screaming taut and she arched into him, seeking more of his hands, more of his mouth, more of him.

"You're fantastic." He muttered the words, and moist, heated breath rushed over her, his thumb brushing along her dripping folds. He swirled his tongue around the tiny trove of nerve endings, painful pleasure clenching her body tighter. "I can't get enough of you, don't want to get enough of you."

She danced along the sharp edge of an orgasm, not quite falling over, despite the dual torment of his mouth and fingers. "I want you to fuck me."

Had those words actually come from her lips? She'd never said them before. In her world, good girls, even ones who flirted with the edges of scandal, who got themselves talked about, didn't say them, certainly didn't tremble and throb and burn for him to follow through.

His raw inhale chafed through her and he was gone, leaving her gripping the bed for dear life, eyes closed, afraid of what she'd done with those words. Fabric rustled, twin thuds hit her floor. Plastic crackled and he hissed in a breath before his large hand covered her again, sliding over the wet flesh.

"You don't know how long I've wanted this." His dark whisper flowed over her ears, hips bumping hers, the thick ridge of his erection rubbing along the damp throbbing between her legs. The head nudged at her clit, the warmth of his palm and fingers spreading across her lower stomach, combining with the incredible heat of his body at her back. "How long I've wanted you."

"Troy Lee, please." She pushed against him, wriggling her butt into the cradle of his pelvis. "Stop teasing."

"Make me." Another torturous glide between her thighs. He brushed his nose up her spine, stopping to drop a hard kiss on her shoulder. "Tell me what you want. I want to hear you say it again."

"I can't." She tingled all over, her skin burning, her breasts aching with each sway.

"Angel." He traced whirls over her belly, up her ribcage to roll one begging nipple between his damp thumb and forefinger. The clean, sharp note of arousal invaded her nose, their scents all tangled together, making her only want more. Teeth scraped her shoulder, leaving prickles of pain and shivers of passion in their wake. "Make me give you what you want."

She shifted, trying to place the head of his erection at the opening of her body. His palm flattened against her stomach and he held her still.

"No. Tell me. Make me give it to you."

"Fuck me." She lifted heavy lids and tightened her slippery hold on the footboard. Moistening her lips with the tip of her tongue, she swallowed. "Make love to me."

His forehead rested against her shoulder, only long enough for her to have an impression of warm, damp skin. He moved, hips canted into hers, and pressing forward, he took her, tunneling each delicious inch of hardness into her in a deep, luscious slide.

"Oh." The breathy sigh fell from her lips as her body stretched, adjusted, clung to him.

"God." His voice was broken, strangled. With his hand spread across her belly, fingers resting in the curls atop her mons, he pulled back and bore forward again, easy and slow. "You're so soft, hot and soft and...damn, you're wet. It's so good, baby, love how you feel around me."

"More," she whimpered on a shaky moan. "Harder."

"I thought about this." He thrust, driving deeper, harder into her, his tempo increasing. His words emerged as harsh gasps, punctuating his strokes. "About what it would be like to be inside you, having you come around me, but this is so much better, Angel, so much more than what I imagined." He licked at her back, nibbling, suckling. "I want you to come for me. I want to feel you coming all over me."

She ground into him, taking everything as he lunged over her in a hard, even rhythm. With every forward motion, his scrotum tapped into her clit, her lips, teasing, propelling her closer to climax. Cupping her belly, he used the pressure to pull her more fully into his momentum. She met him, twisting her swollen sex into each rolling shove of his hips.

"Oh yeah, that's it, baby." He fastened his mouth on the sensitive area where her shoulder and neck met. "Take me, Angel. Fuck me, sweetheart."

The rough growl put her over the edge, pleasure searing into shards that pierced her whole body, forcing a scream from her throat, blanking her mind. Sweat dripped from his neck, hitting her back, and he plunged harder against her, callused fingertips strumming further notes of pleasure at her clitoris. She stiffened as the arousal pitched in her body again, rising to a sharper, razoring climax. On a raw gasp, she slammed down on him, and his hold tightened to a painful level. A hoarse shout spilled from his throat, vibrating over her skin, and he pushed higher into her, hardness pulsing within her.

Huffing for oxygen that simply wasn't there, she melted in his arms. He spun them to the mattress, his chest heaving beneath her. She threw out her arms above her head, her body one big live wire, teeming and buzzing with electricity.

Oh Lord. She'd never...not twice...well, twice in one night, but not twice during one bout...

His arms tightened about her and he rubbed his face against her shoulder. His humming sigh, redolent with male satiation, puffed over her skin. A pure, sweet emotion trembled in her, threatening to bring tears to her eyes. She liked this, being with him this way. He raised onto his elbows and peppered light kisses across her collarbone.

"Bathroom?" He sounded winded, as if he'd run several miles and was panting for breath.

Not possessing the capacity of speech, she lifted a languid hand and pointed toward the back of the house.

"Be right back." He brushed his mouth over her shoulder

and rolled from the bed.

A hand over her thundering heart, she stared at the ceiling and tried to gather her thoughts, her wits, herself. Laughter bubbled up from her throat. She'd thought Mark Cook was hell on wheels in bed? Shoot. Jim didn't even make it into the starting lane of this comparison. She pushed damp hair away from her forehead. If she'd known it was going to be like this between them, she'd have tossed his long, lean self on that prep table in her kitchen two weeks ago.

The mattress dipped and he sprawled out beside her. He propped an elbow on either side of her neck and kissed her, his skin hot and damp with perspiration, before he flipped to his back, their sides perfectly aligned to touch shoulder to knee. He stretched with an elaborate groan of satisfaction.

She poked his side. "You have a bad-boy side hiding under that deputy's uniform, don't you, Troy Lee?"

One corner of his mouth hitched up. "You like it?"

"Um, yeah." She flattened her hand on his abdomen, relishing the feel of hard muscle there. Her body quivered with aftershocks of his possession, a feminine soreness pulsing between her legs. She could smell him on her, smell herself on him. "You could say that."

A chuckle vibrated under her fingers and he closed his eyes. "I'm bringing you fortune cookies more often, that's for damn sure."

Laughter fizzed in her once more, ending in a replete sigh. After several silent moments, Troy Lee rolled to his side and levered up on an elbow. His gaze lingered on her face, trailed down her throat, caressed the length of her legs and back again. Angel squashed the instinct to squirm under that look, with its note of worshipfulness. Something about the glint in his blue eyes spoke of long nights spent thinking of her, of fantasies come true beyond imagining. That glint made her buzz and burn all over again.

Silent, he touched her jaw with a single finger, letting the rough pad take the same journey his gaze had. The sense of being cherished, worshipped deepened. She couldn't recall anyone ever looking at her, touching her, with such reverence. With his fingertip, he drew a line up her stomach, circled the silhouette of one breast, then the other. Under the simple feathering caress, her nipples tightened, breasts feeling more sensitive to touch than she ever remembered, and a rush of desire became a sweet pang low in her belly, the tender flesh between her thighs swollen and wanting.

She swallowed and darted her tongue out to moisten her bottom lip. "Are you trying to start something, Troy Lee?"

In a slow, languorous movement, his gaze lifted to hers, passion and emotion shining in the blue depths. "I think we started something weeks ago, something I don't want to see end."

He couldn't say these things, couldn't dangle the temptation of finally being or finding something more before her. "Troy Lee—"

"Don't. I told you, no holding back, Angel." The maddening digit found the hollow of her collarbone, slid to the wild pulse in her throat, shaped her bottom lip. "Baby, do you really think we were ever just about fun and a good time?"

She tried to laugh and failed. "What about no expectations?"

"Sweetheart, you are so much more than anything I ever expected, I can't stand it."

"I'm scared." She wished the too-revealing words unsaid as soon as she blurted them. "Afraid of not being enough—"

"Stop."

"—of wanting this too much, letting myself fall, then losing it, losing you."

"Stop." He pressed his finger against her lips. "I already told you, I'm so yours it isn't funny. You won't lose me."

She wanted to let go and believe, but it was still too soon. Jim's broken promises still rang in her head, and even if he didn't matter, the reality of those should slow her down.

"You have the most expressive face." He trailed a finger over her cheekbone. "Comparing me to Jim, weren't you, wondering if you could trust me?"

The quiet words shamed her. "I realize you're not him, Troy Lee, but I don't know you yet, not really."

"Probably better than you think." One corner of his mouth lifted. "Why didn't you ever marry him?"

How weird was this, to lie naked with the man who'd just taken her in the wildest way and have him ask why her last long-term relationship had failed. She started to sit up, looking for her pajamas, her robe, anything. "The right time just never came along."

With a gentle hand on her chest, he pushed her back to the bed. He curved that palm around the side of her breast. "You were with him how long?"

She swallowed, gaze trained on the ceiling. "Since I was eighteen."

"So it wasn't a matter of finding the right time." He laid his hand over her heart. "In here, you knew he was the wrong man."

"I suppose you're going to tell me you're the right one and I was waiting for you."

The fabulous grin she loved spread across his face. "You said it, Angel baby, I didn't."

"Oh, you..." She rolled over to pounce on him in retaliation. Still grinning, he dragged her down for a long kiss, his arm across her shoulder keeping her clamped to him while he plundered her mouth.

When he lifted his head, she clung to his shoulders, both of them breathing hard. He cradled her cheek in one palm. "I'm not asking you to believe now. I know it's too soon for that, after...well, after everything. If you can believe just for this second, then for the one after that, and after that, soon you're believing in me, in us, all the while. Think you can handle that? This second?"

She smiled, desire pulling at her again. "I can do that."

An answering smile flirted with his mouth. He kissed her. "What about this one?"

"I can do that too."

He lowered his mouth to hers again. "How about this one?"

Under the persuasion of his kisses, his touches, his lovemaking, she gave herself up to believing, just for now.

Angel woke, with a heavy male arm slung over her waist and an even heavier lump sitting in her throat. When she tried to slip away, he grumbled and tried to hold on. She stilled, struggling to breathe through the sickness determined to make her lose her cookies. Lord, she felt awful. Dragging air in through her mouth, she fought off a wave of nausea. What on earth…? Darn Hope and her new crab-dip recipe. This had to be bad seafood because the last time she'd felt this oh-my-Lord-I'm-going-to-be-sick awful had been after a plate of bad fried clams in Apalachicola.

The lump holding her throat hostage grew bigger and moved higher. Oh Jesus, she was going to throw up. She shoved Troy Lee's arm aside, ignored his guttural protest and sat up, legs over the side of the bed. Her head swam and she clapped a hand over her mouth, willing the nausea away. Thankfully, the rush subsided, although she was left feeling distinctly queasy.

"Hey." The bed shifted behind her and he brushed his lips across her bare shoulder. "What's wrong?"

She shook her head, taking shallow breaths through her nose. This wasn't exactly her preferred scenario when she envisioned waking up naked with an equally naked Troy Lee Farr. Naked and nauseous—yeah, that was a great combination. "My sister's bad crab dip."

A big hand covered her stomach in comforting warmth and he rested his cheek against her shoulder. "I'm sorry. Want something? Water or maybe some tea?"

The sick churning was fading. She pulled in a couple more breaths, feeling more herself. "I think I'm okay."

He kissed the side of her neck. "So I'm guessing breakfast at Lisa's and a walk is out of the question."

She pushed her fingers through her hair. "Let me get a shower and we'll see how I feel."

"'Kay." Another butterfly wing touch of lips on her shoulder. "I've got the whole day and I'd planned to just be with you, but if you'd rather I went away so you could veg and feel better, that's all right."

Her eyes prickled with unaccustomed tears. "You're a sweetheart, but that's okay." She turned her head to drop a kiss on his hair, then his ear. "I want to be with you too."

Something deep inside whispered that this time, she'd found the right man, found the one who would see her as something more.

And darn it, while she was believing second by second, she meant to enjoy every minute of it.

ꟸ

Working a double on a holiday weekend wasn't Troy Lee's idea of a good time. The family togetherness increased domestic disputes; too many celebratory drinks led to an increase in drunk drivers on the road.

After he intervened in yet another family get-together gone awry, he drew to a stop under the pecan tree that was his favorite spot to run radar on Gravel Hill Road and pulled his cell from his belt. Lowering the radio squelch, he let a little of the tension drain away. Another hour and he could change clothes, pick up his Jeep and meet Angel at the bar, spend a couple of hours with her there before they went back home to her place. Anticipation settled in him in a heavy rush.

He punched the keys for her speed dial and waited through three rings, that same anticipation filling him.

"Hello?" Beyond her sweet, breathless voice—the way she sounded when they were wrapped up in bed together—the buzzing chatter of voices blended with a Chris Cagle song.

"Hey, baby." Merely talking to her swelled his chest with warmth and pleasure. "What's going on?"

She laughed over a clinking of glass and ice. "I think half the county's in here tonight."

He slumped, more of the day's tension draining away. "Well, I'm dealing with the other half, the ones that have all gone crazy."

"Bad night?"

"Just busy." He smiled. "Looking forward to seeing you."

"Me too." Her tone lowered to a sexy murmur.

"Feeling any better?" The queasiness from her sister's crab dip had lingered on and off for the last two days. He'd been ready to insist she go to the convenient care center tomorrow if it didn't clear up soon.

"Yes. A little...hey, what can I get you? Sorry, Troy Lee. A little tired but not sick anymore. What, Julie? Okay." Her suddenly distracted voice flowed over him. "Listen, I have to go, but I'll see you later. Are you coming by when you get off duty?"

"Sure thing. Later, baby."

He'd no sooner replaced his phone at his belt, when the radio squawked. "Chandler, C-13."

He reached for the mike. God, please not another domestic. "Go ahead, Chandler."

Roger Gentry rattled off the information for a suspicious vehicle report, off Stagecoach Road. Troy Lee shifted into drive and pulled onto the blacktop, accelerating in the direction of Plymouth Bridge. "En route, Chandler. C-13, C-5, request backup."

"10-4, C-13." Chris's voice crackled through the radio. "En route also, Chandler."

Troy Lee slowed as the approached the bridge. The area was rural and deserted, and something about the bridge and the adjacent abandoned church always gave him the creeps. Lights off, using the moonlight as a guide, he turned onto the narrow dirt road by Plymouth Bridge Church. Behind him, the same moonlight bounced off Chris's windshield, his unit proceeding without headlights as well. Low brush and tree limbs scrubbed at the car, and Troy Lee winced. He'd end up on the carpet over scratched paint before it was all over.

Beyond the church, the dirt path twisted a couple of times before opening up onto a sand pit. In the dark, a handful of vehicles surrounded the area and a fire burned in the middle, a bright beacon. Logs had been dragged up to provide seating and a group of kids sat around the flames. Even with his windows up, the music emanating from one of the trucks was audible. On a muffled groan, he reached for the mike, his radio set to the clear channel he and Chris had agreed on earlier. "Chris, you know what this is, right?"

Chris's growl held aggravated disgust. "Another pasture party."

Troy Lee knew the instant the teenagers heard his engine—they tensed and a couple rose, looking poised to flee. He hit his headlights and blue lights instantaneously, as Chris's flared behind him. He angled his car to the left, leaving Chris the right, their vehicles creating an effective block to the only exit. Using his handheld radio, he called in their arrival to dispatch and stepped from the unit. Hound gave an audible whine as Chris left his own car.

As they approached the kids, all chatter quiet, the only sound pounding music coming from a brand new Ford pickup, Troy Lee let his gaze linger on hands, stances, faces, recognizing a few, including Paul Bostick who glowered at him from under a cap bearing the local high school logo. They'd given up any thoughts of running, and most hands were visible and empty. One or two boys had a hand behind their backs, likely concealing a beer bottle or can. At the edge of the circle, Troy Lee rested a foot atop a log and tapped the brim of his hat. "Evening. Y'all are out a little late, aren't you?"

He received various mumbled replies. In the firelight, discarded bottles and cans, from beers to wine coolers, glimmered. He pulled his flashlight from its ring. "We need to see your ID, please."

Keeping a close eye on them, he and Chris started at opposite ends and checked driver's licenses. Not surprisingly, none of them were over nineteen, most of them still in high school. Halfway down the line, a tall, dark-haired youth held out his license in silence, a stoic expression on his face. Troy Lee flashed the beam over it and did a double take. Delbert Blake Calvert. Troy Lee swallowed a sigh. Oh hell, why did he know this was going to get sticky?

He showed the ID to Chris as he joined them, then passed it back to the boy. He and Chris stepped a few feet away.

"They're all underage. Probably half of them have been drinking." He pitched his voice low enough for only Chris to hear. "Easiest thing to do is transport them to the station, call parents to come get them and maybe put the fear of God in them."

"Yeah." Chris passed a hand over his nape. "We're going to have to call someone in to help transport, though. I'll handle that while you make them pour out the beer."

With only the two of them, searching vehicles and interviewing the teens dragged. The quiet kids remained subdued and compliant, a little fact for which Troy Lee was grateful. The last party they'd busted up, he and Steve Monroe had ended up running through the woods after a couple of boys. Yeah, he liked to run, but not through the cold, damp pine forest in the dead of night.

Finally, a pair of headlights swept the clearing. Pouring out the last couple of cans of beer, Troy Lee took his gaze off the teens to glance at the unmarked unit pulling to a stop behind their cars. Wearing jeans and a polo instead of his investigator's uniform, Cookie stepped from the driver's seat.

"What's going on?" he asked, joining Troy Lee.

Troy Lee dropped the cans into the trash bag at his feet. "Mrs. Coker called complaining about suspicious vehicle traffic out here. Chris and I show up to find them having a little party and they're all underage. Figure the best thing is to call parents to come get them."

Cookie's nod was a sharp jerk of his chin. "If it's a first offense, you're right. Anybody we've seen before?"

"Other than Paul Bostick? Nope." Troy Lee darted a look at the group, now seated in silence on the logs. "And Calvert's nephew."

"Blake?" Cookie's surprised gaze arrowed in on the boy. He shook his head. "Del will have a fit."

"I don't think he's been drinking, or if he has, it wasn't much." Troy Lee tied off the bag. "I didn't smell anything on him and he seems cold sober. Not like a couple of the others, who are close to wasted."

Cookie made a noise in his throat. "Lucky you didn't end up chasing somebody through the woods again."

"Yeah. Guess this group is smart."

"What do you mean?"

Troy Lee grinned. "If they run, all they get is tired and caught. This group decided it was better to just be caught."

Cookie's laugh rumbled between them. "All right, let's get them loaded up and back to town so we can start calling parents."

Somehow, Troy Lee ended up transporting a group of four which included a pair of halfway-inebriated, completely frightened and bawling girls. By the time they pulled into the parking lot at the sheriff's department, tension pounded at his temples. Instead of using the jail intake area, they ushered the teenagers into the squad room and set about procuring parent contact information and placing phone calls.

As he replaced the receiver from making his last parent call, his cell phone rang, the Cue Club's landline displayed on the screen. He flipped it open and propped a hip on the empty desk opposite Cookie's. "Hey."

"Where are you? I thought you were coming by here." Angel's voice competed with the bar noises behind her and the still crying girls behind him. Even so, hearing her sent a wave of warmth through him.

"Yeah, so did I." He glanced at the large clock hanging

above the counter running along the back wall. Twenty minutes until one. Nearly eighteen hours on duty. He didn't mind the overtime, but he'd much rather be with her.

"Let me guess...a last-minute call."

"A long call. Busting up a pasture party."

"Kids still have those things?"

"Looks that way." He massaged his left temple, where the throbbing had concentrated. His eyes burned with exhaustion. He hadn't realized how damn tired he was until he stopped.

"So, how long do you think you might be?" Wistful yearning colored her voice, lightening his weariness somewhat.

"Who knows?" He'd be here until all the kids were released to their parents. "Another hour at least, unless I'm really, really lucky."

Cookie strolled in from the conference room, dropped the phone book back in his desk drawer and sank into his chair. He covered his eyes with both hands. From the front desk, Chris's quiet voice murmured as he finished up his set of calls.

"Just for the record, Troy Lee, this part of dating a cop is the pits. I guess this means planning ahead when you're on duty is out of the question?"

"Pretty much." He shifted his position to relieve the pinch of his bulletproof vest at his waist, folded an arm over his chest and rested his elbow on his opposite wrist. "Sorry, Angel baby, but I think it's a case of love me, tolerate my job."

Cookie slanted an amused look at him, his mouth twitching.

"Who said I loved you?" The teasing rejoinder came in a sexy murmur.

"Hey, a guy can wish." He cast a quick look at Cookie, then at the kids behind them and lowered his voice to a whisper. "Listen, I really don't know how long this is going to take, but I want to see you tonight."

"Me too. Do you need to change or pick up clothes first?"

"I do if we're going anywhere in the morning, since someone won't let me leave anything at her place. Afraid her mama—"

"Troy Lee. Behave."

He laughed. "Do you really want me to?"

"On occasion and when it involves teasing me about my mama, yes."

"All right." He rubbed at his tired eyes. "It's almost closing time for you. Y'all be careful and I'll see you later if it's not too late when I get out of here."

She murmured a goodbye and the connection died. He clipped the phone on his belt again and met Cookie's shrewd gaze. Troy Lee spread his hands. "What?"

A grin hitched up the corners of the older man's mouth. "You're smitten."

"Maybe." The wide smile that pulled at his lips was irresistible. Yeah, he was smitten, as Cookie put it, and it had to be all over his face. Damn it, he didn't care. She was the best thing that had ever happened to him.

Down the hall, the front door opened, a blend of irritated and concerned voices wafting to their ears, followed by Chris's quiet reassuring tone. Troy Lee straightened. Time to deal with the parents.

Getting all of the kids released took more than an hour, as he, Cookie and Chris explained and answered questions, helped smooth out parental anger, soothed anxiety. Bubba Bostick arrived and strode into the squad room, livid and stiff with anger. He glared at Paul. "Boy, what am I going to do with you?"

Paul responded with only silent resentment and a mutinous look. Troy Lee shook his head. Glad that wasn't his kid.

Hands at his hips, Bubba huffed and looked at Cookie. "Do I need to sign anything?"

"No." Cookie slid a measuring glance in Paul's direction. "But you might want to talk to him about making wise decisions when he's already been in trouble lately."

"Yeah." Lips thinned with irritation, Bubba gestured at the doorway. "Well, come on, boy. Let's go."

Del Calvert appeared shortly after the Bosticks' departure, his jaw tight and expression less than happy, but he didn't direct his irritation at Blake. Instead, he sighed and clapped the boy on the arm. "Are you all right?"

Blake shrugged, a compact roll of his shoulders. "I'm okay. I'm not drunk, Daddy."

Del shook his head. "We'll talk about it in the morning. Let's go home and get some sleep." He directed a look at Cookie and the others. "Thank you."

Once the squad room emptied, Cookie glanced at his

watch. "All right, boys, let's get out of here."

Troy Lee twisted his wrist to check his Tag. Shit. After one thirty in the morning. Once he went home, cleaned up and grabbed clothes, then drove out to Angel's...if she'd gone home at one when the club closed and gone to bed, she'd be asleep by then for sure. He didn't need to wake her up, especially since she'd been fatigued all week after dealing with that bout of minor food poisoning. He heaved a rough sigh.

"Troy Lee?" Cookie paused in the doorway, watching him with brows drawn into a slight frown. "You coming?"

"Yeah." He tried to slough off the disappointment. Might as well go home and get some sleep. Damn it.

Chapter Eight

The town lay quiet and still under the clear, cold night sky. At the Highway 93 crossroads, Angel paused, foot on the brake. A right-hand turn would take her home. A left offered the opportunity to pass by the sheriff's department or the housing project, see if Troy Lee was still working, or possibly already home.

My Lord, she was stalking him.

She flexed her fingers about the wheel. She wasn't really *stalking* him. They were dating. They were lovers. If she wanted to prove she wasn't fixated on him, she'd turn right.

She hooked the left without flinching.

The small housing project where Troy Lee lived fronted the highway as it passed through the outskirts of Coney. Angel pulled into the tiny parking lot in front of the forlorn row of brick apartments. This late, the neighborhood was relatively deserted, although beyond the low building, a lone figure moved on the basketball court, practicing throw after throw in nearly seamless perfection. Troy Lee's patrol car was nowhere in sight, his Jeep sitting off to one side. She sighed and reached for the gearshift. Looked like she was going home, to sleep alone.

Lights flashed over the building as a white squad car purred into the lot. Anticipation sizzled through her, and she shifted into park. Opening her door, she stepped out and leaned on the roof, watching as he climbed from the patrol car. He grinned at her over the Mustang. "What are you doing here?"

She rested her chin on her crossed wrists. "Stalking you."

He came around the car, keys jingling against his belt, the leather creaking. "Do you know what time it is?"

"Really late." She rested a fingertip on his tie tack and

stepped closer. He wrapped an arm around her waist and tugged her against him.

"You should be home in bed, asleep," he murmured, nuzzling her jaw. "But I'm glad to see you."

She shivered, a combination of the chilly wind and his touch, his fingers playing those teasing little riffs at the base of her spine.

"Missed you." The rich whisper tickled the sensitive curve of her ear and she pressed nearer.

"You too." She tiptoed up to kiss the corner of his mouth.

He darted a look at the basketball court and stepped back, still holding her, but at arm's length. "Come inside while I get my things."

Fingers laced through hers, he drew her along the cracked concrete path to the last unit. She sighed, rubbing her arms, when he released her to unlock the door. It was ridiculous, really, her reticence to allow him to leave clothing at her house. They'd only been together two or three weeks, only been intimate two nights. Granting him a privilege it had taken Jim three years to gain seemed premature. Although he wasn't Jim, and her heart already knew it.

He pushed the door open and stepped back to let her precede him. She stepped into darkness, immediately surrounded by scents: the sharp, fresh soap Troy Lee used, pine cleaner, the dust of old drywall. His hand brushed the small of her back and the door clicked shut seconds before light flooded the room.

Small didn't begin to describe the space. The living room held a plaid sofa, a plain shelf with a television, and just enough room to walk to the galley kitchen on the other end. Two doors on her right led to the bathroom and his bedroom. A large canvas above the sofa dominated the entire room and she stepped forward to study the painting.

Breathtaking. Completely out of scale for the room, but mesmerizing. The muted blues and greens of the seascape pulled her in, the colors blending to a foggy horizon. Pinks and beiges depicted damp sand with a trail of perfectly detailed footprints disappearing over a dune.

"This is beautiful." She glanced over her shoulder at Troy Lee, who stood beside the kitchen bar. He unsnapped the bands holding his gunbelt in place, unbuckled it and slid it free. He laid it out on the counter and removed his handgun.

"It's one of Christine's." He checked over the gun, placed it in a metal box on the counter and spun the dial lock. "My dad's favorite. It used to hang in his office at Georgia Tech."

"She's very talented." Angel turned in a slow pivot, eyeing the further details of the room. A pair of battered running shoes, holes worn in the sides and tops, sat at one end of the couch. On the lone end table, a copy of *National Geographic Adventure* lay discarded, open to an article on ocean kayaking. She watched as Troy Lee pulled his brown tie free. "So this is where you live."

He folded the tie over the back of one bar stool. "This is where I sleep and eat."

She rolled her eyes. "So where do you live, Troy Lee?"

With a shrug, he tapped the center of his chest. "In here."

How was she supposed to argue with that? Arms crossed, hands under her elbows, she watched as he unpinned his collar brass and laid that aside as well. She liked this, the intimacy of watching him peel away the layers of law-enforcement respectability.

Probably because she was fast becoming intimately acquainted with the bad boy beneath the badge.

The familiar burn of wanting him flared, licking at her nerve endings, sizzling low into her belly. She slipped out of her thin jacket and tossed it on the end of the couch. She walked toward him, putting just a little extra sway in her hips, watching as his eyes took on the same burn. "Do you know what I like about you in uniform, Troy Lee?"

The indulgence in his smile didn't belie the heat in his gaze. "What's that?"

"You're all buttoned up, spit-shined and polished." Stopping before him, she laid her finger just above his top button, revealing the white T-shirt underneath. She leaned up until her mouth was a whisper away from his. "It makes me want to rumple you."

He looped his arms about her waist. "Angel baby, you can rumple me all you want. Anytime you want."

"Really?" She tucked her fingers into his belt and pulled him toward his bedroom. "I might have to take you up on that, Deputy Farr."

His lazy grin appeared as she tugged him through the door

and turned on the light, illuminating a bedroom nearly as spare as his living area. He reached for the buttons on his uniform shirt, but she caught his hands.

"Uh-uh." She placed both palms against his chest and gave a light shove, pushing him against the wall. He'd taken charge both nights they'd been together so far. Tonight, it was her turn. Legs splayed, he rested his shoulders against the wall and watched her, all vestiges of weariness gone from his face. She traced a finger over his badge, the metal smooth and cool under her touch, then trailed her fingernail down the raised vertical seam on his shirt, the muscles beneath camouflaged by the bulk of a bulletproof vest. She flicked a glance at him from beneath her lashes. "Do you know how sexy this is?"

"Yeah, brown and tan polyester is hot." Laughter lurked in his tone, but didn't hide the way his words thickened with arousal.

She ignored his teasing and rubbed a finger along the upper edge of his belt. "No wonder all the girls keep breaking the speed limit."

"You're the only one I'm interested in." He tried to tangle a hand in her hair, but she reached for his wrist and returned his arm to his side.

She tapped the middle of his bottom lip. "Not very good at following orders, are you, Deputy?"

"I have a hard time keeping my hands off you."

"So what do they offer you, those girls?" She traced the seam on the left of his torso. Another flirtatious look from under her lashes. "To get out of a ticket."

"You'd be surprised."

"Do you ever want to?" She outlined his belt buckle. "Trade them out, I mean."

"No."

She leaned into him, fingers tucked securely into his belt, mouth close to his again. "You're saying you've never been tempted? Not once?"

"You never offered." His breathing had altered, becoming shorter, rougher. Intense blue eyes locked on hers. "I'd have lost my badge if you had."

With a sultry smile, she brushed her lips over his. "I won't tell if you won't."

He lunged, one arm around her waist, a hand buried in her hair, his mouth hungry on hers. She opened to him, meeting that hunger head on. His hand slid lower, cupping her butt, urging her into him, grinding her against the growing hardness below his belt. She grabbed the front of his shirt and pulled him closer, struggling to free the buttons at the same time.

One came loose and pinged away over the floor. He half-growled, half-laughed against her mouth. "You're sewing that back on."

"Gladly." She tugged harder, separating the fabric, sending more buttons plinking to the floor.

"Those too." He lifted her against him and she wrapped both legs about his lean hips. One second she was high in his arms, the next her back hit the bed and he came down between her thighs, mouth sealing hers.

"No." She insinuated her hands between them, pushed him aside. Her hands went to his belt and she slid to the floor to kneel between his thighs. "This is my show, Troy Lee."

Levered up on his elbows, he watched with burning eyes as she dispatched the buckle, unfastened his slacks, slid down the zipper. His erection strained against the thin cotton of his boxers. She pushed his undershirt up as far as the vest would allow, caressing and rubbing the delineated lines of his hard belly. Hooking her fingers into his waistband, she eased the fabric down until he sprang free, hard and long and enticing.

She touched him, sliding worshipful fingers down the length, and his breath caught on a winded gasp.

"Vest has to go," he muttered, performing an awkward sit-up to struggle out of the uniform shirt. She stroked him, folded a hand around him, and he sucked in a harsh inhale before fighting his way out of the unwieldy vest and dragging his T-shirt over his head. He leaned on his arms, and she looked up at him, holding his gaze as she wrapped her lips around him.

"God." The syllable left his lips on a broken whisper.

The clean, acidic taste of male skin tingled on her tongue, warm, hard flesh sliding against her lips and teeth, brushing the back of her throat. She loved the feel of him in her mouth, loved his small, rough sounds of pleasure. She gave herself over to the enjoyment of pleasing him, flicking an occasional glance up at his face, his eyes closed, the planes tight with painful gratification.

His hand tangled in her hair, gripping, pulling slightly, his hips tilting up in a restless, wanting rhythm. Nothing disturbed the silence of the room but his jagged breaths and her own smothered moans. He filled her, his taste, his feel, his smell.

With one finger, he traced the line of her ear, her jaw. "Ah, Angel..."

Her name on his lips was less than a whisper, a mere exhale of sound, resonant with emotion. Her eyes prickled and she blinked, letting him fall free of her mouth, sliding her tongue along his length in slow strokes, rubbing her lips around the glistening head. His lashes lifted to reveal blue eyes blazing with desire. His palm caressed along her jaw to cradle the back of her head and he tugged her up toward him. "Kiss me."

Straddling his thighs, she wound her arms about his neck and took his mouth. Her short, full skirt blossomed around them, his slacks coarse against her bare thighs, his damp erection sliding against her naked skin. He caught the elasticized edge of her neckline and pulled down, until the cap sleeves freed her arms, until the cotton dress pooled at her waist. Painting her neck and collarbone with kisses, he enfolded her breasts with hot palms, thumbs brushing hardening nipples through thin lace.

"I'm falling so fast for you." He murmured the words over her heart.

The crisp edges of his short hair at his nape delighted her fingers. Her throat closed on answering words and she swallowed. If he could take that risk, so could she.

She framed his jaw with trembling fingers and held his gaze. "A lot of people would say it's too fast. Shoot, I should say it's too fast, but I don't care. There's so *much* with you, all of it good and strong and true."

His familiar, wonderful grin lifted the corners of his mouth. "I think I can handle you speeding, just this once."

Laughter bubbled in her. "Oh, you can, huh?"

"Yeah. But only with me."

She traced the tiny almost-healed scar on his chin. "I don't want anyone else."

An arm came around her waist in a hard band. "Glad to hear it. I like being the only variable in your equation."

"Really? Show me how much."

On a low growl, he spun them, and she found herself flat on the bed and staring up at him. He lowered his head, kissing the corner of her lips, then the pulse point below her jaw. "This much." Another light kiss on her sternum. "And this much." His tongue rasped over one tight nipple. "And this—"

"Troy Lee." She shivered under the sweet torture of his mouth on her breast.

He lifted his head. "Ma'am?"

"Anyone ever mention sometimes you talk a little too much?" She raised her thumb and index finger, holding them a small distance apart.

"Once or twice."

"This is the time to talk less, love more."

His grin widened, his eyes gleaming. "Yes, ma'am."

Deep rhythmic bass pounded into Angel's consciousness, penetrating the fog of exhausted sleep. Even behind closed lids, her brain registered that the angle of light was wrong. She passed a palm over sheets that weren't her vintage embroidered French linens.

Where was she? What was that noise?

Beside her, Troy Lee groaned, rolled to his stomach and dragged a pillow over his head. A memory rose, of his nuzzling her shoulder after they'd made love and he'd collapsed against her, asking if she wanted to go back to her place. She didn't remember making a reply, just the sweet darkness of satisfied sleep.

So she was in Troy Lee's tiny apartment, in his bed, but that didn't explain the heavy beat that seemed to pulse into her chest. Levering up on an elbow, she held the sheet to her bare breasts. "What is that?"

"*That* is Lil' Wayne. Damn it." Troy Lee shoved the pillow aside, rolled from the bed and stalked naked to the kitchen to pound a fist on the wall. "Devonte! Too loud."

The music dropped, still audible through the thin wall, followed by an answering thumping on the studs. Shaking his head, Troy Lee ambled back to bed and dropped to the mattress. He buried his face against her throat. "Morning."

Having his long, lean body pressed all along hers sent

spikes of shivery pleasure under her skin, although it didn't quite alleviate the fatigue gripping her. She sifted her fingers through his short hair. "What time is it?"

He reached across her to lift his watch from the nightstand. "Almost nine."

She closed her eyes on a sigh. If she planned to meet her family at church, she'd need to—

"Let's stay in bed all day." Troy Lee snuggled into her, as much as a six-foot-one male was capable of snuggling. He kissed the side of her neck. "Or at least until I have to be on duty this afternoon. We can sleep a couple more hours, make love, take a nap, make love some more."

"I detect a pattern there." Regret shimmied through her. "And it sounds wonderful, but I have to get up and get moving. Mama's been on me about missing church and I promised her I'd go today. I still have to go home and shower and change."

He propped on an elbow and trailed a knuckle over her shoulder. "Want me to go with you?"

She stared. "You're volunteering to go to church with me and my family?"

"Well, yeah. I mean, I've been to church before, Angel. I don't think the roof is going to fall in or anything if I show up."

"That's not what I—"

"Ah-ah-ah." He shook a finger between them. "We're back to the Jim thing, aren't we?"

"Well, yes, but—"

"I am not Jim Tyre."

"Believe me, I know."

"Good." He caught her chin between his thumb and forefinger. "Now let him go."

"I'm trying." Easing from his hold, she sat up against the headboard, keeping the sheet over her breasts. "I am, Troy Lee, I swear."

"I know." With his arm across her body, he cradled her hip in his palm and rubbed his thumb over the jut of her hipbone. "But how would you like it if I were constantly comparing you to Morgan in my head?"

A wave of jealous pinpricks moved over her skin. "Who's Morgan?"

"My two-year mistake from college. We all have one. Yours

just lasted longer than most." He shook his head, eyes serious. "You have to turn it loose."

She narrowed her eyes. "*Are* you comparing me to Morgan?"

"Not in a million years." His rich laugh hovered between them. "There is no comparison, baby. None at all. As far as I'm concerned, no woman exists but you."

"Right." She shifted to the edge of the bed, careful not to move too quickly, grateful that the dizziness and nausea of the past few days seemed nowhere to be found this morning. She reached down to snag her crumpled dress. "Lord, Troy Lee, I've seen the girls that flock around—"

"Shit, this is old." He flung the comforter aside and vaulted from the bed. He strode into the kitchen, and the rattling of silverware followed the slamming of a cabinet door. Unease trickled down Angel's spine and she slipped her wrinkled dress over her head. Where were her panties, anyway? And what was old? He reappeared in the doorway, stark naked, a jar of peanut butter and spoon in hand.

"You're everything." Peanut butter muffled his voice, but not the irritation lacing it. "Intelligent, beautiful, successful, funny, the best damn lover I've ever had. So why the hell do you believe you're not as good as everyone else?"

She blinked. "Troy Lee, what are you talking about?"

"I tell you I don't see anyone else, and you bring up how many girls throw themselves at me, which you've brought up a lot. I don't really think you believe I'm interested in fucking any of them, so all I can figure is that for some reason you see them as a threat of some sort."

The nausea made a reappearance and she swallowed. "Would you watch your language, please? I don't like—"

"Would you stop trying to change the subject?" He spooned up another mouthful of peanut butter and threw out his hands. "Yeah, fine. Women like me. They have since I was fifteen. Big damn deal. I could probably get laid once a shift if I wanted to, but I don't. Hell, Angel, I'm falling in love with you and I'm not looking for anyone else."

"You might find someone better." The words spilled before she was aware of forming them.

"Better?" He made a frustrated gesture. "What are you talking about?"

"I don't know how to make you understand."

His mouth firmed and they stared at one another in silence. He set the jar aside on his small bureau with a tight, deliberate movement and grabbed the pair of worn jeans tossed over a straight chair. He pulled them on with jerky motions, zipping them but leaving the button undone. Arms crossed over his chest, he studied her with the implacable cop stare until she wanted to squirm.

"All right," he said finally. "Let's have this out and settle it once and for all."

Nervousness intensified the queasiness attacking her. "I don't have time to argue with you. I told you—"

"Your mama will be just fine if you're late or you miss church altogether. Our relationship won't if we don't deal with this. Do not"—he held up a hand as she opened her mouth—"even try to tell me we don't have a relationship. We do and you know it."

She wanted out, wanted away from this slow relentless conversation. Except she was never the one who backed down from a struggle, an unpleasant situation.

Well, she really, really wanted to back down from this one, especially since her stomach seemed determined to rebel and her nerves were jumping all over the place.

Rubbing a slow circle over his chest, he watched her. "If we don't deal with this, it's just going to keep coming up, coming between us. Do you really want that?"

She looked away, blinked, then turned her gaze back to his. "No."

"So tell me what I have to do to convince you that you have no competition."

The nausea disappeared under a rush of anger. "You know, Troy Lee, it's a little hard to put my faith in that, since I've seen how quickly competition can arise, not once, but *twice* in the last—"

"Ah, hell." He rolled his eyes. "Angel. Look at me. I am not Jim Tyre. The man is a certified idiot for even looking twice at—"

"He did more than look. He married her. Explain that to me." To her absolute horror, her voice cracked and her eyes burned. "Explain to me how he could leave one week telling me he loved me, be engaged to me, and come back married to someone else."

"I can't. I don't understand it." Intensity vibrated in his voice. "Because I don't see how a man could want anything but you. Oh, but hell, Angel, it may make me a bastard, but I'm glad he did what he did, because otherwise you'd still be trapped in a train wreck that was never going to make you happy. Tell me something. If he showed up on your doorstep today, would you want him back?"

"No. Of course not."

"What if Cookie turned up, ready to drop Tori for you? Would you want him?"

Where was he going with this? "No. I want you."

"You have me." He advanced on her, setting off a different type of fluttering rush in her belly, the nausea and turmoil forgotten. He reached for her hand, fingers warm on her wrist, and laid her palm flat against his chest. "You *have* me, Angel. Only you, I swear."

"I believe you," she whispered.

"Not here, you don't." Still holding her wrist, he spread his other hand over her heart. "Not yet. I'm not sure why you think you're not on a level with other women, and I'm pretty sure it goes deeper than Jim marrying Rhonda so quickly or Cookie picking up with Tori. Only you know that for sure. Nobody compares to you, not where I'm concerned. Nobody."

His intense blue gaze held hers, willing her to believe. She pulled in a shaky breath. Each second, he'd said. This second, then another, then another, until she believed all the time. She closed her eyes. She wanted to trust in him, in them. Why did it have to be so darn *hard*?

Using his hold on her wrist, he drew her closer, leaned down to rest his cheek against hers. "I'm yours," he murmured near her ear. "You have me. Believe that, baby."

She nodded and slipped her arms about his neck, holding on hard. "I'm trying."

"I know." He rested a hand against her spine, dropped a kiss on the curve of her shoulder. "One second at a time, Angel. We have all the time you need."

The sister was going to be trouble.

Troy Lee had known it since the first narrow-eyed once-over

Hope had given him as he and Angel slipped into the family's pew, with a couple of minutes to spare before the service started. Her measuring of him continued throughout the service and the mingling that took place on the lawn of the small country church, then picked up again as soon as he set foot in her parents' home.

Angel's mother appeared to have no such reservations, first greeting him warmly at church and now putting a glass of iced tea in his hand and pushing him toward the den with Angel's father and Hope's husband. He wasn't much for syrupy sweet tea and would have rather stayed in Angel's presence, but Christine hadn't raised a fool either. This house seemed to hold a distinct set of male and female roles, and he wasn't about to rock the boat his first time there.

"Thank you, ma'am." He lifted the glass, gave her his best smile and followed Ron Henderson and Darryl Owens along the dim hallway behind the kitchen. They stepped down into a recessed room with dark wood paneling. Humor pulled at Troy Lee's mouth. They ragged Chris about his bachelor's pad man-cave, but his little den had nothing on Ron Henderson's. University of Georgia memorabilia dominated the décor, sharing wall space with photos of his daughters and granddaughters. Three plush recliners and a thick couch faced an old-fashioned console television.

Ron sprawled in the center recliner, placed his tea on the adjacent table and let out the footrest with a replete sigh. Darryl took the recliner to Ron's right, settling his tea on the tin TV tray next to the big chair. Troy Lee eyed the third recliner. Why did he just know that had been Jim Tyre's spot?

Damn if he was going to sit in that chair. What the hell was he supposed to do, anyway? Christine and his dad had been big on manners, and sitting without being invited was one of Christine's pet peeves.

"Have a seat, Troy." Ron reached for the remote. The pregame show for the Steelers and the Oilers appeared on the screen. "Take a load off."

Troy Lee swallowed the reminder that he went by both names—Troy had been his father and he'd been Troy Lee since day one—and sat on the edge of the couch. The apprehension he usually only experienced when facing Calvert's displeasure wound through him. "Thank you, sir."

"So you work for the sheriff's department." Ron took a long swallow of tea.

"Yes, sir." Troy Lee started to set his own untouched glass aside on the oak end table beside the couch. Damn, no coaster. He kept the glass in hand. Condensation dripped onto his knee.

"Not from around here originally, are you?" Ron's attention veered to the announcers onscreen. Darryl appeared to ignore them both, his gaze trained on the stats.

"No, sir." Troy Lee lifted the glass to his mouth. Pure sugar exploded on his tongue and his taste buds rebelled. How did Calvert drink this stuff all the time? "I grew up in Atlanta."

Ron nodded but didn't glance his way, gaze trained on the unfolding pregame comparison. "Stanton Reed seems like a good-enough fellow."

"He runs a tight department."

The low grunt Ron made dripped with disparagement. "Someone needed to, after Hollowell and his boys. Bunch-a damn crooks."

Darryl huffed his agreement and the room lapsed into silence broken only by obnoxious commentators and the tinkle of ice as Darryl and Ron sipped their tea. Troy Lee expelled a relieved breath, rotating his dripping glass between both palms. With the other men immersed in Sunday afternoon football, he let his gaze travel over the family photos on the walls, picking out the path of Angel's life.

In the picture of her holding a fishing rod and dangling a small catfish from a line in the other hand, she was sunburned and snaggletoothed. She looked all of seven. Damn, that photo had probably been taken before he was even born.

A shelf by the sliding glass doors, covered by heavy vertical blinds, held myriad 4-H and FFA ribbons and trophies along with more photos—Angel as an awkward preteen, showing livestock. Prom photos, both Angel and Hope's, lined the top shelf, and sure enough, in both of Angel's, she graced the arm of a much younger Jim Tyre.

High school graduation, and Angel wore yellow and red cords, as well as a salutatorian medal. A snapshot of her with her parents on the lawn before the local community college, she in cap and gown and bearing a diploma, her parents beaming with pride. A studio portrait of her and Jim in their early twenties, one of those shots that turned up in the engagement announcements section of the Daily Herald. Shit, they still had that thing on the wall, after what Jim had done? And Angel had to look at that every time she came in here?

No wonder she was having a hard time letting go of what the selfish bastard had done.

Darryl drained his glass and held it aloft, rattling the ice against the sides. Troy Lee frowned. What was that about?

Moments later, Hope appeared through the door with a pitcher. She took Darryl's glass and refilled it, returning it to him. "Daddy, do you need a top off?"

"Sure, baby." Ron handed her the glass.

Holy shit. Troy Lee stared. If he tried that, Angel would kick his ass.

"Troy Lee?" Hope held the pitcher of tea aloft. Her gaze scraped over him.

"No, thanks. I'm good." He returned her stare for stare. If he could take Calvert's Lord-you're-a-dumbass look or face down any suspect out there, he could take her skepticism and mistrust. She could get over it and stop looking at him like that, because damn if he was going anywhere.

She gave a curt little nod, turned on her heel and disappeared down the hall once more.

Thankfully, he was only left staring at the rapidly melting ice in his glass for ten or fifteen minutes before Marie Henderson called them to the table. Angel squeezed his hand once as he slipped into the chair next to hers. At Marie's request, Darryl offered a brief blessing then Marie passed the platter of roast beef and the bowls of field peas, mashed potatoes and squash with onions. Hope's pair of teenaged daughters filled plates with a minimum of food and disappeared into the kitchen, giggling and texting.

A television sat in the nook off the dining room and Ron used a remote to tune in to the beginning of the football game.

Marie handed off a basket of rolls to Troy Lee. "Troy, you're not from here, are you?"

"No, ma'am." He took a roll and passed them to his right. Darryl received the basket without moving his gaze from the television. "I'm from Atlanta."

Hope eyed him again. "Did you go to college up there?"

"I started out at Georgia Tech, then transferred to UGA

when I changed my major to criminal justice."

Angel slanted a glance at him from beneath her lashes while buttering her roll. "What was your first major?"

His attention narrowed to her mouth as she bit into the fluffy bread and licked a bit of butter from the corner of her lips. He dragged himself back to the question, lifted his gaze to her eyes, which glinted with a wicked awareness of what she'd done to him with the innocent action. "Um, physics and aerospace engineering. Mainly propulsion theory."

Darryl turned his head. "What's that?"

"Rocket engine design." He accepted the gravy boat from Marie and drizzled the thick sauce over his potatoes.

"Rocket science." Hope turned toward Angel and some sort of unspoken communication flashed between the two.

"Kind of. A lot of math, a lot of research into alternative energy options."

Darryl frowned, looking at the television again rather than him. "Well, how the hell did you end up driving a cop car down here?"

Images flashed in his head, his father's bruised and swollen face, head swathed in bandages, ventilator tubing invading his mouth, the flatline on the monitor once the life support had been disconnected. "Being stuck in a lab all day, crunching numbers, wasn't for me."

Hope shrugged. "That doesn't explain how you ended up here."

She was seriously beginning to get under his skin. He forced himself to resist the urge to lay his arm across Angel's shoulders, just because he suspected it would get Hope's goat. Instead, he smiled. "I graduated about the time Sheriff Reed was appointed. Two FBI agents with his and Tick Calvert's professional reputations rebuilding a department from the bottom up? I was all over that."

A saccharine smile graced Hope's face. "So what do you do when you're not working? Fishing, hunting?"

Darryl's head swung in their direction again. "Hey, yeah. Ron and I leased some land from the Terrells this year. We're out there about every Saturday."

"Actually, I'm not a hunter." He could have sworn Angel kicked her sister under the table, but only serenity shown on Angel's pretty face. Uninterested, Darryl turned away. Troy Lee shrugged, aware Marie Henderson was hanging on his every word, sizing him up, but without Hope's distrust. "I play guitar with a local band and I run."

"Run?" Marie forked up the last bite of peas on her plate.

"Yes, ma'am. Distance running. Mostly 10Ks, but I've run a couple of marathons. Right now, I'm training for the Atlanta marathon."

"Oh." Despite her polite smile, Marie appeared mystified that anyone would run for enjoyment.

"Mama, did you buy those pillows you were looking at in Dillard's last week?" Thankfully, the conversation turned away from him with Angel's question, but he couldn't shake a familiar sinking feeling.

Fuck, could he blow this any worse?

Chapter Nine

"Hope, what the hell was that?" Keeping her voice a low hiss, Angel closed the guest-bedroom door behind them. Once dinner was over and the kitchen cleaned, with Troy Lee safely ensconced in the den with her daddy and Darryl again, she'd dragged her sister down the hall on the pretext of seeing the room their mother had just redecorated.

"Better not let Mama hear you talking like that." Hope perched on the end of the bed and propped back on her hands.

"I am not worried about Mama. Just what did you think you were doing, interrogating him like that?"

Hope's plucked brows lowered. "Looking out for you, since you're obviously not going to."

Angel rested against the door, arms crossed over her chest. "What is that supposed to mean?"

"You've been seeing him, what? All of two weeks? You're obviously sleeping with him and now you're bringing him home." Irritation and anxiety twisted Hope's pretty features. "Didn't you learn *anything* from what happened with Jim and Mark Cook?"

"Yes. I learned neither of them was the right man for me."

"And he is?" Hope waved a dismissive gesture in the general direction of the den. "Good Lord, Angel, he can't be more than twenty-four—"

"Twenty-six."

"Fine, whatever. He went to college to be a rocket scientist, Angel. A rocket scientist. Do you know what kind of smarts that takes? And he's a marathon runner. Talk about discipline. What exactly do you have in common with this boy, outside the bedroom?"

"You'd be surprised." She tried to shrug away the crushing hurt and disappointment clutching her throat. Tilting her chin, she looked up at the ceiling and blinked hard before pinning Hope with a stare. "Basically, what you're insinuating is that obviously it's not going to last because I'm not enough for him. Not smart enough, not disciplined enough—"

"I never said that."

"Darn it, Hope, you didn't have to."

"Angel." Hope leaned forward, body vibrating with intensity. "What do you have in common with him? What makes him the right man?"

"We value the same things. Hard work, time to play, our families. He makes me laugh and being with him makes me happy. He likes spending time with me, which is more than I could ever say for Jim."

"I don't want to see you hurt again." Hope's voice trembled, and tears pricked at Angel's eyes.

"He's not going to." Disbelief bloomed in Hope's eyes, but stone certainty cemented in Angel's mind. Hugging the sweet conviction to her, she crossed to sit by her sister. "I know you think that sounds naïve, but he won't. He's a sweetheart, Hope, kind and considerate, and he makes me a priority."

"I just wish you'd slow down a little."

"I slowed down for almost twenty years with the wrong man, Hope. How much more of my life do you want me to waste?"

Hope's exhale was long and shaky. She rocked back and forth, worrying her bottom lip with her teeth. Finally she slid a familiar teasing look in Angel's direction. "Distance running, huh? Isn't that all about the endurance?"

"Oh, yeah." Angel laughed. "And he definitely has that going on."

"I'm jealous." Hope flopped back on the bed. "Darryl's idea of endurance is staying awake past Jay Leno."

Angel collapsed beside her. Immediate regret flooded her, as her head swam and her stomach pitched. Geez Louise, she was never touching anything Hope cooked again. She laid an arm across her eyes. Lord, she was tired. This afternoon was destined to be naptime for sure.

Hope poked her in the side. "He'd better be good to you or I'll hurt him."

The idea of her petite sister attempting physical harm to Troy Lee's tall frame struck her as funny and she giggled.

Hope joined her, lifting an arm to flex a small biceps. "Hey, I'm serious. I could take him."

"You probably could." Hope might be the perfectly behaved daughter, but she had a protective mean streak under the mannerly exterior. Angel lowered her arm and examined the tiny crack in the plaster ceiling, the one that had been there since this had been her bedroom. "But you won't have to. He's not going to hurt me."

The deep sense of contentment and security still glowed within her when she went looking for Troy Lee minutes later. She found him in the den with her father and Darryl, and he jumped to his feet as she entered. She leaned against the doorjamb. "Ready to go?"

"Yeah." A hint of desperation darkened his eyes and he rubbed a hand over his hair. "I've got to be on duty in an hour or so."

"Bye, Daddy." She came down the steps to drop a kiss atop her father's head. He touched her cheek in absent affection. "Bye, Darryl."

Her brother-in-law grunted in response.

Troy Lee cleared his throat and offered her daddy his hand. "Nice meeting you, sir. You too, Darryl."

She patted Troy Lee's chest as she passed, and he fell into step behind her. "I need to speak to Mama real quick before we go."

Tension seeped from him in a relieved exhale as they entered the hall. She cringed. She loved her daddy to pieces and accepted his foibles for what they were, but between him and Darryl, and Hope's prickly interrogation, Troy Lee had to think she had the craziest, and probably rudest, family ever. Good thing he seemed determined to hang on to her.

In the kitchen, Mama and Hope pored over the advertising circulars from the Sunday paper. Angel leaned down to brush a kiss over her mother's cheek. "Mama, we're gone."

Her mother spun to wrap her in a quick hug. "Bye, sweetheart. I love you. Troy, it was good to meet you."

His grin seemed a little strained. "You too. Thank you for dinner. It was wonderful."

A pleased expression brightened her mother's features.

"Why, thank you. It's nice to be appreciated. Angel, don't you be a stranger this week."

"No, ma'am. Bye, Hope."

"Talk to you later." Hope glanced up from the JCPenney ad, and Angel was reassured to see the animosity gone from her gaze. "Nice to have met you, Troy Lee."

"Right." He inclined his head, then glanced at his watch. "Angel..."

"I know." She kissed her mother again. "Bye, Mama. Love you."

Outside, she looped her arm about his waist. "Sure you still want me after meeting them?"

"I'm sure." A relieved laugh burst from his throat as they walked across the grass, brown after the last frost, to where his Jeep waited under a pecan tree. "Angel baby, that was brutal."

"You're the one who volunteered to come."

"Yeah, I know." He pulled open the passenger door and helped her climb up. "Your sister hates me."

She waited until he came around to the driver's seat. "No, she doesn't. She's just protective."

"That's one word for it." He gave her a look as he fired the engine. "Listen, about that tea-glass rattling thing...how do I get in on some of that action?"

"Rattle a glass at me just once, Troy Lee Farr, and you won't be getting any action."

He shifted into reverse and looked over his shoulder to back into the drive, that wonderful grin playing about his mouth. "Oh, you'd probably give me a little action."

"No. None. Absolutely none."

Hand on the gearshift, he leaned in, lips a breath away from hers. "Not even a little?"

"No. Not even. I don't do rattling tea glasses." She laid her hand over his chest, his pulse thudding against her palm. "But you'd be surprised what asking me nicely will get you."

"I'll have to remember that." He kissed the corner of her mouth, then straightened, patting her knee before shifting into drive. The warmth engendered by his simple touch lingered long after they'd turned onto the highway.

ꙮ

"I'm telling you, man, it was the worst meeting-the-family scenario you could imagine." With Chris at his side, Troy Lee jogged up the rear steps to the sheriff's department. A cool breeze swirled a few stray leaves across the parking lot. Silence hung heavy in the late-night air.

Chris punched in the code to unlock the heavy metal door and dragged it open. "It couldn't have been that bad."

"It was." Only the soft murmur of jailers' voices drifting from the space behind the holding area disturbed the jail's quiet. An occasional radio squawk and a dispatcher's reply wafted out of the radio room. Troy Lee fell in behind Chris as they started up the narrow stairs to the squad room. "You know that Ben Stiller movie where he's meeting his girlfriend's parents and the dad is the former CIA guy who hates him?"

"Yeah?"

"This was worse."

"How so?"

"Where do you want me to start? I have zilch in common with her dad, her mother looked at me like I was crazy for running, and her sister? Hell." Juggling his ticket book and campaign hat, Troy Lee tugged his wallet from his back pocket and opened it to extract a couple of ones for the soda machine. "She kept looking at me the way Calvert does Cookie."

"Really? How's that?" At Cookie's dry voice, Troy Lee jerked, dumping half the contents of his wallet on the floor. The metallic cover holding his ticket book slammed into the tile with a clatter. F-uck. His face and neck hot, he leaned down to gather everything, then straightened to meet Cookie's intelligent gaze. Cookie dropped a stack of reports in his outbox and reached for another folder. "So? How does he look at me?"

"Like the farmer guarding a hen house against a fox," Chris replied for him. With a slight grin, he slanted a look at Troy Lee. "Is that right?"

Recalling the suspicion glinting in Hope's blue eyes, Troy Lee set his hat and ticket book on the counter. "That covers it."

Cookie's brows lifted in inquiry. "And who's looking at you like that?"

Troy Lee fed a couple of dollars into the soda machine and tossed a can at Chris before popping the tab on his own. "Angel's sister."

"Meeting the family, huh?" Cookie stapled a couple of copies together and laid them aside.

"Yep." The weirdness of this, talking about Angel's taking him home with Cookie, shafted through him. He shrugged it off. In the scheme of his relationship with Angel, Cookie didn't matter, any more than Morgan or any other woman he'd dated did.

"He doesn't fit." Settled in at one of the empty desks, Chris didn't look up from the end-of-shift recap he was filling out.

"Yeah? How so?" Cookie scrawled his signature across a report and slid it in the file.

With a sip of too-sweet cola, Troy Lee dropped into the chair adjacent to Cookie's desk and waited. After a moment, Chris looked up at him and Troy Lee gestured between them. "You don't want to answer this one for me?"

"Smart ass." Chris dropped his gaze back to the paper.

Troy Lee twisted in the chair and reached for his own blank form before he darted a look up at Cookie. "The sister doesn't trust me. The mother doesn't get me. The dad and I have nothing in common."

"Sure you do." Cookie's chair squeaked as he leaned back, arms behind his head.

"Huh." Troy Lee grunted in disagreement. "Like what?"

"You both care about his daughter."

Silently, Chris lifted a finger and made an imaginary tally point in the air. Struck by the idea, Troy Lee paused with his pen over the report and turned the notion over in his mind. Maybe he wasn't as fucked there as he thought he was after all.

"Same with the sister. She'll come around. It just takes time." One corner of Cookie's mouth lifted in a crooked grin. Down the hall, the front door opened, a quiet exchange of voices going on at the front desk.

Chris signed his recap and took it to the copy machine. "And you're saying Tick will too?"

"I will what?" Calvert strolled into the room, dressed casually in jeans and an untucked polo shirt. His bearing spoke of intense exhaustion.

Cookie darted a look up at the large clock hanging over the counter and scowled. "What are you doing here?"

"We've been at the hospital." Calvert collapsed into the

chair at what had once been Jeff Schaefer's desk and dragged both hands down his face. "Cait's catching a nap there and I needed some air. Figured I'd walk over here, see what was going on."

"Something happening with the baby?" Chris's brows dipped in a troubled expression. Troy Lee concentrated on summarizing his shift and keeping his mouth shut. With Calvert in the room, his gut was already jittering, the slight burn starting between his ribs. If he said anything, it would come out wrong and piss Calvert off. Besides, the guy seemed tense and edgy enough without Troy Lee's adding to it.

"He's back on the ventilator." Calvert rested his elbow on the chair arm and propped against his fist. "It's set low, but the longer he's on it, the higher the chances he'll develop a lung infection. Plus, we'd just gotten him off the feeding tube and nursing, and this interferes with that, so Cait's upset and..."

He shook his head, his voice trailing away. Troy Lee glanced up in time to see the look he exchanged with Cookie, who watched him with concern.

"Needed a break, huh?" Cookie pulled his gum from his pocket and extracted a piece.

Calvert nodded, understanding passing between the two. Yeah, they'd be okay. Cookie was right—with enough time, Tick would come around. The lead investigator stretched out his legs on a harsh sigh. "So what's going on?"

"We're getting ready to go home." Leaning on the counter, Chris capped his pen and tucked it in his shirt pocket. "And ragging Troy Lee's ass about meeting the girlfriend's parents."

"There's a girlfriend?" Calvert quirked an eyebrow. "I thought you had a fan club."

Like Calvert paid that much attention to anything other than how he screwed up. Troy Lee sucked in a breath, trying to figure out how to proceed without saying something stupid. His chest hurt and he patted his pocket, seeking and not finding the roll of antacids.

"You're out of the loop." Cookie dropped the last set of reports and files in his outbox. "There's been a girlfriend for two weeks. The fan club is all in mourning. There is great wailing and gnashing of teeth in Chandler County."

Calvert gave a huff of amusement. "So who's the lucky girl?"

Neither Chris nor Cookie jumped in to answer for him this time. Troy Lee signed his report and rose to make a copy. He glanced sideways at Calvert. “Angel Henderson.”

“Really.” Calvert fixed Cookie with a pointed look.

Anger simmered under Troy Lee’s skin. No need to wonder what that was all about. Again, the strangeness speared through him, and once more, he sloughed it off. Whatever had happened that night with Angel and Cookie had been a one-time thing. It didn’t *matter*.

With a jerky movement, he jabbed the original report in the box mounted on the wall then tossed his copy in his own officer mailbox. He turned to discover Calvert watching him with a speculative expression and a half-smile. Irritated, Troy Lee lifted his chin. “What?”

Calvert made that small, amused sound in his throat. “Trying to imagine you and Ron Henderson meeting for the first time.”

Troy Lee released a breath, a grin pulling at his own mouth. “It was uneventful. He was too focused on the football game.”

“I can believe that. Word is that if their preacher starts getting close to twelve-thirty, Ron taps his watch, reminding him the pregame show is about to start.” Calvert dragged his hands down his face again and slumped deeper in the chair. “Sure as hell glad my meeting-the-family days are behind me. Cait’s grandfather likes me.” He grunted. “Although, apparently her brother had, or has, reservations where I’m concerned.”

“My God, the irony,” Cookie deadpanned.

“Shut up.” Calvert crumpled an empty report on the desk and tossed it at his partner, who deflected it back with a laugh and an open palm. “It’s not the same thing.”

“Sure it is.”

Chris tagged Troy Lee’s chest. “Let’s leave them to duke it out. If you want to run in the morning, I’ve got to get some sleep.”

“Yeah, me too.” It might be a good thing Angel had planned an early night. He tended not to get a lot of sleep when they shared a bed. A different warmth spread through his chest. He might not be sharing her bed tonight, but that was okay.

Seeing the beginnings of trust and commitment in her eyes earlier had been satisfaction enough.

Once the younger deputies had cleared the room, Mark studied Tick. Head tilted back, eyes closed, he appeared to be slipping into a doze, although stress and weariness still strained his face. Damn, he looked like hell.

After several quiet moments, in which Mark wrapped up his own end-of-the-day paperwork, Tick blew out a long breath and straightened. "I need to get back over there."

Mark picked up his keys from the desk. "How about I give you a ride?"

Tick rose, a hand over his lower right side. "It's only four blocks."

"Yeah, I know. Come on."

In silence they made the short drive. Mark pulled into the main parking lot, and Tick glanced at him in surprise when he stepped from the driver's seat. Mark shrugged. "Figured I'd walk up with you."

Tick nodded and didn't demur. The lobby was quiet and deserted; the middle-aged woman working the front desk graced Tick with a warm smile of recognition and handed them passes for the nursery floor. In the elevator, Tick still didn't speak, leaning on the wall, his eyes closed, leaving Mark with the impression he was centering himself, gathering his reserves. The door slid open with a soft hush.

Instead of heading straight for the NICU, Tick stopped by a darkened room canted off from the nurse's station. Even in the dim shadows, Mark could make out Falconetti on the cot there, a thin blanket covering her shoulders, her features reposed in soft sleep. Seemingly satisfied, Tick backed out and headed down the hall to the NICU.

After a brief conference with the charge nurse, they scrubbed and gowned. Nearly a month after Lee's early birth, the NICU atmosphere and rules were more familiar and being surrounded by tiny reminders of what he'd lost so long ago didn't twist Mark into quite as many knots.

No longer requiring the enclosed isolette, Lee curled into a modified fetal position on a raised table-bed with low clear sides. Even with the respirator tubing and all the various wires and IVs, he looked bigger, stronger, than the last time Mark had seen him, three or four days earlier.

Tick laid his palm along the thin little back, long fingers

nearly covering him, and leaned down so his mouth was near the baby's ear. "Leebo, Daddy's back again."

The baby didn't respond and over his shoulder Tick slanted a glance at Mark. "They sedated him to get the ventilator tube in."

Mark started to hook his thumbs in his belt, remembered the sterile gown and crossed his arms over his chest instead. "He looks good, still. Bigger than the other day."

"Yeah, he's up a few ounces and an inch or so." Gaze on his son's face, Tick feathered his fingertips across the little nape, stroking, caressing. "You were right, you know."

Mark lifted a brow. "About?"

"I can't control this. I can't make it better for him or for Cait, and it makes me crazy. It's damn hard, Cookie, and some days even the praying's not enough."

"Yeah." It was hell, being caught in a set of circumstances beyond control. He'd learned that the hard way, during those dark days and weeks and months following Jenny's disappearance. "A day at a time, Tick, or an hour. Sometimes five minutes. That's what you do—what you can do—and somehow you come out on the other side."

"Are you there yet?"

"Getting there." He didn't mention Tori's name, didn't bring up how she'd become his guideline in the still-treacherous morass of getting through the lingering grief and guilt.

"I really wasn't prepared." Tick's dry laugh was little more than a huff of sound. "Weird, huh? I loved him before he was even here, and you know how much we wanted this. I just didn't realize how much he'd change me, how much I'd love him. The way I feel about him, the way I feel deeper about Cait now...hell, Cookie, it's so strong sometimes it's scary." A beat fell between them and Tick lifted dark eyes to Mark's. "I don't know how you stood it."

He didn't have to say what "it" was. Even so far away, the loss of his wife and unborn child didn't slam Mark in the chest quite as hard. It hurt, he suspected it always would on some level, but he was getting better, getting through.

"I did what I could do. An hour, a night, a week." Mark eyed the easy movement of Tick's fingers against the baby's skin, thin wisps of dark hair fluffing out from his nape. "It's going to be all right, Tick. You, Falconetti, the baby. You'll be fine, together, and it'll be good. You just have to hang on together."

Tick didn't look at him. "So you think that's what it'll be with you and Tori? Helping one another handle the past?"

Surprise shivered over Mark. He hadn't expected that, the closest thing to acceptance Tick had yet displayed toward his relationship with Tori. He swallowed hard. "Yeah, I think so. Looking to the future together. I'm telling you, Tick, it's real." He grinned. "So real it's scary sometimes."

Tick did look up then, with a wry half-smile. "Yeah. I can get that. Looking to the future, huh?"

"That's right." For once, he regarded the future with something other than resignation and desolation. Didn't matter what it brought, really. Somehow, with Tori at his side, he could face anything life threw at him.

Chapter Ten

Angel woke up reaching for Troy Lee. When her seeking hand encountered only cool linen, she opened her eyes, tempted to laugh at her disappointment.

Her cell phone, charging upon her nightstand, sang out the beginning notes of "Your Man" and she grabbed it. "Hello?"

"I miss you." Troy Lee's rich voice greeted her. "I'm spoiled and I don't like waking up without you."

She laughed, hugging his words close. "It's mutual."

"We're gonna have to do something about this."

"What do you suggest, Deputy Farr?"

"Well, I would say something about letting me move in"—fabric rustled, his voice muffled for a moment—"but since I'm not allowed to even leave a change of clothes over there..."

"You're not moving in." The idea conjured sweet images, though, of waking up with him, sharing simple household chores, hanging out in front of a movie, falling asleep in his arms every night. "Mama would have a fit. The rumors would fly, especially since we've only been together a couple of weeks."

"You worry way too much what people think. They don't matter, Angel. We matter." He sighed. "But I want you to be happy and if that means keeping two households for a while, I can deal."

"Have I mentioned what a sweetheart you are?"

"Once or twice. Listen, I've got to go. I'm supposed to meet Chris in a few minutes. We're going to run, then work the dog before our shift starts. How about if I come by the club after I get off?"

"If you get off on time, you mean."

"Yeah. Exactly." His quiet laugh rose between them, tickling across her senses. "Bye, baby."

The cellular link died and she lay for several long seconds, holding on to the pleasure of connection with him. She stared up at the morning light casting fingers across her wall. Keeping two households for a while? Was she to take that at face value, that at some point, he envisioned a long-term future with her? She hugged those sweet possibilities close too.

Finally, she pushed the covers aside and swung her feet to the floor. She dedicated her Mondays to inventory and getting vendor orders done for the week, and that meant she had a long day before her. She made the bed and ambled through the kitchen and the middle room toward the bathroom. As she stepped into the tiny hallway, inescapable nausea bloomed in her throat.

She scrambled for the toilet, kneeling on the cool tile and retching until every muscle in her abdomen ached. Her throat raw, she flushed the toilet and slumped sideways to lean on the tub. Her body shaky and weak, she blinked hard.

Okay, that was *it*. She felt worse, not better, and as soon as the doctor's office opened, she was calling for an appointment. Breathing through her nose, she swallowed against a fresh wave of queasiness and eased to her feet. A horrid taste lingered in her mouth and invaded her nostrils, and she grabbed her toothbrush, avoiding her reflection. She didn't have to see to know she probably looked as bad as she felt.

An hour later, after a shower and some toast, she felt more human, although the waves of sickness still attacked her at odd moments. Sitting at the kitchen table with a glass of weak iced tea—her mother's remedy for all stomach illnesses—she dialed her doctor's number and sat through three rings.

"Good morning, Coney Women's Health Center. This is Lynne, may I help you?" The pleasant voice of one of her high school classmates washed over her with comforting familiarity.

"Hey, Lynne, this is Angel Henderson. I'm really not feeling well and I was wondering if Dr. Padgett or Marilee had an opening this morning?"

"Oh, hon, I'm sorry you're sick. Let me check." The clacking of computer keys carried over the phone. "What's wrong?"

"I'm nauseous, with some dizziness. I thought it was my sister's crab dip, but now...I'm wondering if I don't have the flu."

"Okay, Dr. Padgett is booked, but I can fit you in with Marilee if you come on now."

Seeing the physician's assistant was fine with her. "I'm on my way."

By the time she pulled into the small parking lot behind the big, converted frame house, her stomach had settled somewhat. Pulling her jacket close against the nipping wind, she hurried to the back door, which led to the doctors' offices. She paused at the reception desk, her gaze sweeping over the already half-full waiting room. "Hey, Lynne. Thanks for working me in."

"No problem." Lynne fixed her with an assessing stare and passed over a clipboard with the standard forms on it. "You do look pale. Here, I need you to update your paperwork, but I promise we'll get you seen as soon as possible."

"Thanks." By the time she'd finished the forms, two of the women waiting had been called back. Moments later, Marilee Young appeared at the waiting room door. "Angel?"

She followed the physician's assistant into the familiar patient intake area. Marilee directed her to step onto the scales, talking while adjusting the slides. "Lynne says you're dizzy and nauseous? How long?"

"Today's the fourth day."

"Getting worse?" Marilee made a notation on Angel's file.

"Yes. It had just been queasiness before, but I actually threw up this morning."

"Okay." After taking her pulse, temperature and blood pressure and listening to her heart and lungs, Marilee made a few more notations and led her down the hall to one of the exam rooms, this one painted in soft eggshell pink and with a Monet print on the wall. At Marilee's urging, Angel scooted onto the examination table. Marilee took the rolling stool and, frowning, flipped through the chart. "Your last period was in September?"

"Um, yes." Angel tucked her hair behind her ear. "But I'm on that new pill, the one that limits your periods to four a year, so I'm not due until December."

"And you've been taking them as directed?"

"Yes." She turned the question over in her mind. "Well, I missed two back in October, but I made them up according to the package insert by doubling the dosage."

Marilee looked up and studied her over reading glasses. "So you didn't have any breakthrough bleeding?"

"I spotted some, maybe a week or so later." Unease kicked over in her stomach and she tried to quiet it. This was ridiculous. Not only had she made up the missed pills, but she'd made sure Jim had worn a condom that last time and with Cookie there'd been no question of his not doing so. "Marilee, I can't be pregnant."

"Probably not, but let's do a test, just in case."

Angel lifted her hands in surrender and let them fall against her thighs. It wasn't like she had anything to worry about, really. "Sure, why not?"

Marilee provided her with a specimen cup, she visited the restroom and followed the instructions, then returned to the room while Marilee unwrapped the stick and performed the test. Angel fidgeted, twisting her fingers, playing with the little amethyst birthstone ring her parents had given her for graduation.

Minutes later, Marilee looked up from the test stick. "It's positive."

"What?" Shock crashed through her, followed by a wave of pure disbelief. "It's wrong."

"We can do a blood test, which is more accurate, but you'll have to wait while I run the sample through the lab."

She couldn't think, couldn't get her scattered thoughts together. She swallowed, trying to still the frightened race of her heart. "Fine, let's do that, but Marilee, I'm telling you. I'm not pregnant."

Sympathy flashed over Marilee's delicate features. "Let me get a quick sample, then."

Lost in a cloud of bewildered fear, Angel barely registered the prick of the needle. Marilee patted her knee. "I'll be back in a few minutes."

Hands in her lap, Angel stared at the Monet watercolor reprint on the wall. The soothing blues and greens were reminiscent of the shades in the ocean scene hanging in Troy Lee's living room. She bit her lip, seconds trickling by. She twisted the thin ring around her finger over and over. Long, glacial minutes later, the door opened.

Even before Marilee spoke, she knew. The quick breath Marilee sucked in, the way she straightened her shoulders...this test was positive as well. “Angel—”

“Another positive.”

Marilee nodded. “Yes.”

“Oh, Lord.” She covered her mouth with a hand. What was she supposed to do now? This couldn’t be. It couldn’t because...

Her stomach revolted and she crossed her arms over her midriff, breathing through the panic and the nerves. Marilee stepped forward, face set in concerned lines. “Angel, honey, lean forward, let’s put your head—”

“I’m good.” She waved Marilee away. Being touched right now...she couldn’t take it. She thrust shaking fingers through her hair, one arm still folded over her belly. “How...how far along am I?”

Marilee watched her closely then picked up the chart. “It’s hard to say because of the suppressed periods. From what you’ve told me, I’d hazard a guess at five to six weeks, maybe seven, but that’s just an estimate.”

That meant...

“I think I’m going to be sick.”

“All right, let me help you.” Marilee moved quickly, ushering her into the adjacent bathroom, where dry heaves attacked her, wringing tears and sobs from her body. Biting down on her bottom lip until coppery blood flowed against her tongue, she forced herself to calm down. Getting upset, giving in to the panic, was only going to make things worse. She rubbed her shaking hands down her thighs and let Marilee lead her back to the exam room.

She gathered her purse and jacket and clutched them to her chest. “Thanks for seeing me, Marilee, but I need to go.”

“Angel, wait. You’re obviously upset—”

“I’ll be okay.”

“Let me get Dr. Padgett and—”

“No.” The word emerged harsher than she intended and she closed her eyes a second, taking a deep breath. “No, please. I need some time to get things together, to get my head straight.”

“At least see Lynne and make another appointment soon, so we can talk about your options and prenatal care.”

“I will. I just...I need to go.”

Somehow, she managed to get through talking to Lynne, managed to drive home, although later she didn’t remember the trip. She let herself in the front door, dumped her keys and purse in the floor, slid down the wall next to them. Chilly wind whipped in the open doorway, fluttering her skirt, flirting with her hair.

She stared up at the plaster ceiling, picking out whorls and patterns. Five, six, maybe seven weeks. She set the words to a sick rhythm of eeny-meeny-miney-moe in her head. Five, six, maybe seven weeks.

Six—no, seven—weeks ago, she'd been in bed with Jim. Twice.

Five, almost six weeks ago...she'd been in bed with Cookie. Just once.

Resting her arm across her knees and her other elbow on that arm, she covered her face.

"Lord," she whispered, "please help me."

In her purse, her cell phone jingled, the distinctive notes of "Your Man" rising from the jumbled interior. She cringed, pain crashing over her. Moments later, the music died away, the last of her hopes draining with it. Yes, believing second by second, trusting in them, was really going to help her now.

Dropping her hand, she grabbed her bag, dragged it close enough to retrieve her phone. Ignoring the new voice-mail icon, she scrolled through her contacts and dialed, waiting through five rings until another voice mailbox picked up. "Julie? It's Angel. Call me please. I'm not feeling well and I need you to open the bar. Thanks. Talk to you later."

She dropped the metallic rectangle to the floor. Levering both hands on the wood, she pushed herself up, first to kneel, then lurching to her feet like an aching elderly woman. With a listless movement, she pushed the door closed. Her throat hurt, raw and sore from retching, tight and closed from fear.

In the mirror over the table by the door, she caught a glimpse of her reflection: red eyes, disheveled hair, trembling mouth, too-pale skin. "You don't have to do this," she whispered to the frightened woman in the mirror. "You don't."

Wasn't that the easiest thing to do? To make it simply go away?

"No one would have to know." She wrapped her arms close, tight, tighter, as tight as she could get them, and addressed herself again. "Not Jim, not Cookie." She darted her tongue over dry, chapped lips. "Not Troy Lee."

You'd know, the bruised blue eyes seemed to whisper back from the glass.

"Don't you get it?" The words came in a fierce hiss. "Jim's married. Cookie has someone new. And Troy Lee..."

She couldn't get the words out, couldn't articulate what she knew was done and over and lost now. On a shuddering sigh, she touched a fingertip to the glass. "What the hell am I going to do?"

"You're whipped."

Troy Lee frowned at Chris's amused commentary. "What are you talking about?"

"How many times have you called her today?" Chris placed three white canvas bags under a trio of low red crates. From his "stay" position at the bottom of the steps leading to the prisoner exercise yard, Hound watched with eager eyes.

"Twice." His face burning, Troy Lee returned his phone to his belt, hoping he didn't look as sheepish as he felt. Angel hadn't called him back, and yeah, checking his phone every few seconds was stupid. Mondays were busy for her; he knew that. A trickle of sweat made its way down his back. Even under the weak winter sun, the damn vest was hot. The muscles in his thighs twitched with the afterburn of running miles of hills. "But this call was legitimate. I needed to know if she wanted to go to the holiday party with me so I could RSVP."

Chris paced a few strides from the crates and shot him a mock-pitying look. "Miss Lydia doesn't need that list for another week. I repeat, you're whipped."

Hound stared longingly at the red containers, shifted his limpid gaze to Chris and made a low whine, big canine body quivering with anticipation.

"What would you know?" Troy Lee lowered to sit on the second tread from the top. "You haven't had a date in so long, people think you're gay."

"Heh." Mild amusement colored the sound as Chris flipped him off. The door behind Troy Lee clanged open and Chris jerked his chin toward the top of the steps. "Hey, Cookie, how many times have you called Tori today?"

"I haven't." Cookie stopped on the step next to Troy Lee. Chris fixed Troy Lee with a "see?" expression. "Texted her a couple of times this morning about the holiday party."

Smirking at Chris, Troy Lee waved a hand between them. Chris shook his head. "Y'all are sad."

Troy Lee rested his elbows on the step behind him. "You're just jealous."

"Hardly." Chris turned his attention to the dog. "Hound, search." The German Shepherd responded immediately, springing forward, running around the three crates, nosing them under Chris's stream of encouragement. "Atta boy, Hound, find it. Hsst. Where's it at, huh? Where's it at, boy, find it. Hsst. Hsst. Come on."

With a whine, Hound paused at the middle crate, pawing and scratching at the top before sitting and eyeing Chris with adoring expectation. Chris stopped on the other side of the red box. "Is that it?"

Hound laid a big paw atop the crate. Chris leaned down, lifted the plastic and pulled out the white bag. He held it aloft so Cookie and Troy Lee could see "cocaine" written across the front in large block print. "Good boy. Good dog."

He pulled a tennis ball from his BDU pocket. Hound perked up but didn't leave the sit position. Chris tossed the ball across the worn grass. "Go get it."

Watching Chris reward the dog with play, Troy Lee shook his head. The guy's most meaningful relationship was with a four-legged furry beast and he was ragging Troy Lee about being whipped?

"How do you feel about having me for a ride-along this afternoon?"

He startled at Cookie's quiet question. Nerves jumped in his gut, and he came to his feet. "Am I in trouble again?"

"Nah." Cookie laughed. "My unit's going in for routine maintenance. Figured if I tagged along, you could fill me in on that chase-response training you took over in Tifton."

"Yeah." Relief filled him, the tension draining away. Man, he had to find a way to get beyond the constant fear of screwing up. He rested his hands above his gun belt and looked sideways at Cookie. "I can do that."

"Come on then." Cookie tilted his head toward the department building. "Let's go 10-8 and get started."

Unable to bear being inside the silent house, Angel fled outside to the yard and worked herself ragged. She attacked the gingko tree at the back corner of the house with the pruning shears, even though it was the wrong time of year for that. She divided daylilies, not caring that doing so in the cold would shock the roots. She weeded already immaculate beds, tunneling beneath the damp mulch with her bare hands to dig out the tiniest of sprouts. Through it all, she kept her mind a careful blank.

After replacing the shears in the shed, she grabbed a rake and tackled the gravel area around the small building, dragging precise circles in the small stones. Maybe she should open the bar herself after all, call Julie back and tell her she felt better. Maybe if she picked up and went on, pretended everything was normal, it really would be.

She gazed at her hands on the rake handle, nails jagged and broken, dirt embedded under them. Lower, soil stained her turquoise boots and streaked her bare legs. Lord, she hadn't even changed, had just marched out here in her brown cotton dress, legs and arms exposed, wearing her beloved custom boots. A giggle burbled up from her tight throat, morphing into a rough sob. Hot tears burned her eyes and she buried her face in the curve of her arm, braced atop the rake. Breathing in hard, she forced herself back into control. No thinking, just work.

Yes, she needed to go do her own inventory, go open the bar. With a shaky inhale, she lifted her head and brushed at her face, leaving gritty trails on her skin. She replaced the rake on the tool rack and locked the shed. Leaning down, she rubbed at the dirt on her legs, achieving no more than merely spreading the rich black soil.

A shower, a night working, time spent pretending everything was normal and okay.

She could do that.

"It's all about assessing the risk." Troy Lee slowed to swing onto Tuton Road from Highway 112. Cookie lounged in the passenger seat, an elbow propped on the door, his gaze alert and interested. "Like an equation, you know?"

Cookie rubbed his forefinger over his mouth. "An equation."

"Yeah." Warming to the topic, Troy Lee relaxed, navigating the familiar road with one hand on the wheel. "You take the variables you know—the roadway, the traffic, whether it's a felony offense—and you combine them with the ones you don't, and you come up with a risk ratio. If the ratio is too high, you drop out of the chase, try a different tactic."

"Makes sense. You should redeliver that. I'll talk to Tick, have him set it up on the training schedule."

Troy Lee swallowed a rude retort. Somehow, he doubted Calvert would trust him to redeliver anything without screwing up the entire department. He braked for the crossroads at US 19, continued across on River Road, swerving to the other lane to avoid the rumble strips before the railroad.

"Troy Lee." Cookie cleared his throat. "He'll come around to you, but you have to give him a chance."

"Right." Troy Lee took his gaze from the road long enough to glance narrow-eyed at Cookie. "Two and a half years, Cookie. I'll own my screwups. I got caught up in the excitement of that first chase and ran the engine hot. I fucked up the Schaefer warrant. Yeah, there's other stuff too. He can't see beyond any of that. He doesn't want to see beyond it."

"He's forgotten what the learning curve can be like." Cookie tapped a knuckle against the window. "But I think he's got a whole new one and that'll open him up with you."

"Maybe I don't want him to open up with me." Shit, now he sounded like Ellis when she was pouting about one of Christine's rules. "Maybe I just want him to leave me the hell alone."

"We both know that's not true." Cool calm blanketed the quiet words. "You want to be like him."

"Maybe I did." Troy Lee pressed the brakes harder than necessary, the car sliding a little as it came to a rest at the Highway 3 stop sign. He glanced both ways, tapping his fingers on the wheel. On 3, a Honda swung around the curve, approaching the intersection, fast. "Maybe not anymore."

"You've got a damn stubborn streak a mile wide, don't you?"

"Get it from my dad. He called it persistence." The Honda flashed by in a blur of gray paint and Florida tags. "Holy shit, he's flying."

"Yeah. Turn after him." Cookie gestured with a finger, but Troy Lee was already turning in behind the small car, closing the gap with a hard foot on the gas. Brake lights didn't flare as Troy Lee had expected, but the driver's head bobbed. Checking the mirrors. Instincts pricked to life all down Troy Lee's spine.

"Call Chris." Troy Lee stabbed a finger toward the radio and flipped on his blue lights. Still no brake lights. Sure enough, the Honda sped up rather than slowing down. Troy Lee's speedometer crept upwards as he kept pace. He spun the chase variables through his head, the logic blending with the instinct. "There're drugs in that car."

"I think you're right." Cookie already had the mike in hand, rattling off Chris's call number and a request for location, following that with a call to dispatch, asking for a run on the Honda's tags. "You gotta stop him before he hits town too."

"Somebody needs to meet us north of town, to put out the spike strip before he hits those double bridges—"

"Chandler, C-3." Deb's calm voice from dispatch cut him off.

"Go ahead, Chandler."

"Tags are registered to a 1992 Honda Accord, Brad Richards out of Tampa. Has active felony wants and warrants."

"10-4, Chandler." Cookie's words faded into a stream of syllables, Troy Lee's concentration focused on navigating the twisting back highway and watching the other driver's every move. Chris's quiet voice came across the radio as he called in his location and his intention to cut across the PSC service road to intercept the chase.

"C-8 to C-5." Vann Starling hailed Chris. "I'm south of you on 3, right around the curve. Stopping to deploy the spike strip."

"Chris needs to come on this way." Troy Lee shook his head, steering tight into the double S curve before the Stinson place. Adrenaline surged into his system, sharpening his senses, slowing time around him. "This guy's gonna shoot right onto Haven Road."

"No, there's no way—"

"Cookie, he'll take Haven and try to lose us. Tell Chris to come on."

His tone tight, Cookie complied. Sure enough, as they cleared the curve and headed into the straightaway, the Honda jumped forward and Troy Lee pressed harder on the accelerator to stay with him. White flashed beyond Dale Jenkins's pecan grove, a glimpse of Chris's car before he came around the upcoming curve. Brake lights flared briefly on the Honda and it veered to the right down the red clay surface of Haven Road.

"Shit," Cookie breathed, and triumph spurted through Troy Lee, blending with the mix of anger and adrenaline. He took the same right, hard, with Chris falling in behind.

Red dust bloomed behind the Honda, obscuring the road. Damn, he was glad he'd driven this sucker as often as he had, in endless patrol circles. He could map out the geography in his head, the way he could envision notes on sheet music when he played. After the first curve, the dirt road opened up enough to allow him passage around the Honda. If he got out in front, he and Chris could hem the son of a bitch in, force him to stop.

Driving with one hand, he snatched the mike from Cookie's surprised hold. "Chris, we're gonna stop him after the curve, before the Harris place."

"Got your back."

As soon as the way opened up, Troy Lee punched it, coming along side the Honda. Shit, they needed a third car, to make a true box, but they could do this. He pulled slightly forward, eyeing the access points as he did so. All he needed was a damn tractor or a pickup to pull out in front of them.

Like silk clockwork, Chris angled in behind him, the two of them working in tandem to force the Honda to slow and finally come to a sliding halt in the ditch.

"He's gonna bail." Cookie unlatched his seat belt as Troy Lee slammed the gearshift to park. Metal clanged on metal, paint scratching with a shearing sound as the Honda's driver's door banged into the passenger door of Troy Lee's unit.

Troy Lee didn't take time to cringe, lunging out of the unit and into a sprint as the suspect scrambled across the Honda's trunk and up the ditch incline to scale the wire fence. Shit, why did they always run?

With Hound's excited yelping and Chris's voice calling in radio codes, he vaulted across the ditch, scrabbled for purchase on the slick clay, braced a hand on the fence post to jump the wire. The skinny kid had a slight lead on him across the pasture, but with a burst of speed, Troy Lee closed the distance. Hell if he was gonna tackle him and risk blowing his knee. Instead, he grasped a handful of T-shirt and slung the guy down, belly first. The impact wrung a grunt from the suspect.

"You want to run from me again, man?" Cuffs in hand, Troy Lee planted his knee in the middle of the young man's spine and captured one wrist, pulling it down to close the other cuff. He dragged the kid to his knees and kicked one ankle over the other. "You wanna run?"

"Fuck you." Hell, the boy was winded. And he'd planned to outrun them on foot? Shit. "You hear me? Fuck you!"

"Fuck me? Fuck *me*?" Troy Lee searched him, retrieving a pocketknife and sticking it in his own back pocket to be inventoried. "Dude, I'm not the one in cuffs and about to go to jail. Word of advice for next time—don't run from me. I take it personal, and I *will* catch your ass."

The kid responded by trying to spit on him. Sure he was secure, Troy Lee used the pressure points at his wrist to force him to his feet and turn them toward the road, just as Cookie reached them. He passed the knife over to Cookie, his gaze traveling beyond Cookie's shoulder. Chris and the dog worked over the Honda, Hound's tail wagging furiously as he hit on the trunk area. Two county units arrived and slid to a stop. Vann Starling and Steve Monroe climbed out to join Chris and take in the scene.

Cookie's gray eyes glittered with conquest and adrenaline. "You did good, kid."

Troy Lee returned Cookie's wide grin with one of his own. Man, he couldn't wait to tell Angel about this one.

Chapter Eleven

Tori peeked through the NICU window. Sure enough, she spied both Caitlin and Tick. Before she could buzz, Dawn Monroe appeared at the doorway. "Hey, Tori."

"Hi, Dawn." Aware of the slumbering babies, she kept her voice low. "How is he today?"

"Pretty good." Dawn ushered her into the adjacent washroom so she could scrub. "We got to swap out the ventilator tube for an oxygen feed and his breathing seems stabilized."

"That's great." Tori slipped her arms into the sterile gown Dawn proffered.

"Mama and Daddy in there are exhausted, I'm sure. If you could get them to take a break, eat something, that would be good. They need it."

"I'll do my best." She crossed to her brother and sister-in-law. Dawn was right. They looked completely dragged out. Caitlin sat in a rocker, her tailored cotton blouse open so Lee, clad only in a diaper and with his tubing artfully arranged to be out of the way, could rest with his tiny bare chest over her heart. They'd draped a thin blanket to offer a modicum of privacy, but his dark head remained visible. Tick had dragged up a chair, his fingers laced through Caitlin's. He'd leaned his head back, eyes closed.

"Hey, y'all." Tori leaned down to feather a caress over Lee's head. "Kangaroo care, huh?"

"Yes." Caitlin smoothed the baby's back. "We just swapped out. I think he"—she nodded in Tick's direction—"finally dozed off."

"Not asleep. Resting my eyes." Tick's voice emerged as a

drowsy murmur. With a yawn, he straightened and rubbed a hand over his stubbled jaw. "What's up?"

"I had a meeting with the new head of counseling services here and thought I'd come take y'all to lunch." Under her fingers, Lee heaved a shuddering little sigh. His lids lifted a moment, then dropped again. A rush of love, mingled with a sharp longing, swirled through her. Could he be more precious? The too-familiar fantasy, the one that had only recently taken root, of holding her own baby, Mark's baby, rose and she suppressed the maternal desire. Way too soon to be thinking about that. Although she was. A lot. "Or, if you two want to grab something alone together, I can stay with Lee."

Her eyes filled with affection and a new uncertainty, Caitlin slanted a look at Tick. "I think I'd like to sit with him a little longer, since we're going home tonight, but why don't you go, Tick? You didn't eat this morning."

"You sure?" He gave her fingers a squeeze and let go.

"I am." Her voice was as soft as her gaze on his face. "Y'all can bring me back something."

"Okay." He leaned over to brush his mouth across Lee's tiny cheek. "We won't be long."

In the hallway, Tori wrapped her arm around his waist and hugged him on their way to the elevators. "So what sounds good? My treat."

"Anything's fine. We can walk down to the diner." He punched the call button. He cleared his throat as the car arrived with a quiet ding. "You could call Cookie, see if he has time to join us."

She stared at him as they entered the elevator, then smiled. "I'm sorry. What did you say? I don't think I heard you correctly."

"Tori." He leaned against the wall, weariness etched into each movement. "Just call him if you're going to."

With a light laugh, she retrieved her cell from her purse, and using the speaker function, dialed Mark. He picked up on the second ring, but didn't give her a chance to speak.

"Not now, honey," he said, his words competing with a burst of excited male chatter and what she thought was Stanton Reed's full laugh. "I'll call you back."

The line went dead and she stared at her phone. This was what she hated about dating a cop, the way it infiltrated every aspect of their lives. She lifted her gaze to Tick, who'd come to full alertness, speculation in his dark gaze.

"Wonder what that was about?" Not wanting to admit how miffed she was, she dropped the phone in her bag with a nonchalant air.

"No clue." The elevator shuddered to a stop and he held the door with a hand to let her precede him. A grin played about his mouth. "But we can go by the department on the way to the diner."

She rolled her eyes. She should have known he wouldn't be able to resist.

The walk to the courthouse square only took a few minutes. Tick mounted the steps two at a time, stopping to hold the door for her. Even in the small foyer, a cacophony of laughter and energy swelled from the squad room.

"Hey, Miss Lydia." Tick stopped to kiss her cheek. "What's up?"

Lydia waved toward the hallway. "They made a drug bust early this afternoon and they're playing the video from Troy Lee's car."

Tick's brows lifted. "Troy Lee made a drug bust? Come on, Tor, I gotta see this."

Tori trailed him. She didn't get this part, the way they enthused over an arrest. The laughter and conversation grew louder as they approached the squad room, blending with the tinny sound of recorded voices.

"I'm telling you, it was *beautiful.*" Sheer glee colored Mark's voice. He leaned against his desk, gaze trained, like every other man's in the room, on the portable TV-DVD set up on the counter. "Textbook chase technique."

On the screen, driver's-vantage footage from a patrol car played, depicting a small car racing down Highway 3. Curvy, dangerous, widow-maker Highway 3. From the voices, she could tell Mark had been in that car with Troy Lee at what looked like incredible speeds.

And they were excited, laughing about it, like it was nothing more than an amusement-park ride. She didn't get this part, either, and she wasn't sure she liked it.

"Exactly how fast were you going?" Arms crossed over his chest, Stanton leaned forward for a better look.

"On the curve, about eighty-five. When we hit the

straightaway, close to a hundred." Troy Lee grinned and held up his index fingers, a few inches apart. "The road looked like it was about that wide."

Steve Monroe nudged Mark's shoulder. "Has your ass unpuckered yet?"

A ripple of male laughter moved around the room. Mark shifted, pointing at the television. "This is where he takes off on Haven Road."

Stanton caught sight of Tick and waved him forward. "Hey, Tick, come here. You have to see this."

Tori followed behind him, watching as the car sped onto a familiar dirt road, Troy Lee still in chase. Noticing her, Steve moved from his spot next to Mark. With a quick glance in her direction, Mark pulled her closer, his arm behind her, hand resting lightly on her hip. He landed a quick kiss somewhere in the vicinity of her mouth, his gaze straying back to the television. "Hey, baby. Watch this. It's unbelievable."

That was certainly one word for it.

Dust obscured the action, the patrol car slowing, the Honda visible at the edges of the video as it came to a rest in the ditch. The camera shook, metal grinding on the audio as voices tumbled over one another.

"And Troy Lee destroys another patrol car." Chris Parker's deadpan comment brought forth another swell of laughter.

"The car isn't destroyed. It just damaged the paint on the door. How is that my fault?"

"Because you were there and it's easy to blame you?" Steve offered.

"I think this makes up for killing the first patrol car, Troy Lee." Stanton tapped Tick's chest with the backs of two fingers. "Almost fifteen pounds of marijuana, several thousand dollars street value in bagged meth, and nearly five grand in cash in the car. Kid driving the car has felony warrants in Florida for multiple drug charges. Guess he was using 3 as the back way into Florida, to avoid I-75."

Tick nodded. "Good deal, Troy Lee."

Tori nudged Mark's side. "We were going to get something to eat and thought you might like to join us."

Mark's brows lifted and he met Tick's gaze before Tick shrugged in one of their silent communications she'd witnessed more times than she could count. A smile quirked at Mark's mouth. "Yeah, I could take an hour."

Outside, she paused to pull her sunglasses from her bag. Tick and Mark descended the steps behind her, talking in low voices.

"So *has* your ass unpuckered yet?" Fairly certain Tick's words weren't meant for her ears, Tori shook her head. Men.

Mark laughed quietly. "Man, he wasn't kidding about how narrow that road looked at that speed. Let me tell you, I don't like not being the one behind the wheel."

"And you call me a control freak."

She turned to pin them with a look. "Can we go, please?"

Once they reached the diner and ordered, she ran a fingertip around the rim of her tea glass. "I can't believe you're this excited over something so dangerous."

In the booth beside her, Mark stilled. His gaze lifted to Tick's, then shifted to her. "Honey, this is what I do."

"Well, I get that, and I get it's dangerous sometimes." She frowned. "But I don't get why you're all acting like it's the greatest thing since sliced bread."

"Adrenaline." Tick sipped at his coffee. "It's hard to explain, Tori, unless you get a rush from it."

"Tori, baby, listen." Atop the table, Mark took her hand in his. "Troy Lee handled that car better than anyone I've seen in, well, ever. I was as safe as possible and everything went well. Don't worry."

"It's kind of hard not to, when you're off—"

"Hey, Cookie, heard that chase on the radio earlier." The paramedic who stopped by their table had a pleasant, earnest face under close-cropped sandy hair. Jim...something. Tyrone, Tyrell. Something with a T and a y. The smiling blonde holding his hand seemed familiar, but it took Tori a couple of seconds to place her. Rhonda, the new teller at the bank. "Sounds like y'all had some excitement going on."

Mark shifted and rubbed a hand over his mouth. "Yeah, guess so."

"Hey, have you met my wife?" With a proud, eager grin, he drew her forward. "Rhonda, honey, this is Mark Cook—we all call him Cookie—and Tick Calvert. They're with the sheriff's department." His gaze jumped to Tori. "And I'm sorry, I don't—"

"Tori, right?" Rhonda extended a hand. "You've come

through my line a couple of times at the bank."

With a warm smile, Tori shook her hand. "That's right. So you're new to Coney?"

"Yes, and I love it." Practically glowing, Rhonda turned into Jim's side, patting his chest, providing her wedding rings with maximum exposure and sparkle. "Jimmy and I met while he was in Biloxi, and we had a whirlwind courtship."

"She's the best thing that ever happened to me." Jim touched her cheek with a reverent fingertip.

"How romantic." Tori's smile widened. They were so *cute* together. Mark coughed into his hand, and she turned to find him and Tick doing the unspoken communication thing again, with a series of looks and lifted brows. Ignoring them, she focused on Jim and Rhonda again. "It was nice meeting you."

"You too." Rhonda waggled her fingers in a wave, again flashing the diamond on her left hand and pulled Jim toward an empty table. "Come on, honey."

Tick shot a quick glance at Mark. "Is that the same ring he—"

"That would be the one." Mark lifted his water for a slow sip.

"What an ass." Tick stared after the couple with disbelief glinting in his eyes. "He's not even sorry."

"What are you talking about?" Tori shook out her napkin and placed it in her lap. "And what was with the eyebrows and the—" She gestured to indicate invisible words. "Y'all were almost rude. They're cute as all get out. What does he have to be sorry for?"

Mark's utter stillness beside her sank in and she looked sideways to find him sitting, eyes closed, elbow propped on the table, while he pinched the bridge of his nose. She swung her attention to her brother, who was suddenly the picture of discomfort, pulling his wallet from his back pocket and looking anywhere but at her.

Foreboding shivered through her. "*What* is going on?"

"I'm going to head back to the hospital." Tick slid from the booth.

Confused, Tori turned over a palm, face up. "You haven't eaten yet."

"I'll get Shanna to pack it to go for me and eat with Cait."

Mark dropped his hand to glare at him. "Thanks a lot, man."

Fixing him with a hard look, Tick shrugged. "Hey, you made your—"

"Don't. Say. It." A muscle flicked in Mark's jaw, and Tori shifted, the swift, rolling animosity between the two making her stomach flutter.

Tick lifted both hands in surrender, but his expression didn't soften until he leaned down to kiss Tori's cheek. "I'll see you later."

He strode to the counter, waited a moment for his sandwich to be packed up with Caitlin's, then disappeared outside. Tori counted slowly to ten, lining up her silverware while she did so. Once the wild nerves in her belly were calmed, she took a breath and looked up to meet Mark's shuttered gaze. "Do you want to explain that to me? I'm utterly lost, but I don't like what just happened."

He jerked his head toward the back corner, where Jim and Rhonda were canoodling. "You don't know Jim well, do you?"

"No. I've seen him at the ER couple of times when I was working an assault, but that's it. Why?"

"He was engaged, for the most part, to Angel Henderson."

Oh no. Not that name again. She closed her eyes as her stomach dropped, suddenly hollow and hurting. Maybe she didn't want answers after all. Maybe she just wanted to forget Angel Henderson had ever existed. She exhaled, counting once more.

"Tori." At his quiet voice, she lifted her lashes and met his gray eyes with reluctance. A small frown drew his brow together. "Please don't."

"So what does he have to be sorry for—" She dropped the question, dates falling into place. "You said he *was* engaged to Angel, and you said, that night..." She swallowed, pushing the words out. "That night, she was on the rebound."

He nodded, his gaze steady on hers. "Jim went to Biloxi one week, came back with Rhonda the next, asked Angel for the ring."

Ouch. She darted a look at the lovey-dovey couple once more. What had seemed romantic now appeared tarnished, a little sordid and tattered around the edges. "Tick's right. He's an ass."

With a harsh sound of disgust, Mark lifted his glass. "That makes two of us."

She covered his wrist, caressing, soothing. "At least you apologized, and you said she was okay with that."

"Yeah." He set the glass down with a thump and turned to her, his eyes stormy. "I'd undo it if I could, Tori, make it so it never happened. But I can't."

"I know. It just feels like every time I turn around, we're running up against it again. I end up feeling jealous and insecure, and I hate that because I don't want to be those things." She ran her fingertip over the slight cleft in his chin and sighed. "I just want to be with you."

"I know, baby." He tugged her into his arms and folded her close. "I'm sorry, I really am, Tor."

She toyed with the hair at his nape for a second, then pulled back on a wave of regret. Coney was a gossipy small town and he worked in a political job. Shanna appeared with their food. With some of the edginess gone, Tori lifted the bread and sprinkled pepper over her tomato. "At least we don't move in the same social circles, so we're not constantly bumping into one another. That would be awkward."

Mark froze in the act of spreading mustard on his bun. "Yeah, about that..."

All well-being evaporated. "Oh Lord, Mark, what now?"

He cleared his throat. "Troy Lee's dating her. Pretty seriously too."

"Which means we *will* be running into her socially." Shoulders slumping, she dropped the top piece of bread back on her BLT. Great. Just...great. She tucked her hair behind her ear and summoned a smile for him. She would darn well learn to deal with this. The insecurity was her problem and she'd conquer it, even if it killed her. She wouldn't let it push him away. "Well, Mama says what doesn't kill us makes us stronger."

He returned her strained smile with one of his own. "You know that applies to us as a couple too, right?"

"Yes, I do. We'll be okay." She patted his knee. "Now eat your sandwich. We both have to get back to work."

The pounding bass of Big & Rich spilling from the jukebox did little to help Angel's tension headache. Although Monday was a busy day for her, it normally was the bar's slowest night. However, tonight a larger-than-normal crowd answered her prayers to be kept busy. Even with the noise and the people, her mind weaseled out of its box of blankness.

She smiled and teased and bantered with her regulars, pulled boxes from the supply room, helped Shanna, who worked two jobs and was the best waitress she'd ever had, wait tables. Through it all, her stubborn brain circled back and around and over itself.

Five, six, maybe seven weeks. Do this, don't do this. Do this and keep it. Do this and give it away, to a couple who could...

Another twisted game of eeny-meeny-miney-moe. Chilled, she rubbed her palms down her arms. And she'd thought herself so damn *responsible*, so careful, taking precautions. She was no better than the girls they'd all talked about in high school, the ones who let a guy beneath their skirts then paid the price of whispers and ruined lives.

"Wow. Good thing you felt well enough to come in after all." Julie settled a box of Jim Beam on the bar and began stocking. She had to yell over the din. "Do you believe this place tonight? Who opened the floodgates?"

"Stop complaining. This is what I like to see. This is what makes your paycheck, baby." She moved to the end of the bar to take an order. She darted a look up at the clock over the mirrored wall with its glass shelves full of liquor bottles. Eleven twenty. Before today, she'd have been vibrating with anticipation, knowing Troy Lee was off duty, knowing she'd see him soon. Tonight, each minute after eleven filled her with a sick dread.

Yes, getting involved with him, letting herself fall deeper and deeper into him so fast...that had been responsible too. Guess speeding got her in trouble in other places than the roads.

"Your man's here." Julie nudged her on the way back to the storage room.

Dismay crashed through her and she closed her eyes. Lord, please.

"Hey." Energy and pleasure vibrated in his voice. She couldn't avoid this forever, might as well just deal with it. She lifted her lashes. The beauty of his grin, the sparkle of those gorgeous blues, slammed her with loss, and she sucked in a harsh breath, her throat hurting all over again. He leaned across the bar to kiss her. "Angel baby, wait until I tell you about my day."

She wanted to wrap herself around him and cling. Instead, she folded her arms over her midriff and dug her nails into her skin. "Good, huh?"

"The best. Only thing that makes it better is you." His thumb rubbed across her jaw in a firm caress. She swallowed. He couldn't say these things, couldn't be this way, not when she had to tell him... He jerked a hand over his shoulder. "Chris and Cookie came with me. We're going to have a beer and hang out while I wait for you."

Sweet Jesus. Her gaze shot over his shoulder, to the back booth Cookie always chose. Sure enough, he and Chris Parker sat there, Chris talking with his hands while Cookie nodded, grinning.

Somehow, she dragged up enough presence of mind to straighten and try to appear normal. "Corona for you, Bud Light for Cookie. What does Chris drink?"

"Bud Light for him too."

"Here you go." She pulled the bottles, her hands shaking only a little, and set them before him.

He leaned forward to kiss her again. "Thanks, babe."

She watched him walk away, threading his way through tables and patrons to meet his coworkers, his wonderful grin flashing as he joined in on whatever minicelebration was going on there. Her eyes prickled, her nose stuffing up as a wave of tears swamped her. Watching him walk away for good, losing him for good, was going to be so damn *hard.*

The last hour of the night dragged, her every synapse tuned in to him with excruciating awareness. She hurt, all over, as though her confusion and misery manifested itself physically. As the clock ticked nearer to one, patrons drifted out, and Shanna and Julie started on nightly cleanup. Angel busied herself, tallying the day's paperwork, preparing a deposit, shoring up her flagging nerves.

Troy Lee's warm, rich tones wafted over her as he walked Shanna and Julie to their cars. The big wooden door closed behind him and his footsteps whispered over the scarred floor. Her stomach plummeted. Lord, this was it.

He wrapped strong arms around her from behind, hugging her to him. The solid heat of his chest against her back tempted her to lean into him. He kissed the side of her neck, his laughter shivering over her.

"I've been dying to get close to you..." His voice faded. She bit her lip, holding her body stiff in his embrace, and he went motionless, a sudden tension vibrating through him. "What's wrong?"

She pushed his arms away, trying to get words beyond the tightness in her raw throat.

"Angel?" He touched her shoulder, a tentative, feathery contact that made her want to cry, to scream.

"I'm pregnant." Saying the words aloud, even in a small, shaky voice, sent the reality crashing through her all over again. Eyes closed, she dug her nails into her palms and waited for everything to fall apart.

He hissed in a sharp breath. "What?"

"You heard me." Lifting her chin, setting her jaw, she turned to face him. "I'm pregnant. Somewhere between five and seven weeks, which means...which means..."

He stared at her, gaze darting over her features. A hard swallow bobbed his Adam's apple. "Which means it's not mine. We weren't...it's only been—"

"It's not yours." She rubbed at her arms. Sweet Jesus, she was cold.

He glanced away and chafed a hand over his nape. A frown pulled at his brow. "So five to seven weeks...it could be Jim's or Cookie's."

"Exactly."

Her voice cracked, and his too-pale face softened. He reached for her. "Ah, baby."

"Stop. Don't." She fought his easy hold, his efforts to draw her close. "What are you doing? Don't you *get* this?"

"I get it." He didn't give in, pulling her to him with a gentle, inexorable grasp.

"Troy Lee." His name broke as it crossed her lips. "Do you hear me? *I'm pregnant.* I don't know who the father is—"

"Sshh." Holding her close, he pressed soothing kisses to her temple and cheek. Tears seeped beneath her lashes, all of the day's fear and pain gathering in a huge sob welling in her throat. "Damn it, why didn't you say something earlier? Today had to be hell for you."

"Why are you doing this?" Weeping in earnest, she wound her fingers into the soft cotton of his shirt.

"Doing what?" He rubbed his hand down her back, his cheek pressed to her hair.

"This." She uncurled her fingers, planted her palms against his chest and levered away. Panic twisted through her. She waved between them, tears still spilling from her eyes. She sniffled. "Being like this."

"Angel, you didn't think..." He grabbed a couple of beverage napkins from the stack under the bar and pressed them into her hand. While she blew her nose, he folded one arm around her shoulders, sheltering her, while he wiped at her wet cheeks. "You didn't think this would change how I feel about you?"

With damp napkins crumpled in her hands, she looked up at him. "How can it not?"

Confusion darkened his blue eyes. "Because it doesn't. This doesn't change who you are—"

"Who I am?" She laughed, the sound strained and mirthless. "You mean a white-trash slut who tumbled from one bed to the next and got knocked up and now doesn't even know which one it was?"

Anger tightened his features, and his jaw ticked. "Don't you ever say that about yourself again."

"It's true." She swung an arm out in an expansive gesture. "Isn't that what everyone is going to say?"

"Screw what everybody says. Angel, I..." He cradled her face in his palm and inhaled sharply. "I love you and nothing about this changes that."

He couldn't say these things, couldn't *do* this. "You don't love me. You can't."

"Actually, I do, and believe it or not, I'm capable of loving. Christine, my sisters, my Grandma Shirley." His mouth hitched in a half-grin, although his eyes remained serious. "You."

She stared at him, thoughts tumbling over themselves in her fatigued brain. "What am I going to do?"

"I don't know." He pulled her to him, wrapped his arms about her in a tight embrace, rubbed his face against her hair. "But you don't have to worry about me going anywhere. I'm right here, Angel."

In slow motion, she allowed herself to lean in, to link her arms about his waist, to drink in his solid presence. "It's not fair to you. You shouldn't have to deal with this. I can't ask you to."

His kiss at her temple was fierce. "You're not asking me to do anything. I'm here because I want to be."

"I think..." She swallowed and pulled back, brushing her hair behind her ears, not quite able to meet his gaze. "I think we have to slow down, though. Until I figure out what to do. I have to get my head straight."

His hand slipped to her nape, to become a soothing, caressing weight there. "I can get that. You need some time."

She covered her face with both hands, a shaky half-laugh, half-sob escaping her. "You're not normal, Troy Lee."

"Yeah, I know, but I don't think normal is what you need." He kissed her forehead. "Let me drive you home."

"I can drive."

"I know you can. Let me take care of you a little, all right? You look like you need it. You can sleep in, and I'll get Chris to run over here with me in the morning and we'll drop off your car at your place." He tucked her against his chest again, mouth buried in her hair. "Sound good?"

She nodded and sighed into his chest. "Take me home."

Mark's cell rang what felt like mere moments after his head hit the pillow and he shut his eyes. Without opening them, he fumbled for the vibrating rectangle. "Cook."

"Hey." Suppressed tears quivered in Tori's voice, bringing him to instant alertness. "Did I wake you?"

"I just laid down. What's wrong?"

"Can you come over?"

Nightmares, flashbacks of the rape. She didn't have to say it. "I'm on my way."

He tugged on jeans and a T-shirt, slid his feet into loafers and tucked his phone and keys in his pocket. This late the apartment complex was quiet and deserted. The temperature had dropped and a wave of goose bumps lifted on his bare arms. He jogged up the stairs to Tori's second-floor apartment, but she swung the door open before he could knock. Sure enough, in her pale face her eyes glittered with unshed tears.

"Oh, honey." He stepped inside and pushed the door shut with his foot. He tugged her close and she wrapped her arms around him. "Bad?"

"Horrible." She burrowed closer. "I'm glad you're here."

"Me too." He pressed a hard kiss to her mouth. "Come on, let's go to bed and get some sleep."

He made sure the door was locked then, hands at her hips, guided her before him down the hall to her room. The lights blazed there, the snowy white sheets and coverlet rumpled. As she climbed back into bed, he tugged his shirt over his head and shed his jeans. A smile touched his mouth at the memory of the first time they'd shared this bed, one of the first innocent opportunities he'd had to hold her in his arms. She'd been jittery with fear at even that small contact; the proof of her growing confidence in them, in herself, lay in the easy way she turned into his arms as soon as he slid beneath the sheet.

"I hate this," she whispered, face buried in the curve of his throat. "I just want to be normal, Mark."

"You are." He caressed her nape and down her shoulder, lowering his voice to a calming whisper. "Strong, beautiful and absolutely normal. You're perfect just as you are, Tor."

"Perfect?" Her soft noise of dissent puffed against his skin.

"Yes. Perfect." With her settled against him, sleep tempted him.

She relaxed into him, her palm over his heart. "I still worry, you know, that all my issues and my insecurities will be too much—"

"Tori." How could she even begin to think that? His palm under her chin, he tilted her gaze up to his. "I love you."

"I love you too, but—"

"No buts. That's bigger than anything, any issue or problem. I promise."

"I'm holding you to that." She yawned and snuggled into him.

"Okay." He dropped a kiss on her cheekbone. "I promise you, honey, anything that comes, we can handle."

Chapter Twelve

Troy Lee hit the ground running. His mind turning over and over, he ran longer than he intended, making him late to meet Chris to pick up Angel's car. As he'd expected, Chris didn't ask for explanations, merely rode along to follow in the Jeep while they ferried the Mustang to Angel's place. Troy Lee parked it in her customary spot, cast one long glance at the closed front door and headed for the department to sign in for his split shift.

He clocked in and checked his officer mailbox, flipping through a couple of memos and the new Galls catalog.

"So if I get in a car with you today, will I be risking my life?"

At Cookie's voice, he jumped. Shoving the mailer back in the box, he turned to face the investigator. Cookie laid a couple of folders on his desk, sank into his chair and opened a drawer to dig out the phone book. It was a normal, ordinary, one-in-a-thousand interaction, and the reality Troy Lee had been dodging since the night before careened into him.

The baby growing in Angel's body might be Cookie's. Troy Lee rubbed a hand over his mouth, a raw spurt of primal possessiveness shooting under his skin. Jealousy wasn't his thing—he'd always equated it with insecurity—but this sure as hell felt like the green-eyed monster.

Or maybe protective anger, because something that hadn't meant anything, that shouldn't have mattered in the long run, had reduced Angel to tears and doubt and fear.

"Troy Lee?"

He shook himself free of the tide of emotion and focused on Cookie, who watched him with a slight frown, his brows dipping into a V. "Yeah."

"You all right?"

"I'm fine." The words sounded curt even to him.

"You're sure?"

"I said I was fine."

Cookie shrugged and dropped his gaze to the phone book, flipping a couple of pages. "You act like something's under your skin."

"Nothing's under my skin. I'm just..." He tried to expel the unreasonable resentment in a deep breath. He scrawled his initials across the memo and thrust it into the department inbox. "I'm edgy today."

"No kidding."

"Look, just drop it, okay?"

"Getting it off your chest might help."

Fury sizzled through his brain. Even if he could talk about it, he couldn't to Cookie. The quagmire tangled him a little bit tighter. "You know, Cookie, dating a therapist doesn't make you one."

"She's not a therapist." Unperturbed by the animosity, Cookie scribbled down a number on his desk blotter and dropped the phone book back in the drawer. "She's a crisis counselor."

"Whatever."

"Get your emotions off your sleeve, kid." Cookie looked up to fix him with a steady gaze. "Giving into it takes away your focus and that'll get you hurt."

The word *kid* grated, but he swallowed a retort. Turning his attitude loose this morning probably wasn't a good idea. He breathed through another flow of antipathy, centering his attention on the bulletin board across the room. He was going to have to deal with this. Might as well start now.

"Neat trick." Cookie's voice washed over him, and this time the bitterness stayed at bay. "Where'd you learn that?"

"Running." He shrugged. "Something my dad taught me. I used to let the other runners freak me out, if I could hear them breathing behind me. So I learned to focus on the center point and let everything else slide away."

"You never answered the question. If I get in a car with you today, am I putting my life at risk?"

"Life is always a risk. You think things are going to go one way, then life happens. You can either fight or learn to roll with it."

"You're a genius at more than math, aren't you, kid?"

"I'm no genius. I've just figured out that there are always variables you can't control." He lifted his chin and met Cookie's incisive gaze head on. "I'm not a kid anymore, either."

Cookie studied him for a long moment. "No, I don't believe you are." With a sharp nod, he pushed up from the chair. "Come on, Troy Lee. Let's go to work."

ꙮ

Clad in bra and panties, Angel paused in the process of dressing and stared at herself in the bureau mirror. Turning sideways, she pressed her palm over her lower belly. She didn't *look* any different. Other than the nausea and fatigue, she didn't *feel* any different.

And yet, the child growing beneath her shaking fingers made everything different. A baby. Her child. Under her hand, one of her sweetest, most private dreams was unfurling. Shouldn't she be thankful for this tiny life?

Desperate hope took hold. Last night, Troy Lee hadn't turned away. His reaction had been so much more than she could have dreamed. Maybe she could have both, her baby and the man she loved.

She was pretty sure she did love him. She closed her eyes, the sweetness of his declaration winding through her once more. The heck of it was, she believed him. So maybe...maybe she could have everything. Maybe she hadn't ruined it all.

A knock sounded at the door and drew her from the reverie. She snatched up the red dress and jerked it over her head before padding barefoot to the front door.

She opened it to find Troy Lee in full uniform, standing on her porch and regarding her with a serious expression. She wrapped a hand around the door, rubbing one ankle with the bare toes of her other foot. "Hey."

He didn't smile. "Hey."

Oh, this didn't feel good, this quiet, serious reserve of his. She tightened her grip on the door. "Thank you for bringing my car by this morning."

"You're welcome." His gaze traced her face and his features softened. "I should have called first, probably. I don't have to sign back on until seven, and I thought I'd see if you wanted to grab a bite before you opened the club."

Relief flooded her, leaving her knees trembling and weak. "That sounds great. Let me get my boots."

He followed her to her bedroom door. "So how are you today?"

She tugged on one sock and boot and looked up at him. "I didn't throw up this morning."

One corner of his mouth lifted. "That's good."

"That's very good." She slid on her other sock and boot. She rose, smoothing her skirt. He leaned in the doorway, one shoulder propped against the jamb, and she studied him, acutely aware he had yet to touch her. Sadness tinged her relief. Already, things were changed between them. She cradled her elbows. "Ready to go?"

"I'd be more ready if you'd get over here and let me kiss you."

"What happened to the Troy Lee who didn't ask for permission?"

"You told him you needed time."

"I also need him." She crossed to link her arms about his waist and turned her face up. "And I really, really like his kisses."

"Good. Because they're all yours." He lowered his head, mouth molding to hers in an easy caress. She drank in the warmth and affection of that kiss. He lifted his head, thumb caressing her shoulder, exposed by the square neckline. "Grab your coat and let's get something to eat."

By tacit agreement, they picked up sandwiches from Lisa's and took them to the small riverfront park, as they had that first morning together. However, this afternoon, he slid onto the bench beside her, stretching his arm along the pavilion railing, sheltering her from the cool breeze. They ate without words, and occasionally he fingered the ends of her hair. Under the silence, and in his steady presence, she relaxed, more of the tension seeping away.

Hands wrapped around her cup of warm strawberry tea, she leaned into him. "I've been thinking today, about whether or not to tell them."

"And?" He trailed a knuckle along her neck, a long soothing sweep of contact.

"It's too soon. I can't...I can't face that yet." She blinked hard, the brown river shimmering before her gaze. "You probably think I'm a coward."

"I think you're the only one who can make those decisions right now." The rough warmth of his knuckle traveled along her jaw. "And coward is the last thing I'd ever think about you."

"This situation and us being together...it puts you in a bad place at work, doesn't it?"

"I can deal."

She twisted, facing him but pulling away far enough to draw one knee up sideways on the bench. "I don't want to mess up your life, Troy Lee."

"I can really only think of one way you might do that, Angel, and this isn't it. Listen to me." He curled his hand around her nape. "I'm here. I'm here because I want to be. I'm not naïve. I know this is hard for you, that it'll probably be hard for us. It's bound to be, but I'm here and I'm not going anywhere."

"But this could really mess up theirs."

"Yeah. I know."

She laid a hand on his knee, rubbing her fingernail along the razor-sharp seam on the front of his brown slacks. "Do you think I'm wrong then, not telling them?"

"I..." He paused, his Adam's apple bobbing on a sharp swallow. "I think if it was me, I'd want to know, so I could deal with it. But this is your decision. I can't tell you what to do."

She almost wanted him to, wanted some of the overwhelming responsibility lifted from her shoulders.

"I'll stand by you." He whispered the assurance close to her ear, his warm breath stirring her hair. "I'll be whatever you need me to be. You can count on that."

She circled her thumb over his knee. "So what do we do? How do we make this work?"

"We believe." Tightening his hold at her nape, he drew her toward him, touching her lips lightly with his. "One second." Another brief mingling of mouths. "And another."

She smiled against his lips, the first genuine smile she'd had in nearly two days. "And another, right?"

"Exactly." Sighing hard, he wrapped her close. "I can do it if you can, Angel baby. We'll make it work. I promise."

ꙏ

"Hear that?" Dr. Padgett ran the small transducer over Angel's belly. A rapid *whomp-whoosh-whomp* filled the exam room. "That, my dear, is your baby's heartbeat."

Awed, Angel drank in the sound. "That's amazing."

"It's also a very healthy heartbeat." Dr. Padgett lifted the wand, the pulse stopping as she did so. The nurse wiped the clear gel away from Angel's skin and offered a hand to help her sit up. "Your blood pressure is good, and everything looks great so far." She consulted Angel's chart. "Since the heartbeat is audible, I think we're looking at a nine-to-ten, maybe eleven week pregnancy, which means sometime in July, you'll be a brand-new mom."

Still the dratted two-week gap. Angel tugged her skirt into place over her thighs. "I don't suppose we can narrow that down yet?"

"I wish I could." Dr. Padgett shrugged in apology. "I'd like to use both crown-rump length and the biparietal diameter to get a more accurate date with an ultrasound. That'll be at your next appointment, when you're over the thirteen-weeks range."

Which meant more weeks of uncertainty. Lord, the last month had been bad enough, as she lay awake, next to Troy Lee or not, wrestling with the right thing to do where Jim and Cookie were concerned. Running circles in her head hadn't gotten her anywhere but exhausted; she was no closer to an answer now than she'd been at the beginning.

"So you're good until I see you again in early January. I'd like you to limit the lifting at work, maybe have someone do that for you, but otherwise, there's no problem with continuing your normal activities." Indulgence colored Dr. Padgett's smile. "Including sex, if you're so inclined."

Oh, she was, with Troy Lee hanging around, constantly touching, even if they had held back sexually ever since she'd discovered her pregnancy. He remained his normal affectionate, hugging, kissing self.

"Do you have any questions for me?" Dr. Padgett's gentle

voice pulled her free of the reverie.

"Um, not really." She tucked her hair behind her ears.

"If you have any later, don't hesitate to call." Dr. Padgett scribbled across a prescription pad. "This is for prenatal vitamins. See Lynne at the desk on your way out to set up an appointment for next month."

"Thanks." She slipped the prescription into her purse, took a moment to tug on her boots, then walked through to see Lynne.

While Christmas music played softly in the background, Lynne hit a few keys at the computer, printed off an appointment card and slid it across the counter. "All right, you're good to go. We'll see you January tenth."

Outside, an icy wind tossed dried leaves about the parking lot under low gunmetal clouds. Shivering, she flipped open her phone and tapped in a quick text message to Troy Lee, a simple "everything okay". By the time she'd reached her car and slipped into the driver's seat, he'd responded with his characteristic "good deal" message. Suffused with the sense of warm well-being he always inspired, she rubbed her thumb across the screen before folding the phone and dropping it on the passenger seat. She wished he were here, that he could have shared in the absolute joy of listening to that incredibly rapid little heartbeat.

Except she couldn't be sure he wanted to be that involved in her pregnancy. He was concerned, caring, solicitous...about her. Still, the fact he hadn't attempted to broach the subject of her pregnancy or accompanying her to this appointment ate at her, taking little bites out of her confidence.

Why should he? The nasty little doubt whispered in her head. *It's not his baby. You think he's going to want to be involved, to really stay around?*

She bit her lip and fought down the uncertainty.

"One second," she murmured, finally inserting the key in the ignition and firing the engine. "Remember that. One second at a time."

A smile tugging at his mouth, Troy Lee returned his cell to his belt and relaxed into the diner booth, letting Cookie's own quiet cell-phone conversation drift over him. He hated that he'd not been at this appointment, her first official prenatal check, but hadn't been sure about asking to go, either. He wasn't this baby's father, although he found himself awed by the subtle changes taking place in her body already.

He was willing to step into that dad's role, though. He worried about her, wanted to protect her and the tiny life inside her, an emotion he'd not encountered before. Besides, didn't he know from personal experience with Christine that biology had nothing to do with loving a child?

Two teenage girls, one wearing a fast-food uniform, the other a grocery-store smock, claimed the adjacent table. The first, a tall blonde, slumped in her chair and picked at the artificial flowers crammed into a mason jar. "I hate him."

Her companion brushed auburn hair behind her ears. "Two days ago you loved him."

"That was before he asked *her* to the winter formal." The blonde's mouth trembled and she blinked hard. "And before he called me white trash and told me the reason he never took me anywhere was because he was ashamed to be seen with me."

"He's a jerk and you're not white trash. Maybe you're not in the same 'society' as him"—the redhead made air quotes and grimaced in disgust—"but you work hard and you're pulling down a four-point-oh. If anybody's trash, he is."

"Easy for you to say." Genuine hurt lingered in the blonde's voice. She continued fiddling with the fake daisy. "Your daddy works at the bank and you go to the right church. Nobody's going to call you trash."

Their voices died as Shanna arrived to take their order. Troy Lee frowned, rubbing his thumb around the rim of his mug as Angel's torn voice echoed in his head.

A white-trash slut... Isn't that what everyone is going to say?

"Yeah, thanks for calling." Cookie snapped his cell shut and looked across the scarred Formica table at Troy Lee. "You about ready?"

He nodded and downed the last swallow of coffee he'd added too much sugar to. He slid from the booth and pulled a bill from his wallet, tucking it and their ticket under his empty coffee mug. Over the past few weeks, this had become their routine, Cookie spending part of each shared shift in the patrol car with him, mentoring, smoothing out the rough spots in his techniques, talking out scenarios over a quick meal as they'd done over breakfast that morning.

With a slight scowl twisting his brow, he glanced back at the girls on his way out. The overheard conversation and Angel's choice of words niggled. Was that was going on in her head? Stupid small-town classism? Shit. One thing was for damn sure, if that was the issue, he'd find a way to knock down that misconception and fast.

On the sidewalk, Cookie jerked his head toward the other side of the courthouse square. "Listen, I need to walk down to Hodges Jewelers for a minute. You want to tag along?"

"No, I'm going to stop in the bookstore, see if that book on conditioning I ordered is in."

They skirted the newly sodded courthouse lawn, parting ways at the corner. A wave of lavender and sage wafted over Troy Lee as soon as he opened the heavy glass door of the small bookstore.

"Be with you in a second." Lacy Friedman's voice drifted from the storage room at the rear of the old building.

He browsed a minute, his footsteps creaking on the polished hardwood floor. He thumbed through a couple of books in the science section before Lacy appeared, smiling. "Hey, Troy Lee. What can I do for you?"

"I thought I'd see if that book you ordered for me was in."

A small frown of concentration wrinkled Lacy's brow. "I don't think so, but let me go check this morning's shipment. Be right back."

"Take your time." He slipped the book he held back on the shelf and continued looking while Lacy disappeared into the backroom again. The medical section caught his attention and he slid a colorful book on expecting mothers from the shelf. He flipped through, skimming the section on the first trimester. The baby was minuscule, about the size of a lima bean, maybe a large shrimp. He or she would have an audible heartbeat now—damn it, had he missed hearing that this morning? Angel would still be feeling fatigued—yep. She'd fallen asleep, in midsentence, against his shoulder Sunday afternoon while they'd watched a movie. Might still have morning sickness—yep again—although that should be gone by her fourth month or so. Unless the doctor said otherwise, sex was a go too. He'd given Angel a copy of his last blood test results, from his physical in early October. He hadn't wanted her to worry that he carried anything that posed a threat to her or the baby. She should have the results of her own tests back today and God knew he missed making love to her.

Except she'd told him at the beginning she needed time to get used to things and he didn't want to push. He couldn't keep his hands off her completely, but—

"What are you reading?" Cookie's lazy question startled him and he fumbled the book, closing and shelving it as fast as he could.

"Nothing." Face hot, he rolled his shoulders in an awkward shrug. "Get what you needed at Hodges?"

"Yeah." A grin quirked at Cookie's mouth, his eyes glinting with good humor.

"Hey, Troy Lee." Lacy stopped in the doorway, her expression apologetic. "It's not here. I'm sorry. I'll call you as soon as it arrives, okay?"

"Yeah, sure. Thanks, Lacy."

"Let's hit the road." Cookie gestured toward the door. "I'm supposed to meet Tori at her mama's for dinner and I promised I wouldn't be late this time."

Glad the discussion of his reading material seemed dropped, Troy Lee followed him outside, with one last wave at Lacy. "You should know better than to go making promises like that."

"Listen, I can hope for a quiet day. Right?"

"I guess."

Cookie rode along for his first uneventful patrol round. After that, he dropped Cookie back off at the department and began round two. The quiet of Chandler County when there was absolutely nothing going on drove him nuts, giving him too much time to think about Angel, to worry that the way they felt wouldn't be enough to overcome her fear.

He turned left onto 19 and pulled off into the median. Radar log on his lap, he took his calibration reading. With the required check out of the way, he sat back and waited. This area of the four-lane highway didn't produce many tickets—he spent enough time in this spot most of the locals had learned to slow down, which was his intent on this stretch anyway, not revenue generation. Dale Jenkins rumbled by in his farm truck and waved. A couple of the local girls, ones who came out on Saturday nights to watch him and Clark and the boys play did likewise. He chuckled to himself. Why he even calibrated the radar for this area was beyond him. He couldn't write a ticket here if he tried.

Twisting his wrist, he checked his watch. Almost eleven thirty. Man, it was going to be a long, tedious day.

A red Ford pickup topped the slight hill and the radar-unit numbers flashed—eighty-one, eighty-two, eighty-one. He locked in the speed and shifted into drive to pull out behind the truck as it screamed by. Brake lights flared, about the same time the vehicle's familiarity sank in. Shit, Paul Bostick again. Troy Lee flipped his blue lights on and for a moment thought the kid would rabbit. However, after that brief pause, the brake lights shone again and the Ford pulled to the shoulder.

Stopping behind him, Troy Lee considered the vehicle for a moment, Paul's darkly mutinous expression plain in the outside mirror as the boy lowered the window. Troy Lee's instincts whispered that this wasn't going to go well. Checking to make sure the dash-cam was engaged and recording audio, he lifted the mike, calling in his time and the tag number. Still eying the mirror reflection, he keyed the mike once more. "C-13 to C-3."

"Go ahead, C-13."

"You busy?"

"No."

"Request your presence for a stop, about a hundred yards north of the Gethsemane Church of Christ."

"En route, C-13."

Troy Lee grabbed his ticket book, pushed the door open and settled his campaign hat atop his head. As he approached, Paul stared sullenly up the highway.

"I need to see your license and proof of insurance, please."

"I wasn't speeding." Malevolent discontent poisoned the just-changed-to-manhood voice.

Keeping his stance relaxed yet authoritative, making sure his expression was damn-well impassive, Troy Lee held the boy's gaze. "I need your license and proof of insurance, please."

"I called my daddy before you even got out. He's on his way, so you might as well climb back in your little police car and leave me the hell alone." A sneer twisted Paul's mouth. "He's gunning for your badge anyway, asshole."

Troy Lee swallowed the bile of anger created by the blatant

disrespect. He flipped open his ticket book. Engines sounded in the distance, Cookie's unmarked unit topping the hill right before Bubba Bostick's truck appeared at the Flint crossroads and headed for them.

Cookie stopped behind Troy Lee's unit. He paused, bending down to study the radar unit through the driver's window as he passed. Bubba turned sideways across the median, leaving his truck in the grass, and hustled across the blacktop.

"What did you do now?" Bubba threw out his hands, his features set in a mask of disgust as he glared at his son. Troy Lee shook his head and kept writing.

"Daddy, I told you—he's lying. I wasn't speeding this time."

Troy Lee checked off the boxes at the bottom of the ticket for the road conditions: dry pavement, highway. First he was an asshole, now he was a liar. Really, all he needed was Calvert to appear, so he could go for the Triple Crown and be a fuck-up too.

Bubba turned his attention to Cookie. "Do you know what's going on here?"

"Radar is locked in at eighty-one." Cookie appeared completely unruffled. He cocked an eyebrow at Troy Lee. "Did you calibrate it?"

"Yes, sir. Log's on the front seat."

"Camera's on?"

"Yes, sir."

Cookie nodded. "Bubba, let's walk back and take a look."

Bubba slanted a look at his son. "Come on."

At Troy Lee's car, Cookie checked his calibration log, showed it and the locked radar to Bubba, whose face tightened with each second. Settling in the driver's seat, Cookie ran the digital recorder back, playing the video from the moment Troy Lee locked his radar on Paul's truck. For once, Troy Lee was damn glad Calvert had been so hard on him—he'd learned to rein in his emotions, keep them off his face and under control, all of that showing as Paul refused to hand over his license and insurance paperwork.

Bubba turned a slow, glacially cold glower on his son. "Give him your license and insurance card. Now."

"But, Daddy—"

"Goddammit, I said now."

His mouth set in a taut line, Paul passed the items over to Troy Lee. He completed the license check and filled out the remainder of the ticket while waiting for Deb to come back with the license and insurance status. Once that was done, he extended the ticket book for Paul's signature, jotted a number three in the upper right-hand corner and tore the yellow copy free for the kid.

Bubba narrowed his eyes at his son. "Go home. We'll talk later."

With a sizzling glare at Troy Lee, Paul stalked to his truck and pulled onto the highway. Bubba ran a hand over his balding head. "I'm sorry about this. I don't know what's gotten into him lately." He pointed at Troy Lee. "He won't give you any more trouble."

With a brief goodbye, he glanced for oncoming traffic and jogged to his truck, pulling off in the opposite direction. Troy Lee stared, made sure his mouth was closed, then shook his head on a rueful laugh. "Did I just see what I think I did? Did he let the kid drive home?"

"Damn sure did." Cookie tucked his thumbs in his belt. "If I ever have a kid..."

He let the commentary trail away, but the icy reality showered over Troy Lee. Hell, Cookie might very well be having a kid and not know it. The sheer magnitude of what he was helping keep from Cookie tried to steal his breath. Troy Lee rubbed a hand over his nape and tossed his ticket book on the passenger seat. Except he wasn't helping to keep it a secret, not really. It wasn't his place to tell.

He still didn't know for sure what his place was.

"Thanks for backing me up." He glanced at his watch. "Now you're going to be late."

"Anytime. Tori will understand. I hope." Cookie pulled his keys from the ring at his belt and tossed them in the air a couple of times, watching them with a contemplative expression. "I think you did the right thing, calling me."

"Yeah, me too." He was pretty sure Bubba's attitude might have been different if Cookie hadn't been present. Paul's taunt about his father gunning for Troy Lee's badge echoed. In his experience, kids didn't just come up with that kind of stuff on their own. Although it galled him that he hadn't been able to make Paul comply without intervention, he'd also figured out early on that cops who tried to do everything solo usually ended up in trouble, one way or another.

And trouble was one thing he was trying his best to avoid.

Chapter Thirteen

Angel opened the door to the salon, her newly hyperaware sense of smell recoiling from the layers of hairspray, peroxide and ammonia. Her mama looked up from trimming Miranda Holton's hair and smiled. "Hey, honey. What are you doing here?"

"Hey, Mama." She brushed a kiss over her mother's cheek and waved at her sister, who was involved in applying foil highlights to one of her regulars. "Just thought I'd drop by and see you on the way to work."

Mama made a fake smirk and winked at Miranda in the mirror. "Feels guilty because she's too wrapped up in her new young man to come see her mama like she's supposed to."

"Oh, Mama, you know better." She sank into the shampoo chair and picked up a discarded magazine. "I've just been busy."

"Busy cozying up with Troy Lee Farr," Hope teased, painting another section of hair.

Oh, way to start a rumor, Hope. Angel glared the silent statement at her sister.

"Are you feeling better?" Hope closed a piece of foil about the section and started on another.

"I am." It wasn't a lie. She'd discovered that her mama's universal stomach remedy, weak tea, did help, especially if she drank it along with a breakfast of dry toast. As long as she didn't let her stomach get empty during the day, she could keep the queasiness at bay.

Hope fixed her with a critical eye. "Your roots are showing a little. You have time for me to touch them up?"

"Um, not this afternoon." Angel made a show of checking

her watch. Was she even supposed to have her hair colored while she was pregnant? She'd have to call Dr. Padgett's office.

"Maybe Saturday, then." Hope slanted a pointed look in her direction. "Unless you have plans."

"I don't." If Hope was closer, Angel would pull the ends of her hair in retaliation, the way she'd done when they'd been really little. "Yet."

Miranda made a small, sad sound of reminiscence. "Marie, they sound like Madeline and Autry when they were girls."

"How is Autry?" Mama skillfully diverted the subject, holding one hank of Miranda's hair aloft to check the length. "When is her baby due again?"

"March. Everything seems to be going well." A proud smile touched Miranda's mouth. "It's another little girl."

"Well, I know you're thrilled." Mama's wistful sigh hung in the air a moment like a fading daydream. "I miss having a little one around. You know, my granddaughters are fifteen and sixteen now."

"That's right." Miranda let Mama tilt her chin down slightly. "Hope's eldest was born right before Del's twins were, and they just turned sixteen."

Angel's mama laughed. "Do you remember how beside herself Lenora was over those babies?"

"She's the same way over each new one. I tell you, she's so excited now that Tick's baby boy is home from the hospital, she can't stand it."

"I'm sure. I can understand. I was that way when Hope brought Jordan and Brittany home."

Her heart squeezing, Angel pretended to be engrossed in her magazine. Her parents loved their granddaughters, and she had no doubt they'd adore her baby, once the initial surprise and dismay wore off. Darn it, here was another minefield. She couldn't very well inform her family yet, until she dealt with Jim and Cookie. Her mama would start calling friends and family, and then the news would be all over town. She couldn't let it get back to either man that way.

She was going to have to tell them. Waiting wasn't an option any longer. So she'd tell them and let them deal with the fallout, just as she had—dead on.

"Marie, did you hear about Sue Tyre?"

Angel glanced up at Miranda's mention of Jim's mother.

"Well, I know she had a fall, but I haven't heard anything else." Mama executed a couple of neat snips near Miranda's nape. "You know we haven't been talking very much lately, considering."

Angel rolled her eyes at Mama's coy façade. Her mother and Jim's had not talked much, ever. They'd tolerated one another for Angel's and Jim's sakes.

"Well, it's a broken hip and she's in the hospital. They're worried about complications from her diabetes. I hear Jim's been staying at the hospital with her every night."

Mama made a tsking sound and kept trimming. Angel laid the magazine aside. Well, maybe she wouldn't be telling Jim anytime soon, not while his adored mother was sick. Maybe she'd start with Cookie, ask him to keep it quiet until she could inform Jim as well.

Male voices, low and intent, drifted into the hallway from the squad room. Troy Lee stepped through the door to find Calvert and Chris bent over the counter, reviewing what looked like a copy of the department schedule. Chris looked up briefly with a two-fingered salute of greeting.

Tired and glad Calvert seemed too engrossed to notice him, Troy Lee returned the gesture, settled at an empty desk and started on his end-of-shift paperwork.

"I'm just not sure how many days we have to cover." Frustration roughened Calvert's voice. "I'd move Steve over there, but he's going out of town."

"Vann's working a double the day before and the day after, to cover Steve's time off."

"Yeah."

Troy Lee didn't look up from his report. "What day do you need covered?"

"Friday, seven to three, and Saturday, three to eleven," Chris replied, distracted.

Troy Lee shrugged. "I'll do it."

Calvert frowned. "Yeah, but that's eight days in a row for you and you're already working Christmas."

"I can handle it." He laid his pen aside. "Who are you trying to cover?"

"Cookie." Calvert scratched through a note on the schedule and made another.

Troy Lee frowned at the odd, tight quality to Calvert's voice. "Something wrong?"

Calvert and Chris exchanged a quick look, followed by Calvert's almost imperceptible nod. Chris cleared his throat. "Some skeletal remains were discovered over in Echols County, and the GBI thinks it may be his wife."

Troy Lee felt his jaw drop. "He's married?"

"Was married." Calvert fed the corrected schedule through the copier.

Cookie had a wife? A wife he'd never mentioned, who might be a set of skeletal remains. What the hell? Troy Lee rapped his pen on the desk. "What happened?"

"They married young. She was pregnant, and she disappeared at a town festival in Florida a few months before their baby was due. The case went cold."

F-uck. Troy Lee focused his attention on the recap, although the words didn't register. His brain stuttered its way through Calvert's revelation. So not only was Cookie married, but he'd spent years not knowing where she was, what had happened to her. Dealing with his dad's death had been hard enough. He couldn't imagine the not-knowing, the constant uncertain hell of living a cold missing-person case. Cookie walked around with that every day. "Damn. So he lost a wife and a baby."

"Yeah." Calvert removed the old schedule from the smaller bulletin board next to the officer mailboxes and pinned up the new copy. "If it's her, he'll need a few days."

"I bet." Signing off on his recap, Troy Lee ran the requisite copies and filed them.

Calvert paused in the act of pouring a cup of coffee to glance sideways at him. "Cookie's been riding with you, right?"

Unease slid under his skin. "Yeah, part of our shared shifts. Why?"

With a negligent shrug, Calvert slid the carafe back into the coffeemaker. "You want me to ride along in his place while he's out?"

Hell, no. Troy Lee swallowed hard, sudden anxiety kicking his heartburn up to nausea level. "Up to you."

"I may." On a quiet laugh, Calvert lifted his mug to his mouth. "I'm rusty after the past few weeks. Being your ride-along should get me back in practice."

Rusty at what? Giving him hell?

He'll come around to you, but you have to give him a chance. Cookie's calm advice, and at least Cookie had never steered him in the wrong direction. Troy Lee dragged a hand across his nape, chafing the skin there. He forced himself to meet Calvert's gaze. "Sounds good."

What looked like it might be a genuine grin quirked at Calvert's mouth. "Great. We can start with the first couple of hours of your shift tomorrow."

Troy Lee dug in his shirt pocket for the remainder of his last roll of antacids. Yeah, this was going to be just *great.*

"Hug me."

Laughing at the mock desperation in Troy Lee's voice, Angel turned to find him leaning on the end of the bar. "What?"

He held his arms wide, faded Gin Blossoms T-shirt riding up to give her a glimpse of his lean, muscled stomach. "Just hug me."

How was a girl supposed to resist that?

She went into his arms, wrapping her own about his waist and squeezing. With a muffled groan, he hugged her, rocking her side to side for a moment. Palpable tension vibrated out of him with a quiet exhale, leaving him more relaxed in her embrace. She smiled against his chest, sure they probably had the attention of every patron in the bar and really not caring.

"What's this all about?"

"I can't just want a hug?" Her hair muffled his voice.

"You always want a hug. You're needy that way." Under her cheek, his muted laughter rumbled. She pulled back enough to look up at him. "But this feels different. You feel...stressed."

"That's one way to put it." He released her with a reluctant sigh. "I get to ride around in a patrol car with Tick Calvert tomorrow."

"Why is that a problem?" She glanced at him over her shoulder as she moved away to grab a beer for one of her regulars. "He's a nice guy."

"A nice guy? I don't think we're talking about the same

person. The one I know hates me."

"Stop pouting. I really doubt he hates you."

"I'm telling you, I breathe his air. Me and him in a car together is not going to be a good thing."

"Give it a chance." Coming back to his end of the bar, she tiptoed up to brush her mouth over his. "And if it doesn't go well, I'll kiss you and make it better."

"Promise?" His mouth hitched in a lazy smile.

"Promise." She set a Corona before him and watched the way his hands moved while he inserted a lime into the neck. A tiny frisson of desire trickled over her. She loved his hands, loved the suppleness of his callused fingers, the way he touched her, made her feel sheltered and feminine and unique. Darn it, she missed having him touch her that way. She lifted her gaze to his. "Come home with me tonight."

He choked, sputtering. "What?"

"Unless you don't want to." She smoothed her palms down her thighs then lifted a shoulder in an uncertain shrug. "My blood tests came back clean, but I...I can understand if you don't want me that way right now, since it's not your baby."

With his mouth slightly open, he stared at her until she shifted. Why didn't he say anything?

Finally, a small puff of sound that might have been a laugh escaped him. "Not want you?"

"It's a logical conclusion, Troy Lee."

"No hell, it's not." He laughed again and shook his head. "Of course I want you. You said we should slow down, that you needed time, and I figured I'd give you some space."

Relief sent champagne bubbles fizzing through her. "Kind of stupid, huh, both of us assuming what the other was thinking?"

"Definitely stupid." He leaned forward, his gaze on hers. "I definitely want to go home with you tonight."

"Good. I can't wait."

The last hour before closing time lagged. While she waited on the handful of regulars hanging out on this weeknight, Troy Lee sat on the edge of the bare stage, strumming out a song or two, his voice a steady seduction. Once her girls were gone and she'd locked the door behind everyone, she crossed to sit in the chair closest to him, listening while he meandered through familiar lyrics about being alone together with all the time in the world for loving.

His voice trailed away, the music dying also as he ceased strumming. Angel rubbed damp palms over her knees. "Troy Lee? I'm going to tell them, as soon as possible. I need to be able to tell my family, and I can't do that, not until they know. I can't tell Jim just yet; his mama's in the hospital, but I can start with Cookie..."

Something about his expression stopped her, stirred uneasiness to life. He cleared his throat and laid the guitar aside. "About Cookie."

"Yes?"

"There was a body, a skeleton, found over in Echols County today, and the GBI thinks it was his wife."

"What?" Shock grabbed her throat and she swallowed. "What are you talking about?"

"He was married a long time ago and she went missing. They think these remains over by Statenville might be her."

"Oh, my God." She passed a hand over her mouth. All those years, all those conversations, and she'd never even suspected... "I didn't know he'd been married."

"I don't think a lot of people did." His mouth firmed a moment. "Angel, she was pregnant when she disappeared."

The shock whooshed from her in a small, muffled sound. Pregnant? Cookie was facing a dual loss, wife and child. Like she could turn his life upside down now. Sweet Lord, what he must be feeling.

"That's terrible." Sympathy tightened her chest. "How horrible for him."

"Yeah. Calvert was reworking the schedule earlier, making sure Cookie had a few days if he needed them."

"I can't tell him right now, not if he's dealing with this." Dismayed, she met Troy Lee's solemn gaze. "I don't have any control here, do I?"

"It's life, baby. How much control do we have over anything?"

"You're not helping."

"Come here." He jerked his chin in a come-hither motion. She went to him and he pulled her onto his lap, arms around her in a loose embrace. "It'll be all right. Give it a few days, let things settle down with Jim and Cookie. Okay?"

"Okay." Warmed by his nearness and reassurances, she turned her head to bring their lips together. He caught her chin between his thumb and forefinger and opened his mouth beneath hers. The kiss whispered between them, soft and shimmering with promise.

After a moment, he tipped her gently from his lap. "Come on. Let's get out of here."

Later, they lay together, naked in her bed, and talked in drowsy voices. Replete after a lovemaking as slow and easy as his song had been earlier, Angel wrapped an arm around his waist and rested her cheek on his chest. She rubbed her fingers along the indentations of his ribs and abdominals.

"Stop." He caught her hand on an exhausted laugh. "I'm ticklish."

Her own giggle was devilish. "I know."

"Tease." Arms folded about her, he flipped her to her back in a careful, controlled movement. He reared up on his elbows, then shifted to trail a gentle touch down the center line of her belly. "Did you know she's only the size of a large butterbean right now?"

"No, I didn't. How did you know that?"

"Read it in a book today. Her heartbeat should be audible too."

"It was." She stroked a fingertip over his wrist. The awe on his features echoed her own, winding strong threads of intimacy around them. "Her, huh?"

"Yeah." He bracketed her abdomen with his palms, rubbing his thumbs over her skin. His grin contained more than a hint of sheepishness. "When I think about it, I just kind of assume it's a girl, but a boy would be great too."

Her breath caught, almost as much from his reverent touch as his words. She swallowed, moistened her lips with the tip of her tongue. "You sound like you plan to be involved with this baby."

He looked up with a small frown. "I thought we'd already established that."

"I knew you wanted us to be together, at least for now, but—"

"Angel. Baby." His lashes dipped and he shook his head, a rueful smile tugging at his lips. "There's no 'at least' here. I want..." He sucked in a deep breath, his hands tightening a little. "I want it all with you."

"Define 'all'."

"I want what my dad and Christine had." Resting on one elbow, he slipped a hand up to cradle her jaw. "I can see that with you, and this baby."

"I do not understand you." Suppressing the trembling happiness his words evoked, she waved a hand between them. "Most guys would be all bent out of shape because I—"

"I'm not most guys."

"—am having another man's baby."

"DNA doesn't make a parent, Angel. Christine didn't give birth to me and she was more of a parent to me than my biological mom ever was."

She levered up on her elbow to face him and trace the lines of his features with one fingertip. "She's really special to you, isn't she?"

"Christine? Yeah." He kissed her finger when it came into contact with his mouth. "She's great. My mother, my natural mother, probably shouldn't have had a kid to begin with. She wasn't a bad person or anything; she just wasn't interested in motherhood in general and me in particular."

"I'm sorry." It hurt her heart, the picture of him as a little boy whose mama didn't have time for him.

"Don't be. I was only two when she and Dad divorced, and I lived with him. He met Christine when I was four, married her a year later. She..." He laughed softly, affection softening his eyes. "She started from the beginning treating me like I was hers, but she was so insistent about not infringing on my other mom's place. I remember, how careful she was about that."

"So what about your 'other' mom?" She feathered a caress over his cheekbone. "Do you have a relationship with her?"

"She died when I was seven."

"I'm—"

He stopped her words with a swift kiss. "Don't be sorry. The point is, I don't have to be this baby's biological father to love it or be the kind of dad it needs, the kind of man you need."

"This whole conversation scares me."

"I know. One second at—"

"We can't one second our way through this baby's life, Troy Lee."

"We won't. It's just a place to start, Angel, until you're ready to let go and risk, let go and believe."

A boldfaced hypocrite. That's what he was. Troy Lee refused to grip the steering wheel in a stranglehold. All his talk with Angel about letting go, taking risks, and what was he doing today? Hiding behind silence, like a kid pouting because he hadn't gotten his way.

You have to give him a chance.

Damn it. As bad as he hated to admit it, maybe part of the issue with him and Calvert, who sat just as silently in the passenger seat, was him. Maybe he'd made it all worse by not confronting the situation head on. So how the hell could he expect Angel to take a risk, when he was hiding behind his own fear?

He hated when his mind worked like his father's. F-uck. Now he was going to have to do something about it. He flexed his fingers, knuckles aching, around the wheel. He pulled in a deep breath, centering himself as if he waited for the starting pistol. "You make me nervous as hell."

Calvert turned his head quickly. "What?"

"You make me nervous." The words came out even and matter of fact, thank God. He swallowed, keeping his gaze on the road. "So I start overthinking everything and then I screw up."

"Why do I make you nervous?" A sideways glance revealed Calvert facing forward as well, bouncing his thumb off his knee.

Troy Lee's chest seized up. This was different from opening up with Angel. Is this how she felt, poised on the precipice of belief and afraid to look over? He drew in another centering inhale. "Probably because I admire you professionally. You and Sheriff Reed, you're the reasons I came down here."

Calvert made an uncomfortable sound in his throat. "Are there less screwups when I'm not around?"

"Kinda." Troy Lee shrugged, slowing to make the right onto Ferry Road. "I'm not perfect. I'm still learning."

Amusement colored Calvert's grunt. "We're all still learning.

It's not like you master everything in a year or two. It's new every single day."

Silence fell between them, broken only by the crackle of radio transmissions. After a couple of minutes, Calvert cleared his throat. "I haven't made it easy on you. Cookie thinks we're too much alike."

Troy Lee shot him a look. "Uh, no. We are *not* alike."

What appeared to be a genuine grin quirked at Calvert's mouth. "That's what I said."

"Damn straight."

Another silent moment passed. Calvert resumed thumping his knee. "So why did you hang in?"

"You want me to go?"

"No. I'm just asking. A lot of guys would have tossed it in after the Schaefer deal."

"My dad didn't raise a quitter."

"I can understand that. Mine didn't either." After a pause, Calvert stretched out his legs. "My nephew's taking a math class with your sister."

"Yeah, Ellis." He shrugged. "What of it?"

"Nothing. I mean, they're friends, I guess, and his impression from her was that you'd gone into law enforcement because of your dad's death."

The familiar grief gutted him, followed by the wave of mind-numbing anger. Yeah, he was supposed to get beyond that, but the whole damn thing was so senseless, such a damn waste of his father's warmth and intelligence, his fucking *life*. Simply thinking about it pissed him off all over again. He wrestled the anger down and locked it away, keeping his voice even when he spoke again.

"His impression would be the correct one."

"It's hard, losing a parent like that." Old sorrow lurked in Calvert's quiet voice.

"Yeah." Troy Lee swallowed, more against the tightness in his throat than the slight burn in his chest. He forced a laugh, trying to clear his throat. "Maybe we do have some stuff in common."

"Maybe." Calvert's deep chuckle held real humor, a hint of male ribbing. "But don't push your luck, kid."

"Wouldn't dream of it."

Chapter Fourteen

"Tell me again why I have to go." With irritable movements, Angel tugged the black halter dress over her head and smoothed it down her hips.

"Because I have to go." Visible in the mirror, Troy Lee lounged, shoulders propped against the wall.

"It's your job. Not mine." She cast a critical look at her reflection. The black silk made the silvery highlights in her hair shine, and the velvet rose design along the waist hid the tiny little pooch she had there now. With one hand, she adjusted her neckline. Thanks to her pregnancy, she had awesome cleavage.

"No, but I'm yours." He moved to stand behind her, palms warm on her bare shoulders. "Tell me why you don't want to go."

She glared at him in the mirror and lifted her diamond studs, the real ones she'd bought as a celebration when the Cue Club had first started turning a profit under her ownership. "You have to ask?"

"No. Not really." He lifted one hand to jerk his thumb toward her closet. "Which shoes do you want out of there?"

"Stop changing the subject."

"Stop trying to pick a fight with me so you'll have an excuse not to come with me."

She narrowed her eyes further, bad temper spiking all under her skin. "I don't need an excuse."

"Right." His snort bordered on rude. He crossed to survey her shoe collection. "If you could find one that would hold water, you'd be laying it out and I'd be going alone."

Lord, she hated when he was right. Maybe seduction would work, since feminine pique hadn't. Coming up behind him, she trailed her fingernails through the short hair at his nape. "Troy Lee..."

"It's not working, Angel baby. Office politics. I have to put in an appearance." He held aloft a pair of open-toed heels, more rhinestone straps than anything else. "Hey, I like these. Very sexy."

"I'm not wearing those." She snagged them from his easy hold and tossed them toward the bed. One thumped on the floor. Aggravated, she scanned the closet until she found what she was looking for and reached up to pull down the sedate pointed-toe pumps.

"Those?" Askance, Troy Lee glanced from the shoes in her hand to the eff-me pair she'd discarded.

"Yes. These." She slipped into one, then the other. "I'm not wearing hooker shoes to your work's holiday party."

"Hooker shoes? Hardly. Call-girl shoes, maybe. You know, classy and sexy. It's not like anyone's going to look at your shoes—"

"Will there be wives and girlfriends there?"

"Yeah."

"Trust me, they'll notice." Her stomach lifted and turned over, and she fought against a wave of nausea definitely caused by something other than early pregnancy. She couldn't remember the last time she'd felt this sickly nervous about going anywhere.

"Babe, you have nothing to worry about. You should have seen the dress Calvert's wife wore last year. Your shoes are tame compared to that thing. It was like this really short black slip and there were these beads..." He gestured from torso to thigh and she rolled her eyes.

"That's different, Troy Lee." She shook her suddenly sweaty hands. Sweet Jesus, she was going to die before this was all over.

"Why is it different?" A tight note invaded his voice and she looked up into his too-alert gaze.

"It just is."

"Shit." He looked away, his rough exhale reeking of irritation and disgust. "We're back to that not-as-good-as-everyone-else thing again, aren't we?"

"Well, on some levels it's true." To her absolute horror, the words wobbled. She resisted an overwhelming desire to hunch into herself the way she had in middle school.

"The hell it is." His irritation flared into anger. "Damn it, Angel, I don't understand you. Give me one example of someone we'll see tonight who's above you?"

Uh, maybe everyone? Glimpsing the very real ire in his blue gaze, she kept that smart little retort to herself. Instead, she smiled and shook back her hair. "I thought you didn't want to fight tonight."

"I changed my mind. Some things are worth fighting about. Answer the question."

He wasn't going to let this go. With an exaggerated roll of her eyes, she lifted her hands. "Oh, I don't know... Autry Reed. She's a lawyer."

"Okay. She's a lawyer. Big deal."

"Well, yeah, it is. She went to *Mercer*."

"I'm not getting this, Angel."

"It's not rocket science, Troy Lee."

"Obviously not. If it was, I'd understand." He splayed his hand against the wall and leaned his weight on it. "Honestly, I don't understand anyone being intimidated by Autry Reed."

"It's not just her." A fiery blend of anger and dread swirled over her nerves. "It's...come on, Troy Lee. Countywide emergency personnel and their significant others?"

"Yeah?"

She almost growled at him in frustration. God, he was so *dense* to be so smart. She sank onto the end of the bed, using her fingers to mark off names and facts as a visual aid for him. "Is Tick going to be there?"

"I don't know. Maybe. His baby just came home right before Christmas." Confusion twisted his brows together into a snarl.

"He graduated in the top of his class at UGA—"

"So did I."

"And his wife, who works for the FBI, has a doctoral degree."

"I think so."

"Okay. Cookie's going to be there."

"Um, yeah. Probably." His perplexity didn't clear.

"Tori Calvert is working on her doctorate. What about Steve Monroe? Will he be around?"

"He said he was. What—"

"His wife Dahlia? She teaches out at the high school and wrapped up her master's degree at Valdosta this last semester."

His lips parted for a second in slack surprise and he shook his head. "How do you know all this stuff?"

"My mama does hair for half the county. She knows everything about everybody."

"Sweetheart, is this about education? I don't get how—"

"It's about education and respectability."

"Baby, you went to college."

"Two years at the community college, Troy Lee." She dragged a hand through her hair, mussing the layers she'd spent thirty painstaking minutes drying and smoothing and setting. "It's not the same thing."

"Angel, I swear to God, I'm about to get seriously pissed off."

"Don't swear. It's a sin."

"So is extramarital sex and you don't seem to have a problem sleeping with me. We're not changing the subject."

She twined her hands together in her lap. "Why are you angry?"

The swiftness of his moving stole her breath. He knelt before her, both of his long hands covering hers. "Because you don't see what I do."

"You see what you want to see."

He ignored her. "Talk to me about respectability."

Her shoulders slumped on a weary exhale. "Oh, come on, Troy Lee, surely you get this part. Do you know what I did after community college?"

"You worked days at McGee's and waited tables at the diner at night."

It was her turn to stare at him in shock. "How do you know that?"

"Mr. Hubert at the diner." He named one of the town's elderly residents, a World War II veteran who spent his days sipping tea and talking to anyone who'd pass the time with him. "He adores you. And you saved your money and when the Cue Club went up for sale, you wrote a business plan, secured a loan, turned it into a profitable venture when no one thought it was possible. So no, I don't see how the hell you can be intimidated by anyone or anything, Angel Henderson."

"But I am," she whispered, tears stinging her perfectly shaded and mascaraed eyes. "I don't want to be, but I hold up the bar against who they are, what they do and there's no comparison."

"You're right, there's not." He seemed to breathe the words, a pure emotion glinting in his gaze as he looked up at her. "You took nothing and you made something out of it, just like Christine and those balls of clay she starts with when she's sculpting. It takes a rare and unique talent, you know, to make something great out of nothing, and you have it."

She closed her eyes, trying to pull her wild feelings together. He moved, the fine cotton of his shirt rustling, and pressed his cheek to hers. "Don't discount it, baby. Be proud of it."

On a trembling sigh, she lifted her lashes, finding his gorgeous blues close to hers. A shift of her head and their lips met in the mingling she cherished. He pulled back, rubbing warm hands over her bare knees. He stared at her, his eyes alight with a fierce passion, his expression serious. "I'm not going to ask you to do something that makes you sincerely uncomfortable, but I would like to have you with me tonight and I'd damn sure be proud to have you with me."

He rose and extended his hand, palm up. Holding his gaze, Angel sucked in a deep breath and wrestled the fear down.

She laid her hand in his and let him draw her to her feet. His fingers tightened around hers and she moistened her lips, probably messing up the lipstick she'd painted on with painstaking care. Damn it all, if she was going to do this, she'd do it on her own terms. She kicked out of the pumps she'd never worn because they really weren't her.

"Get me the darn hooker shoes then."

His pleased laugh rumbled over her and she caught a glimpse of pride shining in his eyes as he leaned in to kiss her. "You got it, babe."

"They are too cute for words." Leaning as far forward as her pregnancy would allow, Autry Reed rested her elbow on the table and her chin in her hand, a wistfully romantic expression on her face.

"Who?" With a grateful breath, Tori slipped her shoes off,

hidden by the tablecloth, and peered around, following the direction of Autry's gaze. As crowded as the Radium Spring's ballroom was, though, it was hard to pinpoint who Autry referred to.

"Angel and Troy Lee."

Tori finally located the pair, alone at a table across the packed room. A pair of strappy sandals lay discarded next to Angel's chair, and Troy Lee cradled one bare, slender foot against his thigh, rubbing his thumbs across her arch as they talked. His grin flashed at something Angel said, and even from a distance, the adoration on his face was apparent. A little more of Tori's insecurity where Angel was concerned drained away.

"They are sweet," she concurred.

"I'm glad too." Autry smiled. "She deserves to have someone look at her like that, especially after what Jim did."

A tiny frown pulled at Tori's brows. "Do you know her well?"

"I know her to speak to." Autry relaxed into her chair, rubbing a palm over the growing bulge of her second child. "Her sister Hope cuts my hair and her mother has been doing Mama's hair for years. Your mama's too, for that matter."

"She's Miss Marie's daughter? I didn't know that."

"Yes, she's Miss Marie's daughter. Her oldest. I would've thought you'd know her. She graduated with Tick." Autry's soft laugh was indulgent. "I forget that you lead an isolated life, Victoria."

"I do not. I was like eight when Tick graduated from high school. All I remember about that is having to sit through a bunch of boring speeches and all those people being called to get their diplomas." Her gaze tracked back to the couple across the room. "She does look happy with him."

"Very much so."

Fiddling with her engagement ring, Tori scanned the room for Mark, finally finding him near the bank of French doors that opened onto the balcony. He stood with Stanton Reed and a couple of men from the city police department, all of them deep in conversation. He still looked tired and drawn, and worry rippled through her.

"How is he?" Matching concern laced Autry's quiet question.

"Better, I think. He's not sleeping well, but that can be

normal." Thinking about Mark's quiet wrestle with his grief for his wife and unborn child made her own heart ache. He'd mourned them for years after Jenny had vanished, but even so, facing the reality of their deaths had hit him hard. "I think for him believing something is true and knowing it's true are two very different things. He's hurting, but there's a finality he didn't have before."

"Sounds like a double-edged sword."

"Exactly. A very sharp one."

Across the room, Clark Dempsey stopped at Troy Lee and Angel's table, smiling at her, slapping Troy Lee on the shoulder with a persuasive expression. Troy Lee shook his head, then grimaced and rose. He leaned down to kiss Angel quickly before following Clark to the stairs. Angel followed his progress, then reached for her drink. A disconcerted look flitted across her face as she glanced around the room before hiding behind taking a sip of what looked like sparkling water.

Empathy flashed through Tori. Lord, she knew that feeling well enough—being nervously alone, out of place and step with life going on around her. Funny she'd find that little glimpse of sisterhood with Angel Henderson of all people.

Angel reached down to slide on the sparkly high heels. She rose, smoothing her skirt, and slipped into the alcove where the restroom entrances were. Tori lifted her own sparkling water and looked around to check on Mark. He leaned against the wall, seemingly concentrating on something Coney's police chief was saying.

A familiar, willowy blonde detached herself from another group and headed for the restrooms with a purposeful stride. Tori frowned.

"Isn't that Jim Tyre's new wife?" Autry asked.

"Yes." Unease lifted its head. Something about the way Rhonda moved, the set expression on her face raised red flags all over the place. Tori pushed her chair back, urgency springing to life. "Autry, I'll be right back."

Angel washed and dried her hands then leaned toward the mirror to check her makeup. The vintage lighting was pretty, but not nearly bright enough. She ruffled her layers a little and sighed. They'd never get out of here tonight, not now that Clark had charmed Troy Lee into getting his guitar out of the Jeep.

But he was having a good time, and she could...deal. She *would* deal.

She straightened, drew in a calming breath, and adjusted her neckline. The door opened as she turned to go, and she found herself face-to-face with Rhonda Tyre. Angel made herself smile as she attempted to pass the other woman. "Hey, Rhonda."

Her eyes glittering with a feral light, Rhonda wrapped her hand around Angel's upper arm. "What do you think you're doing here tonight?"

Angel glanced down at Rhonda's cupid-pink nails against her skin. Oh no, she didn't think so. "Let go of me."

If anything Rhonda tightened her grip, digging little half-moons into Angel's arm. "I don't know what game you think you're playing, if you're out to make Jim jealous or what, showing up here with that boy, but it won't work—"

"I said let go." Using the technique she'd learned years ago in one of Tick Calvert's self-defense classes, Angel pressed down hard at Rhonda's inner elbow, forcing her to release her hold. She backed up a step, gauging the distance to the door. Darn if she was staying here with the crazy bitch. She lowered her voice to the easy, authoritative tone she used with difficult drunks. "I don't want Jim, Rhonda. I've moved on, okay? He's all yours."

Rhonda sniffed, eyes narrowed. "I've seen the way you look at him."

Sweet Jesus, what had the girl been smoking? Well, Angel had learned a long time ago there was no reasoning with unreasonable drunks, and even though Rhonda seemed sober enough, Angel didn't plan on wasting her breath.

With her index finger, she gestured toward the right. "You need to move."

Rhonda's chin lifted. "I'm not moving and you're not going anywhere until we come to an understanding. Jim is *mine*."

"Yes, he is. He married you, Rhonda. He's yours. You won't get an argument from me."

Touching her index fingers together then separating them in an arc, Rhonda drew an imaginary line between them. "Then stay away from him."

"I—"

"Hey, Angel!" The door swung open and Nikki Pantone's enthusiastic greeting saved her from replying. The EMT who worked the shift opposite Jim and Clark breezed into the restroom, effectively separating Rhonda from Angel by hugging Angel's neck. Nikki wrapped an arm around Angel's waist and ignored Rhonda. "I've been trying to get over to speak to you all night."

"Excuse me." Rhonda flipped back her hair. "We were having a conversation."

"No, you were being a bitch." Nikki delivered the correction in a relaxed tone. She pointed behind Rhonda. "There's the door. Don't let it hit you in the ass as you leave."

"You—"

The door opening once more interrupted Rhonda, frustration twisting her pretty features into an unattractive mask. Angel didn't really need Nikki's intervention, but she was glad for it and the supportive arm about her waist regardless. The ugliness of the encounter seemed determined to weaken her knees, and the shakiness of aftermath began to set in.

Tori Calvert stepped into the small room, and Angel swallowed a trembling laugh. Well, darn. Wonder who else had an invitation to this private little get-together?

"I'm sorry," Tori said, although she didn't sound the least apologetic, her dark eyes roving over the trio to light on Angel with something like concern. "Am I interrupting?"

"No." Nikki smirked in Rhonda's direction. "Mrs. Tyre was just leaving."

Arms folded over her chest, Rhonda slanted a killing look at all of them, pushed by Tori and stalked out.

Nikki shook her head as the door closed with a snap. "That bitch has snakes in her head."

Tori's big eyes widened and Angel giggled, although it sounded shaky even to her. God, she adored Nikki, always had, even if she didn't see her often now that Jim was out of her life. She held onto Nikki, as her knees went watery and her head went dizzy. "I'm glad you showed up."

"Oh, you could have taken her." Nikki sketched a careless gesture. "Although I saw her follow you in and I figured what was happening in here was probably more interesting than trying to convince Chris Parker I'd be a great lay."

Again, Tori looked shocked and Angel took pity on her. She disentangled from Nikki's gently supportive arm. "Behave."

Determined to appear unaffected, Angel moved to the sink

and ran cold water over her wrists. She glanced up at her reflection, only to find Tori watching her carefully. The younger woman stepped forward but didn't invade Angel's space. "Are you all right?"

"I'm fine." She pressed cool fingers to her cheeks. An ironic laugh bubbled from her throat. "She thinks I want Jim back."

"She thinks everybody wants Jim." Nikki rolled her eyes and hopped up on the counter at Angel's elbow. The already short skirt of her party dress rode up to reveal lace-topped thigh highs. "Hell, she thinks I want Jim. How crazy is that?"

"Crazy."

"He doesn't realize it yet because he's all starry-eyed-in-lust, but she's going to make his life miserable."

Angel closed her eyes a second. Oh, hell. She might have to deal with this woman for the rest of her life. Even worse, what might Rhonda be like with Angel's baby? She shuddered.

"Angel?" A touch even softer than Tori's voice drifted over her shoulder. "Are you sure you're all right?"

"No." She opened her eyes, meeting Tori's dark gaze in the mirror. She dredged up a smile from somewhere. "But I will be. Thanks."

"We should probably get back out there." Nikki slipped from the counter, giving them a flash of hot pink panties as she did so. "If Troy Lee finds out she upset you, he'll go ballistic."

Angel snorted. "No, he won't."

"Yes ma'am, he would." Nikki nodded, long rhinestone earrings swinging wildly. "He's crazy about you, and he definitely has that wild-boy side that would go nuts if his woman was threatened."

"You're the nut." Angel exchanged an amused look with Tori, who held the door for them. She surveyed the room, seeking Troy Lee. He stood at the shiny grand piano, deep in conversation with Clark, guitar case at his feet.

"My God, he's beautiful. I just want to lick him or something." Nikki gave a dramatic sigh. "I'm jealous as hell that you're fucking him."

Angel's laugh covered Tori's small choking sound. With her tension effectively broken, she hugged Nikki. "Nik, thank you for rescuing me, but go away."

Nikki plopped a kiss on her cheek. "Later, sugar."

Tori watched her walk away. “Is she always so...?”

“Yes. Always. What you see is what you get. She’s utterly confident in herself, doesn’t care what anybody thinks, and I love her to death.” Angel crossed her arms over her midriff. Across the ballroom, Clark settled at the piano and Troy Lee unpacked his guitar as Emmett Beck, the young city cop who played bass and fiddle, joined them.

“Must be nice, to be that secure in oneself.” Tori fiddled with the square-cut diamond ring gracing her left hand. She drew herself up and turned a dazzling smile in Angel’s direction. “Listen, speaking of confidence. About Rhonda...don’t let her get to you. She obviously has insecurity issues and that has nothing whatsoever to do with you.”

“Wow, you could have fooled me ten minutes ago.”

“It’s not about you. The insecurity, the problem, whatever it is, lies within her.” Tori’s shoulders moved with a deep breath. “She’s just displacing it and you’re the most convenient target.”

“That’s reassuring. She doesn’t seem the type to be self-aware enough to deal with it.”

“I owe you an apology.” A hint of embarrassed desperation tightened Tori’s expression. “Probably you and Mark, both—”

“What?” Angel shook her head. Lord help her, could this night get worse? She wasn’t standing here, having this conversation with the woman Cookie planned to marry. “No, you don’t. Believe me.”

Clark rippled his fingers over the keys, and a familiar murmur of anticipation swelled in the room.

“I do, but now’s not the time or place.” With a light touch, Tori tried to usher her toward the table she and Mark had shared most of the night with the sheriff and his wife. “Come sit with us since Troy Lee’s abandoned you to sing, which by the way, I’ve never heard him do, despite all the good things everyone says about his voice. I’m excited.”

Angel cast a despairing glance at the table. She had a couple of choices here. She could balk like her granddaddy’s old mule, refuse to go, make a scene as Troy Lee and Emmett tuned up and the room hushed. Or she could do the graceful thing, put on a smile and pretend sitting with them wouldn’t leave her sick with nerves.

Darn it all, why did being graceful have to be so damned hard?

"Come on. They're getting ready to start." Like a high-heeled bulldozer, Tori moved her inexorably toward what had to be the second-most place that she didn't want to be. At least she wasn't being ushered over to sit with Jim and Rhonda. That was the only thing she could think of that might be worse than this.

Lord help her.

She didn't miss the flare of surprise in Cookie's eyes as they reached the table and Tori made swift pseudo-introductions. Every nerve in her body stiff and singing with tension, Angel perched on the chair next to Tori's and tried not to think too hard about the reality before her. At her sides, she clenched her hands around the edges of the wooden chair, hidden by her skirt, and focused her gaze on Troy Lee as he settled onto the end of the piano bench. He strummed opening notes, Clark picking up the melody and Emmett soon joining in with the violin.

The crowd didn't exist for them tonight, Angel soon realized, just the music and the joy of it. Troy Lee sang of love and longing and intense desire, of loss and healing and falling. Raw and powerful, his voice swelled to match with Emmett's violin. With his song, memories flashed in her head—the way he touched her, his insistence that she mattered, the look on his face when he talked about her baby, about their future.

Certainty shimmered through her, shiny and bright and full of hope. The man singing before her with such emotion and passion, the man she'd been falling into for weeks now...this was the man she'd been waiting for. The right man for her, the one Jim or Cookie or anyone else could never be.

And he loved her. She hugged that sweet knowledge close. If he loved her as she was, thought she was good enough for him, then darn it, that was all that mattered.

Chapter Fifteen

She couldn't keep her hands off him.

Angel buzzed with it, this pulsing, palpable need that spread throughout her entire body until she was one exposed wire. Standing behind him as he unlocked the door to her house, she wrapped her arms around his waist, rubbing her hands over his abdomen and chest. He fumbled the keys, laughing, as she pressed herself to him and chafed her fingers across hardened male nipples.

"I don't know what's gotten into you," he said, finally managing to throw the lock, "but I like it."

Inside, she pushed him against the wall the moment the door closed. Biting the tip of her tongue, she attacked the buttons on his dress shirt, craving the feel of his bare skin. He widened his stance and pulled her into him, his hands at her waist.

"So what did I do to deserve this?" He nibbled his way along her jaw to her ear, the resonation of his voice sending desire down her spine, swirling into the heat already suffusing her belly. He nipped her earlobe. "Tell me so I can do it again."

On the fourth button, she fumbled too hard and it tore loose, pinging away on her hardwood floor. His husky laugh growled near her ear. "What is it with you and ripping off my buttons, anyway? Not that I mind, but you're hell on my wardrobe, Angel baby."

His dimple flashed with a lazy smile, and desire smoldered in his blue gaze. She spread her fingers over his chest, his skin hot against her palms, and looked up at him. "I love you."

His eyes flared and his lips parted, but no sound emerged. Giddiness bubbled through her, a sparkling flow of sheer happiness. She'd left him speechless and he looked at her like she'd given him the finest gift of his life. The next breath, he crushed her to him, that beautiful mouth of his taking hers in a kiss both ravenous and reverent.

"Tell me again." Cradling her face in both hands, he scattered tiny kisses over her cheeks, her nose, her brow. "Say it again so I know I didn't dream it."

"I love you." She breathed the words into the curve beneath his chin, lifted her head to find his mouth. "I love you."

"God, baby. I love you so much it hurts sometimes." He moved with decisive swiftness, sliding one arm beneath her knees to swing her into his arms.

She wrapped her arms about his neck, liking how being held high against his chest made her feel dainty and feminine. Cherished. "What are you doing?"

"Carrying you off to bed." He angled them through her bedroom door. "Hearing those words from you? That deserves a grand romantic gesture."

He set her on her feet by the bed and reached for the tiny hook at her nape. She finished off the buttons on his shirt and tugged the tails free of his slacks before gliding the fine cotton down his arms. He shrugged free of it, the garment whispering to the floor, and slid his fingers over the bare length of her spine to find the series of fabric-covered buttons at the small of her back.

"You're so beautiful." He touched his mouth to hers and smoothed the dress down over her hips. She caught it, stepped free and laid it over the hope chest at the end of the bed while he shucked his pants. Kissing her again, a light series of caresses and nips, he backed her toward the bed, until she sat on the edge. Kneeling before her, he lifted one foot, stroking her ankle before releasing the rhinestone strap there and slipping off the sandal. He pressed a kiss to the side of her arch, one palm curved around her calf, then lifted her other foot to do the same. "So strong."

She blinked away a blur of tears and leaned forward to frame his face and pull him up to her. "I don't know how I didn't see earlier that you were everything I didn't know I wanted."

"You were blinded by my runner's physique." His chuckle murmured over her lips. "Or my sexual prowess, maybe. You know, the endurance."

Laughter bubbled up as she hugged him to her and fell back on the bed, the urgency of her need not diminished but somehow tempered by the knowledge that they had forever now. "Probably that twisted sense of humor of yours."

On a satisfied groan, he rolled to his side and propped on his elbow. He picked up her hand and pressed his mouth to her palm, kissing each finger. "You have no idea how long I've waited for this, how long I've wanted this."

She trailed a touch down the center line of his chest. "How long?"

"Since the first time I met you."

"When you pulled me over on Highway 3?" That had been forever ago.

"Yeah." He laid an open-mouth kiss on the inside of her wrist. "Well, actually, that was probably sexual attraction. You were wearing this great red lipstick and I had a hell of a time concentrating on writing that ticket. There were all these fantasies kicking off in my head, about you—"

"I can imagine." She pressed her fist against his stomach in a playful mock punch. The muscles didn't give.

"Hey, I am a guy, babe. We think that way, although it's not great practice during a traffic stop. That's how cops get killed." He nibbled at the tender underside of her thumb. "Then Clark introduced me to you at the bar and every time we were playing or hanging out, there you were, all beautiful and funny and smart, and I just got sucked in deeper and deeper."

His exhale vibrated between them, traveling over her skin. He rubbed his cheek into her palm.

"I figured if I waited long enough, Jim would do something stupid—he's too much of a dumbass not to—and maybe I'd have a chance to get you to see me as something more than the cop who wrote you tickets or the guy who played your bar on weekends. And then he did and as much as I wanted to pound his ass for hurting you, I thought hey, here's that opportunity you've been waiting for. Back off, give her some time, be there when she's ready."

His voice faded into a rough cough, and her heart twisted. Somehow she knew what was coming. "Troy Lee, I—"

"I just didn't figure on Cookie being the wild variable in the equation. That night..." A hoarse, humorless laugh lifted his chest. "I turned the corner at the motel, saw him leaving about the second I spotted your car, and I thought I'd die. I'm not a jealous guy normally, but I seriously wanted to kill him. I spent the rest of that shift, and most of the ones for days afterward, driving around, thinking about what had gone on between you two, madly trying to figure out how I could have missed Cookie as the variable. I never expected him to even be in the picture because you were so different from his other women, and I even started wondering if I'd been wrong about the way he looked at Tori Calvert, that maybe he didn't want her after all, and that I'd lost any chance with you."

She closed her eyes at the raw pain in his voice. "I'm sorry."

"No, baby, don't be." He tugged her closer, so her shoulder nestled at his chest, her hip into the cradle of his thighs, his arm a heavy comfort over her waist. "It's over and done, and one thing I learned for damn sure...you're too valuable to risk losing. I kept telling myself if I got a chance, one opportunity to have you look at me, I'd make the most of it."

"I was right from the start. You are a sweetheart." She snuggled into him, kissing him, letting the love and passion and hope color the touch of their lips. "And I'm so yours, Troy Lee."

"That's good." He rested his face against her neck. "Because you own me."

"Really?" She pressed her fingertips between his ribs, catching the ticklish spot. He coughed out a laugh and squirmed beneath her marauding hand. "I've never owned six feet of man before. Whatever shall I do with you?"

He captured her wrists and rolled, stretching her arms above her head, looming over her. "Making love to me sounds good."

On a soft giggle, she twisted free of his easy hold and rubbed at his shoulders. "It does, doesn't it?"

He touched her, skimming his hands over her skin with awed hunger. The emotion resounded in her, finding an answering need in her own heart and body. For long minutes, they put the playful teasing aside, charting one another with hands and lips and tongues.

"Troy Lee, please." His name passed her lips on a moan. She arched into him, threading her fingers into his hair as he made her crazy, playing those riffs on responsive flesh between her thighs. "I want you."

He moved, wrapping her legs around his hips and surging inside her. The sudden sensation of being stretched around him took her breath on a wave of pleasure. His moan of satisfaction came out with a hissed breath and he withdrew, easing home again, setting a slow rhythm that she matched with subtle thrusts of her own.

Resting on one elbow, he cradled her face with his palm and brought their mouths together. His lips traveled over her jaw, to her temple. "Love you, love you, love you..."

His mantra washed over her, and she whispered her own words of love. She arched closer, wanting more, wanting it all, as desire and sensation coalesced, swirling out, eddying, until they blended and crashed into a climax that left her clinging to him and gasping out his name. She held on, nails digging into his biceps, her gaze fixed on his face as he pushed higher, deeper within her, his lashes coming down as the intense pleasure-pain of climax tautened his features.

He collapsed into her arms, his face against her neck, hot breath searing her damp skin. Tiny aftershocks of pleasure vibrated through her, and she ran her hand down the indention of his spine. "Oh, Troy Lee Farr, I do love you."

His answer was a deep male mutter, as though he was winded and beyond words. She hugged him close and smiled against his hair. She didn't need the words then.

She had him.

"Mmm." Angel turned into Troy Lee's warm, naked body as he tossed the covers away and made to rise. She tucked her leg over his thighs and tried to pull him back to her. "Don't go yet."

"I don't want to." He hooked his hand around the back of her knee and nuzzled her ear. "But I have to. I've got to go home and shower—"

"Shower here." She cracked one eyelid. Darkness still hovered beyond the windows. "Troy Lee, it's not even dawn yet."

"Baby...I've got to get moving. I missed my run yesterday and I need some miles this morning." He kissed a hot trail down her throat. Beneath her leg, his half-hard penis twitched. "I have to put together a fresh uniform, plus there's drive time between here and my place. But, I'll see you tonight." He blessed her collarbone with open-mouthed kisses. "And I'm off for three days at New Year's."

"Ooh, you can watch football with my daddy."

He closed his teeth on her shoulder in playful retaliation. "Or I could take you to Atlanta to meet my family."

"Maybe." She traced the ridges in his spine. "Staying in bed all day sounds good."

"Damn good." He growled and kissed her cheek. "But I can't be late for work today."

He shifted to sit on the side of the bed and pull on his boxers. She rolled to her side and levered up on an elbow, watching the muscles play in the dim light filtering in from the living room. "Why don't you bring some things with you tonight? You know, clothes and stuff to leave here."

"Sounds like a great idea to me." He stood, picked up his slacks and tugged them on. The zipper rasped and he slipped his arms into his shirt, leaving it half unbuttoned. With a grin, he rested his knee on the mattress and bent down to kiss her. "Love you, baby." Moving lower, he nudged the sheet aside and dropped another kiss below her navel. "You too, baby."

Her eyes prickled at the pure emotion in his voice and she sat up, winding her arms about his neck and kissing him with everything in her heart. After a moment, he pulled away and bumped his nose against hers. "Later."

She tangled her hand in his collar and tugged him close for just one more. "I can't wait."

Angel parked her Mustang beneath the spreading oak tree next to the EMS station, just as she had dozens of times before. Jim's familiar F-150 waited nearby and she swung out of the low-slung sports car, rubbing her damp palms down her thighs as she headed up the brick walkway to the neat building.

The bays stood open, revealing both ambulances. A radio played a popular country-music station, and good-natured teasing accompanied the familiar routine of the EMT teams preparing to change shifts, Jim and Clark inventorying their bus while Nikki and her partner cleaned their own. Nikki spotted Angel first and paused in the middle of running a squeegee over the windshield, surprise flashing in her green eyes. "Hey, Angel."

"Hey, Nik." At Nikki's greeting and Angel's reply, Jim straightened, nearly hitting his head against the open metal door on the lower side of the ambulance. His face froze into a deer-in-the-headlights expression and her hopes that this might not be as bad as she'd feared took a serious nosedive.

"Jim, can I talk to you a minute?" She folded her arms, rubbing above her elbows, and tilted her head toward the side yard.

He gestured at the supplies scattered beside the vehicle. "I'm kinda busy."

She lifted her chin. "It's kinda important."

His mouth tightened and he glanced around at his colleagues before his gaze landed on Clark's impassive face. "I'll be right back."

Not waiting to see if he followed, she turned and strode toward her car. Nerves jittered in her stomach, trying to edge their way toward nausea, but she concentrated on breathing through her nose, deep calming inhales and exhales.

"What the hell is so important?" Jim joined her, nearly hissing the words, and she was glad she'd chosen this as the venue for her revelation. He might not be happy about what she had to say, but he'd watch his damn manners with his coworkers near. There'd be no yelling. "Rhonda would have a fit if she knew I was talking to you."

Angel could only imagine. She smothered her snippy retort and tightened her hold on her arms. She'd come to do this and she was just going to do it. "I'm pregnant."

Jim scowled and threw out his hands. "So?"

Anger dazzled through her and she narrowed her eyes at him. "What do you mean, 'so'? So you might be the father."

A rude snort exploded from Jim. "More likely it's that boy from the sheriff's department you're fucking around with."

She dug her nails into her own skin. She was not going to go white-trash-crazy-ex-girlfriend on his ass, no matter how badly she wanted to or how badly he deserved it. Instead, she settled for a too-sweet smile. "Hardly, since I was already pregnant before I ever slept with him."

"Well, you said *might*." He spit into the neat mulch surrounding the oak tree. "Goddamn, Angel, how many of us *might* there be?"

At the insult, she straightened her shoulders. "Just one other, and to tell you the truth, Jim, I hope to God it's his."

"Yeah, I'm not that lucky." Hands propped at his hips, he glared at her. "So it's not too late for an abortion, right?"

The air whooshed from her lungs and she tried to quell the crushing pain and fury his callous comment brought. Okay, even she'd thought that at the beginning and she was seriously complicating his life, but overlaid with his hard reaction was the memory of Troy Lee leaning down to whisper a kiss and words of love and acceptance over an unborn child that wasn't his.

"I mean, that's what this is about, right?" Jim's jaw tightened, taking on a pugnacious angle. "You want money for an abortion?"

She stared, sure her mouth was hanging open. He thought she wanted...? She laughed, although it was an ugly, derogatory sound even to her. "I don't need your damn money, Jim Tyre. Hell, the club brings in more on a good Saturday night than you make in a month—"

"Lord, you're a bitch." Anger flushed his face, his nostrils flaring. Yeah, it was a good thing she'd chosen to tell him here. Somewhere private and she might have ended up like one of those poor girls her mama was always talking about from the Nancy Grace show, the pregnant ones whose former lovers murdered them and tossed the bodies. "Then what the fuck do you want from me, Angel?"

What had she ever seen in this selfish bastard? Maybe it was what she'd hadn't seen, all the pettiness and the innate self-centeredness that she hadn't really perceived for what they were, until Troy Lee and his open, giving presence in her life.

She shook her head. "I don't want anything from you, Jim. I just...I wanted to do the decent thing and tell you."

"Decent." He looked away, his shoulders shaking on a silent, repulsive laugh. "Like you even know what that word means—"

"Stop." She shoved the word out from between clenched teeth. "I did what I came to do. You know, and that's it. You've made it really plain you want nothing to do with this baby if it's yours, and that's fine with me."

"Yeah, you say that now, but when it's here, you'll be asking for child support, just wait and see."

"Sign off on your parental rights when it's born and I won't ask you for a dime."

"Get me the papers and it's done."

Would it really be that easy to have him out of her life, out of the baby's? She wasn't going to push the point further today for sure. "I'll talk to a lawyer, see what we have to do."

"You do that." With a hard nod, he turned away. After a couple of steps, he spun to face her. "You listen to me, Angel, and listen good—as far as Rhonda and I are concerned, this baby doesn't exist. Hell, Rhonda doesn't even need to know. You got that?"

"Yeah, Jim, I get it." She waited for him to walk inside and slowly uncurled her aching fingers from around her arms, surprised to find her hands shaking and red spots of blood under her nails. She expelled a trembling giggle that was closer to a sob.

Lord help her, she still had to tell Cookie.

"Here you go. That'll be one-thirty-six." Shanna leaned on the diner counter while Mark pulled a couple of ones from his wallet and scrounged for a penny. A speculative light glinted in her startlingly blue eyes. "So I hear Tori got a ring for Christmas."

He handed over the money. "Um, yeah."

"Never thought I'd see the day when you'd get married." Shaking her head, Shanna opened the till and made change. He waved it back at her and she slid it into her apron pocket. A grimace twisted her mouth. "Of course, I never thought Tick would either."

He reached for his coffee with a noncommittal sound. Shanna had been Tick's current trying-to-forget when Falconetti had come back into his life, and Mark wasn't touching that comment. He lifted the large cup in a farewell gesture. "Thanks, Shanna."

At the door, he picked up a copy of the local complimentary real estate magazine. Tori was hell-bent they were going to live on the lake after they were married, and since she had him wrapped around her finger alongside her brothers, he might as well start looking. Scanning the listings on the glossy back cover, he nudged the door open with his elbow and took a cautious sip of the strong, freshly brewed coffee. God, he needed the caffeine jolt today. Since the confirmation of Jenny's death, sleep had been hit-or-miss, and he was feeling the miss bad this afternoon.

Huh. This one possessed potential. Three bedrooms and a study, a hundred feet of lake frontage, dock already in place...

"Cookie?"

He startled at Angel's hushed voice, coffee sloshing dangerously. He held the cup aloft, steadying it. "Hey. Troy Lee's not with me if you're—"

"No, I was looking for you." She darted a look around, the street and sidewalk quiet and nearly deserted on this Saturday after Christmas, her bright yellow Mustang the only vehicle parked on this block, other than a couple of county employee vehicles. "Have you got a minute?"

"Sure." His instincts pricked up. Something was off—she was pale, looking everywhere but at him, rubbing her palms over her elbows in a nervous, repetitive gesture. If her red-rimmed eyes were anything to go by, she'd been crying. "What's up?"

She sank her teeth into her bottom lip and shook her head. Fresh tears shimmered in her eyes.

Oh, hell. He did a quick visual survey of her, looking for anything to explain her distress. Other than her tears and overall shakiness, she looked like the same Angel he'd always known—turquoise boots, a brown print dress, silver hoop earrings. The only thing missing was her customary denim jacket, and she had to be cold, with her arms bare like that—

Little red bruises, fresh ones, dotted her arms, the skin broken in a couple of places. Like someone had grabbed her, hard. Scenarios flipped through his brain, none of them pretty.

"Angel? What happened?" He set his coffee on the windowsill of the vacant building next to the diner and reached for her arm with a gentle hand, turning her slightly to give him a better look at the marks. Son of a bitch... "Did someone hurt you?"

She burst into tears. *Shit.* He caught her chin as gingerly as he could and tilted her gaze up to his. "Angel, I need you tell me what happened. I can understand if you don't want Troy Lee, but if it will make it easier for you to talk to me, I can call Tori—"

"No!" She tugged her arm free and covered her eyes in an obvious attempt to get herself together. A spurt of hysterical laughter burst from her lips. "God, no."

"Okay, but you have to—"

"I'm pregnant." She dropped her hand and met his gaze, a hint of defiance in hers. He stared back at her, his lungs refusing to work at all. Everything rolled a degree or so off kilter, but the weekend activity of Coney continued around them—a semi loaded with chickens rumbling through the intersection, a pair of women walking laps around the First Baptist parking lot, even a couple of birds chirping in the big oaks behind the sheriff's department.

His chest tightened further, until he thought for sure he'd suffocate. Hell, he remembered this feeling from the day Jenny disappeared, when the realization that she was really missing, that she wasn't coming home, slammed into him with the deadly devastation of a speeding freight train.

He'd felt like this the day Tori had told him they were over too, when he'd believed he'd lost everything pure and good and wonderful that had come into his life.

"What?" Eyes narrowed to slits glittering with unshed tears, Angel glared at him. "You don't want to ask me if I'm looking for money for an abortion?"

His lungs uncramped long enough to let him pull in a modicum of oxygen. His gaze dropped to her arms, folded tight, her fingers digging into the skin above her elbows. She looked even more off-balance than he felt.

He dragged a hand over his nape. "Is that what Jim did?"

"Yeah, and I'm a selfish bitch, out to ruin his life." Something bitter and ugly, like hatred, dripped from her voice. "Like I asked for this."

"Did he do this?" He indicated the marks on her arm.

"No." She shook her head, her expression set in tense, dejected lines. "I did."

"Angel, I—" He rubbed his mouth. A sigh worked its way up from his aching chest. "I don't know what to say."

"Well, there's another difference between you and Jim."

He darted a look at her. "I'm sorry he gave you a hard time."

"I'm fine."

"No, you're not." Hell, neither was he. His knees wobbled, wanting to give out on him. *Shit*, what was he supposed to do with this?

What was Tori going to do with this?

The question sent fear crashing through him. She was already insecure where his involvement with Angel was concerned, and even though she'd shocked the hell out of him by bringing Angel to sit at their table the night before, he didn't have a clue how she'd react to this.

"I don't expect anything from you." Angel spoke in a low, intense voice, hurrying the words out as if she wanted this over and done, wanted to crawl away and hide to nurse invisible wounds. "But I had to tell you. I need to tell my parents and I didn't want it to get back to you through the gossip grapevine."

He nodded, his brain having a hard time sifting through the input. A thought reverberated through his head, offering another explanation for her tears. "Does Troy Lee know?"

"Yes." The first hint of real calm flickered in her eyes. "He's known, almost from the beginning. I don't want you to be angry with him. It wasn't his place to tell you—"

He waved her to a stop. "I'm not angry with him. I'm just...hell." A rough laugh scraped his throat and he rubbed at his mouth. "My brain doesn't want to work."

"I'm sorry, Cookie." Absolute misery coated her words.

"Don't be." He attempted a smile, but was pretty sure it came off more like a grimace. "You didn't do it on purpose."

"I don't want her to be someone's problem, Cookie. It's not fair to make that her life." A hard swallow flexed the muscles in her throat. "I understand if you're not interested in being involved."

"Her?"

One corner of her mouth lifted and she gave a half-hearted shrug. "Troy Lee thinks it's a girl."

Even with the surreal quality of the conversation, the reality of the situation was settling in around him, on him, heavily. "Angel, I need some time to get this straight in my head. Can you give me that?"

"Sure." She tilted her chin toward her car. "I promised my mama I'd come by today and I need to get myself together before I do, so I'm going."

"Yeah." He tried to shake himself out of the walking-through-gelatin sensation. It didn't work. "Drive carefully."

"I will."

He closed his eyes. Her boots thumped on the sidewalk then stopped. “Cookie?”

His lids felt too heavy to lift, but somehow he managed. “Yeah?”

“Thank you.”

He frowned. “For what?”

Sadness glimmered in her eyes for a split second. “For being you.”

With that cryptic statement, she spun and strode to her car. The engine fired and she pulled out, soon disappearing down Durham Street.

God. Mark pressed the heels of both hands into his eyes. What was he supposed to do now?

Chapter Sixteen

Behind the wheel of his unmarked unit, Mark made turns as random as the thoughts bouncing through his head. His thinking refused to line up straight, and he needed that more than anything right now.

The familiar landscape of Long Lonesome Road flashed by and he braked for the next drive on the left. An ironic laugh scoured his throat. Like he'd find any answers here, of all places.

Regardless, he turned down the long gravel drive. Tick's truck was absent, but Mark pulled to a stop behind Falconetti's Volvo. The quiet murmur of the river beyond the tree line greeted him when he stepped from the vehicle. Some of the comfortable calm surrounding the home settled into him.

He rapped a quiet knock at the back door and waited. Moments later, Falconetti appeared, warm welcome blooming on her face. "Hey, Cookie."

"Hey." She stepped back to let him enter and he rubbed at his jaw, trying to pull himself together. He glanced around the living area. "Where's the rugrat?"

"Asleep. It took me half an hour to get him settled." She pointed at the bassinet next to the leather chair. "Please don't wake him up."

An unwilling smile pulled at his mouth. How Tick, of all people, had fathered an infant with a temperament like unstable nitroglycerin was really beyond him.

"Do you want something? Coffee?" She pulled a couple of mugs from an overhead cabinet, movements colored by her easy elegance.

"Sounds good." He'd never finished the cup he'd gotten

from the diner. Hell, he didn't even think it had made it into the car with him. He couldn't remember. He hooked his thumbs in his gun belt and surveyed the array of photos lining the living room wall. His gaze fell on a snapshot of Tori and Tick sitting on the dock at their mother's home. Her eyes sparkled with good humor, the impish smile he adored curving her pretty mouth. His chest seized up all over again.

"Here you go." Caitlin presented him with a painted mug full to the brim with steaming black coffee. She gestured with her own cup of milk. "Would you prefer to sit in the living room or at the dining table while you spill your guts?"

He darted a glance at her, the cup halted halfway to his lips. "What are you talking about?"

"Oh, please." She pinned him with her Fed look, not softened at all by her casual appearance—jeans, thin T-shirt, hair piled in a haphazard knot. "You're not here looking for Tick. So you just stopped by in the middle of a shift to admire Lee? I don't think so. I've interviewed death-row inmates hours before execution who looked less haggard and shell-shocked than you do right now. Something is wrong and you're looking for someone you can trust."

He released a shuddery exhale. "I hate when you do that."

"So I've heard." She tilted her head toward the table. "So sit and spill it."

With one last glimpse at Tori's image, he obeyed. He wrapped his hands around the mug, hoping the warmth from the pottery would transfer to his chilled spirit. It didn't. Caitlin didn't speak, the silence around them broken only by the slight whistle of the wind whipping under the eaves and Lee's occasional snuffle.

He sipped. The hot liquid didn't soothe his too-tight throat, either. He chafed his thumbs around the rim. "I just had a conversation with Angel Henderson."

"Should I know her?"

"She owns the Cue Club."

"The cute blonde with the turquoise boots."

"That's the one." He felt Caitlin's steady gaze on his face but didn't look up. Instead, he bracketed his mug with both hands and studied the pattern of veins and lines and scars on their backs. "I've known her a long time, since she bought the bar. When I was at DCPD, the guys and I would hang out there on our nights off, play pool, watch the game, that kind of thing. Angel and I…we flirted. She was engaged, I wasn't interested, it didn't mean anything, you know? It was just some stupid thing we always did."

He lapsed into silence. Caitlin didn't prod him, but sat patiently, sipping her milk. From the corner of his eye, he caught the flash of sunlight over Tick's rings on her hand. He cleared his throat.

"So a couple of months back, one night she tells me her engagement's off. He'd married someone else on a lark while he was in Biloxi. So I said, hey, why don't we go out sometime then. I wasn't expecting her to take me up on it."

"And she did."

"Yeah. I thought, why not? It's just dinner and a movie. Except I got called out to work a domestic at the ER with Tori and…I don't know. Angel made a move and I followed through on it. It was the stupidest goddamn thing I've ever done." He propped his elbow on the table and buried his mouth in his hand. "She's pregnant."

"Oh my God." Caitlin's dismay didn't make him feel any better.

"If this baby's mine, I can't turn my back on that."

"Of course not." She folded her fingers around his. "No one who knows you would expect you to."

He looked up then, into dark green eyes soft with concern. "You believe in fate, Falconetti?"

"Not per se." She lifted one shoulder in a shrug. "But I agree with Tick, that there's a plan for our lives if we look for it."

"Part of me keeps hanging up on the insane idea that somehow, I'm being given back what was taken from me."

"Just not in the way you expected."

"Right." He dropped his hand from his mouth and glanced away. "Crazy, huh?"

"Not at all. Makes perfect sense to me." Her gaze dwelled a moment on the nearby bassinet before tracking back to his. "You said if it's yours. Is there a question?"

"It could be the ex-fiancé." The memory of Angel's defeated demeanor, her tears and hurt, swam in his mind. "Might be better for most everyone if it's not."

"For most everyone?"

He scuffed at his nape and stretched back in the chair, seeking movement to relieve the god-awful tension gripping him with iron tentacles. "This could...I don't know how Tori will take this."

"I wondered when we'd get to that."

Eyes closed, he fought the squeezing sensation in his chest again. After a moment, he lifted heavy lids. "She could leave me."

"Yes, she might."

Reaction to her calm statement crashed through him, a torrent of hurt and anger and fear. "Damn it, Cait, you're supposed to tell me she won't."

"You came looking for someone to trust, Mark, not to bullshit you." She didn't look away. "She's unpredictable, and I can only begin to imagine how she might respond."

"Shit." He leaned forward, face pressed into both hands.

"Does Tori know you slept with her?"

"Yes."

"How did she react to that?"

"Not well." He lifted his head. "She's insecure about Angel. I thought she was moving beyond that, but this might be too much."

"She's insecure about Angel," Caitlin repeated. "Not other women in your past?"

"No, not really."

"So her uncertainty is fixated on Angel." She tapped a fingernail on the table, her brow wrinkling in familiar concentration. Mark shook his head. Nice to know the soap-opera nightmare his life had turned into in a matter of minutes could provide fodder to hone her profiling skills. "Who just happens to be the last woman you had sex with before becoming involved with her."

Maybe she'd just rather open his wrists for him. "Falconetti—"

"That's it."

"What's it?" he snapped.

"She's experiencing a sexual awakening with you, but she probably hasn't come fully into her sexuality, not yet. It's still too soon. She's missing the confidence that comes along with that, and Angel represents everything she's not."

"It's great that you figured it all out, Falconetti, but how does that help me?"

"It doesn't." She bit her bottom lip and her apologetic gaze met his. "You're probably screwed."

"Great." He'd been afraid of that. "Now what am I supposed to do?"

"You have to tell her, today, before it gets out and she hears it from someone else."

"Yeah." He let his lashes fall briefly. "I know."

The distinctive rumble of Tick's truck sounded in the drive, and Mark tried not to cringe. Shit, no telling what trouble this was going to cause there either. He could see the rift in their partnership getting wider by the second. Damn it, all of this because of one careless, stupid action, because he'd been—

"Cookie." Caitlin touched his wrist, brought him out of the self-recriminations. "Don't."

He nodded, taking a quick moment to gather himself. A key grated in the lock, and the door swung open.

"Hey, precious." Tick dumped his keys, the mail and a grocery bag on the island. The small box he juggled on his forearm toppled to the floor with a quiet bang. In immediate response, a coughing cry rose from the bassinet, building rapidly to a wail. "Holy hell, I didn't mean to wake him."

Caitlin slanted a you're-a-dead-man look in Tick's direction and hurried to lift the angry baby into her arms. "You must find a quieter way to enter this house, Lamar Eugene."

"Hey, Cookie." Tick leaned against the island, handheld radio near his ear. "What are you doing here?"

"He dropped by to see me." With the baby tucked beneath her chin, Caitlin swayed him from side to side.

"You're not listening to this?" Tick pointed at the radio and adjusted the volume higher.

"No, I went 10-6 for a while." He patted his side, where his radio should be. Hell, had he left it in the car? Was he that far gone today? "Left my radio in the car. What's going on?"

"You never leave it in the car." Tick looked at him askance then shrugged it off. "10-80 out of Whitman County, that new guy who's been over there less than a month. Just came across the river bridge, headed this way. He's requesting interception."

Mark frowned. "Who's he chasing?"

"Late-model red F-150 with Chandler County tags. Deb's running them, since he's going through our dispatch now."

Oh, hell. A new red Ford? Foreboding hurtled through Mark. Surely not...

"Chandler to Whitman 806, registration comes back as James Isaac Bostick, 113 Schley Road, Coney. No wants or warrants on the vehicle." Deb's calm voice filtered through the slight crackling.

"10-4, Chandler. Continuing pursuit, approximately two miles from county line, request assistance."

"Damn it," Mark muttered. Ten to one, Paul Bostick was driving, even with his license suspended. Apprehension curdled in his gut. This was not going to be good. He lifted his gaze and found his own uneasiness reflected in Tick's dark eyes.

"Chandler C-13 to Whitman 806." His tone cool and capable, Troy Lee broke into the radio silence. "Discontinue pursuit. Suspect won't stop if you continue. We're aware of the suspect's domicile, will 10-91."

Mark nodded along with Troy Lee's suggestion. He didn't see Paul stopping, and they could easily pick him up at home.

"Negative, C-13." A siren wailed behind the Whitman deputy's voice. "Suspect is traveling in excess of ninety."

"806, suspect is known and will not stop. Repeat, suspect will not stop. Discontinue pursuit at the county line." Natural authority laced Troy Lee's voice.

"Negative again, C-13. Just crossed the line, passing Long Lonesome Road."

"What?" Tick frowned at the radio. His gaze jerked to the windows. "There's no way. We'd have heard them come by and even at ninety—"

"He's confusing Old Lonely with Long Lonesome, which means he's chasing that kid straight onto Highway 3, north of the second S curves." Disquiet shivered over Mark's already stretched nerves. "Tell that son of a bitch to stop and get Troy Lee's twenty. Chris's too."

"Chandler C-2 to Whitman 806, cease 10-80 immediately. Repeat, cease 10-80 immediately. C-2 to C-13 and C-5, 10-20."

On his feet, Mark tagged Tick's chest as he headed for the door. "Come on."

"Precious, I'll be back." Radio at his ear, Tick followed him outside as Chris responded with his location.

"C-5 to C-2, southbound on Highway 3, approximately seven miles north of the Flint crossroads."

Troy Lee keyed in behind him. "C-13 to C-2, northbound on Highway 3, just passed PSC Road."

"They're gonna cross over each other." Mark strained his ears, listening for sirens. Nothing. "If he was passing Old Lonely Road, doing ninety, they should be...where?"

"Hell, I can't do that math in my head. Probably...near the Flint crossroads. Troy Lee's closer than Chris." Tick lifted the radio to his mouth again. "C-13, can you intercept with the spike strip?"

"Negative, C-2. If they passed Long Lonesome, suspect is headed in opposite direction. C-5 should be able to intercept."

Mark ground his teeth. "But he didn't pass Long Lonesome—"

"Whitman 806 to Chandler, suspect traveling south on 3, in excess of a hundred." A buzz of static accompanied the deputy's voice.

"That son of a bitch didn't stop when I told him to, in my county?" Tick bounded down the back steps two at a time. "I ought to kick his ass."

"We'll do it together." Mark jogged to the driver's side. He fired the engine and pulled into a three-point turn. He tried to pin down a mental map of the county. His back tires squalled on the pavement as he entered the roadway. "They're going to cross over Troy Lee near the curves, but they're going that fast, no way he has time to put out the strips."

"I know." Tick bounced the radio against his thigh, his jaw tight. "I want Troy Lee in between them and this idiot from Whitman County, to make the stop. And then I want that asshole's badge."

He brought the radio to his mouth, but the Whitman deputy keyed in. "Whitman 806 to Chandler, approaching the curves on 3. 10-20 on assistance...oh, shit!"

Mark's gut heaved to his feet, sending a surge of adrenaline into his chest.

"Chandler, Chandler, Whitman 806. Suspect vehicle is 10-50. Repeat, suspect vehicle is 10-50. Chandler unit 10-50 also. Did you hear me? 10-50, suspect vehicle and Chandler unit."

"Holy hell," Tick muttered. Mark punched the accelerator. Shitshitshit...that had to be Troy Lee. It had to be.

Chris's unit screamed by at the intersection, his voice calling in ETA to dispatch as Deb reported ambulances and wreckers en route.

"Try to raise Troy Lee. See if he's all right." A 10-50 accident call could be anything, including Troy Lee merely putting the unit in the ditch, but Mark didn't like the ominous absence of Troy Lee's voice on the radio.

"C-2 to C-13, copy?" Only Deb's voice and that of responding emergency personnel crackled on the frequency. Tick's mouth tightened, the skin around it pale, and he keyed the mike again. "C-13?"

Nothing. Mark held the wheel tighter. *Damn* it.

Ahead of them, Chris swooped around the first of the curves. His brake lights flared. Mark slowed as he entered the curve and the short straightaway before the second curve, the wicked one with the dip in the road. Blue lights atop Chris's car and the Whitman County unit sparked in the watery winter sunlight.

The scene, what he was seeing, twisted metal and smoke, broken glass and still-spinning wheels, slammed into Mark's brain.

"Oh, sweet Jesus," Tick whispered.

The salon door squeaked as Angel pushed it open. Peroxide and hairspray tickled her nose, but something else entirely made her eyes burn. She was hollow and hurting, and sometimes a girl just needed her mama. She dropped her bag on the bench under the window.

"Hey, baby." Mama looked up from organizing her roller tray. Her gaze sharpened. "What's wrong?"

Angel walked into her embrace and buried her face against the neck that always smelled like Avon Night Odyssey. A sob tried to escape and she closed her raw throat, holding in the wail. "Oh, Mama, it's been the day from hell."

Mama rocked her side to side and patted her back. "Trouble with that young man of yours?"

"No, he's fine. He's great." With a rough sigh, Angel pulled back and knuckled fresh tears from under her eyes. "It's just...stuff. Is Daddy home?"

"Not yet." Still eyeing her with maternal concern, Mama went back to sorting rollers and rods. "He should be here soon. I've got a perm to do before supper."

The door leading to the hallway between the salon and the house swung open, and Hope's oldest daughter Brittany flounced through, her arms full of folded towels. "You're mean, Mama."

"Yes, I am," Hope agreed, settling a load of empty color bottles on the shelf over the sinks. "Get used to it."

"We were just going riding at the river." Brittany shoved towels in the baskets by each salon chair. "You could have let me do that."

"And *you* could just follow the rules." Hope snapped her fingers sideways for emphasis.

"I am so going off to college, just to get away from you."

"Great. In two years, I'll help you pack." Hope pointed toward the hallway. "Right now, go vent your teenage resentment in the laundry room and fold the rest of those towels."

Brittany huffed through the doorway. Hope sank into her salon chair. She graced Angel with a saccharine smile. "Don't you wish you had one of those?"

Angel wasn't touching that one. She perched on Mama's chair. "What's she mad about?"

"She told us she was at one of her friend's houses the other night. Turns out, she was riding around with Paul Bostick. Darryl 'bout had a fit. So she's grounded and she's pissed at the world, especially since he called her earlier, wanting her to go to the river with him and some other kids." Hope shook her head. "I don't like the idea of that boy around her. He's a senior and way too fast for her, if you get my meaning."

Mama slid an ironic look in her direction. "Chickens do come home to roost, you know."

Hope rolled her eyes. "Thanks a lot, Mama."

A big diesel engine growled outside, followed by the thump of boots on the hall floor. Mama tilted her head to the side with a smile. "There's your daddy."

He burst through the door, his beloved scanner in hand. "Marie, where's my power cord? Damn batteries won't hold a charge."

"In the basket on top of the refrigerator." He disappeared back down the hall. Angel and Hope exchanged a look of affectionate amusement. Mama called after him, "What's going on, honey?"

"Bad wreck out on 3." He came back, fiddling with the cord. He plugged the scanner in and finessed the tuning until it squawked and emitted Chandler County's dispatch. "Jeannette was talking about it when I stopped at the Tank and Tummy. Said it just happened."

"Do we know who it is?" Mama stacked racks of rollers in the cart.

The scanner emanated a steady stream of rapid conversation, a series of ten codes and terse voices. Daddy raised the volume. "Jeannette thought it was Bubba Bostick. Said there was a deputy involved." Brows lowered in sudden concern, he looked at Angel. "Your boy's not working today, is he?"

Angel nodded, nerves fluttering in her belly. She strained to make out the voices coming from the black rectangle. That was Tick, calling in arrival-on-scene codes for him and Cookie. She thought that was Chris Parker's voice responding. If it was a bad-enough wreck, all officers on duty would respond, unless they were busy elsewhere. That was it, Troy Lee was busy.

That's the only reason she didn't hear his voice.

Instincts and experience overrode the fear and horror. Mark angled the unit to the side, blocking traffic but leaving room for emergency-response vehicles. He popped the trunk and jumped from the car before Tick finished calling in their arrival. He caught a flash of fluorescent orange—Chris pulling a vest over his head, hazard triangles in hand. Tick met him at the rear and Mark shoved the second first-responder kit at him. "Check the truck. I'll get Troy Lee."

Kit in hand, Tick jogged toward what remained of the red pickup. Sirens screeched closer. Mark took in a quick scan of the scene, committing the details to memory. The truck, pointed north now, wrapped almost in a U around the base of a large oak in the stand of trees on the east side of the road. Thick black skid marks slid sideways over the pavement. Another shorter set marked the road just south, deep ruts scarring the shoulder where Troy Lee had left the roadway.

Mark hurdled the run-off ditch and sprinted across the rutted field. His heart thudded in his ears. Adrenaline pumped into his bloodstream, worry and fear threading tight tentacles around each nerve. The mangled white sheriff's unit rested upside down, yards from the highway, slowly spinning tires giving it the air of a toy car carelessly discarded by a child. Scars and gashes marred the earth, evidence of the number of times Troy Lee had rolled. Glass from shattered windows glittered in the dirt and squad-car paraphernalia strung a path like Hansel and Gretel's breadcrumbs—black Maglite, metal ticket book, blank report forms, handcuffs.

Smoke curled in a lazy stream from the engine compartment. A powerful green tractor idled in the field, and a jeans-clad farmer sprinted toward the car. Mark drew closer. The driver's window no longer existed. An arm extended onto the dirt, vulnerable fingers stained with blood curling upward.

Please don't be dead. God, Troy Lee, please *don't be dead...*

More engines rumbled beneath the scream of sirens. Voices shouted at the roadway. Mark dropped to his knees. He fumbled the kit open and snapped on gloves. Ah hell, this wasn't good. He slid his fingers over Troy Lee's wrist. The pulse beat beneath his fingers, uneven but there. "Troy Lee?"

"Is he alive?" Dale Jenkins, who farmed the surrounding land, knelt by him.

"Yeah." Penlight in hand, Mark rested on his shoulder to get a better look at Troy Lee. God. The seatbelt remained intact, holding him in the seat with his neck and head at an awkward angle, but blood spattered his uniform and the deflated airbag, covered his face, dripping down to soak into the headliner. Small bubbles popped through the crimson with each labored breath. The dash crushed inward, the steering column pinned against his chest.

They had a pulse and he was breathing. That much was good.

"He did it on purpose." Dale's gruff voice seemed breathless with shock. "I saw it."

Mark pulled the lock on the door but didn't attempt to open it. "What?"

"That's Bubba's boy in the truck, isn't it?"

"What do you mean, he did it on purpose?" He wedged his arm farther into the cab and shone the light on Troy Lee's face and torso. Was all that blood coming from his mouth? That wasn't good.

"The truck was on his side when he came around the curve. He went off the road to keep from hitting it."

"The pickup didn't hit him?" Hell, he couldn't assess him like this. They had to get him out. He tried the door, but as he'd suspected, it was jammed shut and wouldn't open.

"Nah, he hit the broken culvert and flipped. I swear, I didn't think he'd ever quit rolling." Dale patted both palms against his thighs in a nervous tattoo. "What can I do to help?"

The trunk had popped loose during impact and more equipment littered the surrounding area. "There should be a crowbar. Find it."

Behind him, the muted roar of the Jaws of Life ripped the air. He glanced over his shoulder. Two EMTs ran toward them across the pitted dirt. Firefighters and more EMTs swarmed the truck. He caught a flash of blue plastic, recognized Tick's dark head in the mass of county officers and state troopers. They tarped the vehicle, shielding the interior from the view of passersby, usually a sure sign of fatalities.

A wet groan burbled at his ear. He jerked his gaze back. "Troy Lee?"

No response. Mark curved his hand around Troy Lee's neck, supporting but not moving. "Hold on for us, Troy Lee. Just hold on."

"Daddy, I don't hear him." Angel forced a false calmness into her voice. A rising panic gripped her throat, but she refused to give in to it.

"Now, honey, that doesn't mean anything." Mama rubbed her shoulder. "He could be busy somewhere else."

"You're right." She tucked her hair behind her ear and tried to laugh at her own fear. She was overreacting, probably because her nerves were stretched thin. "Stupid, isn't it, getting worked up over nothing?"

Mama's comforting rub changed to an affectionate pat. "You just care about him, that's all. We worry about the ones we love." Reflected sunlight flashed through the window. "That must be Sue, for her perm."

"No, it's Darryl. He just ran over Mama's daylily bed." Hope rose from her chair. "What on earth…?"

Running footsteps thumped on the steps and Darryl slammed the door open, his face set in lines of frozen fear. “Where’s Britt?”

“Darryl, what is wrong?”

“Where’s Brittany?” He grabbed her shoulders, his voice cracking. “Where is she, Hope? Tell me you didn’t let her go anywhere.”

“Of course not.” Eyes wide, Hope twisted one arm out of his grasp and gestured behind her. “She’s in the laundry room, folding towels.”

“Oh, thank You, Jesus.” He collapsed, leaning on the counter with a hand over his eyes. A weak laugh escaped him and he looked up. “I tell you, I ain’t been so scared since...hell, since I don’t know when. I was at the hardware store and heard about that wreck. All I could think about was Brittany, her wanting to be with that Bostick boy. Lord, I didn’t even think about calling. I just left my stuff on the counter and came on.”

“So it was Bubba’s boy?” Sympathy loaded Daddy’s sigh.

“That’s what they’re saying. You know Eddie Stowles is a volunteer firefighter. He went running out of the store. Said the kids in the truck were dead. That’s all I had to hear.” Darryl levered away from the counter and opened the small fridge beneath it to retrieve a bottled Coke. The cap popped off with a small hiss. “They’re saying it’s a bad one, that a deputy was killed in it too.”

Panic flushed the back of Angel’s neck with heat, her pulse fluttering like a trapped bird at the base of her throat. A small sound pushed past her lips.

Mama’s firm hand came down on her shoulder. “Now, Angel, we don’t know it’s him.”

“Oh shit.” Darryl paused with the bottle halfway to his mouth. “Is he working today?”

Hope nodded. “She didn’t hear him on the radio earlier, either,” she whispered, half-turned into her husband as though that would protect Angel from the truth.

“He’s probably just...” Darryl motioned with the Coke. “You know, working or something.”

Did that sound as weak to the others as it did to her? Angel slipped from the chair. “You know what? I’m just going to call him, see where he is.”

She snagged her purse from the bench. Her skin crawled

with the weight of all their eyes on her. This whole thing felt weird, like standing on the sidewalk with Cookie had, the way everything after that confrontation with Jim had seemed like a movie. She pawed through her purse. Where was her phone?

"Mama." Tears in her voice, Brittany appeared in the doorway. Instead of folded towels, she carried her cell phone. Her hands shook wildly. "Lyssa just called me. She said Paul and Kaydee and them were in a wreck, and they're all dead. Mama, that's not true, is it? It can't be true, can it?"

Hope hurried to enfold her trembling daughter. "There's been an accident, yes, but we don't know if they're dead." With Brittany pressed to her heart, she looked across the room to hold Angel's gaze. "We don't."

"I just talked to Kaydee this morning, right after I talked to Paul." A horrified moan erupted from Brittany's mouth and she covered it. Tears flowed down her cheeks and her shoulders heaved with silent sobs. "Mommy, Kaydee was texting Lyssa from the truck. A Whitman deputy tried to pull them over and Paul wouldn't stop. She was scared and he wouldn't...and when Lyssa tried to text her back, Kaydee didn't answer. She'd answer if she could, right?"

She dissolved into tears and Darryl joined them, wrapping strong arms about his wife and daughter both. Angel clutched the phone to her chest. Dear Lord in heaven.

"That's Sara Davis's daughter." Mama sank onto her chair, her face gray. She glanced at Brittany. "Baby, who else was with them, do you know?"

Brittany lifted her wet face from Darryl's chest. "Devonte Richardson was coming. Probably Kari and maybe Santana. Lyssa wanted to, but she's failing math and Mr. Del won't let her go anywhere. I don't know...I don't know if there was anybody else. Lyssa had to go because her mama's all upset. They heard from somebody that a guy from the sheriff's department was killed and they don't know if it's Lyssa's uncle or not."

Eyes closed, Hope held on to her, whispering quiet prayers into her glossy hair. Angel glanced from her mama's pale face to her daddy's. Her heart turned in on itself, but she made herself sit down calmly. She flipped her cell open and scrolled through to Troy Lee's contact info. "I'm just going to call him and see what I can find out."

The phone rang and rang and rang again. On the sixth ring, Troy Lee's voice filled her ear, strong and resonant.

"Hey, this is Troy Lee. I can't take your call, but if you leave your name and number, I'll call you back as soon as I can..."

Chapter Seventeen

"So are y'all talking about a date yet?"

"Other than sometime next year? No." Tori accepted the can of soda Layla extended and grimaced. "Mama wants a big wedding."

"Mama wants?" Layla nudged her in the side as they entered the hall leading to the ER. "What about what Tori and Cookie want?"

"We just want to get married." Tori dodged a gurney next to the wall. "Although I wouldn't mind doing so in a really great dress."

"And in front of a hundred guests, with six bridesmaids in purple tulle and Cookie in a tux," Layla teased.

"That too. Except the purple tulle." Tori made a moue, then completely ruined it by laughing. "I was thinking eggplant satin instead—"

"Layla, I need you." Jay Mackey appeared at the end of the hallway and waved them forward. Urgency tightened his face. "Tori, glad you're here."

Her stomach knotted before the cool ease of experience slid into place. "What's going on?"

"Multiple-injury accident, possible fatalities. Ambulances en route, ETA three minutes." He talked rapidly, holding one push-through door open for them. "Nancy is over in Valdosta at a seminar. Tori, think you could do family counseling for us?"

"Of course." Nancy was the new grief counselor, and before she'd arrived to replace her predecessor, Tori had performed double duty by stepping into that role.

"Great. As soon as we have positive victim identification and patient status, Lorraine will help you get started." He pulled a thin disposable robe over his scrubs. Layla shoved her arms into a similar garment. While he tugged on gloves, she lifted the receiver on the wall phone, paging doctors. Jay swung open the ambulance bay doors and stepped onto the dock, arms over his chest. Sirens wailed closer and closer.

The first ambulance turned onto the side street and into the bay. Clark Dempsey jumped from the cab and rushed to open the back doors and assist his partner in unloading the patient. They pushed the gurney inside, Jim Tyre rattling patient information as Jay directed them to a room. "Seventeen-year-old male involved in collision, pulse is eighty-five, BP is one-ten over eighty, respiratory twenty, severe head trauma, fracture to the right arm..."

Layla appeared and the four of them shifted the moaning boy to the exam table. Layla looked up from checking his airway. "What's on the way?"

"Three teens. Critical with prolonged extrication," Clark replied. "And a deputy. They were pulling him out as we left."

Deputy? Unnerved, Tori glanced at him, but before she could ask, a second ambulance thundered into the bay. Jay pulled his gloves and grabbed a fresh pair. "Layla, you know what to do. I've got this one."

"Do you have his personal effects?" Layla palpated the boy's chest, her hands moving with gentle efficiency. Jim produced a manila envelope and Layla tilted her head in Tori's direction. "She needs those."

Ambulance doors clanged open, followed by the metallic ring of a stretcher being unfolded. More male voices wafted into the hall as rubber wheels whispered on waxed tile. "Sixteen-year-old female involved in collision, no pulse, no respiration, BP is not measurable. Massive thoracic and skull trauma involved. Intubated at the scene, defibrillation attempts unsuccessful."

The plaid curtain separating the two cubicles fluttered. Tori caught a glimpse of Jay checking the girl's pupils. Tick was there, bagging the teenager, while an EMT performed chest compressions. Blood matted long blonde hair, soaked a Chandler-Haynes High cheerleading hoodie. Shaken, Tori averted her gaze and opened the envelope to extract a wallet. She flipped it open.

James Paul Bostick. Oh Lord, Bubba Bostick's son?

"Tori." Lorraine touched her shoulder and indicated the hall with a tilt of her head. "I've got the girl's ID. Come on and you can use the phone in the staff lounge."

"Thank you." She glanced at the driver's license in her hand. Kaydee Sierra Davis. She spun to glance back at the girl lying so still while they tried hard to bring her back. That was Kaydee?

"Tori, are you all right?" Concern creased Lorraine's broad face.

"I know her." Covering her mouth, Tori blinked hard. "I used to babysit her. Her mother is my first cousin."

"I'm sorry, hon." Lorraine patted her shoulder.

"I need to..." Tori drew herself up, gathering reserves. "I need to start making these calls."

More medical personnel rushed down the hall to meet yet another ambulance. Lord, when would it stop? Chris Parker accompanied this gurney, bearing a frighteningly still teenage boy. The paramedic bagging him talked rapidly. "Seventeen-year-old male, no pulse, no BP, no respiration. Massive skull trauma, suspected spinal cord injury..."

Chris went as far as the exam room, then backtracked with another manila envelope in hand. His eyes wilder than Tori had ever seen them, he jerked his chin at her in greeting and extended the packet. "His effects plus the cell phones we found in the vehicle. They're ringing and buzzing constantly."

"Word's out in the county then," Lorraine said. "Worried parents will be calling here next."

"Chris." Tori caught his arm and he flinched. She released him immediately. "One of the paramedics said there was a deputy involved?"

"Yeah—"

A new gurney shoved through the doors, Nikki Pantone reciting patient information to a young doctor. "Twenty-six-year-old male involved in collision. Pulse is fifty-seven, BP ninety over sixty, respiration fifteen, no breath sounds on the right side. Nasal fracture, oropharyngeal airway in place with intubation, severe thoracic trauma, suspected haemothorax..."

As they passed, Nikki still talking, Tori glimpsed dark brown hair and a familiar tan uniform spattered with blood. Swelling and the bag valve mask obscured his face. "Is that Troy Lee?"

Chris nodded. Mark strode through the bay doors, rifling through another manila packet. He pulled out a cell phone and lifted his head, shuttered gaze tangling with hers for a split second before tracking to the identification she held. "Are you notifying families?"

She nodded and he pressed the slim silver rectangle into her palm. "This is Troy Lee's. He'll have his next of kin programmed in as an emergency contact—"

"His stepmother," Chris said. "Her name is Christine."

Mark's fingers curled around hers for a moment, warm and real in the surreal chaos of the afternoon. "Will you call her?"

"Of course."

He pulled his gaze from hers and tagged Chris on the chest. "I need you to come with me. We've got to find Angel."

"Yes, ma'am, I understand you can't tell me where he is." Desperate fear bit into Angel. She clutched the phone so hard her hand hurt and concentrated on keeping her voice steady. "I just want to know if he was involved in an accident."

"I'm sorry, Ms. Henderson." A mask of cool professionalism cloaked the dispatcher's voice. "But I have to follow procedure and it's against department policy to release any information about an officer to unauthorized persons."

Angel killed the call and pressed the cool metal to her forehead. She wasn't an unauthorized person. She was the woman he loved, the woman who loved him, and damn it, no one would tell her anything. She'd gotten the same song and dance from the hospital, when she'd finally been able to get through to the jammed switchboard. No, they couldn't tell her if a Troy Lee Farr was in the emergency room. No, they couldn't tell her if he had been admitted. No, no, no...

"They won't tell me anything." She dropped her hand and looked at her family. "He's not answering. He's not calling me back. No one will tell me *anything.*" Her voice rose, a note of hysteria audible even to her, and she clasped a palm over her mouth. "What do I do now?"

No one replied, but Hope straightened, her gaze riveted on the window. Unsettled by her sister's expression, Angel spun. An unmarked silver unit purred up the driveway. The bottom of the world fell away, and she waited for the abyss to swallow her up.

The car stopped next to Darryl's truck, and Cookie and Chris Parker climbed out. Cookie jogged up the walkway toward the front door. Freed from her painful paralysis, Angel burst out the salon door. "Cookie?"

He turned in her direction, his face haggard and strained. Her gaze locked onto the front of his shirt, stained with dirt and dried blood. Her knees gave and she sagged to the top step. Lord help her. It was true. It was him, and it didn't matter how many messages she left.

"He's dead." The whisper slipped past her lips, the words unreal, nasty in their wrongness. She lifted her gaze to Cookie's as he reached the steps. "He's dead. Isn't he?"

"No." He shook his head and bent to kneel below her so they were eye to eye. "No, he's not."

The tears came, silent sobs tearing her throat. Cookie wrapped her close, tucking her face into the warmth of his neck. His familiar spicy scent enveloped her, and he held her, not the right man, but still her friend after all.

"He's alive, Angel, but he's hurt, pretty badly," he murmured near her ear. "We need to go."

She nodded, scrubbing the dampness from her cheeks. "And you'll tell me what happened on the way?"

"I'll tell you anything you need to know." With gentle hands, he pulled her to her feet. "I promise."

"I need to get..." She turned toward the house, but Hope was already there, pressing her purse into her hands.

"Go on." Hope kissed her cheek and hugged her tight.

In the car, Cookie gave her a brief rundown of the accident. She twined her bag's strap around and around her hand. Troy Lee had left the road at approximately sixty miles per hour, struck a culvert, flipped end over end, then sideways over and over. Horrific images enhanced by every adventure movie she'd ever seen played in her head.

"He was unconscious when we pulled him from the car." Cookie darted a glance at her in the passenger seat. Chris Parker had ducked into the backseat and remained a silent presence behind her. With capable hands, Cookie drove quickly, the unit eating the miles. "But he's responding to pain and he was making sounds before we intubated him, and that's good. The front of the car crushed inward on impact, and the steering column...he has chest and abdominal trauma from that. The

EMTs think he has facial fractures. Chris and I left the ER as they were taking him back, so I don't know much more than that."

Nodding, Angel closed her eyes. With fear holding her by the throat, she couldn't have spoken if her life had depended on it. Imaginings invoked by Cookie's description of Troy Lee's injuries flickered on her eyelids. Memories overlaid them, seconds and seconds of belief, strung together in a montage of hope and love—a chilly night in a parking lot and his mouth descending for that first kiss, her porch light glinting off his hair as he grinned at her and held a fortune cookie aloft, strong arms around her as she revealed her pregnancy, blazing awe in his eyes when she told him she loved him, the feathery touch of his lips on the skin above her unborn child.

She held on to those moments, falling into them.

Vehicles spilled out of the small parking lot adjacent to the emergency room. People, many of them teenagers, milled on the steps outside. City officers directed the flow of traffic and performed crowd control.

"Jesus," Chris breathed.

"Yeah," Cookie responded, his voice tight. A Coney police officer waved him into the area behind the hospital, reserved for authorized personnel. Patrol cars—county, city and Georgia State Patrol—lined the back fence. Somehow, Cookie managed to jockey his unit into that row as well. Groups of uniformed officers dotted the area outside the ER, including the long, wide concrete ambulance dock.

Angel tucked her hair behind her ears and looked up at Cookie as he opened her door. "What are they all doing here? I thought there were only two vehicles involved."

Cookie nodded. She stepped from the car and he took her elbow. "They're here for Troy Lee."

The show of brotherhood and respect left her breathless. As the wide doors drew closer and the reality beyond it bigger, gratitude grew for Cookie's steady hand beneath her arm. Her whole body seemed weak and shaky, ready to collapse.

"Are you all right?" he murmured above her ear, fingers tightening.

She met concerned gray eyes. "No."

Several officers spoke to him and Chris along the way. He nodded and made brief responses, but didn't stop. Dodging the big doors, he guided her to a smaller side entrance and hit a buzzer there. Moments later, the lock clanged, and he tugged the door open and ushered her inside.

The chaos outside had only been a precursor. The ER interior bustled with urgent movement and imperative voices. A nurse ran down the hall to a cubicle, her arms laden with supplies. Outside that doorway, a small group of Chandler County officers, in uniform and out, hovered.

Cookie locked gazes with Tick Calvert as they reached the gathering. "What do we know?"

"They're still working on him. His breathing is abnormal and his blood pressure is falling." Tick jerked his chin toward the doorway. A pastel plaid curtain blocked their view. "They're doing a sonogram, looking for internal bleeding. Tori called his stepmother. She and the sisters are on their way."

His weary gaze flicked to Angel then back to Cookie's, leaving the impression he'd say more if she hadn't been there. Cookie squeezed her elbow. "It may be a while. Let's get you out of the hallway."

"I don't want to leave him."

"I know, but you've had a rough day and you have to take care of you too." He urged her toward the nurse's station. "Come on."

"Tori? The Davises are here."

At Lorraine's subdued voice, Tori lifted her head from her folded arms and nodded. "I'm coming."

She scrubbed a hand over her burning eyes and rose from the hard plastic chair. Lord, she didn't want to do this. Earlier had been bad enough, calling Troy Lee's stepmother, hearing her fear and horror over the phone. What had followed had been even worse, when a hospital volunteer, violating every regulation in the book, had allowed two of Kaydee's friends in to see her body. Calming the hysterical girls had been next to impossible.

As she followed Lorraine, she twisted her engagement ring around and around her finger. With each revolution, a prayer for strength and the right words beat in her soul. Lorraine stopped outside the tiny staff lounge. "I'll be right out here if you need me."

Tori pressed her hand. "Thanks."

With a sharp inhale, she pushed open the door. Sara Davis, seated on one of the same plastic chairs, jumped to her feet, and her husband Trace spun from his post at the window. Sara pressed a hand over her heart, her brown eyes wide and wild with apprehension. “Oh, Tori, thank God. Where’s Kaydee and what is going on? The nurse who called said there’d been an accident, and there are all those people outside. They’re saying some kids were killed, but that can’t be the same accident. It can’t. My Lord, Kaydee just had that little wreck before Thanksgiving and it demolished her car, but she was fine. *Fine*—”

“Sara. Let Tori talk.” Trace laid his hand on her shoulder and she stepped out from under it. He gazed at Tori with calm steadiness. “What can you tell us?”

“There was an accident and Kaydee was involved.” Tori swallowed and indicated the table and chairs centering the room. “Why don’t we sit down?”

“I don’t want to sit down.” Sara’s voice rose and she backed up a step. “I want to see my daughter.”

“Honey, please. Let’s hear what she has to say.”

Sara glanced at his outstretched hand and stepped past him to sink into a chair. She folded her hands on the table, knuckles white with tension. Trace’s eyes lingered on her down-bent head, then a visible shudder ran along his body and he pulled out the chair next to hers.

Tori took the chair on Sara’s other side. “Kaydee was with Paul Bostick and some other teens today.”

“No.” Sara shook her head, an emphatic negative. “She’s not allowed to be with him—”

Trace’s gentle hand at her shoulder stopped her. He lifted his gaze to Tori’s. “Go on.”

He knew. The knowledge shivered through Tori as the agonized awareness dawned in his eyes. Tori swallowed. “A Whitman County deputy attempted to stop Paul for speeding. Paul didn’t pull over and the officer pursued them into Chandler County and onto Highway 3. The truck they were riding in hit a tree. Kaydee was in the front passenger seat. She wasn’t wearing a seat belt and she had to be extricated from the vehicle.”

“Jesus Christ.” Trace closed his eyes.

Sara’s throat convulsed. “What are you saying?”

Tori leaned forward, hands out. Sara wrapped cold fingers around Tori's. "She didn't have a pulse at the scene, and the paramedics performed CPR between there and the emergency room here. When she arrived, she was still unresponsive and attempts at resuscitation failed. I'm sorry, Trace, Sara, but she died."

"No. Oh no, please." Sara clapped a hand over her mouth, her spine-chilling moan lifting the hair on Tori's arms. "No! It's not true."

"Sweetheart." Trace tried to put his arms around her.

"Don't touch me." Sara jerked away from him. She turned fierce eyes on Tori. "I want to see her."

"Of course." Tori rose and gestured toward the door. "Lorraine and I will take you. I should tell you that her appearance will be altered—"

"I don't care." Sara's face crumpled. "I just want to see my baby."

Tori held the door. His features set, Trace didn't attempt to touch his wife again as Lorraine escorted them to the cubicle. She held the curtain for them to enter, keeping the fabric at an angle where others passing by couldn't see in.

Sara stopped short, hand over her mouth again, gaze locked on Kaydee's battered face. "Oh..."

She moved in slow motion, trailing alongside the gurney, touching her daughter's ankle, her knee, her hand. Finally, she curved her palm around Kaydee's jaw, stroking the tangled hair from her forehead. "Oh Kaydee darling, my baby...my beautiful, beautiful girl..."

Tori closed her eyes, trying to keep a wave of burning tears at bay. She wasn't supposed to get involved, she wasn't, but how could she not?

"Tori." Lorraine whispered at her ear. "The deputy has arrived with Miss Francie, Devonte Richardson's grandmother, and she's at the nurse's station. I'll stay with the Davises so you can talk with her."

"Thank you," Tori murmured. She opened her eyes, catching a glimpse of Sara as she leaned to press kisses across Kaydee's forehead. Tori's heart squeezed. She slipped into the hall and turned Mark's ring about her finger.

Lord, please, get me through the rest of this day. Help me, give me the words, the compassion...

When Mark returned to the hallway, several of their colleagues had drifted away, leaving only Chris and Tick waiting. Tick leaned against the wall, cell at his ear, as Mark joined them.

"Yeah, precious, I'm all right. Just tired." Tick rubbed a hand over his mouth. "I don't know how long I'll be, but I'll call you. Love you." He clicked the phone closed and returned it to his belt. He nodded at Mark. "Angel okay?"

"No." She was a big bundle of fear and nerves, ready to collapse. Mark hadn't wanted her caught up in the chaos in the waiting room. Instead, Lorraine had arranged for her to wait in the nurse's lounge, where they could check in on her, but she wouldn't witness what was going on with Troy Lee's care. Mark jerked his head toward the cubicle. "Any word?"

Chris didn't take his eyes off the curtain. "Layla came by a couple of minutes ago. Part of his ribcage broke and separated. He's bleeding into the lung cavity and maybe his gut. They're pumping blood into him and draining his chest, but Mackey wants to manage it without surgery."

Tick dragged both hands down his face. "They're having a hard time keeping him stable."

Mark nodded. "What about the kids?"

"Paul Bostick is upstairs in surgery. Head injury and ruptured spleen." Tick's mouth tightened. "They LifeFlighted Santana Mixon to Tallahassee. Kaydee Davis and Devonte Richardson were dead on arrival."

"Damn."

"I knew Devonte was gone when I got to the truck. He was...there was just no way. But Kaydee... I thought she might make it if we could just get her out. Santana got thrown forward and trapped under the dash, and they had to extract her before we could take Kaydee out." Tick talked in a monotone, staring into the middle distance. "She was talking, not really coherent, but talking. She was bleeding and I was holding, um, keeping pressure on the artery. To stop the flow, you know? I thought, if I could just hold on long enough, hard enough, if they could just get her out...she kept asking for her mama. Sara's my cousin, did I tell you that?"

"No, you didn't."

"She passed out before they could cut through the door."

Tick shook himself free of the memory, his gaze losing the faraway look. “I bagged her all the way here and Denny did CPR, but there was...it was too late.”

Footsteps squeaked on the tile. Mark glanced down the hall. A state trooper approached, accompanied by a Whitman County deputy.

Visible tension gripped Chris’s body. Tick straightened away from the wall, his gaze freezing over. A matching icy anger chilled Mark, the memory of Troy Lee’s bloody face flashing in his mind. He took a step forward and stopped. Probably not a good idea to get too close to the guy. If he did, somebody might get hurt.

“Boys.” Keith Hickey, the trooper who headed up the accident-reconstruction team out of Post 40, removed a notebook from his chest pocket. “I need to get your statements since I missed you all at the scene.”

“You son of a bitch.” On a low feral growl, Tick ignored Keith and advanced on the Whitman deputy. The man’s throat moved in a hard swallow and he backed up.

“Calvert.” A note of nervousness colored Keith’s voice. “Wait a minute—”

“He told you to stop.” Teeth clenched, Chris spoke from behind Tick’s shoulder. “Twice, Troy Lee told you the kid wouldn’t pull over. Told you to stop. You ignored him.”

Unease flickered over Keith’s face. “Boys—”

“I fucking told you to stop.” Tick shoved his shaking index finger into the deputy’s chest. “Those kids are dead. My officer’s in there, his chest crushed. Because of you.”

“It’s not my fault.” His back against the wall, the deputy shook his head. “That boy didn’t have to run—”

“And you didn’t have to bring that chase into our county after you were told to stop.” Mark took up position at Tick’s other shoulder. The deputy’s gaze flicked over the three of them. The skin around his mouth went pale. “Man, this is your fault and you know it.”

“Your guy turned off the road. He didn’t have to—”

“You’re blaming Troy Lee?” Chris lunged at him, but Tick’s raised arm brought him up short.

“No. This isn’t the time or the place.” Tick pushed his finger into the deputy’s chest once more and kept him pinned with his glacial gaze. “I’m going to have your badge. Then I’m going to see your ass in jail for this. If he dies...you're ours." With deliberate dismissal, he glanced sideways at Keith. "You want your statements, fine. But you get this son of a bitch who's not worth the sweat off Troy Lee's balls out of here first. He doesn't deserve to be here."

"Angel?" The soft inquiry pulled her from yet another intricate pleating of her purse strap. Heart pounding, Angel looked up. Cookie stood inside the door. Strain and weariness dragged at his features.

Angel came to her feet, the unrelenting fear trying to choke her. "Do you know something?"

Cookie shook his head and held out a hand. "Troy Lee's family has arrived and Dr. Mackey is going to meet with them in a few minutes. I came to get you, see if there was anything you needed."

She needed Troy Lee. "I'm fine. I just really want to know what's going on."

Cookie squeezed her hand. "Let's go then."

Over the past couple of hours, Lorraine and Tori had brought her water or tea she didn't drink and occasional empty updates, simply more of the same. The crowds had drifted away, the teens and their parents going to the homes of the deceased teenagers. Hope and Darryl had come but after an hour had taken Brittany to Kaydee's family home, where her friends gathered. Paul's family and friends waited upstairs in the surgical unit. The main waiting room now held isolated groups of cops and other emergency personnel, Troy Lee's friends.

Cookie touched her shoulder and spoke near her ear. "I'm going to check with Lorraine, see where we need to be. I'll be right back."

She folded her arms as he walked away. The small bruises above her elbows ached and she glanced down at them. That afternoon, when she'd put them there, seemed a lifetime away, those problems that had seemed so huge paling beside the fear of losing Troy Lee. He'd been right, with his insistence that they were all that mattered, that everything else would fall into place.

Clark Dempsey separated himself from a small group and approached her. "Hey, Angel."

She made herself smile, although it was a stretch. "Hey, Clark."

"I'm really sorry about this."

"I am too, but thank you." She glanced around for Cookie. He'd said he'd be right back. Impatience and worry gathered beneath her skin.

"You couldn't have picked a better man."

"What?" Distracted, she looked up at Clark. He gazed back with eyes both serious and gentle.

"Troy Lee. I knew he'd treat you right if you ever gave him the chance. Why do you think I started bringing him around the bar?"

Her lips parted in surprise and a small smile lit his face. He leaned forward and lowered his voice. "You didn't really think I was going to let you marry Jim's selfish ass, did you? You deserved better."

"Angel?" Cookie appeared at her side. "Come with me."

With his hand at her back, he ushered her toward the nurse's station. The frustration of being a pinball, slammed and pushed around by a cosmic whim, took hold. People kept moving her, taking her here and there, but never really giving her anything to hold on to.

Beyond the nurse's desk lay a smaller waiting room. There, a handful of Troy Lee's closest colleagues gathered, along with a woman with short blonde hair and two girls, whose shiny brown hair and vivid blue eyes echoed Troy Lee's. The younger of the two girls, her face tearstained, clung to the woman's arm.

Clad in wrinkled scrubs, Jay Mackey stepped in through the opposite door. "Mrs. Farr?"

The blonde nodded. "Yes."

"I'm Dr. Mackey. I'm sorry you had to wait." He focused in on her. "The first thing I want you to know is that Troy Lee is stable and we're preparing to move him from the trauma center to a room."

"Thank God." Christine Farr laid a hand over her heart, the intense relief on her face mirroring that coursing through Angel.

"However, we still have several days ahead of us." A cautionary note entered Dr. Mackey's words. "Our main concern right now is the injuries to his torso. Impact with the steering wheel broke a section of his ribcage free, a condition we call flail chest, which causes unequal pressure in the pulmonary cavity. We've wired the ribs and they will heal on their own with time. We can treat the pressure problem through the use of a ventilator, although we'll have to be vigilant, as prolonging the time spent on the ventilator can increase the chances of infection and injury to his lung tissue. The bleeding in his chest is controlled at this point, and the sonogram showed no bleeding in his abdomen, another positive."

"So the bleeding from his mouth...that was from the chest injury?" Christine wrapped her arm around her daughter, who continued to cling to her. Her other daughter hovered near her shoulder.

Dr. Mackey shook his head. "Somewhat, but he sustained some facial injuries, mainly a nasal fracture and a blow to his jaw. Again, the positive is that there is no skull fracture. When you see him, though, he probably won't look like himself because of the edema and contusions. He's been in and out of consciousness, and he's surprisingly alert when he's awake. We won't be using narcotic analgesics, but rather a nerve block, so that level of alertness should increase. However, he won't be able to talk because of the ventilator."

With a tremulous laugh, Christine rubbed her hand up and down her daughter's arm. "Oh, he'll find that totally frustrating, won't he?"

The girl giggled shakily and turned her face into Christine's neck. A smile touched Dr. Mackey's normally serious visage. "I'll send Lorraine to let you know as soon as he's in a room. He can have visitors." He glanced around at the small crowd. "But let's restrict it to one or two of you at a time and keep it short. He's going to tire easily." He inclined his head at Christine. "I'll be by on rounds later to check in on him. If you need anything before that, have the nurse page me."

"Thank you." As he exited and the others left with murmured goodbyes, Christine turned to Angel, her green eyes glowing beneath a sheen of tears. "You have to be his Angel. I am so very happy to finally meet you." She stepped forward to wrap Angel in a tight hug. "I wish it were under different circumstances."

"Me too." Angel held on a moment, needing contact with this other woman who loved Troy Lee, and let go. She brushed disheveled hair from her face. "I've heard a lot about you."

Her mouth trembling, Christine bracketed Angel's cheeks. "Oh, you're everything he said you were."

"Mom." The younger girl nudged Christine's side.

With an indulgent expression, Christine drew her forward. "This is my daughter Ellis."

"Hey." Ellis wiggled her fingers in a wave and wiped tears from under her eyes, smearing heavy mascara. The angle of her chin was reminiscent of Troy Lee's.

"And I'm Montgomery." The other girl, a little taller, extended a hand as elegant as the lilt in her voice. "He is so in love with you."

"Yes, he is." Blinking against obvious tears, Christine stroked a palm down Montgomery's hair. "I just talked to him this morning and he was so excited...oh, that reminds me."

While she turned to dig in her voluminous fabric purse, Angel rubbed damp palms down her thighs. She was glad to meet them, but the day was telling on her, the stress and the worry and the lack of food leaving her edgy and nauseous. Her head spun, the world tilting off kilter.

"I'm probably stealing his thunder, but I don't care." Christine turned, trying to smile through a veil of moisture. Angel concentrated on breathing through her mouth, trying to ward off the weird waves of shadows at the edges of her vision. "He sent me all the way across Atlanta this morning to retrieve this and I know he planned to pick it up this weekend. He wanted you to have it and I don't think I should wait to give it to you. You need it now."

Needed it now? What was she talking about?

Christine pressed a small, soft square into her hand. Angel opened her fingers and stared down at the burgundy velvet ring box. Swallowing, she lifted her gaze to Christine's and opened her mouth on a protest. Her ears buzzed.

"Mom..." Concern trembled in Montgomery's voice and she edged toward Angel.

"Angel, are you all right?" Christine reached for her, hands warm on Angel's suddenly clammy skin.

"I think so." Clutching the box in one hand, Angel fumbled for the chair behind her. "I'm just lightheaded."

"I can't imagine why." Christine sat beside her and smoothed the hair from her forehead. "You've had a horrid day, obviously, and then I spring that ring on you...that was thoughtless of me."

"No, it wasn't. It simply surprised me." Feeling less like she was going to fall on her face, Angel rubbed her fingers across the plush box. She'd certainly never expected this. Now she was afraid to open it, wasn't even sure she should. Shouldn't she wait for Troy Lee to offer it to her?

"I wish they'd hurry." Ellis spoke from the window that faced the hallway. She traced the edge of the blinds. "I want to see him."

You and me both, honey. Angel glanced at the clock. Almost eight.

What was taking so long?

Chapter Eighteen

The pain had disappeared.

Troy Lee's eyes snapped open. He stared at the same hospital ceiling that had drifted over him whenever he'd come to before. The ceiling was the same, but the overwhelming pain in his chest and face, the agony that had made him want to scream, but had drawn only broken whimpers from his throat, was simply gone.

It scared the hell out of him. He tried to swallow against the wash of panic and couldn't. Voices hovered beyond the bed, and he tried to call out to them. Nothing emerged. He couldn't use his throat.

Intense pressure remained, pushing in and out of his chest with each breath. Another sound leached into his consciousness, a rhythmic, sickeningly familiar hiss and click. The panic detonated into full-fledged horror. A ventilator. The pain had gone and he was on a ventilator. The nauseating sense of rolling in the patrol car, the stomach-turning crunch of the steering wheel slamming into his chest blasted into his brain. Had he broken his back?

He tried to breathe through the fear and couldn't, each inhale and exhale controlled by the hated machine. Not being in control of his own breathing was intolerable. He flexed a hand, grateful to find he could move, and reached for the tube invading his mouth.

"No, no, no." Layla wrapped firm fingers around his wrist. "Leave that alone."

Anger and alarm swirled into one entity within him, and he struggled free of her, going for the tube again. His elbow slammed into the IV rack, knocking it sideways. The intravenous tube tore loose from his hand, the stinging a sharp burn under his skin.

Thank God he could still feel something.

"Calm down." Trying to subdue him, Layla tossed a glance over her shoulder. "You guys want to help me here?"

"Troy Lee. Stop it." Cookie placed gentle pressure on his shoulder, Calvert pinning the other just as gingerly. They looked down at him with pale, tense faces. "Just stop, okay? You're gonna hurt yourself."

He strained, without much success, against them, but managed to twist his wrist away from Layla before she could replace the IV line.

"Damn it," she muttered. She laid a hand on his brow and held his head still. "Troy Lee, look at me. *Look* at me."

His pulse beat under his skin. He could feel the panicked thumping throughout his body. He focused his gaze on the ceiling, seeking the midpoint, needing to breathe on his own.

"Look at me." She gentled his forehead and finally he moved his gaze to hers, finding her dark eyes soft and soothing. "Listen. You have to be on the ventilator right now. You have fractures to your ribcage and we have to keep the pressure equalized."

Hiss, click, pause. Hiss, click, pause. The wrong damn rhythm, everything out of his control.

"I need you to calm down and cooperate, or we'll have to sedate you." Layla continued to stroke his brow, her fingers firm and warm at his wrist. "You don't want that, I know. Much better to be awake."

He squeezed his eyes shut, a scream of frustration building, a scream he couldn't release.

"Come on, Troy Lee, calm down." Cookie's hand circled over his shoulder. "Focus and get it together. They want to move you upstairs, and you've got people waiting to see you."

Angel. He'd thought he'd heard her voice, once, when he'd come to while Mackey manipulated his chest and abdomen. His lids snapped up and he focused on Cookie's steady gray eyes.

Calvert squeezed his other shoulder. "Let Layla put your IV back in and we'll go upstairs with you."

He blinked rapidly and stared up at the ceiling wavering before his eyes. He relaxed as much as his quivering muscles would allow. Slowly, Layla released him and within moments had the line restored to his hand.

"All right." She smiled down at him. "How about we let these two push you upstairs?"

Like he had a say in or control over any of this.

The ceiling pattern—tile, tile, light, tile, tile, light—passed above him down a hall and into an elevator. Reality washed in and out, waves of drowsiness ending in a piercing moment of awareness soon washed back into overwhelming exhaustion. He'd been less tired after finishing a marathon.

"Here we go." Layla's voice pulled him from the lethargy and he opened his eyes to find himself in a cookie-cutter hospital room, although he couldn't see much more than the ceiling and the hideous floral valance over the big windows. She left the rails in place but elevated him to a half-lying, half-sitting position and arranged his tubing out of the way. She patted his arm. "Dr. Mackey will be by on rounds shortly. I'm going to go get your family, okay?"

He hated her damn rhetorical questions. He couldn't answer her. He closed his eyes, trying to block out the frustration. He wanted off the ventilator and out of this damn bed, and he wanted Angel, not necessarily in that order.

"We're going to go and let you rest." Cookie spoke somewhere over his left shoulder. "We'll see you tomorrow."

Troy Lee tried to nod and realized here was yet another form of communication denied to him. He lifted a finger in affirmation without opening his eyes.

Calvert made a small sound of amusement. "One finger for yes, two for no, huh?"

Troy Lee raised a different single-finger salute. Calvert chuckled and laid an easy hand on his shoulder. "You did good, Troy Lee. We couldn't have asked for better."

The acceptance and approval in that weary voice warmed him, but he really needed the warm-and-fuzzy of having Angel close. He held aloft an affirmative finger and moments later the door swished closed behind his colleagues. He would have sighed, but all he got was a hiss, click, pause. Hell, he couldn't even grind his teeth.

This was going to be a bitch.

He dozed in fits, his muscles jittering and jerking him awake, the fatigue pulling him back under. A nurse appeared to adjust the ventilator and put him flat on his back again, a move that irritated the hell out of him. Finally, he drowsed once more.

"Oh, Mom." Ellis's tearful voice seeped into his consciousness. "He looks like when Dad..."

Her words trailed away. He opened his eyes, blinking, to find the room dimmer than when Layla, Cookie and Calvert had brought him up.

"He's awake," Montgomery whispered. She leaned over him, brushing a kiss across his forehead. "Hello, Troy-boy."

She sounded as shaky as Ellis. Remorse stabbed at him. They shouldn't have to see this, not if it raised memories of their father's death. He lifted a wobbly hand to touch a finger first to Montgomery's cheek, then Ellis's. She caught his wrist and pressed a kiss to his palm.

"Hello, my darling boy." On his other side, Christine bent and pressed her cheek to his brow. Her loving caress fluttered along his jaw, where a mild soreness throbbed, and she pulled back to look down at him with soft, luminous eyes. "We've been so very worried about you."

His gaze tracked from her face to his sisters. He loved them all, was glad to see them, but where was Angel?

Christine touched his face with gentle fingers. "You look tired. I'm going to take your sisters and get them something to eat, check into a hotel." She directed a smile over her shoulder, toward his feet, beyond his range of vision. "That way the two of you can have a little time alone together. I'm sure you need it."

After more kisses from his sisters, Christine ushered them out. His lids fell as he tried to gather what reserves he had left. There wasn't much.

"Oh, Troy Lee." Angel breathed the shaky words next to his ear, her cheek just touching his. She stroked his neck, his temple, as if he was made of the finest, most fragile glass. "I love you. I was so frightened..."

She was crying. He could hear it in her voice, feel the moisture of her tears on his skin. He fumbled for her hand. The frustration of enforced silence seared him again. He wanted to return those words of love, reassure her. She twined her fingers through his and rested her lips against his temple. Weariness swamped him, his lids too heavy to keep open.

She whispered something, but he only caught part of it, about realizing the only things that really mattered. He squeezed their hands together and fell into the waiting slumber.

A damp chill wrapped around the night air. Mark dragged in a lungful, hoping the cold would hit him with a charge of energy. It didn't. He was wiped out, physically, mentally, emotionally.

He sank onto the one of the benches that dotted the covered area in front of the hospital and patted his chest pocket. Damn it, no gum. Wonder where he'd left that? Probably the same place his jacket was. At the station, maybe. He'd run by there and pick it up after he took Tick home. Elbows on his knees, he leaned forward and rested his face in his hands. Stupid, really, to be concerned about trivial stuff like gum and jackets and even giving Tick a ride.

Wasn't like he didn't have bigger things to worry about.

The electronic entrance doors swished open, and light footsteps clicked on the concrete. He didn't lift his head.

"What are you doing out here?" Tori touched his nape. "It's cold. Where's your coat?"

He shrugged. She feathered her fingertips through his hair. Against his fingers, he squeezed his eyes shut. She straightened and skirted the bench to sit next to him. A well-placed elbow to his midsection nudged him back and she lifted his arm to curve around her. She curled into him and pillowed her head against his shoulder. He didn't open his eyes. All he wanted was to wrap her up close and hold on for dear life, never let her go.

"This has been a horrific day." Each word puffed warm breath against his neck. She squeezed his knee. "How are you holding up?"

An ironic half-chuckle worked its way up from his throat. Holding up? All he was doing was putting one foot in front of the other, trying to stay on his feet. It would help if the blows stopped coming, but he didn't hold out much hope there.

She yawned. "What time is it?"

He rotated his wrist and studied his watch. Giving Keith Hickey his statement three different times had taken longer than he'd thought. "Just after ten."

"Do you know what sounds good?" She laid her palm across his abdomen. The fluorescent light sparked fire off the diamond on her finger and his chest clenched. "Let's go home and lie down together." She lifted her head, trailing a knuckle along his jaw. Stubble rasped against her skin. "Don't go home alone tonight, Mark. I think we need to be together."

In the past week, since the recovery of Jenny's remains, they'd spent their nights apart, in their respective apartments. He hadn't wanted his nightmares and insomnia to disturb her. Hell, if he'd known what was coming, what he stood to lose...he'd have had her with him every night, storing away memories.

He pulled his arm from around her, rested his elbow on his knee, pinched the bridge of his nose. "We need to talk."

"Oh, Mark, can't it wait? You have to be exhausted and I know I am—"

"Tori." He lifted his head, meeting her gaze. "It's important. What I have to say...this could change everything, change how you feel about me."

"Mark, honey, nothing could—"

"I'm serious."

The pretty line of her mouth tightened and her throat moved with a swallow. "You're scaring me."

"Well, that makes two of us."

Her delicate brows dropped into a V. "What's wrong?"

He turned his head, staring out over the nearly deserted parking lot. A fine mist of cold rain danced beneath the halogen lamps. A shudder worked through him. "Angel's pregnant. She told me today. She's pregnant and there's a chance I could be the father."

Silence shivered between them. A funny little sound, almost like a wounded chuckle, emerged from her throat. She propped her elbow on the back of the bench. "Mark, when I said I wanted your baby, this isn't exactly what I had in mind."

He couldn't help himself. He laughed, burying his face in his hands as gulping breaths caught between laughter and sobs shook his shoulders.

"Mark, don't." Tori embraced him, resting her mouth against his nape. She stroked his hair. "So how do you feel about it?"

"I really hate when you ask me things like that," he mumbled into his palms. He raised his head. "I don't know. I spent the afternoon being scared to death you'd leave me once you knew. Then I spent the rest of the day being scared to death Troy Lee would die."

She traced the edges of his hair at his neck. "Kind of cosmic, isn't it, to learn this so soon after finding Jenny and the baby. Like you're being given something for what you lost."

He turned sharply to look at her. She blinked. "What?"

"Nothing." He shook his head, a slow side-to-side motion. "Just...nothing."

She tugged at his hair, lightly. "You thought I would leave you?"

"Honestly? I didn't know how you'd react." He chafed the heel of his hand across his mouth. "Yeah, I thought it was going to be over for good."

"Heh. You made the mistake of giving me a ring, Mark Cook. You're stuck with me now." She nudged his shoulder with her own, a familiar playful gesture that lightened the boulder that had taken up residence in his chest. She sobered on a soft exhale. "I had to tell Sara and Trace Davis their daughter was dead, then watch Miss Francie fold in on herself when we told her about Devonte. It seems like any new life should be celebrated today, even if it complicates our lives, you know?"

A smile tugged at his mouth. He nudged her shoulder. "You sound like your mama."

She groaned and buried her face against him. "Please don't say things like that."

Index finger under her chin, he tilted her mouth to his. "I love you, Tori."

"I love you too." She laid her palm along his cheek. "No matter what. If this is your baby, we'll love it too and find a way to make everything work."

He crushed her to him, relief making him a little rough, but she didn't protest, merely curling closer. After a moment, she pulled back. "I want you to myself for a while. Go find my brother and take him home to his wife. I'll be waiting for you."

"Your place or mine?" He dropped a kiss at the corner of her mouth.

"Yours." She smiled against his lips. "The bed is bigger and the sheets smell like you."

Where the hell was Tick anyway? Mark rapped his knuckles on the nurse's station. "Lorraine, you sure you haven't see him?"

She put her MegaGulp cup aside and gave him the look. "I'm sure."

He expelled a frustrated breath. He was tired, damn it, and he'd been given his life back. He wanted nothing more than to go home and crawl into his bed with Tori, and Tick wanted to play a little game of hide-and-seek.

Maybe he'd gone back to see Troy Lee.

"He ain't up there." Lorraine shuffled some files and laid them in the inbox for the upcoming shift. Mark glanced at her, surprised. Hell, he was out of it enough he was talking to himself aloud now? "Layla just came back from checking him one more time before she goes home. Nobody's in that room but his little blonde. Even his mama and sisters have gone. Did you text him?"

"Yeah." Mark returned the look. He'd texted him, tried to raise him on the handheld, all to no avail. "Four times."

"And?"

"Nada."

Lorraine shrugged and slipped into her thick sweater. "Maybe he caught a ride with someone else."

And not told him? No, that didn't sound like Tick, normally courteous to a fault.

His cell phone rang and he lifted it to find Falconetti's number on the display. "Cook."

"You were supposed to bring my husband home. Have you misplaced him?" Caitlin teased.

"Yeah. You could say that." He glanced around the now-deserted waiting room. "I'm assuming he's not with you."

"No, and he's not answering his cell."

He wasn't responding to Falconetti either? Mark frowned. Okay, now he was worried.

"He's deliberately avoiding me." Caitlin's voice pulled him back.

"What?"

"He doesn't want to bring the afterburn home to me. Why, I don't know." Disappointment invaded her husky voice. "Actually, I do know, but I won't bore you with it. God, he makes me crazy when he gets stubborn like this."

"You too?"

She sighed, and he didn't miss the way it trembled with worry. "Just take care of him, all right?"

"I have to find him first, Falconetti."

"I know. I'll let you go. And Cookie?"

"Yeah?"

"If he's smoking when you find him, you can tell him I'll kick his ass."

"Will do." He snapped the phone shut and returned it to his belt. The hell with this. He'd wait at the car. Sooner or later, Tick would decide it was time to go home.

Keys in hand, he exited through the waiting room. The temperature had dropped in the last hour and the wet chill slapped his bare arms. He shivered. It was cold as a well-digger's butt. He cut the corner on the hospital and an ironic laugh built in his throat. Son of a bitch. The one place he hadn't thought to look.

Tick sat on the unmarked unit's trunk, his gaze lifted toward the stars half-hidden by high wispy clouds. An unlit cigarette dangled between his fingers.

Mark leaned on the vehicle next to him. "Falconetti says if you smoke that, your ass is hers."

"Yeah. I could probably get away with coming home smelling like another woman before I could one of these." Tick held the crumpled smoke up and sighed. "I bummed it off Dix Singleton before I realized I don't have a lighter anymore."

"There's one in the car."

"Someone had the keys." He expelled a harsh sigh. "So how much trouble am I in for not answering her calls?"

"Probably not much." Mark kicked at a loose piece of gravel. "She's worried about you."

"Yeah. I know." Tick turned the cigarette between his fingers, rolling it like a baton. "I can't...I have those sounds and images in my head. I keep hearing Kaydee Davis asking for her mother, keep feeling the way she shuddered under my hand when she stopped whimpering and I knew she was dead...I can't take that home to her, Cookie."

"Yes, you can. She's one of us. She'll get it better than anyone."

"No." Tick shook his head, a familiar stubborn slant to his chin. "Not anymore."

"Man, what are you talking about? She had a baby, Tick, but that doesn't change who she is—"

"You don't get it." The words came from between clenched teeth. "You weren't there."

"The hell I wasn't." Anger flashed along Mark's nerves, so hot he was surprised his skin didn't give off steam in the icy night. "What do you think it was like for me, trying to get Troy Lee out of that damn car before he choked on his own blood?"

"That's not what I mean." Tick came off the trunk to his feet in a tense, edgy movement. He paced a few feet away and jerked a hand through already disheveled hair. "You weren't in that delivery room when she went white—not pale, *white*—and passed out before I could get another breath. She could have died and there wasn't a damn thing I could do about it—"

"Tick."

"You weren't in that NICU all those weeks, when she was living on every breath he took, when we weren't sure he would take another one some days, when I knew if we lost him, it would destroy her and I couldn't do anything about that either—"

"Lamar." He half-shouted before he remembered where he was. Frustration burned over the nape of his neck.

Tick glared. "What?"

"Get in the damn car."

They stared at one another in impasse for a moment. Tick tossed the unlit cigarette aside and stalked to the passenger door. He jerked once on the handle. "It's locked."

Mark hit the remote unlock. Tick yanked the door open and climbed in. With a deep breath, Mark opened the driver's door and sank behind the wheel. He jammed the key in the ignition. "She needs to kick your ass. Somebody ought to knock some sense into that damn thick head of yours before you mess around and screw up the best thing that ever happened to you."

"What are you talking about?"

"You know, you're not normally this stupid." A harsh laugh wrung itself from Mark's throat. He shook his head as he pulled onto the side street. "Hell, you said Troy Lee had the common sense of a fence post. Turns out he's smarter than both of us."

Tick glared at him but didn't reply.

"He pegged it. Said you could either fight life or roll with it."

"You need some caffeine. Or some sleep. You're not even making sense."

"I'm not making sense? Look in the mirror, partner. You're the one who won't go home out of some misguided sense of male protectiveness. I got news for you though, man. That's one woman who's not going to let you treat her like a fragile hothouse flower. You might as well give in and start getting things back to normal. Quit obsessing about all the things that could've happened or might happen, and live your damn life. Be Falconetti's husband and that boy's daddy and enjoy every second of it. I'm sure as hell going to."

"You make it sound so damn simple." Again the sense that Tick spoke from between clenched teeth. "And it's not."

"Because you're fighting. Stop trying to control everything." He slowed for the traffic light at 19. A left and then a right took them onto 112, away from town and deeper into the rural landscape around Coney. The shadows of dark houses and even darker woods flicked and danced beyond the windows.

Tick thumped his thumb on his knee. "Where are we going?"

"You'll see."

Silence hovered for all of three seconds. "I don't try to control *everything*."

Mark snickered. "Only because Falconetti won't let you."

He swung the patrol car onto a nearly abandoned red clay road. Eroded ditches rose on either side. He pulled to one side and killed the engine, but left the headlights on. The twin beams stretched down the road, throwing a pool of illumination around them. Mark climbed from the vehicle. After the heater's warmth, the cold bit even worse.

The passenger door slammed. Tick rested both hands on the hood. "Want to tell me what we're doing out here?"

"You're going to want to take a swing at me. I'm giving you the privacy and the opportunity."

"Why would I..." Tick's gaze sharpened. "What did you do?"

Mark rested his hands at his gun belt and regarded him steadily. "Angel's pregnant."

They stared at one another across the car. The underbrush atop the ditch rustled, eerie green eyes appearing for a second and darting away.

"Holy hell." Oxygen rushed visibly from Tick's lungs, puffing into mist in the cold air. He scraped a hand through his hair, and he turned his back on Mark to rest against the hood. "I knew it. I freakin' knew something like this was going to happen."

"Yeah, life does that sometimes." Fury detonated in Mark's chest, decimating the tightness that he'd carried there all day, sending explosive heat under his skin, burning his nape. "Kinda like forgetting the condom once when you're about to go undercover for a year."

"What did you say?" Tick rounded the car. A matching rage vibrated off him. "What the hell did you just say to me?"

"I'm not taking any damn grief off you over this, Tick. Got that? It was an accident. They happen. You of all people should know that."

"Don't even try making this the same thing."

"Oh, I'm not. I took precautions and got caught. You were just stupid and careless. The difference is, if this kid is mine, I'll actually be here, not off in damn Mississippi—"

"Son of a bitch." On the low growl, Tick planted both hands on Mark's chest and shoved, hard.

Mark picked up the invitation. He grabbed Tick's collar in a cross-hold and slammed him against the car. "Don't make me hurt you, Lamar."

"Yeah, right—"

"Go ahead and say it," Mark gritted. He tightened his grip and dragged Tick's gaze closer to his own. "Do it so we can get it over with."

Tick glared. In the dim light around the car, his dark eyes glittered, mutinous, enraged. He didn't open his mouth, the skin there tight and pale.

"Say it. It's been eating at you for weeks." Mark gave him a slight shake, shoved him against the car and let go. "Say I'm not good enough for her."

Tick didn't reply, still eyeing him with simmering resentment.

"You can't, can you? You want to, but that damn honest streak of yours won't let you," Mark taunted. "Because deep down, you know it's not true. In here"—Mark tapped his chest with one finger—"you know that I'm what she needs, that I'm just as good for her as she is for me."

"Yeah, this is going to be really good for her." Tick straightened his collar. His back still against the car, he folded his arms over his chest. "So how long have you known?"

Did he really think that deceptively casual tone wasn't transparent? The narrow-eyed way he glowered gave him away. Mark held his gaze. "Since about an hour before Troy Lee's wreck."

"Which is why you were at my place. Talking to Cait."

"Not like I could confide in you."

"Does Tori even know yet?"

"What do you think? Do you really think I'd tell you before I told her?"

Silence stretched. Tick coughed into one fist. "How did she take it?"

"She said it wasn't exactly what she had in mind when we talked about having a baby."

Tick chuckled, Mark figured probably completely against his will. "Sounds just like her."

"Yeah." Remembered dismay and fear bounced through him once more. "I thought for sure she'd leave me."

Even he could hear the pain vibrating in his voice. Quiet fell between them, then Tick cleared his throat roughly. "No, when she commits to something, that's it. She's stubborn like that."

"No clue where she gets that trait."

"Kiss my ass, Cookie. It can be a really good quality, unless you're applying it to the wrong things."

"Wow. That sounds almost like a self-revelation."

Tick's long-suffering sigh hovered between them. He pushed both hands through his hair, which already stood out at weird angles. Hell, Mark could *feel* the need for that discarded cigarette emanating off him. Letting down his guard, Mark ambled to the car and leaned against the hood next to his partner. He rubbed the pad of his thumb across the edge of his opposite thumbnail. "She thinks, after everything that happened today, this baby should be celebrated."

"They all should be." Tick chafed his palms together and blew into them. "She sounds like Mama. She—Mama, that is—told me once that sometimes we have to look for our joy. That sometimes it comes out of our greatest pain. I figured out on my own that losing something or someone important makes you value your second chances all the more."

"I can get that." Again, the shimmery idea that this baby might be an unexpected blessing of reparation whispered through him.

"Yeah." Tick dragged both hands down his face. "After today, a little joy would be nice."

Mark made a vague noise of agreement in his throat.

"You said if it's yours…is there a question?"

"It could be Jim's."

Tick's snort defined rude. "Like Jim needs a kid."

"Like Angel needs to deal with him for the rest of her life." He traced the edge of his nail again. "She and Troy Lee are good for one another. He's…there's a lot to him under that pretty-boy face of his."

"I'm seeing that." This time, the silence suspended between them felt comfortable, like, well, like before. Tick cocked a sideways glance at him. "Learning to roll with it, huh?"

Mark nodded. "Yeah. I spent too much time hiding from it instead of fighting, which is probably the same thing, and I've lost too much to throw anything else away, you know?"

"Sounds like Troy Lee's not the only smart one." Tick's quiet laugh emerged as the barest huff of humor. "Guess that makes me the dumbass this time around."

"You said it. I didn't."

Tick pushed away from the car. "Let's go home, Cookie. After today, I really need to hold my family for a while."

With Tori waiting at home for him, Mark could get that. "Sounds good to me."

Chapter Nineteen

Fucking nuts. That's what he was. The whole click-hiss-pause rhythm invaded Troy Lee's brain until he could focus on nothing else. He'd woken and found himself alone when the nurse came in to check his vitals and adjust the bed. So it had just been him and the ventilator for the last hour, and the damn machine was winning.

Watery sunlight peeked in around the blinds. Midmorning, according to the angle. One night down. Mackey was talking about days on the respirator. It was like being at mile one of a marathon.

The door whispered open. He shifted his eyes, catching a glimpse of Chris's and Cookie's serious expressions as they slipped into the room. Man, they looked rough—tired, wrung out, worried.

Chris peered down at him, blue gaze roving his face, clearly concerned. "Brought you a present."

Troy Lee grasped the smooth rectangle, about the size of a picture frame. The roughness of a hook-and-loop fastener dragged at his fingers. He held the object up. He'd have grinned if he could have. The dry-erase board from Chris's dash.

Cookie proffered the marker. "But you probably can't write as fast as you talk."

Troy Lee cut his eyes at him, a visual screw-you-buddy. Chris studied the monitor screen, a slight frown drawing his brows together. "Layla was at the nurse's station. She says you're doing good."

Resting the small board against his thigh, Troy Lee scribbled and held it aloft.

"*Want off the machine*," Cookie read aloud. His gray gaze

lifted to Troy Lee's. "It's got to be a bitch, but Mackey knows what he's doing."

Troy Lee focused on the ceiling for a second, gathering his nerve. He swiped his wrist across the board to wipe out his previous words and scribbled again. He held it up.

Kids OK?

The look Cookie and Chris exchanged was answer enough. Cookie muffled a cough with his wrist. "Paul's in the surgical ICU upstairs. Santana's at Emory and it's kinda touch-and-go with her. Kaydee Davis and Devonte Richardson were DOA."

Devonte? Shock sheared through him, leaving an emotional pain that rivaled the physical agony the nerve block kept at bay. Eyes wide, he looked to Chris for confirmation, hoping he wouldn't get it. Cookie had to be wrong. Not Devonte, not when he had so much going for him.

Chris's miserable blue eyes and stiff nod slammed the reality into him. He lifted his hand to press the heel against his forehead. Fuck. What a damn *waste...*

He smeared the words away with his fingertips and scrawled again, holding it up for Chris. *Miss Francie?*

Chris wrapped his fingers around the bed rail, skin tight over white knuckles. "She's taking it hard. I went by to see her last night."

Cookie was right—he couldn't write as fast as words and questions formed in his brain. The frustration dragged at him while he cleared and wrote again. Cookie leaned to read the board. *Knew would be bad why didn't he stop?*

Cookie lifted his gaze to Troy Lee's. "Paul?"

Troy Lee raised two fingers as a negative. Cookie nodded. "The deputy."

One finger. Cookie shrugged. "I don't know. Tick's all over that. The guy's only been at Whitman a little while. He's not even fully POST certified yet. He came over from Alabama, where he's been at five departments in the last six years."

"A gypsy cop." Disgust tightened Chris's tone.

"Tick and the sheriff are pushing McMillian to charge him, pending the outcome of the ART's findings." Cookie cleared his throat and a look passed between him and Chris.

Troy Lee frowned and scribbled across the board. *Not telling me?*

Another pointed visual exchange. Cookie looked up at the ceiling, as if unseen answers might be written there, then dropped his gaze to Troy Lee's. "Bubba's kicking up a fuss, trying to take the heat off Paul."

The marker slipped between Troy Lee's suddenly sweaty fingers. *Blames me.*

"Yes."

Not my fault. On my side. Swerved to miss—

Cookie's hand on his wrist stopped the frenzied script. "I know. Dale Jenkins saw it happen. He's already given the ART a statement. Everything'll be all right. We just have to wait it out, until the reconstruction team's report is final."

"Gentlemen?" The nurse, out of Troy Lee's line of sight, spoke from somewhere near the door. He recognized that voice. The sadistic one, who'd about made him come out of his skin checking the wires in his chest and then nudged his broken nose while she messed with the tape around the ventilator tube. "I'm sorry, but your time is up."

"We'll check in on you later." Cookie patted his arm in an awkward goodbye. "And don't worry. Everything will be okay."

Easy for him to say. Eyes closed, Troy Lee lifted an affirmative finger. Chris murmured a quiet farewell, and the door whispered shut. F-uck. Everything would be okay? Not from where he was. No, everything—*everything*—spiraled out of his control, and he couldn't roll with any of it because he couldn't get his feet under him long enough before something else knocked him down and winded him. He sure as hell couldn't fight against it.

All he could do was lie flat on his back and wait. Oh, hell yeah. He was loving this.

Angel snagged another fry from her McDonald's bag and scrolled through her contacts. With the fry clenched in her teeth, she sank onto one of the benches scattered before the hospital entryway and typed in directions to Julie. Thank God she'd had the foresight to train Julie in the day-to-day operations of the bar. The automatic doors behind her whooshed.

"Do you think it was a good idea to tell him?" Doubt laced Chris Parker's familiar voice.

"Wouldn't you want to know, if you were him?" Cookie

replied.

"Probably."

Their quiet conversation, not meant for her ears, shivered foreboding over already taut nerves. She dropped her phone in her purse and looked up as they approached where she sat.

"Hey, Angel." Chris met her eyes briefly and nodded, his gaze darting away in the manner she'd grown accustomed to.

"Chris." Her own gaze flicked to Cookie's. "Is he awake?"

Cookie nodded. "They'd only let us stay a few minutes. He was pretty alert, though."

"He was last night, the couple of times he woke up." The moment lulled, and she wanted to ask about the exchange she'd overheard but held the words back.

Chris coughed and glanced at his watch. "I'd better get going. I'm supposed to meet with McMillian at eleven."

"I'll catch up with you later." Arms folded over his chest, Cookie met her gaze once Chris departed across the parking lot. "So how are you holding up?"

She clasped her hands around her knee. A half-hearted smile tugged at her mouth. "Better than the couple of times you saw me yesterday."

"Do you mind?" He indicated the bench and she slid to give him room to sit. He leaned forward, wrists between his knees. Fingers laced, he tilted his hands to study his palms. "I told Tori. And Tick."

She swallowed a facetious reply. Instead, she fiddled with her hem where it hit her knee. "I'm sure that wasn't easy for you."

"Pretty sure it hasn't been a picnic for you."

"Yes, well, it kind of pales in comparison to yesterday. I've discovered I have much to be thankful for."

An ironic smile flitted over his face. "That's along the lines of Tori's reaction."

"It can't have been easy for her either."

"She handled it okay. She's pretty good with the hard stuff. How did Troy Lee take it?"

"He's been great. Very caring, very supportive." Sheer affection warmed her chest. "You know him. Troy Lee is...Troy Lee. He's not like any man I've ever known."

"That's one way to put it." Laughter lurked in the dry

remark.

Angel cut her eyes at him in a suppressing glare, the way she'd done dozens of times over the years when he'd been teasing. "I guess it's my turn to support him."

"He'll probably need it. He's facing a hard few days."

She pulled her purse onto her lap and gathered her empty McDonald's bag. "I should probably go up and—"

"Angel." He turned serious gray eyes in her direction. "When will you know?"

"Maybe another month." She twisted her purse strap around her hand. "The measurements from my sonogram should narrow it down, although you're not supposed to use that dating to prove paternity, from what I read on the internet. If I have an amniocentesis, which I think I'll have to have because I'm over thirty-five, they can do a DNA test from that. That would be in a month or two."

He nodded. "If it's mine...I'll want to be involved. I'll be a father to her, take care of her. You won't have to worry that she's made to feel like anybody's mistake. I'll love her, Angel."

"There you go, just like Troy Lee. Her, when it could very well be a boy." She used the flippancy to cover a very real urge to cry. She touched his wrist, lightly. "Thank you."

He cleared his throat. "So I guess you need to get upstairs."

"Yes." She rose, turned to look at him. "Does it make me an awful person if I hope it's you and not Jim?"

"No. Not at all." His face softened a moment, then he pushed up from the bench. "I've got to get to work. Go check on Troy Lee. I think he's going stir crazy."

"Knowing him?" A puff of laughter escaped her lips. "Most likely. Something tells me he's a horrible patient."

"You know, I can imagine that." Cookie's quiet chuckle rumbled between them. "Later, Angel."

"Bye." Her spirit lighter by one encumbrance, she watched him walk to his patrol car. Slinging her purse over one shoulder, she turned away and headed inside, impatient to see Troy Lee. When she reached his room, after checking in with the nurses for permission to visit, she found him awake, staring at the ceiling, his entire body rigid and vibrating with tension.

Looking at him hurt her heart.

At his bedside, she smoothed his hair with a gentle hand

and leaned to kiss his forehead. "Hey."

Vivid blues brimming with frustration and anxiety locked on hers. He fumbled with a small dry-erase board, slashing words across it then turning it toward her. *Can't do this.*

"Yes, you can." She touched his cheek, stroked his temple. "I know you can."

A vicious swipe of his wrist across the surface, more scribbling. *Can't breathe.*

"What?" She darted a look at the respirator. It functioned the same way it had the night before. She reached for the call button, but he caught her fingers. The marker squeaked over the shiny surface.

Need to do it myself.

"No." With a touch as soft as her voice was firm, she caressed his shoulder, almost bared by the hospital gown. "You need to get well. Right now, that means living with the ventilator. I know you hate it, but I want you to get better, Troy Lee."

Out of control.

She wasn't sure exactly what he was talking about, but his agitation grew more and more apparent, through the stiffness in his body, the dismay radiating off of him, the rapid flutter of his long lashes. She rubbed her thumb across his biceps, hoping to smooth away some of the stress.

"I brought you something." She dug through her purse and retrieved his iPod, which had been lying on her coffee table where he'd forgotten it the morning before. Hard to believe that had only been yesterday, when she'd been trying to lure him back to bed. "Maybe this will help."

She slipped the buds into his ears, adjusted the cord and placed the small rectangle in his hand. Eyes sliding closed, he passed his thumb over the control pad. Some of the visible strain eased from his long body. She pressed her lips to his ear. "Better?"

He scrawled words on the board. *Yes.*

"Good." She stroked his hair. "Now, rest and concentrate on getting better. Everything will be fine."

She continued touching him, calming him, as he fell into uneasy sleep.

An hour later, Christine and the girls arrived. Eying her

with a critical maternal gaze, Christine coaxed Angel away for a cup of tea, leaving Troy Lee under the watchful presence of his sisters.

"So how is he this morning?" Christine rubbed her arm with soothing affection as they boarded the elevator.

"Edgy. He was upset earlier, I think about the ventilator." The memory of his anxiety and frustration bit deep, cutting because she could do so little to alleviate any of it.

"I'm sure." Christine selected the lobby level and leaned against the wall. She watched the numbers above the door, a distracted, faraway expression on her delicate features. "He's very much like his father, and Troy was always horrible about being incapacitated in any way. He wanted to be up, doing things."

An affectionate smile touched Angel's lips. "That sounds like Troy Lee."

"Hmm." The elevator arrived with a tiny jolt. "Yes. He caught chickenpox when he was seven. I finally gave up trying to keep him in bed. When he had the flu at twelve, I didn't even try. The best I could do was getting him to sit in the armchair in Troy's office with a quilt."

Fondness colored the memories. Christine held the door and gestured for Angel to precede her. Angel darted a glance at the older woman from beneath her lashes. "You adore him."

"That charmer? Oh, yes. I always have. Troy used to tease that I'd only married him so I could have Troy Lee for my baby." Christine's light laugh trilled between them and she winked. "He was probably half right. I fell in love with both of them at first sight. I never understood how Vanessa—she was Troy Lee's mother—could prefer a research lab over that beautiful boy. She was used to statistics and experimental theory, and I'm not sure she knew what to do with the reality of him. He was a handful, always into something."

Angel could just imagine. If he had half as much mischief in him as a child as he did as a man...that house had never known a dull moment.

"I think I have photos." Christine dug in her purse as they approached the cafeteria. She removed a strip of plastic-encased photos from her wallet and handed them to Angel after they'd placed their orders. The first picture was a family group, taken on the beach before what looked like the Tybee lighthouse, all of them dressed in khaki shorts and white shirts. A younger Christine sat on a weather-beaten log with what looked like an older version of Troy Lee, a man with slight silvering at his temples and stylish spectacles. The children gathered at their feet, Ellis a toddler, Montgomery a beautiful little girl, and Troy Lee a grinning boy.

She flipped past that to find a shot of him at four or five, big blue eyes glinting with mischief beneath tousled brown hair. Christine tapped his wide smile with a fingertip. "How could I not fall in love with that?"

Tucked beneath a photo of Montgomery at the same age was a snapshot, cut down from a bigger picture. A recent candid of the siblings, gathered on a plush sofa, each holding a Chinese food container. Angel traced the line of Troy Lee's jaw, tearful laughter pushing into her throat when she saw he held a fortune cookie aloft. "He is beautiful."

"Inside and out." Christine paid for their tea and nudged her toward a table. "That's why he's the child of my heart."

"What?" Angel met her gaze over a cautious sip of hot tea. Peppermint exploded on her tongue.

Christine waved a negligent hand in the air. "My standard answer when asinine people made a big deal about the fact that I wasn't his 'real' mother. I'd tell them he was my child by choice, the child of my heart, and that usually shut them up pretty quickly. Of course, he took that and ran with it. He spent years torturing his sisters with the fact that I'd chosen him and just gotten stuck with them."

"That sounds just like him."

"Doesn't it?" Christine wrapped both hands about her cup. She looked up, her eyes serious. "He loves you. I hope..." Her voice trembled and her lashes fell briefly. "I hope you understand how precious that is, how special and wonderful and beautiful that sweet heart of his is. I want you to treasure him as much as we do."

"I do." Angel blinked hard and bit her lip, trying to stop the quivering of her chin. "I feel like I've waited my whole life for him, waited to get to this point where I could appreciate and value him most."

"That is so...oh, my God." Her eyes filling, Christine touched her fingers to her mouth. She dropped her hand on a shaky laugh. "When he wanted me to get that ring, I asked him if he was sure and he said yes, that all he'd been waiting for was you to realize you'd been waiting for him."

Troy Lee jerked into awareness, much as he had all during the previous night. His body seemed constantly poised on the edge of panic, yanking him from an edgy rest to jittery wakefulness in seconds. Everybody kept telling him to rest, but being checked over at least once, if not twice, an hour precluded any real respite.

Cognizant that he was alone again, he stared at the ceiling and dug his fingers into the sheet. He brushed paper and lifted two folded sheets from Montgomery's sketchpad. He unfolded the first to find Ellis's girlish handwriting: *Angel and Troy Lee, sitting in a tree, k-i-s-s-i-n-g...*

Such a brat. He refolded it, tucked it beneath the dry-erase board, unfurled the second. If he'd been able to breathe on his own, the little drawing would have taken his breath. One of Montgomery's distinctive tattoo designs, the ones she did for fun and gave away to a friend who owned a tattoo parlor. He traced the ephemeral angel with his eyes, awed at the way Montgomery had captured the essence of his Angel in just a few lines, shy and bold, innocent and sensual, playful and loving all at once.

Oh, yeah. He was getting that inked on his shoulder, as soon as he got out of this damned bed. Carefully creasing the paper back into a smaller rectangle, he slipped it beneath Ellis's teasing rhyme.

The problem with being laid out this way was having too much time to think. To ponder what had been in Devonte's head in the moments before he died. To grieve for everything the boy had been and would have done. To hurt for Miss Francie, who'd lost the only family she had left.

Too much time to wonder how long it might be before the ART report was in. To worry that it wouldn't matter, that he might find himself without a badge, his career gone. Somehow, over the past three years, he'd *become* a cop. Not his job, but who he was, the way his dad had been a mathematician.

What was he supposed to do if he lost what he was?

Mark rested his elbow on the chair arm, a hand over his mouth, and trained his gaze on the television in the conference room. Deeply aware of Trooper Keith Hickey's attention to the screen, he tensed as the images and sound flickered to life. Roger in dispatch had downloaded Troy Lee's shift video from the server to a DVD, cueing it to begin moments before the first radio transmission from Whitman's deputy.

Watching the events unfold from Troy Lee's perspective leant the experience a surreal quality. Winter sunlight filtered through trees and slanted across the rural road in front of the squad car. The dialogue replayed, the Whitman deputy's refusal to stop at both Troy Lee's and Tick's requests coming in loud and plain.

"C-13, can you intercept with the spike strip?" Tick's voice as the straightaway before the curves opened up, and Mark tensed further, knowing what was coming.

"Negative, C-2. If they passed Long Lonesome, suspect is headed in opposite direction. C-5 should be able to intercept." Troy Lee, sounding calm and collected, entering the first curve. On the second, Paul Bostick's Ford flashed across the line, a blur of red paint and glimmering chrome. "Oh, fuck."

Palpable shock colored Troy Lee's brief expletive. On screen, Paul's truck slid sideways, the tail end coming around, into Troy Lee's path. The arc of blue sky over the adjacent field spun wildly, the ditch rising before the windshield. The view rocked in a violent quaking, dark ground slamming into the glass. Then sky and earth rolled over and over one another, a crazed tumble filled with a shower of broken glass, flying objects and Troy Lee's muffled grunts. At last, the dizzying spin came to a rest, the screen depicting only freshly turned soil and crumpled white metal. A gurgling groan rattled and Mark's skin crawled, his mind flipping through horrifying flashbacks of Troy Lee's bloodied face, his arm protruding from the broken window and lying motionless against the dirt, his awful stillness as they'd extricated him from the vehicle.

Tick pointed the remote at the television, the screen fading to black. Hickey leaned back in his chair and fixed them both with a measuring look. "Well, I've seen enough."

To her relief, when Angel slipped back into Troy Lee's room after Christine's visit with him, a quiet pensiveness replaced Troy Lee's earlier anxiety. With the bed elevated, he scribbled across a notepad and she caught a glimpse of sketchy sheet music on the top page. His gaze flicked to hers, and the glow of contentment and love there kindled an answering warmth in her. A prayer of gratitude whispered through her mind, that he was alive and doing better than Dr. Mackey expected.

As she approached the bed, he laid his pen aside. She stroked her thumb across his wrist. "Don't stop on my account. I just wanted to be with you."

Gaze on hers, he rotated his hand to squeeze her fingers then reached for the dry-erase board. *Christine says you have the ring.*

Her breath hitched, and lips parted, she nodded. The little burgundy box resided in the side pocket of her purse, zipped securely away.

He quirked one eyebrow. *Well?*

"Well what?" She ran her fingers along the inside of his elbow. She leaned down and lowered her voice to a teasing whisper. "Just because I have it doesn't mean I've peeked. That's like unwrapping Christmas presents early. I was waiting for you."

He touched a finger to the ventilator tube and slashed words across the board. *Mind waiting a little longer? Want to be able to do it right.*

"I'd wait forever for you." She feathered her fingertip along one of his eyebrows. "But you, Troy Lee Farr, do everything right where I'm concerned."

Pleasure glinted deep in his eyes. He lifted his hand to caress the corner of her lips, the softest of kisses in the contact. She blinked away a wash of tears at the sweetness of that touch.

He gestured at the ventilator and reached for the board once more. *Mackey says two more days, maybe three. Can't wait.*

"I know." She laid her palm under his jaw, just below the bruising there, darkening from angry red to deep purple. The shivery what-could-have's shuddered through her mind. With her thumb, she traced the outline of a tendon in his neck. "You should—"

The hushed click of the door handle turning drew their attention. He tensed under her hand, but the palpable stiffness drained as Cookie stepped into the room. His gaze darted over them. "Hey. Brought you something." He held up a small sheaf of papers. "Preliminary ART report."

Beneath her palm, Troy Lee went rigid all over again, his brows dipping into a worried scowl.

"Relax," Cookie said, his voice firm and soothing. "It's good. See for yourself."

He approached the bed and Angel stepped back so Troy Lee could take the proffered papers. She tapped his knee. "I'm going to step out for a second and let you talk."

His heart thudding to a higher rate, Troy Lee skimmed over the first page. Despite Cookie's reassurance, he couldn't get away from the fact that these papers could very well hold the key to his future, or lack thereof. The summary of the accident and scene conditions bogged him down. Frustrated, he flipped to the second sheet and ran his finger along the lines of typed script.

Two thirds down the page, he found the line he sought. A shudder worked over him.

Deputy Farr is not at fault.

He closed his eyes on a wave of relief, the papers crumpling slightly under the pressure of his fingers. Cookie patted his shoulder. "Told you everything would be fine."

Troy Lee fumbled for the dry-erase board. *Bostick?*

"Paul's looking at charges from driving with a suspended license to vehicular manslaughter. Tick and the sheriff are meeting with the county attorney now, and they're supposed to get together with Bostick and his lawyer later today. It'll be okay, Troy Lee. It's in the best hands and they'll do everything they can to shut Bubba's mouth down."

Troy Lee lifted an affirmative finger. He could let go at this point, let Reed and Calvert handle it.

Cookie cleared his throat and rubbed his thumb over the bed rail. "Angel told me about the baby."

Surprised, Troy Lee lifted his gaze to Cookie's. Worry threaded through him, and with all of his protective instincts singing, he narrowed his eyes at the older man.

Cookie's mouth twisted with a hint of ironic humor. "Don't look at me like that. She and I are good. If the baby's mine, we'll work it all out." Cookie clapped his shoulder once more. "I'm going before the nurses toss me out again. Get some rest. We need you back on the road."

Once the door shut behind him, Troy Lee closed his eyes. Even with the hiss-click-pause rhythm filling his ears and his body, he slid into true relaxation for the first time since he'd awakened on the ventilator. Things remained out of his control, but he could roll with that. He still had who he was and he had Angel.

Everything else would fall into place.

ꙮ

Not bad. Not bad at all.

Seated at the dining table, Angel compared December's ending recap to November's. Even with her away from the bar, with Julie running things, the profit margin had gone unaffected. Maybe she could turn loose of the reins a little more. She laid a palm over the tiny pooch beneath her navel. Actually, come July, she was probably going to have to turn loose of those reins a lot more, but if this level of profit kept up, she could promote Julie to manager and give her a raise.

Bare feet whispered on hardwood and a hard male arm wrapped around her neck from behind. She sighed. "You're supposed to be in bed. Resting."

"I've been in bed for more than two weeks." Troy Lee nuzzled her ear as he spoke, his voice still raspy from the mechanical ventilation and the bout of bronchitis he'd fought once it was removed. "You could come to bed with me. I rest better when you're there."

She turned her head to look into those mischievous blues. "If I come to bed, rest is not going to be what you want to do."

He chuckled. "You know me awfully well."

"It's too soon, Troy Lee." She kissed the corner of his mouth, wishing it wasn't, needing that closeness and connection with him, and he levered slightly away. "Your ribs aren't completely healed and—"

Her voice died. He held the little burgundy box, the one she'd tucked in his nightstand drawer, before her eyes. Her surprised gaze met his suddenly serious one.

"Open it."

He pressed the velvet square into her palm. Her fingers shaking with anticipation, she flipped the lid.

"Oh." Awe left her breathless. She touched a reverent finger to the large bluish opal, cut into an oval and surrounded by shimmering diamonds.

"It was my grandmother's." A hint of uncertainty tinged his voice. "It's not the traditional solitaire, but—"

"It's perfect." She lifted her eyes to his and she laid that same reverent fingertip on his bottom lip. "You're perfect."

"I love you, Angel. I love you and I love the Butterbean and I…" On his haunches beside her chair, the kitchen light glinting off his bare shoulders, he swallowed hard, the muscles in his throat moving. "I want you to be my wife."

She smiled, not bothering to blink away the happy tears blurring her vision. "I want that too."

"So that's a yes?" He plucked the box from her hand and removed the ring. He lifted her left hand and held the ring poised before her third finger.

"That's a yes." She laughed through the tears, and he slipped the circle onto her hand. It was a little big, but she didn't care. It, he, *they* were absolutely perfect. Framing his face, she kissed him, carefully avoiding his healing nose.

"Ah, Angel baby, I love you so damn much." He tucked her close to his chest, but not too tight, the just right that was all him. "I want to spend the rest of my life with you."

"Me too." She caressed the line of his jaw, stubble scratching her skin. "And I can't wait."

"There you go," he murmured into the curve of her neck. "Speeding again."

"Oh but, Troy Lee sweetheart, you said you didn't mind, as long as it was with you."

Epilogue

Angel killed the engine and glanced in the rear-view mirror, eying the Chandler County patrol car pulling into the parking lot behind her. The new Dodge Charger sported a dark blue paint job and silver markings, a departure from the standard white and brown. A familiar tall figure emerged from the driver's seat and sauntered toward her Mustang. She lowered the window and he leaned down, his handsome face serious.

"Mrs. Farr, do you know why I stopped you?"

"I'm pretty sure I wasn't speeding this time, Deputy." She slanted a quick check at the console clock. "And besides, aren't you off duty?"

"I am. Just went 10-6, 10-42." White teeth flashed in his wonderful grin and Troy Lee bent farther to whisper his lips across hers. "Figured I'd see if my 10-42 and a half wanted to have dinner." He glanced sideways into the backseat, his blue gaze lighting further. "Hey, Butterbean."

Secure in her car seat, Tatum chortled and kicked her feet. She waved her arms, and the pink stuffed kitty she'd been clutching tumbled into the floorboard. Troy Lee pulled the door open and tilted his head toward the strip mall behind them. "Hop out. I'll get her and we'll grab a bite."

Angel snagged her tote, which served as both purse and diaper bag, and stepped free of the car. The evening sun glared across the parking lot and she slid on her sunglasses. Troy Lee contorted himself into the backseat to extricate Tatum, talking to her the whole time. She responded with a stream of happy, chirping gibberish.

He straightened with the baby in his arms, and she patted little hands against his cheeks, pressing an open-mouth kiss to his nose. He laughed and Angel smiled. Tatum had discovered giving kisses as a new talent the previous week, just days before her first birthday, and Troy Lee and her granddaddy proved to be her preferred kiss-ees. Neither man seemed to mind, as Tatum enchanted Angel's daddy as much as she did Troy Lee.

Tote over her shoulder, Angel tucked her arm through his as they turned toward the little Chinese restaurant at the end of the strip. "How was your day?"

"Oh, baby." He dipped his knees on a self-satisfied groan, making Tatum giggle and pop her head under his chin. "I have been tearing them up today. Had to start a new ticket book."

"There'll be letters in the paper again, about you and your speed traps." She poked a teasing finger beneath his ribs, at the point where his vest ended.

"Speed trap, my ass."

"Troy Lee." She poked him, harder, and he grimaced.

"Ow." He rubbed at the spot. "What did y'all do today?"

"Not much. We went to see Grandma and Aunt Hope, didn't we, Tatum? Then we met Julie to go over the books—"

"Wait a minute. You took my kid in the bar and I get poked for saying 'ass'?"

She rolled her eyes. "It wasn't open."

He lifted Tatum until they were nose-to-nose and eye-to-eye. "Wait until Miss Maureen Sutter hears about this one, Butterbean. There will be scandal all over town and your mama will be right in the middle of it."

"Troy Lee." She shook her head at him as they reached the sidewalk. The mischief glinting in his blue eyes killed his attempt at a serious look. Laughter tickled her throat. Lord, she loved him, even when he teased unmercifully, which was most of the time.

"Hey look, Tatum." He turned with the baby and pointed down the walkway, toward one of the gift shops tucked between the Chinese place and an insurance agency. "There's your daddy."

With her first glimpse of Cookie, Tatum squealed and leaned forward from her perch in Troy Lee's embrace, her arms outstretched. "Dada."

"That's right. Daddy." Angel laughed. Lord help her, the child was never going to say "mama". Daddy, milk, kitty, and something that sounded suspiciously like Troy Lee, but no "mama" yet.

"Hey, little girl." Love and pride lighting his entire face, Cookie crouched on his haunches and held out both hands as Troy Lee carefully set Tatum on her feet. Sucking her fingers, she toddled the few steps to her father. He swept her up in a hug and she chattered gleefully before gracing his chin with a wet kiss. With a satisfied murmur, she rested her head on his shoulder. Cookie rubbed his hand over her back, early-evening sun glinting off his wedding band. "Where are y'all headed?"

Troy Lee slid his arm around Angel's waist and tilted his head toward the restaurant. "China Wall for supper. You want to join us?"

"Wish I could. I'm supposed to meet Tick over at the women's center in a few minutes. First night of the self-defense class. If I don't get moving, I'll be late." He lifted Tatum to buss her cheek and she giggled. "Go eat with Mama and Troy Lee, little girl. I'll see you tomorrow."

The baby went back to Troy Lee's arms easily. After brief goodbyes, Cookie sauntered to his unmarked unit, and Angel steered Troy Lee toward the restaurant. She eyed Tatum, who was intent on figuring out how to release his whistle chain from the button on his epaulet. "You know, the two of you are the reason she is so rotten."

"She's not rotten." He grinned against Tatum's wispy brown hair, just one shade lighter than Cookie's. "She's well loved." He raised their daughter to the nose-to-nose position again and she chortled. "Two moms, two dads, three grandmas, your grandpa, and more aunts and uncles and cousins than you can count. Probably the most loved little girl in Chandler County, aren't you, sweetheart?"

Angel smiled and tucked her hand through his elbow. That little bit of mathematical logic was impossible to argue.

"Goodnight, Butterbean." Troy Lee whispered a kiss across Tatum's brow and settled her in the crib. She yawned, her little lids heavy, and scrunched up against the bumper pad. Her lashes fluttered, and she blinked a few times, as though afraid she'd miss something if she gave in and went to sleep.

At the foot of the crib, Angel folded her hands on the rim and rested her chin on them. "She's almost out."

"Yeah." He stepped back and looked over at Angel. Her blue eyes glittered at him in the dim light, and the squeezing in his chest had nothing to do with the residual pain he still had every so often in his rib cage. No, this was pure, old-fashioned so-in-love-he-hurt, and he absolutely relished every second of it.

Angel straightened and reached for his hands, pulling him toward the door. "So now that our sweetheart is down, are you ready for bed?"

"Well, that depends." A smile hitched at the corners of his mouth.

"On?"

"On what number you had in mind." He dipped his head to kiss her, murmuring against her lips. "Are we doing the experienced older woman seducing the impressionable younger man bit, or—"

"Troy Lee." Her sigh held equal parts exasperation and laughter.

"—even better, experienced older woman trying to seduce impressionable young cop out of giving her a ticket. I'll even put my uniform back on."

"You are so bad." Her shoulders shook with shivery giggles, and he pressed her against the wall, kissing her hard.

"How about this one?" He nudged her nightgown's thin strap aside, giving him access to her shoulder. "Adoring husband ravishes the wife he loves to distraction."

She looped her arms about his neck. "Oh, I like that one, Deputy Farr."

"So do I, Mrs. Farr, so do I." Sliding an arm beneath her knees, he swung her into his arms. Their lips met again. "As a matter of fact, it's my absolute favorite."

About the Author

How does a high school English teacher end up plotting murders? She uses her experiences as a cop's wife to become a writer of romantic suspense! Linda Winfree lives in a quintessential small Georgia town with her husband and two children. By day, she teaches American Literature, advises the student government and coaches the drama team; by night she pens sultry books full of murder and mayhem.

To learn more about Linda and her books, visit her website at www.lindawinfree.com or join her Yahoo newsletter group at http://groups.yahoo.com/group/linda_winfree. Linda loves hearing from readers. Feel free to drop her an email at linda_winfree@yahoo.com.

It's not the past that wounds us...it's the ghosts we hold on to.

Hearts Awakened

© 2008 Linda Winfree

Hearts of the South, Book 6

A lifetime ago Mark Cook's pregnant wife vanished, taking everything and leaving an empty, aching hole in his life. Since then, as penance for his failure as a husband and father, he's refused to allow himself to live. Refused to lay his sleeping heart on the line for any woman.

Enter Tori Calvert, his best friend's baby sister. Suddenly, against his will—and against his better judgment—that same damaged heart seems determined to reawaken. And Mark's not sure he can withstand the pain.

When she was a teenager, a vicious attack ripped away Tori's very essence as a woman. Finally she feels ready to focus her existence on something other than her job as a rape crisis counselor. And to step outside the shelter of her loving, protective family. She trusts Mark more than any man, yet fear holds her back.

Fear that even the healing light of love may not be enough to banish the shadows of the past.

My Bookstore & More
www.mybookstoreandmore.com
Green for the planet.
Great for your wallet.

LaVergne, TN USA
25 October 2009

161971LV00008B/15/P

9 781605 044323

To Jolee + Kirk
Your mom had to
stand in line for this
so make

ROAD DOG

sure you read every
word - all the
best Steve

Stephen Combs ▪ John Eckberg

2/15/03

FEDERAL POINT PUBLISHING

Federal Point Publishing
109 West Groveland Lane • East Palatka, Florida 32131

January 2003
Manufactured in the United States of America
Distributed by Mickler's Books, Inc. • Oviedo, Fla. 32765

Edited by Robert F. Dixon
Cover design by Ron Falkner
Cover graphics by Jonathan Pennell
Cover photo courtesy of WCPO-TV, Cincinnati

Front cover: November 13, 1995. Sgt. Greg Baird steers a just-captured Glen Rogers into the back seat of a Kentucky State Police patrol car. At left is Trooper Ed Robinson.

Library of Congress Cataloging-in-Publication Data
Combs, Stephen M. March 7, 1944 --
Eckberg, John August 23, 1953 --

Details will be furnished upon request

ISBN 0-9668259-1-8

This book is dedicated to two men who gave their lives in service to their community

Randy Bell
July 14, 1953 - May 8, 1998

Ricky Childers
February 16, 1952 - May 8, 1998

Tampa Police Department

Acknowledgements

From both of us, thanks to our editor Bob Dixon, who allowed no detail to go unchecked and no claim to go unchallenged.

Also to Ron Falkner and Chuck Robbins for reading the manuscript. Your criticism, suggestions and encouragement were invaluable. And to our publisher, Jim Mast. Thanks for your support and your confidence in us.

From John Eckberg: To my parents for lessons about truth, to my family for your patient support and to my friends Dann Scheiferstein, Jack Roehr, Randy McNutt and Mike Boyer, whose unending curiosity helped keep this project alive.

From Steve Combs: To Barbara Boyer (now of the Philadelphia Inquirer), who covered the Rogers story when she was a reporter for the *Tampa Tribune.* Thanks for believing in us and for being a pal during those long days of the trial.

Prologue

You could write a story on this one.
— Detective Bob Stephens

The dog hunkered under the back porch, and as he growled and gnawed at a bone, a Kentucky State Police patrol car wheeled up the drive to the house and crunched to a halt in the gravel. The dog barked but did not move from under the porch as the two men got out, their doors closing with hushed thuds, and walked through the fading winter light to the front door. Detective Floyd McIntosh and Lee County Game Warden Larry Hagan showed their badges to Tommy Flinchum and in low voices explained why they had come to his small wood-frame house deep in the Kentucky foothills near Beattyville. It was the fifth house they had visited. They were ready to head home themselves but first a question or two. After a brief conversation, Flinchum led the two around back where the dog was chained to the house.

The animal watched intently as Flinchum came to him. Flinchum stooped, then reached under the porch and hauled him out by the collar, the prized bone still between his teeth. Flinchum grabbed the bone from the hound's mouth, gruffly worked it loose and handed it over to McIntosh. Both officers examined the bone intently, as if it were a talisman from another time and place, and then, satisfied, they dropped the bone into a clear evidence bag, wiped their hands on their pants, nodded a terse ‘so-long’ and headed back to their patrol car.

Beattyville can be a bleak place in January, the naked trees forbidding and stark against a gray granite sky. As the officers drove off, their radio spitting and crackling to life, a cold wind blew down from the hills above the ramshackle house. It picked up a whisper of snow and a few orphaned leaves, then swirled away into the gathering dusk, following the car out of the dale as the dog watched from the shadows.

1

HAMILTON, OHIO • NOVEMBER 1993

Joan Burkart had not seen her father Mark Peters for two weeks and was worried when she arrived at his three-bedroom white house, with the shutters and front porch facing sleepy Fairview Avenue, to find that all the first floor windows were open. It was a cold day, winter clouds were heavy in the sky and snow was in the air. No songbirds were left to brave the Ohio ice that would soon gather.

Those windows, she thought as she walked to the house, why were they open? Her father would never knowingly leave the inside of his house exposed to the elements. The place was empty or at least it seemed that way. Nobody was out back in the garage, which looked like it had been cleaned out. She walked to the back steps and tentatively knocked on the door, then cocked her head and listened. Did she hear something or someone inside? She unlocked the door and entered, calling for her father and wondering why there was no answer.

Joan shuddered when she glanced over at the kitchen sink. Now it was more than intuition that told her something was terribly wrong. The sink was full of empty beer cans and the kitchen counter was a pit. She thought her father had not been drinking for a year. At least that's what he had told Joan's husband, John. So why were those cans in the sink? She made her way through his house, calling his name, worry rising with each step. Nobody was on the first floor and nobody was upstairs, she soon realized, her eyes resting on familiar details: the family photos framed and hanging on the wall next to the grandfather clock, the easy chair her late mother treasured, the dining room buffet overflowing with papers and works-in-process.

Then she realized that all was definitely not right. Furniture was missing. When she went back through the kitchen, her eyes again played across the sink with its pile of beer cans before coming to rest on the basement door. She went to the door and called down. There was no answer. She started to go down the steps but stopped, fearful of what she might find in that dank, musty space. Memories of her loving father, grinning while he picked his guitar, flooded her mind as she began to fear he might forever be lost to the grim face of death. And something else worried her. Was somebody in the basement? Was he down there waiting for her right now, breathing deeply and slowly and purposefully? She whirled out the door and drove frantically to the police station. They would help her find her father.

For months Joan, a devout Catholic, had been saying daily prayers for her father, asking that the Lord would send somebody into his life to care for him now when he needed it. Someone to make runs to the pharmacy for Lasix, to the doctor's office for check-ups of his aging heart, to the grocery or hardware store or just to be there for him through the lonely hours. Her father's needs were not so much burden as worry, and though he had given up the bottle for some time now and was taking better care of himself, even the simplest chores, like the weekly trip to the grocery store, had become more difficult by degrees. He was an old man and old men needed prayers.

On the way to the police station, Joan thought about the last time she had heard from her father. It was mid-October, she realized, just before she had to go into the hospital for minor surgery. Her father sent flowers, which she hanged upside down to dry. After the operation, she and her husband took a short vacation to Tennessee, to take in the glorious colors of autumn and celebrate their October 17 wedding anniversary. Now she was back in town, but where was he?

The Hamilton Police Station is uptown from the Lindenwald neighborhood, but it is not a pleasant drive. The station hunches on the shore of the city's Second Ward, separated from the blue-collar and middle-class Lindenwald by railroad tracks and the segregation that splits many small American towns. Lindenwalders are white. Second Warders are black. To get to the station, one must drive through the Ward, past dirty lots where wine and whiskey bottle shards collect in weeds, past street corners infested by twenty-something crack slingers, past vacant two-story houses built after World War II when Hamilton's foundries churned night and day and a working man could choose his life's vocation.

At the station, she tentatively walked up to the desk. She had never done anything like this before. Where should she begin?

"I'd like to file a missing person report," she told the officer behind the bullet-proof glass. "How do I do that?"

"Who is missing? How long have they been gone?" the desk officer asked. "Are you sure it's not just a vacation?"

She assured the officer that her father was truly missing and he could see that the worry on her face was real. Then she made a request that made him roll his eyes, give her an I've-heard-everything-now look.

Could somebody come back with her to her father's house and look in the basement? She had wanted to search the basement but had a bad feeling about it. She said she knew it was an unusual request but her husband, a fireman on duty, couldn't come with her. While no police department is in the habit of helping people explore a loved one's basement, this time the department would make an exception. Nothing was out of order and they returned to the station. Police were hopeful that her father would soon turn up, they told her; sometimes people take spur-of-the-moment vacations. As other officers probed deeper, their faces went sour. Detectives asked about her father's habits, whom he had been spending time with, his favorite haunts and anything else she might tell them that would shed light on his disappearance. His car was gone, too, Joan said, a newly purchased 1979 LeBaron with temporary tags, and the dog and cat were missing. He would not have taken the animals with him. What's more, the house and garage were cleared of many valuable items. If her father had taken an impromptu selling trip to the south coupled with a vacation with the family pets, which he might have done, well, by now the vacation should have ended. So where was he?

2

Oh he's a smoothie.
— Detective Dan Pratt

HAMILTON, OHIO – JUNE 1993

For Mark Clarence Peters, it was the lighting job of a lifetime. The county wanted to restore the Butler County Soldiers, Sailors and Pioneer Monument above the Great Miami River in downtown Hamilton. Under the al fresco cupola they wanted the Doughboy "Billy Yank" to be the signature symbol of the city. Peters got the job. With downtown on the slide, it had become a point of civic pride. The doughboy, a helmet in his left hand and a carbine at rest, was saluting the onset of peace. Companies could flee the city and residents could head to the greener pastures of Cincinnati suburbs, but Hamilton would always have its doughboy in the night.

Peters knew more than a little about combat. From 1942 until World War II ended in 1945, he fought in the U.S. Army, and it was tenure that would stay with him for the rest of his life. He told few war stories. What was the point? And besides, in his hometown of Hamilton, where he returned after the war to become a respected electrician, just about everybody had a story or two anyhow. Peters' war stories, when he told them, usually were set on Guadalcanal and told of the month-long effort to clear the island of Japanese snipers that guaranteed a nightly bombing. The roar and rumble made sleep impossible and nerves raw as a sergeant's curses.

The days on the island, the action Peters saw while mopping up, brought a deep appreciation of the simple pleasures that a day could hold that endured throughout his life, but particularly during retirement. He found solace in the passing of time. He filled his house with clocks — their ticks and chimes brought a pleasing order to his world. For the rest of his days, Peters would drink in the measured pace and peace of domestic tranquility. A cluttered dining room in a warm household on a winter afternoon with a couple of ticking clocks on the mantle brought a soft reassurance to him: Minutes were passing, time was precious and finite, there were no more detonations in the night.

Throughout his life, Peters had always had an appreciation for mechanical contraptions and a talent for fixing the devices that made living easier for everybody. It started when he was a boy, and it was driven by a curiosity about the unseen. Once, while growing up far from this small town on the edge of a great Midwestern city, Peters decided that what he and his buddies needed was a diving helmet. Their favored pond was a cooling respite in the hot afternoons of August, but splashing and wading, swimming and diving soon became boring. So Peters took a tin bucket from the barn, snipped out a viewing oval and fitted a curved piece of glass from a clear milk bottle to the outside of the bucket. He sealed it with tar and tape and more tar, spot-soldered a valve to the top and from it ran a long hose back to a hand-held bicycle pump. The diver could wear the bucket, the strap under his chin, and look out into the murk of the pond. As long as the fellow up above continued to pump, a rural Ohio farm pond became the coast of Burma and bullfrogs were miraculously transformed into giant squid; — smallmouth bass became man-eating sharks. The helmet worked.

It was a simple and trusting time for those on the fringes of a small American town. Everybody had a cow out back and a hog or two fattening up for market. People arose with the crows and went to bed with the chickens. It was still an America from a different century, but that would all soon change. Hamilton's city fathers decided that the best way to ensure a thriving local economy, to bring the factories that would lure workers from the hills and hamlets of Kentucky in a lemming-like wave of cars and cribs, would be to spurn buy-outs from the captains of industry who owned the regional utilities. They decided to keep the generating plants locally owned and heave the power lines out of town to the farmer's wives in their dowdy dresses who craved light at the flick of a switch. Electricity was coming, kerosene was going and any thinking fellow could figure it out: The guy who could learn to pull wire, string outlets and hang fuse boxes had a job for life, a future so bright he'd have to dip low the bill of his Cincinnati Redlegs cap just to cut down on the glare. Almost no one in the villages, hamlets and crossroads outside of Hamilton had electricity until the middle-1930s. It was an America from a different century but the century was finally slipping away. There was little doubt in the mind of the young Peters that he would become an electrician. And he would become a good one at that.

Installing the lights in the dramatic monument above the regional history museum where Mad Anthony Wayne took a stand for a new nation by building Fort Hamilton more than 200 years before would be a privilege and an honor. Whenever the topic came up as he frequented the American Legion halls and VFW clubs in and around his hometown, Mark would proudly recount his role at the landmark. It was the only veteran's monument for miles around, and thanks to his genious with the lighting, it could be seen at night from all the hills around the city. Mark Peters — electrician, soldier and hometown boy — was proud of his work. Whenever his grandchild Christina, a toddler at the time, passed by the monument in the back seat of her parent's car, she would raise her chubby hand and point through a window to Billy Yank.

"Grandpa lights," she told those in the car. "Grandpa lights."

Though Mark Peters left the Army, Army life never really left him. He loved the handful of service clubs in town: the cheap beer and whiskey prices, the deep lights and wood bars, the jukeboxes with George Strait and Garth Brooks and "The Killer" — old Jerry Lee Lewis — yodeling of love lost and heartbreak, the barstools and faces of the smiling regulars. They were kingdoms, where every man was a charming prince and every lady a queen. Friendship flowed like tap water from a leaking spigot, and Peters' nights had lots of laughs as folks chased alcohol-free O'Douls with a neat glass of Kentucky's finest bourbon and chuckled at the irony of it all.

His family worried some about Peters' fondness for alcohol, his thin frame and rapidly aging face. It would have helped if Peters had sometimes left the house with his false teeth in his mouth, been a little tidier about his personal appearance and cut back on his drinking. He had always been an independent man, so his loved ones kept their worries in check. Peters, too, knew that alcohol was killing him, so on one Spring day in 1993, he decided he could live without it. He quit drinking.

What started as a hobby for Mark Peters, repairing clocks, soon became a passion and something of a vocation fueled by equal parts nicotine and caffeine. He always had his cup of coffee and smoke going, though he knew neither was good for a man pushing seventy. There were dozens of clocks in his living room and the bedrooms upstairs. Clocks adorned the walls and crowded the floors. His family moved to Lindenwald when he was a teenager but Peters would not return until the early 1990s. He just lost a lease on a shop in the Lindenwald business strip. John Lancaster accepted the generous offer of garage space and moved his inventory out back. Peters would take no money. He had no real need for it. He just liked the company and Lancaster with his furniture, the desultory bedroom suites, fading mirrors and squeaking oak kitchen chairs, chairs where generations had sat and banged spoon to plate in petulant impatience, Lancaster brought it all to Fairview Avenue and the home of Mark Peters.

The flea markets led Peters to accumulate other items for his house and for pleasure. He had an extensive coin collection, many from the 19th Century, and whenever he saw a distinctive knife, he bought it. But it was his ability to breathe new life into old wood that led Peters to cross paths with June Elizabeth Von Stein, a 51-year-old woman who had her own upholstery business.

It was in June 1993 when Von Stein entered into her business plan with Peters and then with Peters' housemate, Glen Rogers. Her daughter Michelle was pregnant when they met, and while Michelle's husband frowned on the situation that brought Rogers into his wife's acquaintance, there was nothing to be done about it. "The Guy" was how he dismissed Rogers whenever the name came up, though after they met, he admitted that Rogers seemed nice enough. He had a rough country charm about him that was hard to dislike. But there was something nagging, something vaguely wrong. Rogers walked a little too tall, a Casanova in cut-offs. He fancied himself something of a stud, with his sleeveless athletic shirts and pants a tad too tight. The unspoken misgivings about Rogers soon turned to scattered cautionary asides. Von Stein knew that whatever relationship she had with Rogers was founded on business, not barstools, so she took any hunches about him from her son-in-law in stride. Rogers once spoke of his mother to Von Stein, a surprising personal aside about love and respect. Though Glen's actions toward Von Stein — his obsequiousness and ingratiating way of holding doors had seemed little more than dutiful son — there were times his doting courtesy suggested more, much more, the possibility of romance, even an affair.

Over one meal when he launched into his discourse about love, Von Stein later told her daughter, Rogers went into a deep monologue about duty and family and a mother's love. As usual, it was about two coats of smarm too many, and the conversation soon shifted to other topics. Von Stein did not want this arrangement to get too personal. This much she knew: She wouldn't worry about him. She was not going to date him, and she knew how to handle herself. She could flutter close to the flame and not get burned.

She and Peters decided it would be in their mutual best interests to row their boats in the same direction for a while and see what happens. She'd find the reupholstery work, Peters or somebody he hired would actually do the work. All they needed was a little carry cash and maybe a part-timer to do some heavy lifting when needed.

Von Stein had lots of incentive but not much cash. The business would be her ticket out of Hamilton. Unlike Peters, her heart did not burn with love for the gritty town. Instead she yearned for the lights and opportunity offered in a bigger city, maybe Las Vegas. Reupholstery would get her there. It was an all-cash business for the most part and some of her expenses would be tax-deductible. Finding work would be no problem. There was always some doctor's wife in the nearby band of suburbia called West Chester who was unhappy with her dining room decor, a woman who would change fabric like fingernail polish, and with only a little urging: peach giving way to columbine yielding to cranberry. A larger city like Las Vegas would hold even more. But the key was to get out of Hamilton.

The arrangement worked for Peters, as well, as long as his Lindenwald neighbors didn't object to the comings-and-goings of the van making drops and pick-ups or the arrival of the repair guy. Though retired with a modest pension, he could always use a little more cash and this might bring it in. Freelance electric jobs were few though the quality of his work was high. Everybody with any juice in this town knew or had heard of Mark Peters.

But those jobs were becoming rarer and rarer, as Peters traded the mainstream of the subcontracting world for the backwater of retirement. A deal with Von Stein seemed like it could fly. Flea markets and estate sales out in towns that dotted the map held an endless array of antique tables and settees, from Louis XIV chairs to Whistler's mother's rocker, so Peters sold his restored cars and the garage space was given over to furniture repair.

Peters realized he needed a hand with the heavy lifting. He always used to have a wiry strength but those days were long gone. A strong hired back was what he needed now. Peters was a longtime friend of Edna Rogers, whom he met through the club life, particularly the V.F.W. post out on Smalley Boulevard or the Eagles lodge out on Ohio 128. They dated for a time, but soon split up, though they remained on friendly terms. It was at the Eagles, on a state highway also called Ross-Hamilton Road, that Peters ran into Edna one night in the summer of 1993 and learned that one of her sons was back in town from California with no place to stay and looking for work in a printing shop or as a remodeler. Edna's bungalow on Hunt Avenue was quaint, but that was just Realtorspeak for tiny, so small that a person had to go outside to find enough space to change her mind. Peters could offer up a bedroom in his house in return for help as needed with the business out back. Just for a few days until the son, Glen, could get back on his feet. A few weeks at worst. Employment could last longer if Glen was willing to learn and work. The arrangement seemed to make sense. Rogers had that strong back and was personable enough, though the jailhouse tattoo of DEbI, which looked like the date "1930" upside down across his knuckles, was not exactly the touch of class that some delivery jobs needed. If it ever came up, the tattoo always gave Rogers a chance to tell the tragic tale of his first wife dying and leaving him with two boys, youngsters he was trying to support down in Texas where they were living with cousins.

Even with the compelling story that matched the crude tattoo, Rogers would have to be kept from the clients. Peters thought he was too rough around the edges. But Peters needed the help and Rogers needed the bed. The old man took Glen Rogers in as a boarder as a favor to his former girlfriend.

It was not long before the arrangement soured. Rogers learned little and lifted even less. He hadn't yet bothered to find another crib – jailhouse lingo for one of those nasty apartments near the tracks in a neighborhood that was a hop-skip-and-a-jump from the joint. And he always seemed to be sneaking or lurking about the house. When Peters stopped by the local firehouse to spin a few stories and sip coffee with his son-in-law, Glen tagged along but stayed in the car. Rogers began to spend more and more time alone upstairs in the house and Peters was no longer comfortable with the situation. What was he doing up there all day? Why wasn't he out in the garage learning how to etch old varnish from rococoesque trim?

When Rogers was with Von Stein, it was another matter. He turned on the Southern charm, as if he were an eight-year-old skipping to a church picnic, a carefree and phony display of pleases and ma'ams and opening doors and grins and dipping nods meant to curry favor and attention: Eddie Haskel meets Guns 'N Roses. His manner was too much, too sickeningly sweet. The deal was simple enough. Per-job basis. She found the work and was pretty much the boss. He would be the subcontractor, ready and able to repair and paint. They met to discuss the deal at Ponderosa Steakhouse, living big, or at the Waffle House out on Route 4 in Fairfield.

At the meals, Rogers doted on Von Stein's grandchild, a four-month-old who still took a bottle but was also fond of mashed potatoes and came along with his mother Michelle to soak in the atmosphere. Rogers gave mothering tips to Von Stein's daughter — "Tip DJ's head up when he's feeding so it settles." That advice came as the two sat in the van outside Peters' house while Von Stein ran inside to pay a man for his work. Rogers was genuinely interested in the child, she thought. He had raised a couple of them, she knew, so she took his suggestions to heart and noticed how he could feed a boy in a high chair and maybe prop him up between blankets in the chair.

If no generous deed goes unpunished, then Peters had a few notches due on his ledger. Though business was business, if he caught somebody admiring one of his clocks — or most anything else he owned — he often asked if they liked it. The answer was always yes and Peters would frequently just give the clock away. After all, he had a dining room table full of clocks and such. Club leaders knew the clock market well enough to realize that the sale of one would make a great fund-raiser for the VFW. Raffle tickets sold for two dollars each. The take would surely match the tally from any of the other fund-raisers the club has organized, certainly the regular affairs like the Friday Social fish-fry, where Edna Rogers sits at the door, taking cash and dishing tickets. The event never really started making money until Edna took over the door. Yes, a clock raffle was overdue, and though it would not be in the same class as a golf outing, it would raise a few hundred dollars, buy some Christmas presents for needy kids.

Glen Rogers was not the only new resident at the Fairview Avenue house. Peters took in a small kitten and a puppy, a German Shepherd that one day would grow to 100 pounds or more and keep his eyes and nose on the garage, the coins, the knives, the clocks and the aging Peters. For now it was a frolicking pup and the kitten that hunted dustballs and chased its imagination for plenty of laughs.

Peters soon realized what a great thing this furniture repair business could be. Most of the inventory came from a closed used furniture store out on the strip. Allowing Lancaster into the garage gave Peters something to do and someone to make small talk with. If Rogers had become an inconvenience, had worn out his welcome, well, that too, would inevitably change a week or so after he moved out. Peters called a son in Kentucky, finally, and asked him to come and stay because he had a job for him. Rogers was only supposed to stay a day or two, and now those days had turned to weeks and it was time for him to go.

Peters was worried and wanted his son around when he gave Rogers the heave-ho. Rogers saw it coming. It was only a matter of time, and for Rogers, the time to act had arrived.

3

HAMILTON, OHIO • AUTUMN 1993

Glen Rogers was not the angel Joan Burkart had in mind the one and only time she met him.

It was a fall day and the oaks and maples of the Lindenwald neighborhood were blazing when she had stopped at her father's house, went into the garage where he was nursing a cup of coffee and watching John Lancaster at work. She handed over the plastic pipe for a kitchen sink drain that needed to be replaced. He had asked her to bring it by because the sink was stopped up. Her father invited Joan inside the house and she readily went along to see his new puppy and kitten. On the porch he paused and dropped his voice. He told her that somebody had moved in with him and was going to stay for a short while. He could not remember the fellow's name, only that he was the son of Edna Rogers and that he would not be living there for long, just a few days.

Once inside, she discovered a long-haired, unkempt man working under the sink. He got up as the father and daughter came into the kitchen, said hello, then moved off through the house to his room upstairs. He said nothing else and did not look back. She wondered about the guy as he walked away, and she bent to pick up the kitten. She knew at once that she didn't like him there. She also knew there was little she could do about it.

When she reported that her father was missing, Joan told authorities what she knew about him. He was Edna Rogers' son, a man named Glen.

The officers looked at one another and then back at Joan. There was no point sugar-coating the truth. A low-rung drug snitch known for his vicious temper and for rampages and then blacking out for days at a time, a man with a record dating back to his teens who was as conniving and deceitful as a man could be — he was suddenly back on the radar screen.

When Joan mentioned the Rogers name, police didn't pick and choose their response. They gave it to her straight: Expect the worst, they said. Expect the worst.

The clock finally stopped on the relationship between Glen Rogers and Mark Peters sometime in mid-October. The evening of October 17 they had a disagreement on the front porch of the house on Fairview Avenue. It ended with Rogers getting something of an eviction. They both left in Peters' car, and Peters would never be seen alive again.

It was months before the truth came out about the visitor and his plans.

All the while he lived in the house, Rogers had a scam in mind, a serious sting that he believed would bring him a bundle. That's what he told his older brother, Clay Wayne Rogers, back in October 1993, and it's what Clay would tell Hamilton police on January 1, 1994, while calling them in a clumsy attempt to collect a $1,000 Crime Stoppers reward offered by a local television station for information about Peters' disappearance.

Clay had tried to muffle his voice when he talked to Detective Tom Kilgour for ten minutes. Kilgour and Detective James Nugent were on the Peters case, tag-teaming, but they had very little. Kilgour knew he was talking to Clay as soon as he heard his voice but decided to play out the line and see where it went. Clay spoke in generalities and then said he believed that a guy named Glen did the old man in, a guy named Glen who was now living in California. Within minutes, Kilgour grew tired of the charade. Kilgour had known Clay since they were kids growing up on the west side of town. They attended the same schools, walked the same halls and the same blocks home. Clay was wild and his home life was rough. When they were teens, their paths diverged. Clay fell into a life of crime. Kilgour became a cop. He smirked and shook his head as he talked with Clay from the bullpen desk area of the Hamilton Police Department, a back room loaded with computer printers, ringing phones and large men quietly working at small desks. Finally he could take it no more. Clay was too clumsy for words.

"Clay, what are you doing?" he finally asked.

"Hi Tom," Clay replied in his own voice when he realized the jig was up. "How's it going?"

It was time to come clean, to fill in some blanks and Clay Rogers did not hesitate. His brother was involved with the death of Mark Peters, he said. But he didn't think he killed him – or if he did, it was an accident. The old man died after the two argued and Glen may have pushed him. Old men die easy, especially old guys like Peters who had a weak heart and had spent a few years drinking too hard in the veterans clubs that were his second home. Clay was not sure when it happened but he knew where the body was. Yes, he would come down to the station to talk about it. Living in Covington, Kentucky, at the time with a menial job at a downtown donut shop, he could get up to Hamilton within the week to meet with detectives.

"Now about that reward?" The reward could wait, he was told. "Come to Hamilton as soon as you can."

Clay told police that when he was released from jail on Dec. 12 a month before, he made a beeline for his mother's home in Hamilton and called Glen in California. Glen told him a tale: "Mark Peters is dead and it was an accident," he said. He said it was due to Mark's medication. He told Clay he was in trouble in too many different places and that he could not be connected with Peters' death. Clay asked Glen why he went to the family cabin for two days, though he knew full well why Glen had made the pilgrimage south to the familiar hills and hollows of Beattyville, Kentucky. Glen responded with a chilling statement that danced around the truth like a cat that toys with a moth.

"Glen said I knew why he went there and that I did not need to be involved in this and to stay away from the cabin and property," Clay told police.

Clay claimed Glen told him that Peters caused his own death, that he had been drinking heavily, that his death may have been caused by a mixture of chlorohydrate and alcohol. He told him there were holes already dug in the area, gravesites, and that he had spent four days in Mark Peters' house after the death to clean it out.

Furniture was sold at flea markets in Northern Kentucky and at a Lexington pawn shop. Glen kept some items with him as he traveled the country. As for the car, Glen told his brother that he ditched it in downtown Cincinnati.

Clay agreed to go with detectives to that Kentucky hillside, and said he would go at their convenience. But he left out a key part of his brother's scam. Furniture was not the only thing he stole those weeks he lived in the house. While Mark Peters worked in the garage or visited there with neighbors, Rogers was working in the house, sifting through family records, seeking a false identity. He found one, too. James Peters, a son who lived in California, had a VISA card number and it was not long before Glen had the account, and enough information that he could impersonate the man. It was the jackpot.

There was at least one other lead in the case. The woman: June Elizabeth Von Stein.

When Von Stein stopped home from work that afternoon in late October 1993, she was surprised at the scene in her front yard. Hamilton police cruisers were everywhere. At least five were arrayed across her front yard and on the street in front of her house. "They were all over," she said. "I thought they wanted some upholstery work done but no, they wanted me to go with them right now."

She was a suspect in a case that came to light for authorities only days before when Joan Burkart told them her father was missing. Police now considered his disappearance more than a simple missing persons case. They were investigating a murder, they believed, and they wanted to know more about the relationship between Von Stein and Peters.

It was not a business arrangement in the classic sense of deal: shared assets, a cash arrangement that included the purchase and sale of goods and items or an alignment of efforts to mine a market niche. This arrangement was much cleaner and simpler. Von Stein, who was planning to move to Las Vegas, kept her bulky copy machine at his house until she could make the move. She also visited with Peters, a seventy-one-year-old who seemed even older, drank coffee with him and used his garage to store furniture that needed refinishing. But Peters had been missing for nearly two weeks and now Von Stein was a suspect.

Von Stein, a lifelong Hamilton resident, refused to go, and that gave police something to think about that afternoon on her front porch. But she did not refuse to talk, far from it. The interview would occur, and it would occur that very day but not during business hours. She had work to do. "I'm not going anywhere now. I got appointments. You want to talk to me, I can come to the police station on my own. I don't need somebody to drive me. I don't need to sit in the back seat of a cruiser with all my neighbors watching. I can make it to the station on my own. I know where it's at." And she would come without a lawyer. She had nothing to hide.

When her day ended, Von Stein drove to the station and was taken to an interview room. The meeting soon slid toward antagonism. Von Stein, a woman of strong will who had no arrest record and was accustomed to working in a male-dominated trade, was also used to speaking her mind. Police, poised to find a missing man and suspicious of everything about this petite blond woman, opened the interview with a sneering bombshell.

"So, you like younger men?"

"Well, all you farts are too old if that's what you mean," she shot back. If they wanted to start off smart, she could keep the static coming as good as anybody. Police got to the point. She and Glen killed Mark Peters and took antiques out of his house, they suspected. The allegation was shocking. She always found Peters to be a charming and witty friend, a kind old man who had courtly ways, particularly around her. She was touched by how Peters would rush through the house, ditch the shirt he was wearing and put on a clean one when she arrived unexpectedly. He might even try to sneak in a shave, she said, in the time it took for her to visit John Lancaster — the wood refinisher busy most mornings out in the garage — and then make her way to the house.

"Hey, I liked the old guy. He was a nice guy and I had a lot of good conversations with him. I even did a rocker for him as a going-away gift. They said they had witnesses who saw my van in front of his house. Now if I was going to steal something, am I going to park my van with my business name on the side of the door right in front of the house? I might be blond but I'm not a ditzy blond."

She told police what she knew. The last time she saw Mark Peters was on October 17, a night they spent at local clubs. First stop was the Eagles Lodge. She parked her van in front of Mark's house and rode over in his car with Glen driving. She was going to join the club and the local V.F.W. as well, and she needed to meet with officials at both organizations. At the Eagles she met with leaders, had one drink and signed up. From there, the three headed over to the Campbell Guard Post No. 1069 V.F.W. in nearby Fairfield where she had another drink and another signing session. There she ran into a friend, another Hamilton businesswoman, Betty Stiver, who ran Sunshine Health Foods.

Rogers left an impression on Stiver and others who saw him there that night. "I remembered thinking what an attractive man he was," Stiver said, "except he had a gap in his teeth. He was missing a tooth. I thought what a good-looking man he'd be if he'd only had that tooth." Rogers was on his best behavior that night. He bowed slightly when he was introduced and he did nothing to draw attention to himself.

Von Stein told police Peters was drinking and he was rowdy.

"Mark was the kind of guy that if he got a few drinks in him, he got loud and obnoxious," she said. The bartender came over and told Peters he had to leave. He was far too loud and too drunk. Rogers left the bar with Peters and then returned twenty or thirty minutes later to pick her up.

It was not until months later, as club members looked back on the night, that they realized that when

Rogers returned, he was a changed man. He was nervous and seemed antsy. He acted like he was in a hurry. He did not stay long.

"We didn't think much about it at the time but we talked about it later," Stiver said. Soon, Rogers and Von Stein left. But the evening was not over. "We stopped at the Elbow Room for one drink – I know the owner George – and then we left to go back to Mark's house, where my van was parked. I was going to run in and go to the bathroom."

Once upstairs, she walked past a partially open bedroom door where somebody appeared to be sleeping, though she could not hear any snoring. "It looked like somebody was in there. Supposedly that's the last time anybody saw Mark," she said.

The next morning, she received a call from Rogers asking if she needed him to help. He was being paid forty dollars a day plus meals: good money by bottom-rung Hamilton standards. She told him she did, that she needed to make a few more calls and that she would pick him up in an hour. "I didn't know where he was calling me from but when I got down to Mark's house to pick him up, John (Lancaster) out in the garage said he didn't know where anybody was. He'd been there since 6:30 a.m. and said he hadn't seen anybody," Von Stein said.

Two days later her cell phone rang. It was Glen and he sounded excited. He needed a favor. It was a week after their night in the private clubs. Mark had left in the morning with some lady, he said, in fact her name was Liz, and they went to Cincinnati somewhere. Mark needed a ride back because she wouldn't bring him back to Hamilton. Could Von Stein go get him, he wondered. She said sure, to call back in ten minutes with directions and she would go and get him as long as he was within ten miles of where she was headed. The return call never came.

The interview ended with Von Stein refusing to take a lie detector test. She was troubled by the cops' attitude — that they believed she was a conspiring older woman who hooked up with younger men to con and kill an old man was not the most comforting of assertions. She went home, convinced that police were not going to give up on her. She needed to talk to Glen and needed to do it soon. She would not be disappointed. Within days he called again.Their conversation went something like this:

Where are you? she asked.

Right here in town, he replied.

Don't you know what's going on here? For one thing, they're trying to say you and I killed Mark Peters and took stuff out of his house.

Mark's not missing, Rogers told her. His son had a big fight with him and blackened his eye. Von Stein believed him.

Glen, you do know where he is? Tell him what's going on here. At least let him call police and tell them where he's at.

Von Stein hoped her phone was tapped. The conversation would prove that she knew nothing about Peters' whereabouts. Then if his disappearance was linked to this usually polite man who had been her business associate, police would soon find that out and arrest him. She would do what she could to help.

She forced him to answer her questions. "The day you called me and was in the van, why didn't you call me back?," she recalled asking him. Glen didn't answer. She then told him she not only spoke with police but was cooperating with them, that she went down to the station to tell them what she knew on her own. Glen wanted to know the name of the detective assigned to the case and when he learned it was Tom Kilgour he demanded that Von Stein stop talking freely.

"Don't you dare talk to detectives," he commanded.

"Why not? I'm going to tell them everything they want to know."

"Because I'm a three-time felon and any more arrests would put me in prison for a long, long time."

Von Stein was not moved. "I've never been arrested in my life and I can't really deal with that," she answered. "It's your problem."

Glen flew into a rage. "Don't talk to that fucking prick," he screamed into the phone. "I know that son-of-a-bitch." His venom continued and then the line went dead. Rogers hung up. Von Stein would never hear from him again. A few weeks later, Von Stein made her planned move to Las Vegas. It raised suspicions among police but they had no reason to hold her. She had told authorities what she knew about Rogers and now he was gone. What else could be done?

Across town in Hamilton, Joan Burkart had given up on finding her father alive. Weeks before, she had taken the flowers her father had given her for her wedding anniversary and dried them. She put the blooms, pastels of blue and pink and white, into a vase and set the vase up on a mantel, never to be taken down. It would be a shrine of sorts to a loving grandfather who trusted too much, a reminder that his death would not be in vain.

His killer would be brought to justice — some day. Her Lord would see to that.

4

LEE COUNTY, KENTUCKY • JANUARY 10, 1994

This time, Danny Townsend didn't have much choice.

"OK," he told the caller from Hamilton, Ohio. He would organize a search team to scour the mountain cabin at Old Landing Road and Highway 52, ten miles west of Beattyville on the way to Richmond. Detectives Thomas Kilgour and James Nugent were on their way. They needed help. They were looking for a body.

Two weeks earlier, they had pressed Townsend for assistance and he had held them off. "Right now we've got a couple of inches of snow on the ground," he had told them in that late December phone conversation. Could it wait? On this cold Monday morning, the cops had run out of patience. They would arrive in four hours. On this day they could wait no longer.

And so Danny Townsend, the 55-year-old police chief of Beattyville, Kentucky, did what he had to do. At his desk in the cramped police station of the little mountain town of 1,100, he picked up the phone and summoned his posse.

While Chief Townsend stayed in Beattyville tending to city matters, his volunteers descended on the cabin. They arrived around the same time and parked on Highway 52. There is almost no shoulder on Highway 52, and a slight misjudgment can send an unhappy driver into the roadside ditch that falls sharply from the narrow pavement. The cabin sits fifty yards up the steep hillside from the highway and in summer conceals itself in thick foliage. In winter the careful eye can spot the cabin from the highway. Old Landing Road, a winding and narrow trail of perhaps two miles that serves a few mountain homesteads, begins on the other side of the highway from where they parked and immediately takes a sharp turn uphill to the right.

The roads were clear, but it was cold with spitting snow and just enough of a biting wind to let the searchers know it was January. They had to walk up the hill because dense overgrowth had made the cut impassable. Larry Hagan, the game warden; Eugene Barrett, Lee County rescue squad captain; and Danny Thomas, a Beattyville policeman, were all here not in official capacity but as volunteers. They were joined by Ova (Junior) McIntosh, a rescue squad member, and Larry Barrett, Eugene's son. It wasn't long before three men drove up in an unmarked police car bearing Ohio plates. Two of them introduced themselves: Detectives Tom Kilgour and James Nugent, Hamilton PD. With them was a man in his thirties wearing a jacket, blue jeans and a baseball cap. He did not introduce himself. Nobody asked for his name. But the local volunteers knew something about him, all right. They knew he was the informant who led the Hamilton detectives to this cabin where, he told them, they would find the body of Mark Clarence Peters. The next hour would set in motion a chain of events and a slow unfolding of justice that would fill graves and change lives forever.

Finding nothing inside the dark two-room cabin but a rotted-out floor, caved-in ceiling and piles of rubble — a mattress, broken furniture, trash, beer cans and a whiskey bottle — the team of seven fanned out. Was this a waste of their time, the cynical scam of a goofball?

Skepticism soon faded when Eugene Barrett noticed

a bone — a rib bone, he believed — peeking through a dusting of snow. It could have been an animal's; he could not tell. The searchers soon found more bones scattered away from the cabin that most likely were carried there by dogs. Searching the back room with his flashlight, Officer Danny Thomas was looking for a body and did not realize the rubble he stumbled over concealed human remains. Barnett and Hagan came along and looked closer. On top of a piece of drywall was the frame of a wood chair. Barnett pulled back the chair, lifted the drywall and discovered a bundle on the floor. It was wrapped in a window drapery and bound by forty-two feet of hemp rope, and wrapped again in a Motel 6 blanket. Inside the bundle Barnett found part of a foot, the body's only remaining flesh. Mixed in was a man's Van Heusen shirt with a ticket in the pocket for a drawing for a grandfather clock at a VFW post in Hamilton, Ohio.

Chief Townsend arrived around 3 p.m. and pursued his own search. In the front room he found two *Playboy* magazines on the floor. Next to them he discovered a thin, worn ring. Townsend called the sheriff's office, which contacted State Police Post 7 in Richmond. By late afternoon the cabin swarmed with state police (led by Det. Floyd McIntosh), the Lee County medical examiner and forensic investigators from Frankfort. As darkness fell, McIntosh and Hagan left the scene to conduct a house-to-house survey to find out if dogs had carried home any human bones.

Down the hillside, across the highway and up the other side of Old Landing Road, sisters Clara and Edith Smallwood sat in the coziness of their front room and observed the goings-on. They knew this cabin well. Their cousin Claude and Uncle Clyde had built it back in the Fifties as a weekend fishing and hunting retreat. They watched but they did not intrude.

The wheels of justice had begun to turn.

5

I don't know how long ago that was. Year before last. I lost track of time, I don't know. All these years keep going and going and going and going.

— Glen Rogers, interviewed at Post 7

ON THE ROAD

Glen and his older brother Clay had a name for their years and time together away from Hamilton — five or six years straight running through the Midwest and southland scrub brush of Florida, sometimes together, sometimes apart in the late 1980s and early 1990s. Always running, usually from the law.

They were vagabonds and they called themselves Road Dogs — named for their preferred method of long haul travel — the dog on the side of the bus.

"It's not hard to get out of the state," Glen once boasted. "All I have to do is walk into a Greyhound station. Nobody ever checks it. Nobody asks for I.D. You get on the next bus out, nobody cares. You can rob a bank and walk around the corner and go to the Greyhound station. Nobody ever knows who you were, ever saw you. That's a fact."

Glen went from town to city and back to town and learned the ways and rhythms of homeless shelters and scrap yards and lonely women, sometimes attractive but sometimes not so, divorced and hungry for a man. When he worked, it was always a bit of brokerage. Something for nothing whenever possible.

Glen knew cars and how to steal them and what they were worth chopped up in sections the size of a desk or chair. Hot cars and Glen Rogers went together like smoke and honkytonks. When he was road dogging, he always had some little scam in the works that usually had to do with hot cars or something stolen or drugs. Carnival work was real work and Glen only rolled as a carny for one season, about four months. He was a highwayman and he lived on the back roads of Kentucky, Tennessee and Ohio or haunted the roadhouse motels across the country from Central Florida to Southern California.

He was as dangerous as a man could be, unpredictable and without a conscience. He stalked empty houses and staked them out before entering in broad daylight. A house with no vehicle in sight meant nobody was home. Once inside, he worked quickly and without fear. If anybody ever came home while he was there, he would not be the one who was surprised.

"I'm not the one who's caught," he bragged. "If somebody comes home, they don't catch me. I catch them. They's the one who gets caught. There's no motive. There's no witnesses."

The pair had criminal training from the crib.

"From birth on up we was taught," Clay said. "After you left, you strip and burn everything you had. Glen knew water washed away evidence. So it was always fire and water. You burn it. It's gone. So Glen doesn't worry about fingerprints."

The Road Dogs went to small towns and big cities. Once Glen arrived, he found the lost corners on the side of town with the railroad tracks and spare lots of $100-down used cars and chain-link fence debris. He knew the down-heeled country corners of the Midwest and South because they were the second cousins to his hometown of Hamilton. The river of whiskey joints through the nation was seamless and endless and Rogers knew how to survive on its shores.

By the time he had been in California a couple of years Rogers had been traveling the country for at least a decade — probably much longer — without attracting much attention other than in brief press accounts of routine crime reports. Even in Hamilton, where he settled for a while in 1991-92 and drove a cab, he managed to avoid the public eye. One charge, for which he skipped bail and was never tried, involved a felony in Indiana. Rogers never said where exactly this crime took place, or when, or exactly what happened. Either he didn't remember or didn't want to reveal this detail of his past.

"I woke up in jail on a robbery charge. It was some store or something. And I bailed myself out." And he didn't bother returning to face trial in Indiana. "I knew better," he explained.

Sometime around 1993 while living in Hollywood, California, he went to jail for arson and battery, but the state, unable to convict him in three trials, eventually dropped the charges. It wasn't for lack of opportunity that authorities failed to put Rogers out of business. Between 1982 and 1995 he was arrested or charged with ten felonies and eleven assaults from Ohio to California. He served less than a year in prison for felony breaking and entering and two days in jail for assault.

Though he was in and out of detention as a juvenile and did one stretch at reform school, his juvenile record was long ago purged. Retired police who dealt with him, and Rogers himself, profess to only vague memories of Glen's juvenile career.

Sometimes the incidents amounted to little more than petty squabbles or bar fights, and the complainants were happy just to be rid of him. On February 16, 1993, Glen was a laborer for M. Charles Productions at the Wagon Wheel Flea Market in Pinellas Park, Florida. Heavy drinking among several employees led to an argument and then to a fight involving Rogers and Shane David Bayless. They were chronic trouble-makers, and their supervisor wanted them gone. He paid them off, and they packed their belongings and took a taxi to Gibsonton.

"I was just minding my own business when out of nowhere a fight broke out," Glen explained. He got hit in the eye; by whom, he didn't know. One thing about Glen's life as a drifter is clear, however: how he financed himself. Working for Bentley Brothers in 1994 in Pinellas County, he staged a daring daylight raid on the office and took all the payroll cash.

"I robbed the circus of about $15,000. I just broke the trailer door open and stole all the payroll."

Rogers did nothing to call attention to himself and was never confronted as a suspect. It was classic Rogers: Act as if nothing is unusual, and make no attempt to find the limelight.

"I went right back to work at eight o'clock the next morning," he said, and worked for Bentley Brothers another week before quitting. From there, he and an acquaintance he knew only as "some guy named Sarge" drove Sarge's car to Sarge's hometown, "somewhere in Oklahoma." From there, he migrated to Joplin, Missouri, and worked for about a month at a place called The Club. He stayed with a woman he met at The Club, a woman whose name he cannot recall. Neither could he recall where he went from Joplin.

Rogers lived with many different women during this time. (His preferred source of room and board was lonely, vulnerable women; he was an expert at preying on their emotions.) Prior to the journey that took him from Florida to Oklahoma to Missouri, he lived in California. After he beat the arson rap in Hollywood he lived in nearby Van Nuys for a time, then boarded a Greyhound and moved to Las Vegas, where he claims to have gambled away $20,000. He stayed there about two months and then moved to Utah, where he paid $15,000 for a trailer and four acres. He never explained where his money came from. He lived there with a girlfriend. He could not remember her name.

Everywhere Glen Rogers went, he collected women like trinkets, discarding them when the novelty wore off. (The more fortunate ones survived the experience.) He could not even be bothered to remember their names. Rogers thinks he went to Colorado from Utah. This was sometime in 1994. From there he went to Houston looking for his two children, who became wards of the State of Texas following the death of his wife in 1992. "The bitch wouldn't let me," he said of a state worker who blocked his attempt to visit his children. The court barred him from seeing them, he explained, because his wife had died of "unexplained circumstances."

Debbi Nix Rogers married at age sixteen and died at age twenty-eight in Houston. "They said it was a heart attack," Rogers said, "but a drug overdose is more like it."

Glen got close enough to catch a glimpse of his children, but they did not see him. He made his way up to Oklahoma and found work as a "weeder," cutting wheat and barley. After a short while he migrated south to Texarkana, Texas, and rejoined Bluegrass Shows. He had worked for them on and off for three years. Usually he drove a truck — up the East Coast, down the West Coast.

In his travels Glen pursued many lines of work, never for very long. In California he worked in construction, repairing earthquake damage. He had his own painting business. He and his onetime girlfriend, Maria Gyore, managed a 150-unit apartment building. In Oklahoma he operated a combine.

Glen Rogers was a man of many occupations, and when he roamed, his brother said, Glen sometimes left a trail of bodies. “I know for a fact there’s a body in the desert out beyond the Greyhound Bus Station in Las Vegas,” Clay said. “He got rid of another body in Denver in a tunnel.

“I know it for a fact.”

6

HAMILTON, OHIO • 1980S

Detective Dan Pratt was a patrolman the first time he met Glen Rogers. The call was a breaking-and-entering out on Route 4 near the edge of Hamilton. A burglar alarm had been triggered and Pratt, patrolling the town on a dreary week-night, was called to investigate. He was surprised at what he found when he arrived at the Midas Muffler Shop. Rogers, who had clearly had too much to drink, had managed to break and crawl through a back window, locate the keys to his 1969 yellow Mustang, with its hatchback ready for big bass speakers, and when he could not get the shop door unlocked, had tried unsuccessfully to drive the Mustang right on through it.

It was in the shop in the first place because police had cited Rogers for having a loud muffler when he roared through the narrow streets of the city's Second Ward. By the time the night was done, the car would need more than a muffler. The shop's door was dented, the car was too, and Rogers was under arrest. But a working relationship was born on that night between Rogers and Pratt, who wanted to strap on a shoulder holster and suit and tie and go to work as a detective. Rogers, who had already gone to work for other jurisdictions as a police drug buyer and informer, would be Pratt's ticket up and out.

With limited resources, and saddled with a department of familiar faces, making drug arrests in a town like Hamilton is a difficult proposition. Dealers know the cops. Cops know the dealers. Arrests are few, particularly in the black community, where white buyers are immediately regarded with suspicion and doubt.

For Hamilton police in the 1980s, Rogers was a godsend. Within a few months he became a key player in the local war on drugs, one of the town's biggest police informers who would set up dozens of drug busts. He would turn in acquaintances and friends alike, and Pratt estimated that 100 or more drug arrests through the 1980s and early 1990s involved Rogers. One 1991 bust netted forty dealers. When Glen escaped arrest, the low life of Hamilton knew who was to blame.

One slow afternoon, police estimated how much money Rogers made through informing on buyers. It was in the thousands of dollars. Typically, Pratt would pick up Rogers in the late afternoon and they would drive through town to a bar or house, where Glen knew there were drugs, mostly small-time dealers. Rogers would say that his friend in the car wanted to make a buy. Within minutes, the deal was done. Usually, there would be another buy from the same dealer and a request that this time he wanted more, wanted to climb the ladder of small-time dope dealing. After each buy, Rogers pocketed twenty bucks for his trouble and received a free lesson in police protocol. He wore listening wires and learned what was admissible in court and what was not. Pratt said authorities never let him touch or be near the drugs. They did not want their chief witness tainted, and when the court date arrived, Rogers was a ready witness. No conviction, no cash.

Police had back-up units on some arrests, three or four officers working with Rogers as he prowled the bars and clubs of the county, dozens of places with names like Stumble Inn and The Crystal Bar, The Choo-choo and The Caboose.

It was a part-time job with decent pay and plenty of small town power. Close friend? Family? It did not matter to Rogers. He would work to arrest anybody. The straight-shooters like Pratt, who had to meet with Rogers frequently and use him for the busts, cringed, then went on with the task at hand: getting crack and pot off the streets.

But a drug informant's life carried consequences for an informer. Hamilton was no megalopolis. Drug dealers did their time, typically ninety days or less in the overcrowded red brick county jail downtown. Because budgets are lean and the jail was always full, the drug sellers were usually out on the street long before serving their full sentences. Once out, they came looking for Rogers. Frequently they found him. It was not too tough. Where's Glen? Driving a cab would be a good place to start, they knew. Paybacks were brutal. Rogers was once found by fellow cab drivers, face down and unconscious in the company lot. Though the beatings were few, whenever Rogers crossed paths with irritated dealers, they got their pound of flesh or paid somebody else to get it for them.

From 1986 to 1991, Glen filed eight police reports, claiming to have been beaten or robbed himself. There were times he called police from back room telephones, begging for them to rescue him from the bar because he was about to get the thrashing of his life. Glen was never much of a fighter.

If it got too hot, Rogers skipped town, headed south to Kentucky, to Winchester or Lexington or the cool green hills of Beattyville, where the family's hillside hunting cabin always beckoned. Kentucky was a footloose backwoods corner of the country, and he fit right in. He could get a lumbering job or set out and harvest marijuana plants and run them south to Florida and west to California at will. To avoid running into double-crossed and angry foot soldiers on the bad-guy side of the drug wars, Rogers learned to alter his appearance. He would allow his hair to grow long, then cut it severely and grow a beard. He avoided clubs and bars where particularly unsavory buyers spent their time: PJ's out on Route 4 had a reputation as a biker bar and Glen rarely drank there. It was just too tough, Pratt remembered.

Though a blessing in the drug wars, Rogers was also a hex for local lawmen. From 1987 through 1992 and his last contempt-of-court charge in Hamilton Municipal Court, Rogers was arrested thirty-nine times by seventeen Hamilton officers. He was arrested for failure to appear in court numerous times, disorderly conduct, receiving stolen property, forgery, petty theft, parole violation, simple assault, disorderly conduct by intoxication, criminal damaging, assault, criminal trespass, aggravated menacing, contempt of court, arson, resisting arrest and inducing panic.

His role as a drug informer largely kept him out of jail, despite his many scrapes with police. He came to know policemen the way a wisened mechanic knows a V-8 engine. When he appeared before a local judge, his trial was frequently postponed and Rogers would ignore the date and time of his next appearance. An arrest warrant usually followed. He could ignore that, too, because as every street criminal knew, the local jail was full and there were thousands of arrest warrants that would never be served because there were no empty beds in the jail. The Hobson's choice for the county sheriff was not which ashtray to use or which coffee cup to fill but which criminal each night would go free to make room for the really bad guys: the car thief or the check bouncer, the drunk driver or the bar fighter? Who would be freed to make room for the arsonist?

Rogers, a ninth-grade dropout, became a quick study in police ways and developed a persona that could lead people to believe he was a detective. He was bold. While living in California, he once stormed through a bar looking for his girlfriend, claiming to be a police detective on official business. While a few may have questioned that in their own minds, nobody stopped him. Impersonating the detective was a skill he honed in Hamilton. He worked with police or was arrested by them so many times that it became a cat-and-mouse game he played with skill.

Here, too, is where Rogers learned another powerful lesson: Police, more often than not, do not get their man. Arrests are rare. Mistakes are many. The guilty frequently walk. Luck, rather than competence, usually brings the guilty to the judge and jail.

In 1987, Glen's long string of freedom came to a knot. He pled guilty to breaking and entering and forgery, and rather than receive probation or a mitigated sentence in the county jail, he was slam-dunked two years. The man who once bragged that he had seen the inside walls of every juvenile jail in Ohio was about to see the wrong side of yet another prison. He went to the Warren Correctional facility in nearby Lebanon to begin his stretch on January 19, 1988. Because he was a first-time offender on the books, even though his police record was literally as long as a tall man's arm, and was ironically considered nonviolent, the Ohio Parole Board decided he was a good risk for release into the community.

He was given shock parole on August 22 and again turned loose on the citizens of Ohio. It was not long before Glen showed the board the error of its ways. By November, he had violated his parole and was returned to prison but this time to the Ohio Reformatory upstate in Mansfield. By June 1, 1989, he was free again and ready to roam. A day later, June 2, he was booked again for simple assault, the result of a post-release celebration of freedom no doubt, and the short spell Hamilton police had with no Glen Rogers around was broken.

Main Street remains one of the few classic neighborhood everyman's streets in Hamilton. There are shoe stores and drug stores, men's clothing shops and a poodle-trimming salon. Secondhand fronts offer household items, baby's clothing and other detritus of pop culture: an electric toothbrush that has no bristles, clock radios, candles, bad suits, dresses and other wear from the dearly departed. Antique shops hold china from an old woman in the neighborhood who needs a new furnace, while down the sidewalk a video store offers Tuesday Movie Night.

At the corner drug store, you can still order up a cherry phosphate, and from one of the four classic Naugahyde stools you might have seen Glen Rogers come and go from time to time in 1990. He lived upstairs. The apartment building is large by Hamilton standards, with a live-in superintendent, who frowns and shakes his head slowly from side-to-side as he tries to remember details of Rogers and then stops. He remembers, finally. The guy was trouble in an apartment building that is no stranger to problems. The place fills with children on autumn afternoons as school lets out. The younger ones coyly scramble in and out of doorways and pose questions to visitors like: "Are you two getting a divorce?" Household stability in the eyes of a 5-year-old here is more concept than concrete reality in this sprawling brick building of echoing hallways and cramped bathrooms. That was the way it was when Glen lived here, and that's the way it remains today.

Rogers is not quite forgotten in this neighborhood whose half-dozen long stretch of stores was his boyhood block. Police have a detailed track record of his adult time here and a snapshot of one particular night when Glen's household became a typical study in domestic violence. Fights between Rogers and Angel Wagers were regular and despite police visits, the frying pan-flinging never really abated. Music on the louder side could be tolerated in this apartment building — George Strait droning through open doors — but Rogers' profanity and fighting awakened too many people and brought the law so Rogers and Wagers were told to leave. Locks were changed. Hit the road. Don't bother with a lawyer and fix that hole over there in the living room wall. Glen's behavior was becoming increasingly violent.

Wagers, whose name is tattooed on Rogers' right shoulder, filed a chilling account in 1990 describing one of Glen's rages. Unemployed at the time and drawing $100 per month in compensation from the State of Ohio, Rogers was low on cash and high on stress. He rolled up in his battered Oldsmobile Delta 88 and demanded to be let in. "He is very violent," Wagers wrote in a domestic violence complaint. Rogers arrived at her house just as she was about to leave for work. Her father had to wake her up because she had overslept, and Rogers demanded to know how she could abandon him at the Main Street apartment to return to her parents' home. He then began to beat her, mostly about her face. He grabbed and held her by the arm and repeatedly threw punches, screaming: "Just what the hell are you doing?" He beat her to the floor.

"I do believe he has a mental problem and I don't put anything past him," she wrote in the complaint. "I am terrified of him. He has threatened to kill me and my family and he led me to believe when I would start my car it would blow up."

Since Rogers was seventy percent grease monkey,

police took his threats to blow up her car seriously. They immediately dispatched an officer, whose first act upon arriving at the scene was to pop the hood of Wagers' car.

"I am really afraid for my life," Angel wrote. Rogers was tracked down and arrested — another night in jail and he was back out on the street. The report and the red flags it should have raised were filed and forgotten.

Another police encounter in the 600 block of Ludlow Street in 1991 was spectacular for one twist. Rogers had barricaded himself and a hooker in the house and threatened to shoot anybody who came through the door. This was no time for pizza delivery men and it was no time for Lieutenant Dan Lang to do anything rash, either. He was the shift supervisor called to the east side of town and he took a few minutes to sort it out: Former petty police drug informer who has a decades-old record of barking but not biting goes off the deep end and actually blows away a cop.

Rogers, reported neighbors, had a hammer and was beating his way through his house and threatening the hooker and anyone else who got in his path. He was smashing doorways, walls and cabinets in a terrifying orgy of fury and mayhem. Eventually, he turned his destructive attention to the front door, and the bassoon of the painted pine bellowed through the neighborhood of World War II-style wood-frame houses. It was an Emmy-winning performance by police standards. By now, Glen was no longer satisfied with the routine.

He found a propane blow-torch in the house, fired it up and aimed for a hole he had bashed in the door.

"Any time anyone approached, he'd shoot those flames out," Lang said. The officer had seen a lot of odd domestic runs in his time on the force: the arguments over spilled salt that escalated into gunloading, the lost set of car keys and the accusations of infidelity immediately followed by fists on flesh. But never, ever, had he seen a man set a door on fire with a blowtorch. Eventually the door caught fire, Rogers lost his head of steam, was arrested and taken to jail. But he did not stay there long.

Knowing that the jail was overcrowded and that the resulting arrest warrant would never be served, Glen ignored his court date and went on about his grim business.

7

HAMILTON, OHIO • EARLY 1990S

Wayne Brockman pulled his dirty Dodge Diplomat, called Yellow 25 by his gravel-voiced dispatcher, up into the bumpy lot at Ohio Taxi and settled it next to Redtop 59, an old Chevy Nova driven by Glen Rogers. It was a hot summer night, and it was not yet closing time for the bars and honky-tonks that lit the corners of Hamilton's Second and Fourth Wards. Brockman looked over at Glen and cringed. He was the last guy on earth Brockman wanted to see. He just did not like Glen Rogers.

Brockman was not alone. Most employees of Ohio Taxi wanted little to do with Rogers. Dispatcher Steve McKay put nothing past Glen. In fact, he believed Glen probably was a killer — though McKay had no hard evidence, only suspicions.

McKay's second cousin, the late Tommy Wolsefor, had shared a studio apartment with Rogers near JJ's bar before Wolsefor's demise. McKay believed Glen killed him. Wolsefor was an alcoholic with advanced liver disease in his last days. He was a cab driver too, and his living arrangement with Rogers eventually would be his undoing. Wolsefor's problem was the same as many who live in a world of reefer, whiskey, pills and impromptu parties. He liked a good time, preferably one enhanced with some street medication. He was a partier and any time of day was okay. Wolsefor headed off to Vietnam like many of his generation and when he returned, he moved back to Lebanon, just east of Hamilton, to marry and raise two sons. He worked as a lineman for the City of Lebanon. He also developed an appreciation for alcohol. Within years, he had lost his job and his family and found himself on the street, only a rung above the homeless and only there because he could still drive a cab, could manage to show up for work sober and on time.

It was while driving a cab that he met Glen Rogers. They hit it off well, as heavy drinkers often do. In the fall of 1990, Wolsefor and Rogers shared the apartment down by the tracks. The arrangement was hardly a tidy one. Wolsefor reported a breaking-and-entering in October and claimed he came home and found Cora McKnight, Rogers' lover. Charges followed but were dropped. To family members, Wolsefor was known as a fellow who had close friends, good friends and unfortunately, trashy friends. Mark Peters was in the first category. Wolsefor's quest for drug-laden and alcohol-laced fun eventually caught up with him — and strangely Glen was there.

"Eventually he had a seizure and Glen was the one who found him," Steve McKay said, but the finding came only after Wolsefor had lain in the apartment for more than two days and nights. Wolsefor was in bad shape. He was in a coma and lucky to be alive when he was taken to Mercy Hospital Hamilton, before being transferred to the Veteran's Administration Hospital in Dayton and then finally, as he began to recover, back to Hamilton to a retirement center.

Within two days of his return, Wolsefor, who lived more than two months after the seizure without incident, was dead. Only a handful of people knew he had been transferred back to Hamilton and one of them was Rogers, who had paid Wolsefor a visit.

During the early stages of his recovery, Jill South,

a sister, made repeated visits, tried to stop by at least daily and despite finding him in a mostly vegetative state, she was not discouraged. She had seen miracles happen, believed they could happen to her brother and was looking for one now. Nobody was beyond redemption. There were times of lucidity but those moments were rare. She said he acknowledged visitors with a light in his eyes that was unmistakable and touching. She would sit and talk to him about her day, about her family, about anything that came to her and he of course, would listen. Wolsefor could not talk but he could listen. He was coming back from the brink and he knew it, but it would not be easy. "He really did know us," Jill South said years after her brother died. "You could just tell."

One startling revelation came the day before his death and shortly after a visit by Rogers. It was late afternoon, just before dinner. Inside Wolsefor's room a devoted sister held her brother's hand and recounted her day on the job as a secretary in the intensive care unit of a nearby hospital. Wolsefor wrenched the corners of his mouth into an oval, looked at his sister and spoke.

"Jill," he said, his voice filled with terror, "Get me out of here!" It was a plea from the depths of despair.

"It was as plain as a person could normally talk," she said. Jill was staggered by the words and took them to heart. Her brother was desperate, though she did not know why. She decided to take him into her house. He had lived with her before and though it was a strain, he could live with her again. The next day, her brother was dead.

Rogers organized a cab driver procession to the cemetery and could not keep quiet about Wolsefor's death.

"Linda over (at) the Choo-Choo Lounge told me Glen went to see (Tommy Wolsefor)," McKay said. "She said he took a fifth of whiskey with him. Tommy wasn't supposed to drink anything. Another drink would kill him. Glen put it in his IV; I am pretty sure he did it. The guy wasn't supposed to have liquor of no kind. That's what Linda told me."

There is only one way Linda could have known how Wolsefor died. Rogers took credit. Charges were never filed.

Tommy was not gone. Not entirely. Two months after his death, a mysterious event occurred one night in Hamilton when police found a man driving erratically through the city. They took him down to the station and booked him for driving under the influence of alcohol. His name was Tom Wolserfor. Nobody thought anything of it, though the names were similar. And Tom Wolsefor was a nobody, recently deceased but already forgotten by police. The red flags, the lights and buzzers never went off.

Three years later, there are plenty of red flags over the arrest. Tom Wolserfor never showed up for his preliminary hearing nor for his trial; a warrant for his arrest is still on the books in the city. How did Glen Rogers' deceased roommate, buried by a loving sister who remembers her brother's last request was to please get him out of that nursing home, how could he end up with a DUI two months after his death? Rogers had stolen his identity and sold it. Ohio authorities issued a new driver's license to a man who claimed to be Tom Wolsefor a month after his death. The new Tom Wolserfor added a letter to his name and used the same Social Security number and date of birth. Rogers had cashed in again.

On that night in the parking lot, as Brockman worked on his smoke, only the hookers were out and they were doing less than a booming business. For some, it looked like the entire evening might end with a freebie, that's how slow it was. The drunks were still inside the joints, singing along with George Jones' laments and marveling at the restorative powers of sour mash. Hookers and drunks owned the streets of this town after midnight. The good folks of the upper west side had long since retired to their homes.

The drunks would be the ones ferried home and that last run was still an hour or more away, so for now, it was quiet. Brockman usually avoided Rogers, particularly during the lulls in customers. After all, Rogers had a quick, even hair-trigger temper, was a bold bullshitter and generally the guy could only be trusted to act in his own best interests.

Brockman had seen Rogers go into his patented rages before — a blind, profanity-laden rampage over the simplest things. Once he launched into a stream of profanities when given a fare he simply did not want. Sometimes the rave came with no warning and with no motive. Brockman wanted nothing to do with a man who was so explosive. He knew that though Rogers showed up for work in a good mood, that mood could turn foul in a flash. And his trips to work on the 4 p.m.-to-4 a.m. shift depended in large measure upon how thirsty he had been for alcohol and drugs the night before. Rogers would party until dawn in his nasty apartment and frequently the afternoon sun would find him in a dead man's slumber.

Brockman dreaded the call by the cab company owners to rustle Rogers out of bed. But because drivers on the 4 p.m. shift were hard to keep and because Rogers, when he was on the job, was reliable, friendly and polite to customers, it was better and easier for the company to rouse him than find a new driver. Getting him there, however, was increasingly becoming another matter.

And there were other challenges with Rogers. Though he was a man of little means, he had been known to arrive at work driving a nearly new car or truck and then offer it for sale to his colleagues. Where did the truck come from? Who owned it before? Where was the title? All were questions that had only fuzzy answers from a congenial cabby. “I remember one time he came in with a pickup truck with Michigan tags,” said Mark Crouch, a fellow driver. “It was a nice truck, too. The contractor’s name was still on it: Mohawk Construction. When I asked about the title, he said he had it in his wallet. He reached for his wallet like he was going to show me. But he never showed me. He never brought his wallet out.”

Rogers got no takers for that truck, and co-workers soon realized that it was probably better not to ask about the roots of the vehicles and certainly better not to buy.

Another night Glen nearly beat to death one of his girlfriends, a hooker, when he believed she was holding back cash. Once, Crouch and Rogers drove around Hamilton looking for the same gal. “We put twenty-five dollars on the meter that night,” Crouch said. “We never did find her.” Crouch was not disappointed, either. The last thing he wanted was a front row seat for a sidewalk prize fight that would end with the brutal beating of a woman who had known more than one beating in her time with Rogers.

But in his time with the company, it was clear that Rogers was something of a draw. Many of the elderly who relied on a cab for transportation to grocers and drug stores began to request Glen as their driver. He had an easy way with riders, was polite beyond measure and always took an interest in their personal affairs. His was a southern politeness, honed in the hills of Kentucky and kept alive through the heat of many Ohio summers. Glen realized he was wanted as well and looked out for that customer base. He knew that even here on the tattered and paint-splotched last rung of the service industry, a niche needs to be tended. He opened and closed doors for customers, remembered his pleases and thank you's and treated them like captains of industry coming and going from a swanky New York hotel. It was rough-hewn marketing and nobody did it better than Rogers.

As he pulled into the lot on this slow weekend night, Brockman did not relish the thought of spending the next half hour talking with Rogers by yellow streetlight glare as the two counted clicks on their car clocks and waited out the long hours before dawn. Since fares were few, Brockman would have no choice. To ignore him or park elsewhere in the lot would have been a slight not easily forgiven.

The next few minutes would hold a conversation that Brockman would not soon forget, one he would recall four years later as if it had happened only a month before. "He was a nervous fellow and I didn't never want to say something out of the way to him because I'd seen him just go off like a madman," Brockman said. "He'd just explode. He was a stick of dynamite about to go off." Brockman measured his words with Glen and fished for a smoke and thought of safe conversational ground. They talked about police and the mean streets of the city. The two sat and talked as the smoke curled and drifted into the dim streetlight of night. They soon moved into deeper water. They spoke of the things that people will do to one another, the evil that is done, the harm that is caused, the lives that are lost to hasty decisions or simple wrongdoing.

It was idle banter, two men passing their time and the night. Then Glen offered up a stunning personal recollection.

"I killed my father," he told Brockman.

"He said it just like that, just like it was nothing," Brockman said.

In Brockman's eyes, Rogers was an admitted murderer and he was free and on the street. The notion that this long-haired, wild-eyed cab driver killed his own father years ago and had gotten away with it never sent Brockman to the police. How could he have done that, bring the heat around with their questions and grim looks and besides, what good would it have done? Claude Rogers was long buried. And how could it ever be proven that this drug addict had whacked his old man? Telling the cops would surely have aggravated Rogers beyond anything anybody had ever seen, and the drivers had already seen plenty from this guy. No, there was just no point in it. Something dark had this man under its wings, and Rogers had the fare for the ride.

Brockman was not the only one who heard and believed that Glen killed his father. Glen's brother, Clay, said he thought Glen killed their father, Claude Rogers, Sr., who died in March 1987, seemingly from natural causes. Clay knows it as sure as he knows the route from Beattyville to Lexington; as sure as he knows the inside of the Lexington County jail.

Their father had led a tough life in Hamilton, but no tougher than the thousands of other lives squandered in the poorer parts of town: the east side where the late actor Ray Combs rose from poverty to the California highlife of Beverly Hills; or over in the Fourth Ward, where domestic violence reports clog daily police logs with threats of bloodshed and gunplay; and in the city's segregated Second Ward, a typical ghetto neighborhood where corner drug sales are as common as sidewalk litter.

When their mother, Edna, married Claude, he was a dashing country boy from the hills of Kentucky, come north to work in the foundries and mills of small-town Hamilton, and she was something of a local beauty queen newly graduated from Hamilton High School.

They were in love. He was the envy of all the local gals, but it was Edna who caught him. They married and began to raise a family. As the children and size of the family grew, however, so did Claude's drinking and carousing.

Today, Edna refuses to dwell upon the abuse she and the children endured as Claude increasingly turned to Hamilton's honkytonks for whiskey and escape. When Claude began to beat Edna, she had little choice but wait for the violence to end, for him to stagger down the sidewalk to a local haunt. When he was gone, she gathered her family into their road-weary station wagon to find a secluded alley where they could sleep out the night.

"There were no shelters for women and families in those days," Edna said years later. "What was I supposed to do? I had a family. We slept in the station wagon." Five children crammed into the car may have made for a closer relationship among the kids but it did not make for a comfortable night. "But Glen was the only one who ever complained," Edna recalled with a fond smile for her blue-eyed boy.

Life in the Rogers household changed dramatically when Claude Senior suffered a stroke while working at a local paper company. With Claude bedridden and unable to work, the family went on the dole. Dollars, never in great supply, now became even scarcer and as for social service relief, well, Edna shrugs, there simply was none. She had nowhere to turn. The memories of those days are not good ones. She frequently had no money for the most basic of supplies. Instead of shampoo, she washed heads with dishwashing detergent. Dinner on some nights, the good nights, was a steaming pot of macaroni and cheese.

The meal became Glen's favorite.

Claude would not live long after his stroke. The last night that Claude Rogers spent on earth, Glen was with him. Clay believes that Glen had finally struck back and Clay later told detectives that his brother killed Claude as payback for torment delivered at bath time. If Clay was to be believed, there were even movies of the abuse. On that March morning in 1987, Claude was dead and Glen, well, he was not.

8

VAN NUYS, CALIFORNIA • SUMMER 1995

Around 10:15 p.m. on June 6 Ramundo Hernandez walked into Le Mirage Apartments where he lived on North Las Palmas Avenue and, his arms loaded with groceries, walked past the elevator to Apartment 101. Hernandez was taken by surprise when suddenly the elevator door opened and out popped a man who grabbed him and pushed him into the elevator. The man placed a knife at the left carotid artery in Hernandez' neck and threatened to kill him — for what reason, Hernandez had no idea.

Hernandez had lived in the apartment only five days. He only knew the man as Glen Rogers, the building maintenance manager and his next-door neighbor.

"He just kept telling me not to move," Hernandez said. Though he spoke no English, Hernandez understood Roger's fierce body language clearly. Terrified, he stood frozen. "If I moved he was going to kill me. I was very afraid and I was traumatized, shocked."

Hernandez knew that Glen lived with a woman named Maria, the apartment manager. This was Maria Gyore, Glen's girlfriend. Hernandez didn't understand what was going on, but he did know his neighbor was acting wildly and out of control.

"He was talking in a strong manner to me," Hernandez said — yelling the entire time while holding the knife to his throat — "pushing the buttons, he would bring the elevator up and down and would not let me get out."

Glen Rogers had flown into one of his celebrated rages. Someone thought they heard him yell, "Open the door, motherfucking bitch."

On the elevator Glen asked his neighbor, "Do you know the bitch in Apartment 102?" Hernandez did not.

Hernandez finally got free when the elevator door opened on the first floor and Rogers spotted a security guard sitting at his desk. Now Rogers was interested in the guard, a man Hernandez only knew as Mr. Bijiff. First he picked up a stack of newspapers and threw them at Bijiff. Then he reached across the desk and grabbed the hapless guard by the jacket. When he was unable to pull him across the desk he threw the guard down and banged his head on the concrete. Bijiff was about five-eight and weighed around 140 pounds, not much challenge for the six-foot, 190-pound Rogers.

Rogers walked away from this incident with thirty-six months of probation and a restraining order keeping him from the apartment building.

Glen's formal education ended at age sixteen in ninth grade. He continued to learn, though – the ways of the street, for certain – and vocational skills as well. In reform school he learned printing and worked that trade for a time in California, where his employer offered a testimonial to his skill, reliability and friendliness. Glen could succeed in the mainstream workaday world when he wanted to. He didn't just land at Le Mirage Apartments for a place to crash. He took his assignment as building maintenance manager seriously, earning a certificate from the Apartment Association of Greater Los Angeles for completing the "Registered Resident Manager Course" on May 25, 1995. Glen Rogers was a recognized journeyman in his line of work.

Glen lived at Le Mirage from December 1994 until June 1995, when he was evicted over the Hernandez incident. He next surfaced at the end of July at 6645 North Woodman Avenue in Van Nuys. On his rental application he listed Maria Gyore as his wife and said they would be moving in with her two small children.

Glen moved around some during his California years but always seemed to find work. In 1993 and 1994 he lived in Los Angeles. From 1991 to 1993 he lived in North Hollywood. Sometimes he was employed by Maintco Corp., a Burbank property maintenance firm. For a while he was self-employed as Rogers Painting & Maintenance Co., operating out of a Los Angeles post office box. And for some time in 1994 under the stolen identity of James Peters he was employed by William J. Galvin, a licensed painting contractor.

But like all the other places he'd ever lived as an adult, California would never grow roots under Glen Rogers' feet. Always, he kept moving. His lifestyle dictated it.

He walked into McRed's Bar and ordered a beer from bartender Rein Keener. Immediately he began flirting with her, and within minutes he asked her for a date.

Glen was impossible to ignore: dancing blue eyes, long blond hair, neatly-trimmed beard and moustache, cowboy boots that matched his belt, tight blue jeans, and a Southern charm that seemed to stop women in their tracks.

"I don't even know you," said Rein, a 24-year-old student at Pasadena City College.

Glen assured her she would know him real soon. And so, every night for the next two weeks when she worked, he took up the same position in a booth across from the bar, and he worked on Rein Keener.

He brought her a bouquet of peach-colored roses and greeted her with a kiss on the hand. When business was slow they made small talk. Rein said she didn't date much because she attended school full time, hoping to become a prosecutor.

"Oh no," Rogers grunted. "Women make the lousiest prosecutors."

"How do you know?" Rein asked, laughing. "Have you been on the wrong side of the law?"

"No," Glen replied. Then he pulled a badge from his pocket and displayed an official-looking identification card. "I work for the government," he said. "I travel around the country looking for people."

Glen always had the right words, the ones women liked to hear. One night while listening to the jukebox, Rein asked if he liked country music. "Yeah, and beautiful women," Glen replied.

Glen understood the danger of drinking and driving. Perhaps it came from his taxicab days, when he would extract staggering and incoherent drunks from Hamilton's bars and haul them home. Glen knew how to plan ahead, and if he anticipated a long night of drinking, he left his own vehicle behind and took a cab or walked. That's what he did the evening of September 28, 1995.

Glen left his Woodman Avenue apartment and walked south to Victory Boulevard, then east to McRed's Lounge. It was a short walk, nine-tenths of a mile.

Around 10 p.m. Glen asked Rein Keener for a ride home. He had been a regular customer for two weeks by this time and Rein felt she knew him well enough to say yes. Her shift was about to end, and she was ready to go home. They were headed out the door when someone playing darts in the back room called over to her: "Come play one last game with us."

Rein asked Glen if he minded waiting. It would only

be ten minutes, she promised. Glen cooled his heels at his regular booth while Rein threw darts. She told inquisitive friends she wasn't about to embark on a date but merely giving Glen a ride. Then she would head home.

When she finished, Rein walked toward Glen's booth and at that instant an eerie feeling overcame her. Perhaps it was a survival instinct gear engaging; perhaps it was just blind luck. Rein told Glen she had changed her mind. He was twice her size; she felt strangely uncomfortable with the arrangement.

And then she saw a side of Glen Rogers that confirmed her decision as the right one. His face began to well up with a rush of blood as rage began to form. He got tense, agitated. Rein was saved by the ringing bell of the telephone. As if on cue, her relief called in sick. McRed's owner Michael Saliman asked her to work another shift. Rein Keener was off the hook.

Rejected, Glen went back to his booth and poured on more alcohol, and before long he grew loud and obnoxious. Rein waited on his table and continued to serve him, though she knew he was sliding over the edge, out of control.

Sandra (Sammie) Gallagher was in a glorious mood when she walked into McRed's. Thirty-three years old and the mother of three, she had just won $1,250 in the California State Lottery and she came here to celebrate. She lived in Santa Monica and was married, though she and Steve Gallagher were going through a rough period. Sammie was pursuing some independence. At first she rejected Glen's advances but Sammie couldn't ignore him for long. Eventually they were flirting and having drinks together.

Sammie took a liking to Glen, perhaps egged on by the alcohol, and they left the bar together at 1:30 a.m. When Sammie fetched her purse and jacket, Keener, who had stored them behind the bar, warned her to be careful. She and Sammie had just met, but Rein was worried about her new acquaintance.

Nobody in the bar knew this at the time, but Rogers was planning to leave town. Before visiting the bar Thursday evening he sold his furniture for $1,000 to a man named Wilte. He told Wilte he and his friend Istvan (Steve) Kele were moving to Las Vegas in a couple of days.

Sammie and Glen were not alone when they left the bar. Another pair of drinkers went with them — Rogers' roommate Michael Flynn, and a woman named Gilmore. And, it turned out, they weren't just going to drop Glen at his apartment. They decided to get some beer. They drove — Glen and Sammie in Sammie's pickup truck, the others in a car — just a few doors east to the 7-Eleven at the corner of Whittset and Victory, where they bought a six-pack of Red Dog and a twelve-pack of Budweiser. Next they stopped at CJ's Bar, where at 1:55 a.m. Glen went inside and came out with some envelopes.

Next their little caravan headed to Glen's apartment. Both drivers double-parked in front of the building. Gilmore got out of the car and went inside. Flynn executed a U-turn and was stopped by a city police officer. At 2:05 a.m. he was arrested for drunk driving. And by now Glen, fueled by hours of drinking, had completed the transformation from suave Southern gentleman to raging monster. He and Sammie began to argue.

The strong hands enveloped Sam Gallagher's throat and cut off her air supply but she did not lose consciousness instantly. She gasped, reeled around and tried to put up a fight, but she was running out of breath quickly. She had no time to think about why this was happening, or how and when she became the victim of this violent man. Flynn may have been the lucky one, for he had an alibi. He was cooling off in the drunk tank. Gilmore was asleep in Glen's apartment.

At 5 a.m., Gilmore was awakened by Glen, who told her about Flynn's arrest. But then he told her, "I have bigger problems, I have bigger problems, I have bigger problems, I have bigger problems."

Gilmore asked him, "Where is the girl?"

"She's dead," Rogers answered.

At 5:30 Glen went to the Shell station at Victory and Woodman and called Steve Kele from a pay phone.

"I have a dead girl in my car," he told Kele. "I need help."

Kele met Rogers at his apartment at around 6 a.m., then followed him south on Woodman to Victory, then east on Victory, past McRed's Lounge and the 7-Eleven to Morse Avenue. They turned right on Morse and again right into the parking lot behind the Laurelwood Convalescent Hospital. Kele parked his car on the east curb facing north next to the AM/PM gas station.

At 6:30, as had been his routine for fifteen years, a groundskeeper arrived for work at the hospital. The facility sits on a pleasant landscape and occupies a single-story building with ninety-nine beds that serves both as both short-term convalescent home and long-term nursing home. Its parking lot is fairly well hidden from the street.

When he turned onto the grounds, the workman saw a white four-door automobile parked on the southeast corner of Morse Avenue, occupied by a man he later described as "possibly Armenian" who was looking back toward the parking lot. Continuing toward the lot, he next saw a pickup truck parked at an angle in front of the trash dumpster. He saw a white male kneeling on the seat of the truck, moving something inside. Figuring the man was dumping trash, the maintenance man thought nothing more of it. He parked his car and entered the building.

At 6:35 Kele, still sitting in his car, watched as the man from the pickup truck ran from the hospital and approached him. At the same time Kele saw smoke rising from the rear of the hospital where the man was seen in the truck. "Go, go, go," the man called to Kele, and the two sped from the scene. As they left the man told Kele that he had torched the truck to conceal any fingerprints on the vehicle and around Sandra Gallagher's throat. He had strangled her before dumping her body in the truck and setting it on fire.

At this same time a passerby stopped at the hospital, saw the fire and called the Los Angeles Fire Department. LAFD put out an alarm at 6:36 a.m.

Back at Rogers' apartment, his drinking companion from the night before was beginning to awaken. There was a purse on the kitchen counter belonging to Sandra Gallagher, an earring of Sandra's and her cigarettes. When Glen arrived home he didn't explain a lot, only that he was going to Las Vegas for a few days.

Five days later on the second of October, a Wednesday, Rogers arrived in Jackson, Mississippi, by Greyhound Bus and at 9:04 a.m. he checked into the Sun-n-Sand Motel at 401 North Lamar Street. He stayed there until October 11, and during this time made several telephone calls to Steve Kele back in California. Glen told Steve he was in Louisiana. The last time Kele heard from Glen was October 15. He said he had no idea where the call originated.

Fire, water and air — a killer's best friends. Burn away fingerprints, wash away the identity, vaporize the evidence. Jan Baxter did not learn of her daughter's death for a week; that's how long it took investigators to identify her. But careful as the killer was, his efforts did not yield perfect results. Investigators were able to lift a single print from one of the victim's fingers, and that was enough to identify her as Sandra Gallagher. Four years later, it would be used at her killer's trial.

~

They gathered at noon Sunday, October 15, 1995 in the old chapel at Magalia Community Church to pay their final respects to Sandra Souther Gallagher. Though in the future she would be mentioned countless times in newspaper and magazine articles about the murder, there was one final account of her life, devoted just to her and not to her accused killer, reported by the *Enterprise Record* in Chico, California:

> She was the victim of a homicide on Sept. 29, 1995, in Van Nuys.
>
> Mrs. Gallagher was born Nov. 18, 1961, in Montrose, Colo.
>
> She lived in Colorado until she was 14, when she moved with her family to Southern California. She graduated from Fullerton High School.
>
> In the early 1980s she lived in Paradise for a couple of years before she joined the Navy. She served in the Navy for five years and then worked at a submarine base in San Diego.
>
> Mrs. Gallagher enjoyed writing poetry. She also played the guitar and sang.
>
> Survivors include her husband, Steve of Santa Monica, her two children, her mother and stepfather, Wes and Jan Baxter; her father and stepmother, Bob and Delores Souther; two brothers, Duane Souther and Bob Souther; a sister, Jerri Vallecella; and her grandparents, Ed and Ruby Keller.

Time did not heal Jan Baxter's wounds.

"I have never been able to imagine it," Sammie's mother said. "What could she have possibly done that was so horrible that he strangled her and set her body on fire and threw it into that pickup? You would have thought she must have done something really horrible. What did she do, laugh at him or tell him no?"

There were fond memories and the family held them in a white-knuckle grip.

Sammie Gallagher liked to finger-pick her acoustic guitar. She played and sang for her own enjoyment, country mostly, and she would keep the little ones entertained with her music. Singing to her sons was one of her quieter, calmer pleasures. "She had the most gentle voice," her mother said.

9

Linda could fight. She would fight a gorilla if she had to. — Kathy Carroll

JACKSON, MISSISSIPPI • OCTOBER 1995

It's a photograph for the family album — the young woman wearing a smile as wide as her face, brimming with glee and joyously mugging for the camera while her new boyfriend beams in loving adoration. Linda Price was showing off her prize, the hunk with the long blond hair, a neatly-trimmed beard and those stunning blue eyes.

Glen looked as happy. And he had reason to be proud, for he had bagged not just one woman, but two.

"You're the prettiest mother and grandmother I've ever seen," Glen told Linda's mother as he hugged her. And so, Carolyn Wingate was hopeful that her daughter, a single mother and grandmother herself who quit school after seventh grade, had finally found the happiness that had been so elusive.

He introduced himself to Mrs. Wingate as Glen Williams.

"Linda's eyes lit up when she talked about him like she had never talked about anybody in her life," Mrs. Wingate said in her soft, quiet Mississippi voice. "She was happy. I didn't get that close to him, but he was so charming. I was happy for Linda."

It all began on October 6, 1995. At the fairgrounds on the east side of Jackson, the Mississippi State Fair was having its annual run. Linda, a fun-loving but lonely young woman of thirty-four, drove out there that Friday. With all the activity and people around, she might meet someone interesting.

Linda found her way to the Budweiser pavilion, where she met, and immediately fell in love with, Glen Rogers.

"I had seen Glen standing over there to the right of her," Kathy Carroll remembered. "He was a handsome guy." Like her sister Linda, Kathy was taken by Glen's long blond hair and the way he was dressed — white sweatshirt, tight blue jeans and cowboy boots. "When you're walking around you're going to look at people and stuff," she said. Glen Rogers was somebody women would look at, a head-turner.

"When we came back to the table," Kathy said, "Linda had walked back to our table and said, 'I want you to meet somebody I just met. His name is Glen Rogers.' It hurts when they say in these books — these magazines — that she was a slut. They said she met him in a bar. It wasn't a bar. It was a pavilion."

On this very first day of their three-week romance, Linda moved in with Glen in room 241 of the Sun-n-Sand Motor Hotel, a twenty-five dollar-a-night, 1960s-era hotel near the Capitol downtown where lawmakers stay during the legislative session. This was just a temporary residence, for Glen liked to move around. When he arrived in Jackson two weeks earlier, Glen first stayed at the Holiday Motel on U.S. 80, near his new-found favorite bar, the Sportsman's Lounge. A few days after meeting Linda, the couple moved back to U.S. 80 to the Tarrymore Motel, just across the road from the bar. It wasn't long before Glen got them an apartment in south Jackson, at 3630 Rainey Road in the Briarwood South Apartments.

In their three weeks together, they lived in three places.

Carolyn Wingate was as smitten with Glen as her daughter.

"You don't say a man is beautiful, but he is beautiful," she told Jay Hughes of the Jackson *Clarion-Ledger*. "He has the prettiest blond hair and green eyes you've ever seen. And charm? That isn't the word. He made me feel so good."

He also made a lot of promises. He told Linda they would eventually move to his house in the Kentucky mountains. Using her imagination, Linda could envision an idyllic life of simple pleasures far from the big-city rat-race of Jackson, her lifelong home.

Carolyn Wingate felt sure Glen Rogers had just repaired a hole in her daughter's heart.

"She was lonely. She was searching for love that she never had that she needed to find somewhere in this world. Linda was just attracted to people like that. They could charm her. She loved somebody to love her."

Glen even got Linda to ease up on the alcohol, though he continued to drink heavily.

Glen had arrived in Jackson on October 2 from Van Nuys, California. He had boarded a Greyhound Bus in North Hollywood around mid-day on September 30, a Saturday, paid the fare of about $150 and arrived in Jackson one day and thirteen hours later, at 4:15 a.m. Monday. Three days later he bought a red 1979 Datsun King Cab pickup truck for $300 from a man by the name of Skip Sciple, whom he had met in a bar. The next night he got drunk at the No Name Lounge in Jackson and took a taxi home to the Sun-n-Sand. He left his new truck in the parking lot and the next morning discovered it had been stolen.

On October 11 he was hired as a laborer for Larry C. Reeves, Contracting, listing his home address on the employment application as 401 North Lumar, Apartment 401, in Jackson — the Sun-n-Sand Motor Hotel. His wage was $7.50 an hour. For references, he listed John White, with a street address but no city, as a "national service officer," and Skip Sciple, the former owner of his truck, also without a city, as "repair specials." He listed military service as Army, discharged in 1986 with the rank of E-4 (In fact, Rogers never served in the military.)

He listed his last job as self-employed, operating as Rogers Painting & Maintenance Co. from a Los Angeles post office box, from 1993 to 1995. He reported his title as "owener" and said he earned $53,000 annually. Prior to this self-employment, for which he had a printed letterhead, Rogers said he worked in 1992 and 1993 for Galvin Painting in Reseda, California, starting at $3 an hour and ending at $450 a week. In 1991 (Rogers never provided specific dates) he said he worked for Maintco Corp. in Burbank repairing homes and apartments and performing "miscellaneous and maintenance." He reported his earnings as "70% of gross." He showed prospective employers in Jackson a Maintco business card printed with his name.

The next day, October 12, Rogers applied to rent an apartment at Briarwood South. On the application he stated he had been a truck driver one month for Reeves Contracting. He listed his home address as 1353 Woodside Drive in Jackson. On the thirteenth, Linda Price also filled out a rental application for Briarwood. She listed her mother's address as hers and said she had been a printer for the Bruckner family for fifteen years. She signed the application as Linda Rogers-Price. She had known Glen Rogers for six days.

Glen had swept into Linda's world in a flash. Linda knew almost nothing about Glen but he always had money and was willing to spend it, that was for sure. He often paid for drinks with $100 bills.

Though Glen spent a good part of his life in bars and had engaged in who knows how many bar fights, he seemed to have an instinct for knowing when to stay out of trouble. One night he and Linda came into the Sportsman's Lounge and took a table next to the bartender, who was not working then, and her date. Glen knew the bartender from his frequent forays to the bar during his two weeks in town, "nighttime, daytime, anytime," she recalled, and had flirted with her. "I told him right away that this man was my fiancé and then he left me alone. He didn't bother me any more. We just talked a little bit and he seemed very nice, very polite. I never saw him drunk. He was always well behaved."

Patrons at the Sportsman's Lounge said it would be hard to forget Rogers because of his flamboyance. Maurice Robinson said he was at the bar one Monday night when Glen kept the house in drinks for four hours. "When he walked into a place he wanted to be the center of attention," Robinson said. "He wouldn't let anyone buy anything. You never know who's sitting next to you. He wasn't acting ugly or anything, but when he drank he wanted everyone to drink."

Though he drank faster than everyone else in the bar, Rogers ordered a beer for everyone each time he ordered for himself. He wouldn't let the bartender keep extras on ice. Instead, he required her to open each beer and set it in front of the customer. Eventually, everyone in the bar had four or five full beers on the counter, either gleeful over the windfall or too intimidated to tell Glen to ease off.

When he wasn't drunk, Rogers was amiable and made friends easily. Acquaintances he met in bars may have wondered where all the cash came from, but they didn't pry.

Glen had a dark side Linda Price did not know about; the warnings did not register with her.

Denise Hall, a childhood friend, ran into Linda at the grocery store in late October, and Linda told her about moving into an apartment with her new boyfriend. Linda appeared to be nervous and was shaking. "I need to hurry up and go home and cook supper for my boyfriend before he comes homes and kicks my ass," Linda told her friend.

Linda didn't know about California, Sandra Gallagher, McRed's Lounge or the Laurelwood Convalescent Hospital. The clues kept coming — and missing their mark.

At the Sportsman's Lounge on October 30, Monday night, Linda Price and her sister Marilyn Reel were talking. They went to the restroom together, and Linda told Marilyn she was afraid of Glen, afraid he might be involved with the "mafia." Glen had made a call from a pay phone just outside the restroom door, and when the women came out, he assaulted Linda with a verbal flogging about "talking to people about their business."

The next night Sandra Huffman, who lived across the hall from Linda and Glen at Briarwood, overheard an argument about Price's ex-boyfriends. Sometime between 6 and 7 p.m. she heard Glen say he would "lay her throat open" if he heard another word about Linda's ex-boyfriends.

Even so, the romance blossomed. Glen was quickly absorbed into the Wingate clan as if he were already a member of the family. He spent most of his time with Linda and had dinner at her mother's home at least once during his three weeks with Linda. For Glen, whose upbringing lacked even a pretense of closeness between family members, acceptance into the Wingate inner circle was a new and wondrous experience. It was an intimacy Glen clearly was not accustomed to.

It was this intimacy that led to his remark that Carolyn Wingate was the best mother and grandmother anyone could ever want.

Carolyn was very much used to this intimacy. She shared her home in south Jackson with her son Chester, granddaughter Chrystal Price and a nephew. Another daughter, Kathy Carroll, lived just a few minutes away on McCluer Road. Linda, who had moved with Glen into the Briarcliff South Apartments in mid-October, was just around the corner and down Rainey Road not two minutes from Kathy and her family. A family gathering could be thrown together in five minutes. And the family did favors for Glen.

A couple of days after Glen's truck was stolen, police found it. Bold and brazen as always, with a nationwide warrant on his head for the murder of Sandra Gallagher in California, Glen got Carolyn Wingate to drive him downtown. She would be perfect cover for the truck he so badly needed. He walked into the Jackson Police Department, plunked down forty-five dollars in cash and retrieved his truck from the police impound lot. But not until after police checked out the truck through the National Crime Information Center computer. It came back clean and Glen walked out a free man.

The only family member who did not share the joy of Linda's new love was her brother, Chester Wingate, Jr. Chester lived only minutes from his mother's house and stayed in close contact with her and his sisters. Disabled by an injury in his painting business, he lived on a pension and had plenty of time to spend with his wife and five-year-old son. A couple of days before Halloween he stopped by Carolyn's home, where Linda introduced him to Glen.

"When I first met him was in my Momma's front yard," Wingate said. "He went to shake my hand and I wouldn't shake his hand. There was something not right about that boy. He never would look me in the eye. He reached his hand out to shake mine, and when he did, he turned away."

Chester had a warning for Linda. "You can do what you want, it's your business, you're old enough, but I'm telling you, Sis, something's not right about this boy. When a man won't look you in the eye, something's not right."

But Linda knew she had found the man who cared about her.

Wingate decided once and for all that he did not like Glen the night Linda invited Chester and his young son for dinner. Glen was watching "Walking Tall," a rough-and-tumble movie about Buford Pusser, the Tennessee sheriff who never shied from violence when the need arose. Glen refused to turn off the videotape when Linda asked. "Glen, there's a baby here," Linda scolded Glen. Glen was furious. Linda's congenial lover suddenly underwent a change of attitude.

Wingate and his son cut the dinner short. "Linda, we're going on home," he told her.

It was rare for more than a day to pass without personal or telephone contact between mother and daughters. And that is why, on Thursday, November 2, 1995, the dull worry that gnawed at Carolyn Wingate's mind was coagulating into fear. She had not heard from Linda since Monday.

It was also when she last saw Glen. Mrs. Wingate and Chrystal Price had been to the apartment Monday morning, and Glen was sitting in the living room when they arrived. During the visit Linda told Chrystal that Glen had been "fussing at her," but she did not elaborate.

They had plans to next meet on Tuesday, Halloween night. Linda invited Kathy to bring the children over for Halloween candy. Accompanied by her adult son Shane, Kathy took the young ones to the apartment. Nobody answered the door, and Glen's truck was gone.

By Friday, a sense of urgency and full-flown anxiety were squarely implanted deep into Carolyn Wingate's gut. She fretted all day, calling Linda and getting no answer.

Finally, she called Jackson Police.

A policeman would meet her in front of Building 1, Apartment 111, at the Briarcliff South Apartments, 3630 Rainey Road. The family pastor, Reverend Gary Longo, was summoned from his home, where he had already gone to bed. "They called me and told me they were going over there to open the door because they thought she might be in there," Rev. Longo said. "Carolyn knew she was in there, and Carolyn knew something was wrong, because Carolyn hadn't spoken to her in a few days and they spoke every day."

Officer James Roberts was working the 3-11 shift out of Precinct 1 in south Jackson. He took a radio dispatch at 10:23 directing him to the apartment complex regarding "unknown trouble." Arriving at 10:49, he found several members of the Wingate family and a maintenance man, Raymond Thornton, waiting outside Apartment 111. Thornton unlocked the door.

They waited outside as Roberts, finding only a hallway light on, carefully made his way through the apartment, announcing himself as a police officer as he moved.

Of all the fears a policeman encounters, perhaps none makes the heart pound faster than the sound of silence in a dark, unfamiliar room. James Roberts had his ears cocked but the only sound he could hear was the spooky creak of his own shoes as he forced them against their will to move him to the back of the apartment. The shadows from his flashlight danced in wicked delight like ghosts as he peeled his eyes, dilated and big as saucers now, looking for a sign — any sign — of anything that wasn't supposed to be. When you were a kid you could get up and walk out of a theater or turn your head if the show got too scary. Several people waited outside only a few feet away but he was all alone. Roberts did not like this; it was not the kind of thrill he dreamed about when he decided to become a cop. He was met by eerie silence — and the sight of blood stains on the living room carpet. Videotapes were scattered about the floor. In the kitchen he found more blood: splattered on the floor, soaked paper towels in the garbage can, and in the kitchen sink, a mop caked with dried blood. As he cleared the front rooms and moved toward the back, he grew increasingly certain that he was about to discover something very bad. He would give anything right now to be someplace else. A street fight with a drunk or a wild chase would be far preferable to this.

The apartment seemed to be vacant. There was nobody in the west bedroom, nobody in the north bedroom. Roberts was tense, his body pumped by an adrenaline rush. Finally he approached the bathroom, the only room left, and turned on the light. The shower curtain was closed. He pulled it back with his flashlight.

His heart raced. The color deserted his face like air from a popped balloon. She was nude, stabbed three times in the chest. She was lying on her back in the bathtub, her face covered with a washcloth. On the bathroom mirror was a message, written in red lipstick: "Glen we found you."

A cop is trained to keep his emotions out of the picture, Roberts had to remind himself. The sickening coppery smell of blood, the putrid odor of decomposing flesh that pummels the senses like nothing else imaginable, the face of death are part of the program, they come with the territory. But a cop is no different from anyone else. A young person's death never goes down easy.

What would he say to her? Emerging from the apartment, tentatively, nervously, he looked into the anxious eyes of Carolyn Wingate.

"Momma, it's bad," he said. He ached for her.

Carolyn Wingate had hoped for the best. She had feared the worst and got it. She and her daughters became hysterical. Several officers and crime scene technicians had converged on the apartment by the time detectives arrived. Not far behind was the Hinds County coroner, who waited for investigators to process the crime scene and gather evidence before entering to inspect the body.

It was cold that night. The family members moved into a neighbor's apartment, where they stayed for about two hours. Mrs. Wingate told detectives about her daughter's boyfriend, a man who had eaten dinner at her home but whose name she wasn't certain of. He introduced himself as Glen Williams, but someone else said he was Glen Rogers, she told them.

Inside Linda Price's apartment, it appeared that the killer had tried to clean up the crime scene. The bloody towels and mop pointed to some half-hearted effort that would do nothing to conceal evidence. Perhaps it was the killer's signature; perhaps he was so drunk or drugged that he could not perform this task adequately; police did not know. They did, however, find two peculiarities that almost certainly were the killer's signature marks: He covered the victim's face with a washcloth. And he left feces in the toilet, a final insult. His rage, his hatred of women, had to have been deep-seated and enormous.

Police knew they had something horrible on their hands, but as in any crisis in its early hours, they didn't have the bigger story yet. That would come later. Right now all they could do was start putting the pieces together, preserving and collecting evidence, taking photographs, talking to witnesses.

Technicians worked through most of the night. When they left, a patrolman guarded the apartment. Wendy Freeman, who lived in the same building, knew who Rogers was but did not know his name. She took an instant dislike to him the first time she saw him and considered him an unsavory character.

Wendy was the last to see Rogers at Briarcliff South. He was leaving the complex, obviously in a hurry. She waved, but he did not wave back. She watched as he pulled out of the parking lot in his red Datsun pickup truck. He headed north on Rainey Road and disappeared into the congested and narrow, winding streets of south Jackson. Eventually he made his way to Interstate 20 and drove west to Bossier City, Louisiana.

In time, the clues came together.

Among the evidence in Linda's apartment was a black and blue vinyl purse containing a prescription bottle of codeine in the name of Maria Gyore, filled at Thrifty Drugs, on La Brea Avenue in Los Angeles. They also found a camera with undeveloped film. The film came back with the photo of the happy couple, Glen's arm around her shoulder, touching her right breast.

On his left wrist was a man's Shey watch. For Glen Rogers, that watch would become the last thing he would ever want to see in a photograph.

10

If there's four or forty, I couldn't tell you.
— Glen Rogers, November 13, 1995

BOSSIER CITY, LOUISIANA • NOVEMBER 1995

Bossier City was Andy Sutton's lifelong home and the center of her world. Here she grew up, attended Meadowview Elementary School, Green Acres Junior High, and until quitting the Class of 1976 to get married and have her first child at age sixteen, Airline High School. Her entire support system was here, family and friends. Her father died in 1979 and her mother in 1991, but Andy had brothers and sisters either in Bossier or in nearby northwest Louisiana towns. She never found lasting success in marriage or career but she never left Bossier. It was familiar, comfortable.

Later she would obtain a diploma, but with four children and little vocational experience, Andy was confined to low-wage jobs, usually as waitress or bartender. Job changes and unemployment were common.

Her children — two teenage sons from the first marriage and two younger children from the second — lived with their fathers. Andy lived with her friend Theresa Jean Whiteside, who had offered her a place to stay, Apartment 93 in the Port Au Prince Apartments on Preston Boulevard. It was a good central location, in the heart of town, between Texas Avenue and Old Minden Road near the Red River and a short hop into Shreveport.

Andy was an outgoing, friendly woman who made friends easily and who could light up a room just by walking into it. She had lots of friends and made new ones easily. “Annie — her name was Andy but growing up we called her Annie — liked to talk a lot, laugh a lot,” said her sister, Terriea Pullig. “I’ve seen her a lot of times give her last dollar to a friend who needed it.”

In late 1995 Andy, 37 years old and unemployed, wanted to turn things around. She talked fondly of her two older boys and very much wanted to regain custody of the little ones. “She wanted to eventually get her home life established so she could get her kids back,” said Andy’s brother, Willie Jiles. “She was definitely a loving mother. She was just having trouble getting things squared away.”

Steady work would need to come first, and Andy hoped to get a bartending job at A Touch of Class, one of her favorite spots.

On the Friday afternoon of November 3, Andy Jiles Sutton went out looking for happiness. At the It’ll Do Lounge she met Glen Rogers and immediately went nuts over him. Because he was so smooth with women – his smile, the way he showed an interest, the way he complimented them on their looks — it wasn’t surprising that Glen had no trouble talking Andy Sutton into driving him to the Greyhound Bus station just about two hours after they had met.

They made plans for Glen to move in with her. But first he had to make a quick trip to Florida, Glen explained. He had some unfinished business there.

He promised to return in a few days and bring her a car.

Glen talked the ticket agent out of a one-way pass

to Tampa with a sad story about losing the ticket he had bought and was issued a "special needs" ticket valued at $99, fifteen percent off the regular $117 fare. Unlike the brazen behavior he displayed when reporting his truck stolen, Glen was in a stealthy mood this day. For the Greyhound passenger list, which does not require identification, he gave his name as James Peters.

The bus left Shreveport on time at 5:10 p.m. Bus travel offered the twin benefits of anonymity and economy, but it was no luxury cruise. That didn't matter to Glen. He was a highwayman with time on his hands, and the next town, the next con were all that mattered. On the bus, he would nod off or look out the window or bullshit with passengers during the snake-like crawl through hardscrabble Dixie. It was tough to sleep through the jolting stops and starts and the whining of the diesel engine as the bus made its middle-of-the-night calls on forgotten bergs. Emphysemic passengers punctuated their sleep with wheezing. Some were badly in need of a bath, and there was a putrid aroma that sometimes wafted from the chemical toilet whenever the restroom door opened, but this was Glen's chosen means of travel. The important thing was that he blended in like he was part of the fabric on the seats. He was in his element here, comfortable and in control. He was road-dogging again.

His snake-like itinerary on this run covered 1,066 miles, with transfers in Baton Rouge, Tallahassee and Ocala. After all the twists and turns, the layovers and transfers, Glen's bus arrived in Tampa on time at 6:35 p.m. Saturday, November 4. He grabbed his belongings and walked through the front door of the terminal onto Polk Street. He was no newcomer to the region.

Glen had been in Tampa a year before with his brother Clay, Clay said. He claimed the two were unwitting patsies in an old carney con. He said they wooed a pair of sweethearts at the Showtown USA Lounge, spending freely on dinner and drinks through the night, dancing, laughing and getting more and more familiar with their dates. Finally, at night's end, after heading out of the bar in one of the women's small white Ford to a nearby trailer park, the two learned that there would be no big payoff inning.

One of the girls, Tina, was tight with the bartender. The entire night was a big game, and the con men had been conned. Glen went berserk and made a move for a knife on the kitchen counter. His brother stopped him and pulled him out of the trailer before he could kill anybody. Glen left, unwillingly, and he made a vow to himself. He would not forget nor forgive the embarrassment. One day he would return. This was Clay's story.

Today was that day. It was time to get even. Glen hailed a cab.

He knew just where to go — to the Showtown USA Lounge.

Hundreds of miles west in Jackson, Miss., the Jackson *Clarion-Ledger* of Sunday, November 5 held fifteen obituary notices. The youngest of these was Linda Price, age thirty-four, a daughter, sister, mother, a grandmother.

Linda's death notice, by *Clarion-Ledger* staff writer Marky Aden, was as brief as Linda's life:

> "Linda Denise Price, 34, of Rainey Road, a homemaker, died of stab wounds Thursday at her home. Jackson police are investigating the homicide.
>
> "Services are 2 p.m. Monday at Baldwin-Lee Funeral Home with burial in Lakewood Memorial Park South. Visitation. . .
>
> "Mrs. Price was a lifelong Jackson resident. She enjoyed gardening. She was a member of Trinity Gospel Fellowship Church.
>
> "Survivors include. . ."

On a cold Monday afternoon, November 6, Linda's friends and family turned out for her service at the Baldwin-Lee Funeral Home. Though Linda was a lonely woman who desperately searched for happiness in the bars along U.S. 80, or perhaps because of it, every one of the 175 seats was filled for her funeral.

"Linda was a very open, friendly person, towards anybody, as far as I knew," Rev. Gary Longo, pastor of the Trinity Gospel Fellowship Church, told the church on a day that was dreary and cold as winter came to camp in the South.

I don't know if I've ever done a funeral when it was a pretty day, Brother Gary said to himself as he waited for the service to begin. Reverend Jackie Moulder, who would officiate, was a pillar of concentration as he waited for his time at the pulpit, while the organist played *The Old Rugged Cross* and weeping filled the pews. Linda was dressed in a new white turtleneck sweater to hide the gash where her killer had opened her throat — from ear to ear as he had promised not two days before her death. She wore a single ring, one of two her killer had overlooked when he robbed her.

Later, most of her jewelry would end up 500 miles away at the Lake City Fast Cash-Pawn Shop in Tennessee, the pawnbroker unaware he had taken evidence in a murder case.

The other ring went into an evidence bag along with a beret and was kept under guard at the Jackson police station.

Because Linda's injuries were so horrific, just before the service someone made the decision to close the casket, which had been open for the viewing.

> I'm not on an ego trip, I'm nothing on my own
> I make mistakes and often slip, just common flesh and bone
> But I'll prove someday just what I say I'm of a special kind

When He was on the cross, I was on His mind. . .
He knew me yet He loved me
He whose glory made the heavens shine
So unworthy of such mercy
Yet when He was on the cross, I was on his mind
Yet when He was on the cross, I was on his mind

After Rev. Moulder opened the service, Rev. Longo, behind a screen that separated him from the pews, rose to sing:

Carolyn Wingate came to the funeral home on this sorrowful day to fulfill the one obligation no parent ever wants to contemplate, to bury her child. During this time when friends and family came to say goodbye to Linda and console the family matriarch, she had time to reflect on the hurts that had come her way:

Thirty-five years earlier her brother Claude was returning to the trailer park where he lived and noticed his car parked at a neighbor's. Looking through the window, he found his wife in bed with the neighbor, who greeted Claude with a gunshot blast to the head.

Her husband Chester's sister died in an automobile accident, and Chester, a painter and mechanic, died of lung cancer in 1992.

Tragedy found its way into her child's life as well. Linda's husband, Clint, who was Chrystal's father, committed suicide when Chrystal was three years old. Linda met Danny Williams, who helped raise Chrystal, and the little girl called him Daddy. But Danny had trouble with the law and was sent up for burglary. He never returned. He died in prison. Some said it was a payback. Others blamed a drug overdose.

After the service, a long procession snaked its way over to the cemetery. Unintended and unknown to the funeral directors who planned the event, the convoy drove past the front door of Linda Price's apartment which she shared with her accused killer, Glen Rogers. Rev. Longo later took the funeral home director aside and rebuked him for the unfortunate route, "just to remind him that when somebody is murdered, you need to know where the murder took place."

At the top of the hill just beyond the Briarwood South Apartments, the procession turned into the Lakewood Memorial Park South cemetery. All the way to the back of the park it slowly proceeded, through the Garden of the Sermon on the Mount, around the circular drive of the Garden of the Christus, on to the far end and around the bend.

There was a short graveside service of prayer and Scripture readings. And then Carolyn Wingate said goodbye to her daughter. Shannon and Chrystal Price said goodbye to their mother. Chester Wingate Jr., Debbie Spikes, Kathy Carroll and Marilyn Faye Reel said goodbye to their sister. And then, on a gently rolling plain in the company of hundreds of silent witnesses who had come before her, on a cold and gray Monday afternoon in November of 1995 in her thirty-fifth year, Linda Denise Price was laid to rest.

A few days after the funeral Chrystal Price, age fourteen, went with her grandmother and her Aunt Kathy to visit Jackson homicide detective Chuck Lee Jr. He was in charge of the evidence collection, held for a possible trial in Jackson that would never occur. At his office in the detective section, he opened the bag that contained two items taken from Linda's body: the mother's ring she wore, and a beret. Quietly, he removed the mother's ring that Linda Price's killer had overlooked, and he handed it to Chrystal.

11

I always told Tina she was a rebel without a cause – always for the underdog. — Mary Dicke

GIBSONTON, FLORIDA • NOVEMBER 5, 1995

Bartender Lynn Jones, twenty-two and single, had arrived at the Showtown USA Lounge at 11:30 a.m. to begin her shift. She immediately struck up a conversation with the good-looking man sitting at the bar, asking, “Are you with it?” The cocky but congenial man captivated her with his long blond hair, neatly-trimmed beard but most especially those dancing blue eyes. He wore bluejean shorts and a pullover shirt with four buttons at the top, and a red baseball cap.

“With what?” he replied.

“At the carnival,” Lynn said.

“Yeah, I’m a driver looking for work.” Lynn thought his response was odd, for any carnival worker would understand that in the lingo of the business, “with it” meant working in the carnival. The Showtown was a popular watering hole with inexpensive down-home country cooking in a town where carnival workers and operators — show people — spent the winter. Anyone who spent enough time here, even if he didn’t work in the show, would know the special language of the trade.

At first he called himself Brandon and then Randy before finally telling the bartender his name was Glen.

He was just goofing around, hanging out on a Sunday following a long bus trip the day before. What difference did it make what his name was? He could have said his name was Jim, a name he'd used in the past. Upon arrival he ordered breakfast at the bar, moving to a table to eat. Then he moved back to the bar. First he ordered a soft drink, then began drinking Budweiser on tap. He sat at the bar most of the afternoon, paying for his first drink with a hundred-dollar bill.

Rogers had begun his outing late Sunday morning shortly after Donald Daughtry, age 65 and a twelve-year Yellow Cab employee, was dispatched to the Tampa 8 Inn. Daughtry wheeled into the parking lot and honked. Rogers piled inside and said he wanted to go to Carny Town and he wanted to go to the Showtown Bar in Gibsonton. Talkative as usual and in the company of a fellow taxi driver, Glen told of how he was a carnival worker on the East Coast and had come to Florida for the winter. When Daughtry pulled into the north parking lot of the Showtown, Glen gave him ten dollars for the fare and a two-dollar tip.

"He smelled of stale beer and was unkempt," Daughtry would testify eighteen months later. "He looked like he'd been drinking all night long."

Sometime around 3 p.m., four maids from the Ramada Inn at nearby Apollo Beach who had just finished work walked into the Showtown and collapsed at a large table next to the end of the horseshoe bar. With tourists and a convention in town, the Ramada had produced a busy weekend for the housekeepers. Four others and their male boss arrived a few minutes later. They did this occasionally, gather at the Showtown to unwind and talk shop, talk and laugh about the weird things that go on in their line of work.

Soon, sixteen female eyes were peeled on the stranger at the bar, and he was the principal topic of conversation at the table. It didn't take long for his charm to swing into action.

Janine (Jeannie) Fuller got up and walked to the jukebox. Glen — he called himself Glen now — followed.

"Are you married?" he asked.

"Yes I am," Jeannie answered.

"You don't have a wedding band."

"Just because I don't have a wedding band don't mean I'm not married."

They picked out some songs, and they danced.

When they sat down — Jeannie with the women, Glen by the poker machine at the bar — he bought the table a round of drinks. When the drinks arrived, Tina Marie Cribbs and two others walked up to Glen and thanked him, and then started asking about him. He was so instantly likable, and they didn't even know his name. Then he bought another round and served them himself. Every one of the eight women was flirting with him.

Glen flirted back. There was something about those sparkling blue eyes, that smile that would disarm a housemother, the Southern charm, the thank-you ma'ams and the ain't you beautifuls that made it easy for them to flirt with him, just a bit of harmless fun on a Sunday afternoon.

Glen didn't pull punches, though. "I don't like you because you're dark complected and you have black hair," he told a disappointed Ruth Ann Negrete. She understood. Glen liked women with light-colored hair, blond or strawberry. They really did something to him. It wasn't that he didn't like her. He just didn't want her. Besides, Ruthie let on that she had a boyfriend. Glen didn't tangle with boyfriends. Southern gentlemen didn't do that.

Glen asked Lynn Jones if she had a car. He might need a ride later on.

Ruthie Negrete, though not of the right complexion

for Glen, couldn't stop staring at his eyes, those sparkling eyes that said howdy, let's dance and maybe later on get out of here together.

"And we was talking about his butt," Ruthie said. "His shorts were kind of tight. He was well-groomed. His hair was like he was under the sun a lot and was sun-bleached." He seemed to be a nice person.

One by one, Glen eliminated unsuitable prospective dates. Cindy Torgerson and Jeannie Fuller were married. He wasn't paying much attention to Lynn Jones behind the bar, but Lynn was paying lots of attention to him and was trying, without success, to keep his eye.

Finally, Glen got down from his perch at the bar and joined the women at their table, to find out who was attached and who was not, learn who had a car and who did not.

The stranger began to focus on Tina, a slightly plump woman who had a missing front tooth, short reddish-blond hair and wore glasses.

Around 3:45 p.m. Tina took a phone call from her mother, who had just returned home from work and was supposed to meet Tina at the bar. Later they planned to have a family cookout.

Around 4 p.m. Cindy Torgerson, Jeannie Fuller and Ruthie Negrete left. When only Tina Cribbs remained, she joined Glen at the bar and struck up a conversation. She told Ruthie he was kind of cute and had a nice butt. She told Cindy she was going to stay because she was interested in him. She also said he needed a ride somewhere, and that she offered to take him. It bothered Cindy that Tina didn't know where Glen wanted to be taken. Tina was certain it wasn't far, because she had just told her mother, Mary Dicke, she would meet her at the bar.

"I was due to get off at two o'clock," said Mary,

"and because the girl didn't come in, they had to call another girl in. So I was an hour and a half late getting off, and I knew I had missed Tina at the Ramada."

Tina reached her mother at home by phone. "My ass is dragging," she said. "I'm going home. I've had a few to drink. Maybe you'll have to drive me home."

"No problem," Mary replied. "Do you want me to come straight on down, or do I have time to take a shower?"

"No, I just ordered a drink," Tina said. "Take your time."

They joked around on the phone and talked about the cook-out planned for later with Tina's two boys. They bantered back and forth more like school buddies than mother and daughter. That's the way they were, best friends.

Tina wasn't usually much of a drinker. But on this Sunday afternoon she had downed three or four beers and chased them with several shots of butterscotch schnapps.

And although she told her mother she was too drunk to drive, she agreed to give her new friend Glen, whose last name she did not know, a ride over to a residential neighborhood they call Winter Quarters, just across the CSX railroad tracks where show people live out the winter. Glen had a friend over there he wanted to see, he told her. He could have walked, it was so close, but Tina, always ready to help someone in need, agreed to give him a ride, and they got into Tina's white Ford Festiva for the two-block excursion.

"I'll be right back," she told Lynn Jones, and she left her nearly full can of Busch beer on the bar as collateral. "Tell my mom I'll be back in fifteen minutes."

When Mary Dicke entered the south door of the bar, she saw the north door closing but didn't know it was Tina and her new friend Glen.

Mary walked to Tina's usual seat at the bar and

felt the beer can. "I saw a Busch can sitting there, which is what we both drank," Mary said. "It was real busy, and I ordered a Busch. I had already felt the can and it was plumb smacking cold. I assumed she was in the ladies room. The can was ice cold, just like it came right out of the cooler. And by this time all the other girls had gone. And I don't know. I got to shooting the breeze with people we know and what have you, and I thought, 'whoa, wait a minute.' So Lynn came up here and I said, 'Where did Tina Marie go?' Lynn was the one that actually wanted to go with him."

In the meantime, Cindy Torgerson returned to the Showtown to pick up chicken wings she had ordered for her husband to take to work. While there, she overheard Glen ask Tina if she would give him a ride to Nundy Street in the carnival winter quarters.

Lynn was ready to explode.

"Did you know your daughter just left here with the most gorgeous, drop-dead good-looking man?" she said to Mary. "If I never speak to her again it'll be too soon."

Later that evening, the phone rang in Andy Sutton's apartment. It was her new boyfriend, whom she'd met only on Friday at the Touch of Class bar in Bossier City, Louisiana. He wouldn't make it in tonight as promised. He was having an electrical problem of some sort on his truck, and the lights didn't work on the replacement truck the company had given him. He'd be in by Tuesday, for sure, and he assured her again that he was bringing her a car of her very own.

When Tina told her friends she would return in fifteen minutes, she told Glen she would drive and it wasn't a hard sell because Glen was all the way drunk by now. He'd driven a cab long enough to know about the perils of drinking and driving and never fussed when someone else insisted on driving.

Winter Quarters was just across the tracks but Glen

had a better idea. He persuaded Tina to drive up to Tampa, about ten miles north on U.S. 41. He had some reefer and some beer at his motel room. They could go there and party for a while and have sex and she could still get home in time. Her brain numbed by the drinking she wasn't used to, Tina agreed. The family cookout with her mother and two sons somehow phased itself out of her thinking.

Around 10 p.m. Glen walked into the motel office, where Chenden Patel, co-owner with her husband, was on duty. He announced he was staying over until Tuesday and paid her for another night.

Earlier, Robert Thompson, a 29-year-old guest in room 217, was watching the end of the Chicago Bears-Pittsburgh Steelers football game and decided to go outside for a moment. In the parking lot below his room he saw a woman wearing shorts and a man who reminded him of Kenny Rogers, the singer. He walked down the stairs and as he got close he greeted them, to which the man responded, "We don't want no fucking drugs."

"I don't sell drugs," Thompson replied. "Here, have a beer."

"My name's Kentucky," the stranger said. "And don't you forget it." With that, he gave Thompson a hard, strong handshake.

Mrs. Patel also saw the man later that Sunday night and identified him as Glen Rogers, the guest in room 119. He was packing a small white car, and two suitcases sat near the door of his room.

"If you want to stay, don't leave your luggage in your car," Mrs. Patel warned him. Though he'd paid in advance, Glen said he wasn't sure he would be staying over Monday night, and he wanted to be packed.

The next morning, around nine o'clock, Rogers drove out of the parking lot alone in a white Ford Festiva. An hour later Erica Charlton pushed her cleaning cart past the door of room 119 because it had a sign on the door handle that said "Do Not Disturb."

Mary Dicke was beginning to worry the kind of worry that puts a knot deep into your stomach and won't go away.

Tina was not in the ladies' room. She did not return in fifteen minutes as promised. Her automobile with the missing right headlight was gone. And Mary Dicke knew, more than anyone could know, that her daughter would never blow her off this way. Never.

First she went to the trailer park, two blocks from the Showtown, and checked both homes, hers and Tina's. Then she began dialing Tina's pager. One, two, three, a dozen times she dialed. She put in her secret code. Thirty times during the night Mary Dicke called, and never received an answer.

Mary was baffled because Tina would never do this to her. They were just too close. They began each day together over coffee before heading off to work, Tina to the Ramada Inn and Mary to her waitress job. Then usually they met again at day's end for coffee or a Busch at the Showtown. It was handy for Mary to be near Tina's boys, 11 and 13, to help with their care and upbringing, for the two fathers were not in this picture. They both worked so hard — Tina needed the money and always had two jobs and sometimes three going at once. Mary needed the activity. She had recently lost her own husband and this would be her first Christmas without him.

On Monday morning, all the women who had partied at the Showtown reported for work at the Ramada Inn except Tina. In her lifetime she had never failed to show up for work without notification. Mary could not imagine what had happened to her daughter, but she would not let herself think the unthinkable.

She kept dialing the pager and hoping that Tina would surface.

Mary called the Ramada; nobody there had seen Tina.

When the unthinkable turned to reality Tuesday afternoon, it came with the stunning swiftness of a kick to the head from an irritable bull.

Mary had become frantic long before Tuesday afternoon. When Tina did not return home Sunday night, Mary called the Hillsborough County Sheriff's Office to report her daughter missing, and by now she was seriously worried. The story first broke on Tampa radio and television in late afternoon with reports that a body had been found at the Tampa 8 Inn. Police had a suspect almost immediately from the registration card: Glen Rogers, who listed an address of 1250 Frower Drive, Jackson, Mississippi, and said he was representing Farrow Amusements. Using a police unit computer at the scene, Detective Ricky Childers ran the Mississippi driver's license number listed on the registration card. It came back as Glen E. Rogers, with a different address: 250 Farrow Drive. From this information Childers learned that Rogers was the subject of an arrest warrant for murder that Los Angeles police issued on October 17, three weeks earlier.

Before noon, Tampa police had a suspect. They still had no idea who the victim was.

Mary Dicke learned about the murder the way no police department ever wants a victim's family to learn anything — through news reports. Police had not identified their victim and so could not notify next of kin. But they were powerless to keep a lid on the story, given the public nature of radio signals and the very obvious sounds of whole fleets of police cars racing to the motel.

Lynn Jones called Mary at home. "Turn on the TV,"

she said. Over the telephone, Mary told police that the victim in room 119 was likely her daughter.

Det. Bell and Sgt. McNamara had the oft-repeated but never pleasant task of visiting the victim's next of kin. At Mary Dicke's home, they learned first of the jewelry Tina wore, jewelry that was missing. One of the rings had an oval black stone with diamonds around it. The other was a gold-colored Mothers Day ring with three birthstones: two representing her two children and one for herself. Another ring had a black square stone in the center with diamonds around it. Tina also wore a gold watch.

Tina's car, a 1993 white Ford Festiva, was missing. It should have contained a black patchwork purse with Tina's driver's license and $283 in cash from the paycheck she received on Sunday, a checkbook from South Hillsborough Bank in Apollo Beach, and a pack of Marlboro cigarettes. Mary had no trouble describing the Mothers Day ring because she wore an identical one. She had no trouble describing the patchwork purse because she had made it. In the last forty-eight hours, what began as minor concern over a missed rendezvous turned first into anxiety, then fear, and finally devastation.

12

FLIGHT FROM FLORIDA • NOVEMBER 1995

Driving west out of Florida toward the delta land of Louisiana, one hand on the wheel and the other out the window, Glen knew he had forgotten something, but he could not remember exactly what. He had come to Central Florida to repay an old grudge and now that IOU was settled and he felt better. A year before, while traveling in the carnival with his brother Clay, he had spent the night buying drinks for a plain-looking but friendly woman at the Showtown USA Lounge. She took the beers freely and led him and his brother to believe that there would be fireworks in the hours to come back at her trailer. But that never happened.

Glen had to be pleased with himself as he drove through the mid-afternoon haze a year later. Yep, he made it back to the bar, found that woman and paid her back for making a fool of him. She would never make a fool of anybody else ever again, that was for sure. He fixed her, just like all the others. But what was it he was forgetting? It was something important, he was certain of that. Or maybe it wasn't important. His attempt to clean up the crime scene in that motel room were feeble. He'd registered in his own name, too. Why not? There was no crime in that. The cops would know soon enough who they were looking for and why. Registering in his own name would mix them up about what happened and why. It would make it look like he had nothing to hide.

In the meantime, what was he missing? And what time was it? The clock in this piece-of-shit Festiva was broken and the non-stop shimmy was getting on his nerves. This was no Delta 88 or Ford Mustang. Glen smiled as he recalled cars from his past, the ones that flew with a throaty roar. Glen looked out the window and wondered what time it was. He glanced over at his wrist. His watch – it was gone. Where was the watch? He gripped the wheel tighter.

Where was the watch?

13

TAMPA • NOVEMBER 7, 1995

In her fourth floor office at the Hillsborough County Courthouse — government issue, nothing fancy — Karen Cox reached across her desk to silence the ringing telephone. She didn't look up from the project that lay before her, another in a long string of endless tragedies. The phone rang all the time and she'd learned to work through it, taking the calls, getting rid of them quickly, getting on with it. Another phone call. She was busy, pleas to arrange, trials to prepare.

It was Sergeant George McNamara from Tampa PD's major crimes unit. As usual, this wasn't a social call. George talks fast, sounds hyperactive, though he isn't. Type A personality, that's all. Busy all the time. Lots of work to do, it never ends. "Come out to the Tampa 8 Inn on Columbus Drive near U.S. 41. There's a body in room 119."

Three miles from downtown in a seedy section of Tampa's near east side, the Tampa 8 wasn't familiar territory to Karen Cox, though she'd seen its sign without thinking about it thousands of times while whizzing above it on I-4. She got lost but finally found the place, next to the Tropicana Motel, both of them surrounded by chain link fence, their dumpsters part of the landscape, people going from room to room, leaving doors open, senseless noise blaring from ghetto blaster radios. Working girls could usually be found hanging out on the street, and this neighborhood was a pretty good place to pick up a bag of grass or a rock of crack. The rooms were clean, pretty well kept. Tampa 8's owners had fixed the place up some, but the pink and green paint job had 1950s written all over it. Most of the clientele couldn't have cared less. Rooms were twenty-five dollars with free HBO, and that's all that mattered.

Meeting George at murder scenes was a familiar ritual. He was the chief homicide detective, she the chief homicide prosecutor. They didn't call her in the middle of the night (she was pregnant at the time) or when she was in court, but otherwise Karen Cox and George McNamara held all too frequent rendezvous; this was just one of forty-seven murders Tampa suffered in 1995.

She arrived to find a swarm of city police, a still-shaking sheriff's deputy, somebody from the medical examiner's office and a nearly hysterical motel maid, Erica Charlton.

Sgt. McNamara, boyish-looking at 33, his light brown hair coiffed perfectly, dapper, as usual, in slacks and sport coat, greeted her. White female, unknown, thirties he reckoned, stabbed, body in the bathtub. Blood all over the place.

The killings went on but the revulsion never ended. Karen Cox did not go inside to look at the body — that would risk contaminating the crime scene — but she knew too well what lay behind the walls of room 119. She was the consummate professional, trained in the technicalities of the law, not the emotion of the arts, and this was but a job to do. And yet the unjustified taking of a life never made sense and it hit this young mother-in-waiting especially hard.

"When you see someone who's dead in the middle of the day it seems very surreal and horrible," she said. "I did not look at the body but even though you're detached, it's just horrible."

Cox was there not to investigate but to render legal advice when asked.

"Do we need a search warrant?" McNamara asked.

"No you don't," Cox answered. Management had called police, who now had implicit permission to enter. Besides, warrants aren't normally required for crime scenes.

And so, Cox, an assistant state's attorney and the chief of Hillsborough County's homicide prosecution team, had another murder to pursue.

For the previous two days Erica Charlton had honored the hand-lettered "Do Not Disturb" sign hanging from the door to room 119. The guest was a stayover, and the maids did not bother stayovers unless they asked for clean towels and such. On this Tuesday Erica knew from the manifest she carried on her rounds that the guest had checked out. She let herself in with her pass key and thought it was strange the deadbolt lock was engaged. The guest didn't just leave and push in the pin lock. He went to the trouble of turning the deadbolt lock from the outside. Sometimes they leave and don't even shut the door. Sometimes they don't even turn off the water.

At first, she was not alarmed by the bloody towels in the bathroom sink. Or the bloody pants. Or the bloody shoes.

Maybe he had cut himself.

Maybe someone had beat him up. That was not uncommon in this neighborhood.

She looked at the mess, shook her head disapprovingly and turned to the bed, the central collection point for the soiled laundry. She would pile all the towels and pillowcases and wash cloths in the center of the bed and then tie it all up in a bundle of the sheets and cart it off to the laundry. She did all of this, but when she bent over to pick up a towel from the bathroom floor she saw something just barely visible from the bathtub where the curtain didn't quite reach the end.

"As I enter I see, I see a little blood, didn't think nothin' of it," she said. "But I opened the door wide. As I go through the door I see all kinds of bloody shoes, bloody pants, bloody towel on the bathroom floor. Clothes like pants, like tennis. Then the shower curtain was closed. I could just see a little forehead in the shower, just peeping through the shower curtain I could see a head. So I push it wide open and that's when I see the little piece of head lying down in the shower. I didn't really see the whole body. I was shocked when I see a dead body."

Never before had Erica Charlton looked into the face of death and when the fixed gaze of the white woman's lifeless eyes greeted her from the bathtub she bolted screaming from the room as fast as she could make her legs work — Erica's body was not made for speed — and she poured out into the parking lot of the Tampa 8, her thick black arms flailing. She nearly ran into the arms of Sheriff's Deputy Donald Morris.

Morris had been sitting in his patrol car on stakeout for stolen cars. He couldn't make out what Erica was trying to say, the words running together furiously in her normally lyrical Bahamian accent. Something about a bathtub. She was pointing to a room where the door was ajar, probably somebody passed out, drunk maybe. He would check it out and then get back to work.

When he opened the door and didn't see anyone, Morris walked back to the bathroom. There, he used his flashlight to open the shower curtain. As the blood drained from his face and he began to shake, he realized he had failed to check the room properly when he entered. He might not be alone. The pall sickened him. Deputy Donald Morris was standing in the middle of a murder scene. His adrenaline kicked in now, and Morris stepped back, drew his revolver and carefully, quickly, retreated to the door to summon help.

Five minutes after Deputy Morris radioed for help, police were on the grounds of the Tampa 8 Inn like wasps on a windfall peach. First, they had to protect the crime scene. A guard was stationed at the door and nobody not involved in the collection of evidence was allowed to enter.

To detectives it was just another murder, a senseless waste of human life not fundamentally different from so many others. In his thirteen years on the force McNamara had seen all too many of these productions. He sized this one up as just another score settled on society's lowest rungs. Likely somebody whacked over a drug deal gone sour. Probably damn little difference in respectability between killer and victim. Another day, another murder. Work it like any other. Protect the evidence, find the killer and get him off the streets for a while. Move on to the next case.

They needed to round up any witnesses lingering at the scene. Detectives knew even the killer could be in their midst, so it was important to grab everyone in sight. While crime scene technicians from the Tampa Police Department began to comb room 119, officers scoured the parking lots of the Tampa 8 and the Tropicana next door, recording license tag numbers, making note of everything they saw. They needed to get a handle on just what had happened, and, as in the early minutes of any mystery, they had no way of knowing what was important and what was not. They had to study everything. No piece of evidence — no cigarette butt flipped to the ground fifty feet from the door of room 119, no paper scrap, no candy wrapper, nothing in the dumpster — was too small to overlook.

The quality of forensic sleuthing and evidence-gathering right here, right now, might determine whether the State of Florida would get a conviction for first degree murder or leave a courtroom in frustration and failure.

Shortly after noon David Schultz, an assistant Hillsborough County medical examiner, arrived and began inspecting the body. Cox consulted with McNamara. Police interviewed a motel guest, who said that around 11 p.m. Monday he noticed a stocky white male with a full beard and blond hair pacing in the parking lot. He said the man appeared to be angry and kept mumbling.

McNamara quickly assembled a team: His longtime friend Randy Bell as lead detective, and Bell's partner, Ricky Childers. For evidence gathering he assigned another detective, who approached room 119 while scanning the second story balcony overhead. Then she looked to the ground and saw a blue plastic wrapping for Lifestyle Spermicidally Lubricated condoms. Entering the room, she made dozens of seemingly insignificant observations: a partially made bed with the sheets pulled back on the opposite side, cigarette ashes on the top bed sheet and floor, a stain on the mattress cover, several pages torn from a telephone directory on the floor and in the trash can, a television tuned to Channel 10, an October 29 TV Guide opened to page 1, four GTE telephone books, a piece of blue paper under the bed, more ashes on the floor and nightstand, a wadded up tissue in the nightstand drawer, gray tile with pink flowers in each corner on the foyer floor, two drinking glasses sealed in plastic on the sink counter-top in the foyer next to the bathroom, an ice bucket, an unopened bar of Sweet Bouquet soap.

The foyer light was on, the bathroom light off. The toilet contained human feces, blood and toilet paper.

A white hand towel, bloodied, was in the sink, and blood was smeared on the counter. The detective made note of these details and a thousand others, minutiae the untrained eye would overlook or dismiss as insignificant. She saw a pair of Chic brand tennis shoes, blood on the soles, several bloodied towels rolled in a ball, on top of the towels a pair of black jeans, and on top of that, a roll of toilet paper. Dried blood ran down the outside of the bathtub.

She pulled back the shower curtain. Slumped in the tub was the body of a female, a shade on the plump side, with reddish-blond hair. She wore a white golf shirt that had been pulled up under her breasts, white socks and bloodied blue and white panties. Her right arm was extended across her left side with her hand resting on her shoulder. She had a two-inch laceration on her left wrist and new bruises in several places, defensive wounds that spoke volumes about her final moments: She waged a ferocious fight for survival. This was the information prosecutors would need to make a case for the death penalty, a crime that met the standards of cruel, atrocious and heinous.

First, of course, they had to identify and catch the killer.

Between the victim's bloody legs the detective found a Motorola pager. It was caked with blood and did not work.

The assistant examiner went to work. First he took a mental picture of the entire crime scene before he focused his attention on the body. Later, he would perform an autopsy at the county morgue. He inspected the bathroom, then removed the roll of toilet paper from on top of the black jeans and placed it in a large brown evidence bag. He then took away the white tennis shoes. He did not know the victim's identity but could tell just by looking at the blood-splattered walls and the bloody towels and clothing that there had been a fierce battle. The body lay face up in the bathtub — feet at the faucet end. The tile shower walls, shower curtain and sides of the bathtub were smeared with blood. Blood was clotted in the left front pocket of the black jeans and an angular incised cut over the right back pocket matched a cut through the victim's right buttock. She was fully clothed when stabbed and had not expected it. The killer removed her shorts before dumping her into the bathtub.

The killer had pulled up her shirt but not until after the stabbing, for there was a corresponding hole in the shirt where the knife had entered just above her left breast. It was a white shirt with "Ramada Inn Bayside" embroidered on the left side. Her body was damp, and it appeared that the killer might have turned on the shower. Whether this was a signature or a half-hearted alcohol- or drug-numbed attempt to wash away evidence, he could only speculate. That would be for the psychiatrists to figure out later, if and when they ever caught this guy. It was Florida. Killings happened every day. Convictions didn't always follow.

Dr. Schultz next concerned himself with the body itself. He discovered two stab wounds, either of them fatal, from what appeared to be a wide, nine-inch knife or machete. The killer needed powerful arms to restrain his victim, who weighed 165 pounds, and ram the knife into her right buttock, through her lower abdomen, and out the front of her body. The first wound penetrated the right internal iliac artery (a major artery that runs along the pelvis) and the abdominal cavity. This alone was a fatal wound, but the killer was just getting started. He wheeled her around and plunged the knife deep into the left side of her chest from the front, thrust it upward and then twisted it before pulling it out. The knife opened her left lung and the pericardial sac (the membrane surrounding the heart) and went out through her back ribs, causing both a pneumothorax and a hemothorax — that is, air and blood in the chest cavity. This wound, too, was fatal. In the course of this unspeakable violence the killer delivered a numbing blow with his fist to her chest, as evidenced by abrasions and a bruise on her left flank. There was blunt impact to her arms with multiple contusions. He noted the defensive stab wound on her left wrist. There appeared to have been no sexual activity, either forced or consensual; her attacker had only one aim, to kill her.

Though intoxicated by alcohol and marijuana, as lab reports would later reveal, she had put up one hell of a fight. Death did not come instantly. The pain of the knife, made excruciating by the twisting action as the killer pulled it back out — not to say her knowledge that she was going to die right now, right here, that this killer was the last person she would ever see, that she would never again hear the voices of those she loved —- must have seated in her a terror beyond comprehension.

At 12:51 p.m. Dr. Schultz removed a thin gold necklace with a clear stone and a silver necklace with a silver St. Christopher medallion from around the victim's neck. He noticed a bruise on the back of her left elbow and saw a green tattoo of a cross on her left shoulder. Later the jewelry she wore would prove something of a puzzle, for investigators would learn that robbery was part — perhaps a small part but still one element — of the motive.

A crime scene technician took photos of the body, and at 12:56 it was placed in a plastic bag and removed to the county morgue. Underneath the body Dr. Schultz found two dimes, four nickels, a pair of sunglasses, and a Shey brand men's sports watch with a black wristband attached at only one end. It was flashing 8:22 a.m. Monday. The dimes, the nickels, the sunglasses, the watch, were all meaningless to the young medical examiner and yet he knew these objects could mean everything.

In the bathroom sink police found a thin gold necklace and two cigarette butts along with some hair in the drain.

Meanwhile, technicians dusted for fingerprints and took photos. They collected hundreds of pieces of evidence, everything in the room that was not furniture or fixture. It seemed like they had everything. But they didn't have a murder weapon, a suspect, a motive or any idea of who the victim was. It was going to be a long, tense day. Months later, Sgt. McNamara would remember every sad detail:

"There was a great deal of violence," he said quietly. "There was a struggle."

The ease and speed with which police identified the suspect in the motel murder as Glen Edward Rogers astonished even them. Whether it was an act of bravado or stupidity, they did not know. He swaggered into the Tampa 8 Inn and registered under his own, real name, producing a Mississippi driver's license as identification, offering the name of a former employer, and leaving his fingerprints all over the "Do Not Disturb" sign he'd fashioned from a piece of cardboard. They were having no such luck identifying the victim, however. Whoever she was had been relieved of whatever she carried. There was no identification, no wallet or purse, and no automobile. Tampa's newest Jane Doe would have to wait for someone to miss her.

At police headquarters, Sgt. McNamara began the search for information about his new suspect. He typed "Glen Edward Rogers" into the National Crime Information Center computer, and when it came back "wanted for murder," George figured there must be some mistake. Not this one, he told himself. This was just some low-level knock-off, a prostitute who made a fuss over payment, a drug deal gone amiss, whatever. He plugged the name in again.

Rogers had been wanted between March and June 1993 when he worked in food service for Farrow. His employment ended when he was arrested in Noblesville, Indiana. An acquaintence named Jackie bonded him out of jail, but Glen skipped bail and never returned to Indiana.

The computer spit out the sheet on Glen Rogers: Born July 15, 1962 in Hamilton, Ohio; 6'-1"; 180 to 190 pounds; blondish-gray shoulder-length hair, a beard and a mustache. On parole from Los Angeles for beating up his girlfriend. Lengthy record going back to the age of nine or ten. He was a drifter and sometimes carnival worker, a former cab driver and drug informant for the Hamilton Police Department. More gruesome detail followed: The suspect was wanted in California for the murder of a young woman. He was accused of strangling her, throwing her into the cab of her pickup truck and setting the truck on fire. The murder took place September 29. For thirty-nine days he had been on the run, lost in a vast and far-flung abyss of violent fugitives constantly on the move and nearly impossible to track with any consistency. Outside of Los Angeles County, Rogers was virtually unknown. He was well known in Hamilton, but he had been gone from there a very long time and to the local authorities, he was out of sight and therefore out of mind.

While Cox opened a file on her suspect and began to put together what she had learned about the case, Tampa police were getting phone calls from police agencies around the country, checking for similarities to their own unsolved murders. George McNamara carried a reputation for relentless pursuit of anybody he thought worthy of pursuing. Karen Cox, an experienced prosecutor with her eye on a move to the federal courts and no compassion for killers, would steer the prosecution. They would make a good team.

Hundreds of miles away in the North Florida Panhandle, the unkempt man drove west with a can of Budweiser between his legs and Jimmy Buffett cued up loud on the tape player. The white Ford Festiva could not be muscled down the road. It was no Mustang. No big Buick. In fact, the car was trouble. It needed a tune-up. It shimmied at fifty-five miles per hour or faster and because a headlight was out, it could not be driven at night. A dead headlight was a cop magnet, and he could not afford to be pulled over. So the car plodded through the day, its driver sipping warm beer and reaching for a Marlboro Red from time to time. The semi-trucks and workday traffic swept past in a blur of speed and wind. He had money in his pocket — $283 from a purse he had stolen the day before. The purse itself and the wallet with the ID were gone, dumped in a trash can at a highway rest stop near Tallahassee. Nobody would find it there. Nobody, no way. Authorities were looking for him; he pressed onward.

Around mid-morning Michael Pitts, a maintenance worker from a sheltered workshop, was emptying trash cans at the I-10 rest stop. Lifting the lid on one, he peered inside as he pulled the plastic bag tight. Then he stopped and looked closer. It was a patchwork purse. Inside was a wallet and driver's license but no money. He turned it in to his supervisor.

Back on the interstate, the driver of the white Festiva hunched over the quaking steering wheel in the slow lane, the day growing unseasonably warm for fall. He squinted at the road and thought about what lay ahead. He wasn't worried and he wasn't on the run, not really. He had a pocket full of cash and nothing but time. He would be in Biloxi in a couple of hours, maybe hit a riverboat casino and while away a hour or two at the blackjack tables, turn that couple of hundred into a couple of thousand. With his luck, how could he miss? By noon, Florida would be behind him for good. Two states back, in fact, and he would be free and clear. Nobody could catch him. He was on the road, again, and it felt like home.

~

GIBSONTON, FLORIDA • NOVEMBER 11, 1995

On a cool November afternoon, Tina Marie Cribbs was laid to rest. Her teenage boys were there, and her best friend/mother, Mary Dicke. It was a simple affair conducted by friends at the funeral home. They grieved. They prayed. They spoke tender words about the young mother with a heart the size of a barn who would do anything for the underdog. They could do these things, go through these motions, do what you're supposed to do at a funeral, but they could not understand any of it.

After the brief ceremony, her body was cremated. Her friends and mother took the ashes back to the Showtown USA. They placed the urn on a table in the middle of the barroom and tipped one last cold beer to Tina's memory. It was the first time anyone could remember an impromptu wake at the Showtown, the home, the living room, even the kitchen for many of the regulars. Tina Marie was right there on the table for all the world to see. The old friends exchanged hugs and wiped tears for the memory of a woman whose life was hard but not without love.

14

BOSSIER CITY, LOUISIANA • NOVEMBER 7, 1995

When he finally rolled into Bossier City Tuesday evening, November 7, Glen delivered on his promise to Andy. He had gotten a "good deal" on a 1990-something car — some kind of a small Ford — from "a friend." He said the previous owner had not taken care of it, that it was trashed and needed to be cleaned up, the wheels were out of balance and when it went over fifty-five miles an hour the car shimmied. But it would make a nice little car when fixed up. She wasn't aware that Glen's words were one lie on top of another.

Nor did she have anyway of knowing that the car belonged to Tina Marie Cribbs or that two days earlier Rogers had run a nine-inch knife through Tina Marie's buttock and out her abdomen and then whirled her around and plunged the knife through her left lung and dumped her in the bathtub to die, gasping and bleeding. Nor did she know that a week earlier he had dispensed with Linda Price in a similar manner. Or that in September he had strangled Sandra Gallagher and discarded her body in her pickup truck and then set the truck on fire. Or that he was the only suspect in the unexplained disappearance of Mark Peters. Andy Sutton did not know these things because she had a new boyfriend. He left and then he came back. She was in love and he might just be in love with her. After all, he came back. Andy would endure no more lonely days. She knew her life was about to change. No more running from one guy to the next. This time, Andy figured, she'd found her dream love. Finally. She deserved it, she believed.

Terriea Pullig had urged her younger sister to slow down. Andy called Terriea on November 7. They hadn't seen each other for a couple of weeks, but frequent, long telephone conversations keep them close.

Andy couldn't stop talking about Glen.

"Well, I thought I'd call and tell you where I'm living and give you my address and everything," Andy told her sister. "I've met a guy who is just so sweet, you know, so nice."

"What do you know about him?" Terriea replied, skeptical. "Where is he from?"

"He's from out of town," said Andy. In fact she didn't really know where he was from.

"What does he do for a living?"

"He drives a truck."

"He drives a truck, for what company?"

"Terriea, why are you asking me all these questions? He drives a truck."

"Because I kind of want to know who you're seeing. You never know this day and time who these people are, what they're like. Does he own his own truck or something and just pick up loads?"

"Yeah, I guess that's kind of how he does it, because I took him to the bus station and put him on the bus, and he was supposed to go somewhere and pick up a truck."

Andy never would give her sister Glen's last name or his employer, and Terriea felt a growing sense of unease creep into her world, an awful and dark suspicion that all was not right.

"Just kind of be careful," Terriea warned. "I think you're moving too fast, and you don't know much about him."

"I don't understand why you are asking all these questions," Andy answered.

The next morning, Theresa Whiteside, sleeping on the couch because Andy and Glen had the waterbed, awoke when she heard Andy stirring around the apartment, getting ready for a 10 a.m. job interview at Thrifty Liquor. She went back to sleep, then got up and made coffee when Andy returned sometime before 11. By early afternoon Glen and Andy made their way to the It'll Do Lounge, and Theresa joined them later. When she arrived Glen was buying drinks for Andy and a woman named Rhonda, and he bought Theresa a beer.

They did not stay long at It'll Do, however, because Andy got into an argument with the bartender and wanted to leave. The three bundled off to A Touch of Class on Texas Avenue, Glen and Andy stopping for cigarettes at the Airline Food Market along the way.

"I told 'em to pick me up a pack and I'd pay 'em for it when they got to the bar," Theresa said. "And when they come in the bar, I just bought 'em a beer, both of 'em, to pay 'em back for the cigarettes, and she was standing beside me and she seemed kinda disgusted with him for some reason, I'm not really sure. I think it was because he was really drunk, and he had to go home. She had to take him, to give him a nap, so they could get back that night."

As he and Andy drank away the afternoon, Glen underwent a metamorphosis, from Glen the charmer to Glen the argumentative and unpredictable. Later, they got into an argument. This time, she refused to give in and would stand her ground. They were supposed to visit Theresa at Mr. Bill's on Barksdale, where Theresa tended bar. But Theresa warned them to come late, around closing, because Andy had been barred from the place. Glen and Andy left A Touch of Class around 4:30, and Theresa reported for work at 5. She never saw her friend alive again.

Nine hours later, Theresa closed the bar, stopped to eat at Whataburger and arrived home at 3:30 a.m.

"When I got in the door and I shut it, I heard the door shut, so I just assumed they was back there," Theresa said. "And while I was eating my food, I could have swore I heard the commode lid shut — I just assumed they was back there." She did not hear it flush, however ("It's creepy, I mean, it makes noise all the time"). Theresa had good reason to assume Glen and Andy were in the bedroom: A blanket and pillow had been thoughtfully placed on the couch for her.

Theresa went to sleep on the sofa. She awoke around 10 a.m. to a knock at the apartment door. It was Thomas Norman Bryant, Andy's ex-boyfriend. Andy had been ill for a few days and Tommy had come to make sure she was all right. He had tried to call several times but kept getting a message that said the line was being checked for repairs. What Tommy did not know, what nobody knew at the time, was that the telephone line to Apartment 93 had been cut sometime during the night.

"I looked in the peep-hole and couldn't recognize who it was and I said, 'Who is it?' and he said, 'Tommy,' Theresa said. "All I had on was my black shirt, so I went back there and I knew that Andy was with Glen." She let Tommy in and then knocked on Andy's door. There was no answer.

"I opened the door and didn't really know who was in the bed," Theresa said "I just saw one figure lying there. I went over and pulled the covers down. She had a pillow over her head. I pulled the covers down and at first all I saw was her chest and there was blood all over her. I moved the pillow and her arm was above her head and it was still. I moved her and I said 'Andy.'"

Then realization struck and Theresa ran screaming from the room as Tommy checked for a pulse and any sign of life. "She's not breathing," he told Theresa, who was busy putting on her shorts.

He touched Andy's arm. Again he checked for a pulse and then tenderly touched her bloody head.

"Call 9-1-1," he told Theresa.

When none of the phones worked, Theresa ran through the complex, banging on doors, but got no answer. Finally the pair made it to Bryant's truck to use his cell phone. Andy was gone. It was time to figure out why.

How Terriea Pullig came to learn of her sister's murder only added to the tragedy.

"I had just come home and turned on the TV," she said. "The news was on. I was in the kitchen starting supper and I heard the name Sutton and I thought, well, let me go in there and listen to that. And I come in and turned the TV up a little bit, and about that time the phone was ringing and it was my brother, and I was looking at it and he was telling me about it all at the same time 'cause it got leaked out and it was put on the news."

When Willie Jiles learned that something was going on at his sister's apartment, he immediately drove over from Blanchard but police rebuffed him at the door.

"So he was still up in the air," Terriea said. "No one really told him until later. So he had just got out of there and got home and was calling me."

Willie called Terriea and tried to lead with a buffer, but the news hit her without warning.

"We've had another tragedy in the family," Willie told her. "I want you to sit down and hold on a minute. This has leaked out, so it's on the news right now. They've found her body, and she's been murdered."

Bossier City Police faced a big job in Apartment 93 on this day, November 9, 1995. Patrol officers heard the dis-patch at 10:31 a.m., and when they arrived the fire department had already disconnected electric power, thinking the death might be electrocution because of the wet bedroom floor.

When Sergeant Harry Fain pulled back the covers from Andy's head, he quickly determined that this death was not from natural or accidental causes. Dried blood caked her face; the carpet was soaked with a reddish-brown substance. Sgt. Fain told the other officers and firemen to leave the apartment. Evidence gathering would require an uncontaminated crime scene, and nobody — not even the chief of police or the sheriff — would be allowed inside without an investigative purpose.

While Officer Larry Hawkins stationed himself at the apartment entrance, Fain wrapped the place in yellow crime scene tape and told Hawkins to detain Theresa Whiteside and Thomas Bryant. Hawkins asked Theresa if Andy had a boyfriend. Theresa answered, "Yes, his name is Glen," but she did not know his last name. It didn't take Hawkins long to consider the unknown Glen a suspect. His suspicions were further aroused when the suspect's Datsun pickup truck, in the parking lot with no license plate, came back registered to a Glen Edward Rogers, wanted for questioning in murders in California and Mississippi.

While one officer stood guard over the truck, others transported Whiteside and Bryant to police headquarters to be interviewed. At 11 a.m. police began taking video and still pictures. They looked for fingerprints and shoeprints. The search came up empty through the hallway, bedroom and bathroom. But there in the master bedroom was a large mirror which produced at least sixteen prints.

When the prints had been lifted, crime scene technicians moved in to remove anything that might be evidence: Miller and Miller Lite beer bottles, bedsheets and pillows, ashtrays, Doral and Marlboro cigarettes, hair, a Bell telephone with caller ID, a pair of green boxer shorts, clothing, jewelry boxes and a one-dollar food stamp. They also found a treasure trove of knives — a black-handled knife, a steak knife, eleven kitchen knives, two knives in knife blocks and a butcher knife. Later they learned that the murder weapon was among those and had been wiped off and replaced in its knife block after use. Another knife was found wrapped up in a pair of men's pants that investigators presumed belonged to the killer.

At 2:15 that afternoon Brenda K. Reames, a pathologist contracted by the Bossier Parish Coroner's Office, began the autopsy. Dr. Reames' report revealed horrid details of the violence that ended Andy's life and her desperate struggle to survive: ". . .a result of multiple stab wounds of the trunk, several of which caused fatal injuries with extensive internal bleeding. . . fourteen stab and incised wounds of the body with multiple wounds contributing to death, including injury to the heart, left lung and liver (and) four defense injuries."

Andy had thrown her hands up to ward off the blows, taking stab wounds to her right forearm, wrist and hand. The fatal wounds were delivered to her abdomen and chest, causing bleeding in the chest cavity and rupture of the pericardial sac. There was no evidence of either rape or consensual sex. Andy tested negative for drugs, but her blood alcohol level was .024 percent — she was highly intoxicated and now she was dead.

15

I ain't afraid of dying. I ain't afraid of killing. And I wasn't afraid of getting caught.

— Glen Rogers

FLIGHT TO BEATTYVILLE • NOVEMBER 9, 1995

Glen kept driving. It was all he could do.

He rolled up the window in the Festiva against the autumn chill, slipped in the Hank Williams Jr. greatest hits tape and tapped his thumb on the steering wheel to one of his favorites: "I'm So Lonesome I Could Cry." It set off a chain of memories about his childhood in the country-western haven of Hamilton and most all of the memories were bad. Glen faded back through the years to bath night with his older brother Clay. He could see his breath as he sat in the tub and the water was icy cold because the family had no money for gas to heat the water. They both hated bath night and fought and fussed and screamed. Now they both were going under.

It was time to shampoo and both heads were plunged under water. Was their old man going to drown them like puppies? Glen and Clay were both flat on their bellies, and the boys opened their eyes and looked at one another as they held their breath and felt their heads, each boy's hand wrapped up in the other's hair, desperate. The boys tried to raise their heads but they could not. They were going to die. They were going to be drowned and there was nothing they could do about it. In terror, they looked through the cloudy water at one another and a mental bridge was built. And then up and out of the bone-chilling water they were yanked, each coughing and gasping. Bath night.

Glen came out of his reverie and realized that he needed a shower. But it had to be a shower. He hated bathtubs, and deep down inside, he hated his mother and any woman who reminded him of her. He hated the memories of his father, too, memories that never were far, that he could never lose. Most of all, he hated himself and the raw deal that life sent his way.

He shook off the memory, hit the reject button on the tape, and tossed the cassette to the floor, noticing his lucky 1892 coin in the tray. He picked it up and began to absent-mindedly rub it. He kept it in the coin tray, handy. The coin had belonged to good old Mark Peters. What a sucker, Glen thought. He immediately began to feel better as he rubbed the coin between his thumb and forefinger. Everything was going to be all right after all. The cops were too stupid to catch him. Nobody caught him after Peters died. Nobody would catch him this time, either. It didn't matter how many people he killed or where he wrote his name and left fingerprints. They couldn't catch him.

He floored it and the front end of the Ford shook violently. What time was it anyhow? He looked at his wrist, couldn't break the habit. Where is that damn watch? He just couldn't remember, and he didn't like that at all.

16

I got people there in Beattyville. Who'd recognize me there? Probably everybody.

— Glen Rogers

ACROSS LOUISIANA • NOVEMBER 9, 1995

Rogers headed east out of Bossier City on Interstate 20, past Barksdale Air Force Base where at any time of day lumbering, jungle green B-52 Stratofortresses performing touch-and-go landings pass not 500 feet over the highway on their endless circular flight paths. He was on the run, heading for the safety, he was sure, of family and friends in the Kentucky mountains.

Across the northern Louisiana plains — sparsely settled farmland with only an occasional outpost for travelers — he drove. First it was 175 miles east, through Monroe to Vicksburg, Mississippi, then another forty-five miles to Jackson. By now, Rogers displayed a boldness that those looking for him could only marvel at. Wanted by Los Angeles Police on suspicion of murder, he had brazenly walked into the Jackson police station to retrieve his stolen truck. He had moved about Jackson, checking into motel rooms under his own name, seemingly oblivious to the intense interest in his whereabouts. On this day he was the subject of a nationwide manhunt, had been a guest star on the television crime program *America's Most Wanted,* and was sought for killings in California,

Florida, Louisiana and Mississippi. Police had a description of the Ford Festiva. And now he was driving it right through the heart of Jackson, where he had stabbed Linda Price to death eight days earlier.

He continued north, to Birmingham, across the Tennessee River and into Chattanooga. Then he took Interstate 75 north along the western foothills of the Appalachian Mountains, through Cleveland, Tennessee, up to Knoxville and on to Lake City.

Meanwhile, police in Tampa were putting together a frightening profile of their suspect. They contacted a man by the name of Gary Cretors, a taxi driver in Pinellas Park, Florida, who had been a close friend of Glen's and a fellow cab driver in Hamilton in 1991-92.

Cretors told police he had gone to Rogers' house every weekend for a cookout and that he got to know Glen quite well. He said Glen had a girlfriend but he didn't remember her name. He said he heard Glen talk about Mark Peters, that Peters was a very good family friend who had money. Glen told him he would occasionally get money from Peters.

Cretors had not seen Rogers since that time in Ohio. Cretors told police he "had seen Glen Rogers carrying a .357 and on occasion a 9-mm." He said Glen carries a lock-blade knife, "smoked reefer and did acid." Further, he said, Glen is a very heavy drinker with a fondness for Budweiser and Marlboro Red cigarettes.

Glen was again on the move and headed north, to one of only two places on earth where he was just about guaranteed to be recognized. Glen was going to Beattyville, Kentucky, to the family farm of his youth. It was a second home, and he knew he could depend on a loyal cadre of pot-growing and drug-dealing friends to shield him from the tightening net of the law. He could rely on a deep-seated culture of exclusion to protect him, a culture whose roots thread back to the pioneers who settled here in the 18th century. Here were hill people who looked out for their own, who enforced a strict code of silence and who, like these hills themselves, knew what it meant to be silent. Glen figured he would be safe.

Beattyville forms where two winding roads cross in the Daniel Boone Forest, in the foothills of East-Central Kentucky in an area known as the Cumberland Plateau. To the east at Haddix, the aptly named Troublesome Creek meets the north fork of the Kentucky River, while a little to the south the middle fork runs midway between the hamlets Turkey and Shoulderblade. The south fork is the product of several tributaries with names like Stinking Creek that meander through such burgs as Flat Lick, Salt Gum and Goose Rock. The three forks converge at Beattyville to form the Kentucky River proper, which flows northwest past Lexington to Frankfort and on to the Ohio River.

It is rugged territory, though not so unforgiving as the higher Appalachian Mountains to the east. Its people have survived by adapting to the mountain and its ways, for the mountains can never be tamed. Its inhabitants are mostly descendants of the independent free spirits who settled here, and except for the widespread acceptance of welfare, their culture has remained as intact as the giant rock ledges that overlook the canyons and streams below. It is a culture that reflects the isolation of mountain society, a society that plays by its own rules and invites the rest of the world to mind its own business. Revenue Agents have never been welcome here, not in the old days when they came to bust up moonshine stills, not today when they come to uproot the marijuana fields.

And yet, poverty and ignorance remain constant companions to the people who have inhabited these hills ever since the white man first migrated west from Virginia.

When the lawyers and land speculators discovered

Eastern Kentucky in the years prior to World War I, things began to change. The simple hill men were no match for the fast-talking, friendly and well-educated outsiders who came around armed with long, complicated deeds the landowners couldn't read and pockets crammed with cash they could not resist. Enticed by money and promises of regular wages for working the coal from their own land, they began selling off — with little understanding of what they were doing — the mineral rights to their coal, oil and timber. Usually they kept the land itself and the tax liability, but they gave up its economic value. Mineral rights went for pennies on the dollar.

Dotted on the steep, rugged land are reminders of the people who once tried to forge a living in this isolated region: tumbledown shacks, and lone brick chimneys that peek out of the woods from long-abandoned plots. There is some commercial timber — oak, beech, black walnut, buckeye, yellow poplar and pine — but Lee County didn't succeed in the bidding for a wood veneer plant, and the entire timber harvest is shipped to another county for processing.

The area's other cash crop, not tabulated in the economic and census surveys, is marijuana. With its sparse population and rich mountain soil, Lee County is one of the nation's most fertile regions for growing cannabis, which long ago replaced more labor-intensive and less profitable moonshine distilling as the tax-free product of choice.

This part of East-Central Kentucky has long suffered from a shabby image, the stereotype of a forgotten land where everybody is barefoot, snaggle-toothed and can't read. It's an unfair cartoon image, as evidenced by the town's core of hard-working, honest people who greet strangers — cautiously at first — with open friendliness and generosity. But it has this reputation of a people who settle their own scores with no interest in outside assistance. The story is told about Mafia organizers who moved into Lee County in the 1930s with the intent of taking over the moon-shine trade, and how they mysteriously disappeared one day, never to be seen again.

"I don't know if it actually happened, but it's part of the folklore," observed Bob Smith, publisher of the *Three Forks Tradition* newspaper. "It's like the hangings we've had around here. Sometimes you don't know, and sometimes you don't want to know."

Glen was headed home.

From the first of November, Rogers had been a man of death and destruction. He had traveled from Jackson to Bossier City to Tampa and then back across three states to Bossier City. In those three cities he had met and stayed with three different women who turned up dead after he departed.

With a broken headlight in Tina Marie's car, he drove only in daylight and slept in the car as needed, once at a Union 76 truck stop near Jackson. He was in no hurry; he was not running.

And he never panicked. He skulked through casinos in Vicksburg and Jackson. At one stop a waitress showed him a newspaper picture of a man wanted for murder.

"This looks like you," she told him.

"Well, it ain't me," Rogers said, and he quietly left.

He made it to Lake City, Tennessee, north of Knoxville on I-75, on Friday. He registered at the Lamb's Inn Motel under the name of James Peters and was given the key to room 34. That night he entertained himself at the First and Last Chance Bar right behind the motel. On Saturday he went to the Fast Cash Pawn Shop to unload five rings, two microphones and his lucky silver dollar. He had taken the rings from Cribbs, Sutton and Price, and though he hated parting with any of his keepsakes, this time he had no choice. He was running low on cash.

Sunday he drove fifty-eight miles north to Corbin, Kentucky, where he bivouacked for a while in the car at the Union 76 Truck Stop. He filled out an employment application using the name of Rodney Whiteside, an identity borrowed from Theresa Whiteside, Andy Sutton's roommate. It was Theresa's brother's name.

("I only filled out that application so I could go back to the truck wash, so I could steal a tag on a car," he would later explain.)

Then he continued north, leaving I-75 near London, Kentucky, to drive the final fifty-one miles northeast to Beattyville on a narrow, winding mountain road. But first he removed the Florida license tag from Tina Cribbs' car and replaced it with a Tennessee plate he had stolen earlier at a truck stop in Mississippi. He opened the little Ford's rear hatchback and tossed the Florida tag inside with the Kentucky tag he'd also stolen. He would need that Kentucky plate again when he reached Beattyville.

The Florida plate he would keep for later. Who knows, he might head back south in another day or two.

Up north in Hamilton, people expected Rogers to return. When the news that crazy Glen Rogers was on a killing spree through the South filtered back to the barstools of this factory town, he was spotted everywhere. On one week-night at a K-mart on the southeast side of town, a frantic patron told the store management that Glen Rogers was inside shopping. The K-mart emptied in a melee.

"Our problem was that half the town looked like Glen Rogers," Det. Pratt said.

Police believed Rogers would try to make it back to this city. Glen always left and he always returned. This time, with a national manhunt already underway, authorities had no reason to believe otherwise. "That Jimmy Nugent (Hamilton detective) came here and sat there and told me that if he saw Glen, he would shoot him on the spot," Glen's mother said. Police watched bars and kept tabs on family members' homes, but particularly his mother's house.

Behind her bungalow on Hunt Avenue, a gritty corner of the city, one set of neighbors received a knock at the front door. On the porch was a pair of well-dressed but unsmiling men. They wore ties and flashed badges. They were FBI agents up from Cincinnati. "How would you like a trip to Florida," they asked. "A nice condominium vacation right on the beach? Maybe for a week?"

"When?"

"How about right now?"

Within an hour, FBI agents were settled in the house with their sights trained on the back door of the Rogers house. If Glen made it home, they would have him.

The comment about shooting her son on sight from the Hamilton detective set Edna thinking. If one police officer wanted to shoot her son that badly, then how many others out there harbored similar feelings? And what of the phone taps and new cars all over this poor neighborhood? Were there snipers? The likelihood that her son would die on her doorstep was becoming all too real.

Edna hesitated but let her heart lead when she finally spoke about her tragic life to the local news media. The message Edna wanted to convey was simple. "I'm so afraid. I'm so afraid. I'm afraid they're going to hurt my son. I'm begging, please give up," she said. "I love you very much, please, please, please. . ."

It was the telecommunications age. Glen would get the message.

Arriving in Beattyville on Sunday afternoon, Rogers went looking for compatriots. His plan was straightforward, uncomplicated: blend into local society and ride out the gathering storm. Hang out here as long as necessary — a few months, a couple of years, whatever it took.

And though he aimed to lie low, he was confident of his position and resigned that his fate could not be denied. He continued to throw about his brazen, catch-me-if-you-can arrogance.

Glen was anything but reclusive in Beattyville. Brenda Taulbee at the Fill Zone service station on Main Street was tending the register when Rogers arrived that Sunday. He wanted a certain brand of chewing tobacco that she did not have. "They'll just have to settle for this," he told her, accepting an alternate brand. She did not know who "they" was.

"He was real polite," Brenda said. "He had real blue-looking eyes as I remember, and he was sort of a nice — he wasn't cleaned up really good but you'd think this guy would look nice cleaned up."

It took a while for police to piece the puzzle together. Finally, a pattern emerged: The victims were single white women in their thirties, usually with reddish-blond hair, and all had been stabbed with a large knife. The killer left two of the victims in bathtubs and tried to clean up the scene; one was left on her punctured waterbed; one was strangled and then thrown into her pickup truck, which he then torched. Mark Peters did not fit the pattern because his was a killing of opportunity. From nowhere, Rogers shot to the top of the FBI's Most Wanted List and the *America's Most Wanted* squeezed him in at the last minute as an unwilling guest star. All of a sudden, Glen Rogers was a national story. A terse dispatch from Tampa Police to the Regional Organized Crime Information Center underscored the urgency: "Glen Rogers is a serial murderer."

That would not matter much in Beattyville. Folks were accustomed to killing here, had been for decades. Rogers planned to hang with old friends from childhood who could protect him. Though badly in need of repair and without an intact roof, the family cabin offered shelter of sorts, and Glen knew how to make do with what he had. In the past he had found more comfortable accommodations at his cousin Doug Phillips' house on Highway 799 just outside of town. Phillips had his own disagreements with the law and would provide a safe harbor for his wayward relative.

Trouble was no stranger to the Phillips family. In 1997 Doug Phillips was serving time for second-degree assault. His brother was sentenced to prison for accidentally killing his own adult son. Shooting William Tell-style, Jimmy Phillips was trying to hit the Masonic emblem on his son's hat with a rifle shot that instead struck him in the head.

Tooling around the countryside on Sunday afternoon, Glen pulled the Ford Festiva up to a four-way stop sign on Highway 52, where Sheriff Doug Brandenburg and Kentucky State Police Detective Kevin McNally were standing alongside their patrol cars, passing time.

Rogers waved: Hello, fellas. The two waved back. And Rogers drove on down the road.

At first Glen moved freely. After waving to the cops the first time, he came back around, this time with a hitchhiker he had picked up.

At 2:12 p.m. on November 13, Rogers knocked on the door of Youth Haven, a summer Bible camp near Beattyville. Polite but nervous, he asked to see a chaplain. When told the director was not there, he left after about five minutes. His greeters did not recognize him. Sometime before 2:30, Glen sought refuge at the home of the Smallwood sisters, his elderly second cousins who lived across the road from the Rogers family cabin, on Highway 52 at Old Landing Road not far from the mission. Frightened, they refused to let him in. "He only stayed here for about ten minutes," Clara Smallwood said. "We didn't let him in the house. We stayed on the porch and he stood out in the yard. We didn't ask where he had been or where he was going."

The cabin had belonged to Glen's father, Claude Sr., and his uncle Clyde, Claude's brother. They inherited the property from their father, who was a brother of the Smallwood sisters' mother. Originally from this area in Lee County, their father lived in Hamilton and built the cabin as a weekend retreat. Glen spent time here as a boy. He'd never been known to use a gun, knife or any kind of weapon around the Smallwoods. "This thing they are talking about is a side of Glen we never saw," Clara said. "Around us he was a loving relative. He was never violent and was always respectful of our feelings."

The Smallwood sisters had last seen Glen on October 18, 1993, the day after Mark Peters disappeared. Glen had supper with them that night and then moved on. For the next two months, he called about every other week — brief conversations supposedly to check up on them, see how they were doing, "Oh, and had any police been coming around the cabin?" he always asked. "No," they told him. "Why?" He didn't reply. Then, as suddenly as the calls began, they stopped and the sisters lost touch with their relative.

This time there would be no supper for a weary traveler, no protection offered by kin for a shirttail relative. He stood there in the hardscrabble yard near the renegade plastic rooster standing sentinel in a flower bed, long since gone to weeds. He was alone and burned out, more mongrel than sleek road dog. When the sisters would not allow him inside, he knew the game was over. He had been discovered in Beattyville and he had to get out immediately.

"I just wanted to stop and say goodbye and tell you all I love you," Rogers told them. "What they are telling on me is not the truth."

When Glen turned from the driveway onto Highway 52, he looked up the other side of the road to the ghostly remains of the family cabin, the sunken roof, the open windows and doorways, the graveyard of Mark Peters and who knows how many others. It might have been a safe house for him but that was not to be. It was time to move on. As Glen's car disappeared behind the naked trees under the dreary November sky, Clara Smallwood reached for the telephone.

17

McIntosh: Were you still driving this little white car at this time?

Rogers: Yeah.

McIntosh: You think the lady might want her car back?

Rogers: No.

HIGHWAY 52, EASTERN KENTUCKY • NOVEMBER 13, 1995

In the little town of Ravenna deep in the Appalachian foothills of Central Kentucky about forty miles southeast of Lexington, Bob Stephens, wearing blue jeans, tennis shoes and a pullover windbreaker, was driving his bronze 1994 Ford Crown Victoria, an automobile that looked so unlike a police car that he was getting used to being pulled over by local officers whenever they thought he was acting suspiciously, because he had this habit of driving around slowly, taking long studied looks at people.

On this Monday afternoon, Bob Stephens had legitimate business here, but that was news to Chris Cox, a rookie officer on patrol for the Irvine Police Department who didn't like the way the stranger pulled alongside the white Ford Festiva in a no-passing zone. He flipped on his blue lights, and Stephens obediently pulled to the right. So did the Festiva, but its driver took a good look at Stephens and didn't like what he saw. He certainly recognized a cop when he saw one.

The driver, unkempt with a shaggy beard and long blond hair, then threw an open can of beer at Stephens and took off. Stephens peeled out after him. So did Chris Cox. The chase was on.

As soon as Stephens placed his portable blue light on the dashboard, Cox knew his target now was the Ford Festiva, not the Crown Victoria. He had no idea why he was chasing the little white car, because there was no established communication link between Irvine Police and whoever was driving the Crown Victoria. Cox figured it was a state trooper, but he didn't recognize the man. So he jumped into the chase, about to embark on a wild ride along a winding mountain highway that would reach speeds of eighty or more, taking part in one of the greatest pursuits in local memory.

"Oh yes," Cox said. "To this day that chase is still the highlight of my career." Twenty-four years old and a lifelong Irvine resident, Cox had been on the small-town force only since April, having graduated from Eastern Kentucky University in nearby Richmond the previous October with a degree in police administration.

With twenty-six years as a Kentucky State Trooper, Detective Robert G. Stephens figured he had seen about everything. A sex-crimes investigator for Post 7 out of nearby Richmond, he was working a case in Irvine when, at about 2:30 p.m. he heard a radio dispatch: A white Ford Festiva automobile with Tennessee license plates had recently left Beattyville and was headed for Richmond. Its driver was purported to be Glen Edward Rogers, wanted in four states for murder.

Only two roads come into Ravenna, River Road and Kentucky Highway 52, and they meet in a Y near the CSX railroad bridge. Ravenna merges into Irvine. To set up the chase, Stephens had backed up to an abandoned grocery store. He looked out at the low gray sky. It was one of those dull November afternoons when you wonder if you'll ever see the sun again, in the high thirties, showers predicted, though the roads were dry so far. No blinding sunlight. Good day for a chase. Stephens waited, but not long.

"I hadn't been there but three or four minutes and he showed up," Stephens said. "I looked up and there he was."

Stephens knew Rogers' description from a photograph. Heading west, toward Richmond, he pulled alongside Rogers to get a good look, then backed off to wait for help.

Rogers wasn't waiting. He bolted from the intersection and raced through the tiny but busy downtown area of Irvine. Somehow he avoided collisions as he threaded through traffic congestion to the narrow Kentucky River bridge and crossed in the wrong lane, all the while releasing beer grenades at Stephens' car.

"He went through a red light, ran a couple of cars off the road, and then he rolled down the window and started throwing beer cans at me," Stephens said. "He took three or four drinks out of it and threw the first one at me near the courthouse. We crossed the bridge and he threw another beer out. They were just bouncing off my hood."

The chase took the three cars through Irvine, West Irvine, then through Rice Station to Winston on Highway 52, scattering frightened motorists and pedestrians in its path. "Irvine only has two stop lights, and we ran both of them," Stephens said.

About twelve miles down Highway 52 at its intersection with Highway 977 near Waco, troopers were setting up a roadblock. By this time, Rogers had clearly established that he did not wish to be apprehended. He pushed the little 4-cylinder Festiva to its limits, navigating furiously, continually changing lanes, going the wrong way against oncoming, unsuspecting traffic, seemingly oblivious to the danger.

Flying down the mountainside, state troopers on his tail with lights flashing and sirens yelling, Rogers led his entourage into a roadblock that consisted of three police cruisers and a satellite unit from WCPO-TV in Cincinnati (its crew tipped off about the story), with uniformed troopers standing in the roadway. The troopers, Ed Robinson and sergeants Joey Barnes and Skip Benton, all armed with shotguns, knew they faced a tricky and dangerous situation. Somehow they had to allow traffic through the roadblock while they waited, then quickly plug the gap once they saw the flying wedge emerge from the fourth turn on the hillside. Their plan was scuttled when the last civilian car to pass the roadblock in front of Rogers was going too slow to give them enough time to plug the hole.

He barely slowed for the roadblock. It must have given him the feeling of a jalopy racer in a figure-8 race, finding that hole and making a run for it, knowing it could slam shut in an instant. As Rogers tore through the opening, Robinson leveled his shotgun at the Festiva in hopes of taking out a tire. The Festiva kept going. Stephens was on the thrill ride of his life. Rogers, he said, "attempted to force me out of my lane, into the lane of oncoming cars. I attempted to pass him in the three-lane section of the highway and he attempted to run me out of the roadway. I attempted to pass the car again and he pulled into the wrong lane, causing me and other vehicles to run off the roadway. The vehicle refused to stop, and we kept traveling toward Richmond."

At the roadblock, Sgt. Barnes intended to close the highway with his cruiser as Rogers approached. But the slow civilian car creeping through gave him no time. Fearing Rogers would hit him broadside, he pulled away.

"I jumped in my car and it took me 2.3 miles to catch up with him," Barnes said. "I was making an attempt to get around him to set up what we call a moving roadblock. He was driving all over the road. Essentially he would cut me off each time I would try to get around him."

Like the front row of the Indianapolis 500, they chased down the highway three abreast, Stephens on the gravel shoulder, Barnes in the wrong lane, Rogers in the middle.

Stephens hit him first with a glancing blow. Barnes followed with a broadside shot and pushed him off the road, into a culvert.

"Joey had the oldest car, so we used his," Stephens explained.

"Detective Stephens and I both tried to get around Rogers but he continued to swerve across both east and westbound lanes," Barnes reported. "Detective Stephens managed to draw his attention by getting up along his right side. I then struck his vehicle twice, and as his vehicle spun, I hit him broadside with my front. Both of our vehicles went off onto the south shoulder and came to rest facing westbound."

Barnes estimated they were all exceeding fifty miles per hour when they crash-landed. For his efforts Barnes suffered a minor back sprain and his car was badly damaged; Rogers, safely strapped in his seat belt, was unhurt, and the Festiva was barely scratched.

The capture of Glen Edward Rogers ended a nationwide manhunt for one of the country's most wanted fugitives. He had run free — though he was hardly running because nobody was chasing him — for nearly two years following the mysterious disappearance and still unexplained death of Mark Peters. Citing cost, authorities in Hamilton, Ohio, where Peters was murdered, and in Kentucky, where the body was dumped, decided not to follow Glen's trail to California even to question him. He was a career criminal with a long rap sheet going back to his pre-teen years. But he had been ignored. Hamilton police were happy to forget him, relying on an old police adage: If he isn't in our jurisdiction, he isn't our problem. They had enough of their own troubles without worrying about someone who had moved away.

But Glen Rogers could no longer be ignored.

His flight and six-week killing spree ended on a Kentucky road that day, but not before four unlucky women met violent deaths. And evidence suggests that Glen Rogers' homicidal ways may have started many years earlier.

~

RED RIVER PARISH, LOUISIANA • NOVEMBER 12, 1995

At 2 o'clock on Sunday afternoon a somber group gathered in the country north of Halls Summit at the Social Springs Cemetery, more than fifty in all, to say goodbye to their mother and their sister and their friend Andy. It was a peaceful site, on gently rolling land between a meadow and a woods, so calm and quiet, so unlike the turbulence and the violence of her final days. Her sister Terriea Pullig led the twenty-minute service, and all who cared to were invited to speak. There were friends, her four children, an ex-husband, her brother Willie Jiles. Here on a cloudy Sunday afternoon, Andy Lou Jiles Sutton was laid to rest.

18

Stephens: Well, it looks like possession of a stolen car. That's the first one right there.

Rogers: Receiving stolen property, but you can't prove I stole it.

Stephens: That's right. You're right, receiving stolen property. We're gonna charge you with that.

RICHMOND, KENTUCKY • NOVEMBER 13, 1995

Rogers was taken to Kentucky State Police Post 7 headquarters in Richmond, a college town of 65,000. Meanwhile, inside the building, Detectives Floyd McIntosh and Stephens began what would be a nearly three-hour long interview. It was the first and last time Rogers would speak to police, play the game of cat and mouse without a public defender at his side and a jury across the room. There was a lot to talk about, but McIntosh decided early on to talk about the one case he knew: the skeletal remains found on a family farm owned by the Rogers clan where Glen was known to hole up.

"None of us here in this room have the details enough to get into full details of these murders that are coming in from different areas of the United States," McIntosh began. "I want to talk to you about Mark Peters. I'm not satisfied with what you've told me, that you can't tell me more pertaining to his death."

Rogers' answer was cocksure and chilling, brazen

in its simplicity and because it might be true. Not a minute into the interview, Rogers told McIntosh why his memory was fuzzy on the Peters case: "There's been thirty-five or forty between him and now, I don't know."

Those cases could wait. What about Peters? His death had nagged at the corners of most of their days for two years now. Mark Peters had been missing since October 18, 1993, along with an extensive knife collection, coins, guns and furniture. Rogers wouldn't admit that the remains found on the hillside had belonged to Peters. In fact, he said, it was more likely that the remains found on the Rogers family farm belonged to someone else, an "old gray-headed man," a truck driver who was stabbed two years before in a brutal barroom fight in nearby Fayette County by his brother Clay. Glen entertained the detectives with his description of that encounter, staggering for its raw brutality.

"My brother grabbed the knife and the guy jumped up and kicked," Glen said. "My brother grabbed his leg, started kicking, stuck the knife in him, stabbed him, I guess. At that point, I went out and started up the truck. My brother ain't nobody to play with to begin with."

Rogers then told the story of his adult life, or at least the last two years of it: working in construction repairing earthquake damage in California, how he traveled by Greyhound Bus from town to town, how he settled down with one woman in Los Angeles, Maria Gyore, and how she led him to join "an elite group. . .the Hungarian Mafia." He talked about living in Utah, Las Vegas, trying to visit his kids in Houston and always the wandering.

"What about that car out there," Stephens finally asked.

"A girl loaned it to me in Florida," Rogers replied.

"Some girl I met."

The detectives tweaked it out of Rogers that he told the woman he was going to get a twelve-pack of beer and cigarettes but never came back. He denied killing her, admitted that he drove the car north and changed tags on it because he knew he was wanted by police for her murder. He admitted meeting Andy Sutton in a bar near Shreveport and said she was alive the last time he saw her. He talked about working in carnivals, stealing payrolls. He claimed he drove a truck for 84 Lumber, was arrested for stealing a car in Winchester, Kentucky, and for assault and battery. He remembered names of people he lived with and the places. But when it came time to remember the days immediately before his capture or the names of the woman he had been with, Rogers drew a blank. McIntosh was not fooled.

"We talked about where you were last year and the year before last and whether you're completely correct on it or not you say 'Well, I left here and went there, and lived here and done this and done that' but when we start backing up, you can't tell us where you were a week ago," McIntosh said. There was a bank robbery in the county only days before, and police believe he was linked to it, that he robbed the bank, then slipped south to Lake City, Tennessee. Rogers said he robbed no bank, then told investigators that his partner, Steve Kele, might have done it: "He's already been convicted of bank robbery and served twenty-two years. . .he went on a rampage in the early Seventies." He spun a tale of a man who came to him and his Los Angeles woman who needed to get an apartment but "didn't have no credit or nothing."

But the guy was a member of the elite Hungarian Mafia, "they're just — whatever they call themselves — and he made a living by flying around the country, renting cars and robbing banks."

Stephens shifted back to reality, to Glen's last week

of freedom and to his wallet, which provided a ready road map in receipts tracking how he had spent his time on the run. He told police about pawning six rings, two microphones and a "lucky dollar" in Lake City at the Fast Cash Pawn Shop and could not help but sneer at the line of questioning and the pretense of whatever charge was pending against him: grand theft auto or whatever it was. The night and chase were still a big game to Rogers, his very own virtual reality game. The television cameras outside and the newspaper stories and pictures that chased him from restaurants only added to the allure. And the best these boys could come up with was: What did you pawn down there in Tennessee?

"I wish you had me for better than what you got me for," he told them, believing, still, that the interview, now about an hour old, was centered on a stolen car and nearby bank robbery and nothing more. He described his time and the roundabout way he arrived in Beattyville. And then McIntosh shot a question out of the future, about the years of incarceration and how Rogers would likely spend his last days. The killer and the cop got introspective just before dinner break. McIntosh offered a dose of what was in store: "I mean, I realize you probably don't want to spend the rest of your life in prison or something, but. . ."

"Well, that's probably what's gonna happen," Rogers replied.

And then Rogers took the interview in a personal direction.

"Are you getting overtime?" he asked them. His years as a drug snitch taught him how much police value overtime, whether on crowd duty at football games and parades or perhaps on Tuesday night drug buys.

"We don't get paid overtime," said Stephens. "We're dedicated state employees."

"Well, there's always a prick dedicated somewhere," Rogers replied.

Dinner was ordered: fast food.

"A nice home-cooked meal," Rogers wisecracked as it was served.

"Yeah, sure," Stephens deadpanned, in no mood for humor. Glen capped the meal with a cigarette, bummed from an officer outside. He whined about the brand and wondered if he could give a statement to the television crews outside. No, not just yet. Police wanted to get back to their game of cat-and-mouse.

Rogers explained that if he was facing bank robbery charges, he would have to shave his beard and cut his hair, and that would be that — the jury would never convict, he believed. The interview shifted again to the recently murdered women, beginning in California and onward to Louisiana and Florida.

"If you're wanting me to say I killed somebody, I'm not going to," he said. Stephens answered that he just wanted the truth. Glen had a ready reply:

"I can't tell you the truth."

They argued about Mark Peters. Rogers, the interview now nearly two hours old, said he'd read a report about the old man's death. He had nothing to do with it, he claimed. McIntosh then trotted out what was for him the most troubling of details about the case. The murderer had overlooked a cigarette pack in the victim's shirt pocket. In that pack was a raffle ticket for a grandfather's clock with Peters' home address, phone number and initials on it.

"How can personal papers that belong to Mark Peters be in the remains if that's not Mark Peters' body?" McIntosh asked.

"Don't know, got me. Don't know. Got me there," Rogers replied, laughing. McIntosh asked if there were other bodies on the hill. Rogers replied that yes, he knew of other murders that had taken place there as far back as ten years, people who were murdered from the "East, Ohio and Indiana." And then he blamed the deaths on his brother, Clay, and claimed that Clay at times had the cabin full of money, guns and jewelry and killed people, not with a gun or knife but with his hands.

Stephens tired of the charade.

"I talked to California," Stephens said.

"You did?" Rogers replied.

"Yep. And Glen, I want to tell you something. They got some major shit on you out there. They'd like to take you back to California right tonight and start their trial. They say, 'This isn't an O.J. Simpson. We'll win this one.' "

Stephens then talked about Sandra Gallagher and how witnesses said Glen doused her truck with gasoline and set it afire. "That's bullshit," Glen replied, "all bullshit," denying that he ever spoke about her death to anybody and claiming that if anybody said he did it, they were lying.

"When you say they can't bring that stuff out on the tape, you're wrong," Stephens said. "They're all tied together. Every bit of it. From California to Louisiana to Florida back to Louisiana, back to Kentucky. They're all tied together. It's simple. I could draw you out a chart now. It's simple."

"You only got half the puzzle," Rogers sneered.

So police laid out the rest of the puzzle for him, how serial murderers kill people the same way time after time: fire and water, bodies left in bathtubs, "Do not disturb" signs left on doors. Only Rogers knew why all those murders occurred, Stephens pressed. Police knew the facts, but only Rogers knew the motives, knew whether something snapped inside that set him off in a rage, something that had to do with abuse or sex, something that left him empty and confused when it was over, something that maybe left him with remorse as he looked down at the bloody women in the bathtubs and their defensive wounds.

Whether he realized it or not, Glen's world was caving in around him. Back in California his work was meticulous, the way he burned off Sam Gallagher's fingerprints, set her truck on fire and dumped her body into it. But careful as he was, his efforts did not yield perfect results. Investigators were able to lift a single print from one of Sammie's fingers, and that was enough to identify her. Tonight it looked like it would be enough also to bring Glen to trial for her murder.

Glen wasn't going to tell anybody about it, he finally decided, after the detectives skimmed over details of the murders in California and Florida, after they detailed how death row inmates die by electrocution or the gas chamber. None of it moved Rogers. He remained resolute.

"Electrocute me, kill me, that's better than sitting in prison thirty years wanting to die," Rogers said as the interview closed. He was angry and spitting bile.

"You can sit here all night long. You might as well save yourself some time and let them take me where ever they're gonna take me cause I ain't saying nothing else."

Then he made the demand that closes all interviews with killers: "Get me a lawyer," he finally declared.

"I want a lawyer."

19

McIntosh: Well, a man that's a suspect in a murder every two days, you know, he probably changes cars about like we change socks.

Stephens: He hasn't. He's got the same car. That's unusual. You changed license plates, but you didn't change cars.

Rogers: Well, how many two-door Ford Escorts are there in the United States?

Stephens: I don't know. Not many in Lee County, let me tell you.

Rogers: Um. If you're wanting me to say I killed somebody, I'm not going to.

Stephens: I just want the truth.

Rogers: I can't tell you the truth.

RICHMOND, KENTUCKY NOVEMBER 13, 1995

When reporters tired of camping out in the Post 7 yard, they returned to the hills of Beattyville to pester the Smallwood sisters. Edith, then 72, and Clara, 64, suffered from poor health and were not prepared for the media feeding frenzy in their front yard. It was a slow news week, and they would pay.

"People were pounding on the doors, pounding on the windows while I was there," reported local newspaper editor Bob Smith, the only journalist the sisters would allow inside. "News vehicles were everywhere.

The ladies would go to the door and say they weren't interested in talking to them. Reporters would shove microphones up their noses and they just wouldn't leave them alone." It could have come right from Ma and Pa Kettle — an old mountain house with a worn-out mobile home in front of it perched on the edge of the knoll overlooking Highway 52, not much room for parking on the narrow, dirt Old Landing Road that turned sharply from the highway. Never had so many people collected in one spot in this remote area. Perhaps 300 feet across the highway and up the other side of the foothill stood the dilapidated cabin where Glen Rogers allegedly dumped Mark Peters' body in late 1993. None of the media cared. They wanted the Smallwood sisters.

"We know very little about Glen," one of the sisters said. "We were just doing our duty and don't deserve this kind of harassment. You have to wonder if you would do it again knowing that these people won't leave you alone."

The Smallwood sisters never understood what all the commotion was about, why all those reporters were making them miserable. Eventually they fled their own home until the storm died down. It never occurred to them that, after two years on the run, Glen Rogers finally was stopped, not by stellar police work or high-tech forensics, but by the stubbornness of two old ladies who drew a line on the front porch of their mountain home and warned him not to cross it.

In an interview broadcast two days before his capture, Glen's sister, Sue Rogers, said on the tabloid television program *A Current Affair* that Glen vowed he would kill himself rather than surrender. In a telephone call a week earlier, he had told his sister, who is fourteen years older, that he was headed for Mexico. She immediately called police and filled them in:

"Right after Mark (Peters) disappeared, Glen would call me every day." she told police. "He would either call me at home or, when he told me about how Mark died, I was at Mom's and he talked to me there. Glen told me right after Mark disappeared that he and Mark were at the house, Mark's house. He said he had shoved Mark and that he thought he was dead when he fell. Glen said he did not know if Mark hit his head, or if he had a heart attack.

"Glen had been staying with Mark for a while before Mark died. He said he did not mean to kill Mark. He also said he had taken some coins and some other stuff out of Mark's house, but he did not say what he did with the stuff. Glen knows where to take stuff to get rid of it.

"Glen told me that after Mark died he put him in the car. At one time he said he put him in the trunk and took him to a farm that my daddy used to own, but now all the kids own it. He said he wrapped the body up and took it up on a hill to an old cabin or shed that Daddy built. It was an old run-down shack. He said he put the body in it. Glen said that after he got rid of the body he went to California. I do not know where he got rid of the car, but one time when we were talking about it, Glen said that nobody would ever find the car. He said it was an inch high and in a junkyard.

"When Glen got to California, he called my other brother, Craig, and asked him to pick him up. Craig and Glen do not get along and Craig refused to pick him up.

"I think Glen kept Mark in the house — dead — for maybe a couple of weeks before he took his body to Beattyville. About that time, Mark was supposed to give my mom $100. She was going to visit my brother in North Carolina, and he wanted to give her the money to buy souvenirs. . .Mom never picked up the money.

After that, which is right before we knew that Mark was missing, every time somebody would call Mark's house for him, or stop by or anything, Glen would tell them he was sleeping or doing something and could not be bothered."

Sue Rogers said her brother called their mother frequently. One letter came with a picture of Glen with his new teeth, and it showed how he had changed his hair. It was short on top, long in the back, and bleached blond.

"He told Mom he had burnt off his fingerprints so that nobody could identify him."

She said her brother then made a chilling boast: Police had "only scraped the surface." They would soon find a "whole lot more dead people." He ended the conversation by telling her, Sue, that he was coming for her next. He said he had two dead women under his arms as he was speaking and that he was coming for her. Terrified, Sue immediately called Middletown Police to say her brother was headed home for the last time.

After the interview, troopers took Rogers to the Madison County Detention Center. It would be his home for the foreseeable future.

The jail sits in the town square behind the courthouse on Irvine Street. Built of red brick in 1990 to house 130 inmates, it doesn't look much like a jail from the outside, but more like a government administration building or perhaps a telephone office. Its design is clean, but it clashes architecturally with the stately yet modest white courthouse and the century-old buildings that border the square.

Richmond has a Southern flavor that extends even to the jailhouse, at least to the lobby, where Beulah Phelps, the administrative assistant to jailer Ron Devere, greets visitors behind a window and tends to matters of administrative importance. In her fifties, with just a hint of Tootsie in her eyeglasses and hair and Kentucky warmth in her voice, she talked to inmates in motherly tones.

"Did you get enough to eat?" Phelps inquired of one short-timer who came to pick up the funds remaining in his commissary account.

"Oh yeah," the boy replied.

"Do you miss us?" Captain Dunn, the jail matron, a portly black woman in her thirties, wondered playfully. There was no answer. The young boy, clean cut with short hair, was sheepish, polite and of few words. Beulah knew why.

"You didn't want to be honest and hurt nobody's feelings," she explained.

The youth had fifty dollars left. His mother had given it to him. One floor below in the cell blocks, deputy jailer Mike Clark supervised maintenance. Though it's a maximum-security jail, trusties move about in limited freedom to keep the green block walls and sandstone linoleum floors sparkling.

While college students reveled not one block away in the pool halls and pubs that occupy buildings built long ago for haberdashers and merchants and undertakers who often as not lived above their businesses, Glen Rogers had only a limited view of his world, only of guards and trusties walking past, seen through the envelope-size window of his dungeon.

Back at post headquarters, a fax machine was buzzing. One burnt out and a new one had to be purchased. Detectives from other states, Ohio mostly, had begun to arrive and wanted answers: How many people had this man killed? Detectives are always trying to solve cases the easy way — riding the wake of a serial killer. But this time, ties were disturbingly close, and soon a portrait began to emerge. In addition to the most recent string of murders, another trail of bodies might also lead to Rogers' cell:

Carrie Gaskins: The thirty-year-old resident of Bethel, a village in the far-flung eastern suburbs of Cincinnati, was found stabbed to death in her home in 1992. Clermont County investigators Lieutenant Dennis Shannon and Sergeant Barry Jacobson traveled to Kentucky to try to talk to Glen about this red-headed woman who was found slashed to death in her home. Their trip was futile; Glen's lawyer kept them at bay and the case remains unsolved.

Carolyn Branham: She disappeared from Winchester, Kentucky, on December 15, 1994, after calling her father from the Playhouse Pool Room, a local hangout, to say she wouldn't be home that night and that she had a job at South Western Dryer, a tobacco warehouse, in Lexington. The woman who had a rose tattoo on her hip, a "$" sign tattooed behind her ear and "Biker" tattooed on the back of her neck was never heard from again. A year before, she had lived in the Maple Street Apartments in unit No. 5 and made frequent trips to California and Florida.

According to the Clark County Jail, where Glen was incarcerated on September 7, 1993, he, too, lived at the Maple Street Apartments, just down from this biker gal, in unit 12. The tie was enough to later bring Detective McIntosh to Winchester on November 20, 1995, to interview Clarence Branham, Carolyn's father. It was only days after Rogers' capture. McIntosh was chasing every lead. The investigation soon played out. There was only a missing woman. She once lived in an apartment complex. Rogers had lived there at the exact same time. She was thirty-eight. She was picked up in a tough bar. She had reddish blond hair. She was gone, probably dead.

Kelly Lynn Camargo: This 16-year-old Hamilton girl was last seen August 23, 1993, getting into a car in the parking lot of PJ Shooter's, a biker bar on the southern city limits of Hamilton. Two weeks later, hikers walking through a wooded area near the small town of Camden, ten miles north of Hamilton straight up on Ohio 127, found the girl's partially decomposed body. She had been stabbed repeatedly and left in a desolate wooded area far from any city, near a farmer's pond. Glen Rogers became a suspect the day he was captured.

Emerson Skinner: A Hamilton loner who lived on Glen's old street only a few doors down from Glen's old apartment, he was brutally and repeatedly stabbed to death on Oct. 17, 1994. He was a customer of Ohio Taxi and while police suspected his murder was linked to sex, they had no evidence of who did the killing. It was a clean crime scene — only a bloody footprint was left behind as a grim calling card. Skinner had been stabbed twenty-five times. The number of similarly brutal murders in Hamilton through the years could be counted on one hand.

And finally, Thomas Allen Wolsefer. His death certificate listed a blood condition, too many red blood cells, and lingering trauma from a stroke as cause of death on January 7, 1991. Glen confided in a barmaid that he killed Wolsefer by putting whiskey into his IV bag as he lay in a nursing home, but police had only hearsay evidence and no will to investigate.

FBI records show that even though he was wanted for questioning in connection with the Peters case at the time, Rogers had brazenly returned to town in late September 1994 to get a copy of his birth certificate, found in his possession when he was captured near Beattyville. Shortly after Skinner's death, Rogers was also stopped by a Kentucky police officer near Beattyville as a suspicious character. Rogers' bookend sightings before and after Skinner's murder, and the fact that Skinner was slaughtered on the anniversary of the disappearance of Peters, made Rogers a suspect.

As the investigations piled up, so, too did the reporters and photographers, creating a surreal scene around police headquarters. Scores of reporters and photographers — and all their equipment, the TV trucks with their satellite towers — jammed their way onto the yard of State Police Post 7 and its four visitor parking spaces with no roadside parking. They camped out on the lawn while troopers dealt with Rogers inside. The post is prominent, a single-story colonial brick building perched near the entrance to Eastern Kentucky University out on the main highway, two miles south of downtown. Rogers was curious about the reporters. He loved the limelight.

"Is the news still out there or are they gone?" Rogers once asked Detective McIntosh.

"Oh yeah they're out there."

"What they wanna know? Can I give a statement?"

"They want to know if you want to talk to them."

"So they're still out there?"

"They ain't gonna leave," Detective Stephens said. "Oh, gosh, yeah. They ain't gonna leave."

As the press corps clamored for a statement from police or a piece of Rogers himself, the commotion attracted curious local residents and students. It was a boisterous but controlled bunch and a bonanza for local fast food shops. "You went downtown and there was no place to park because of all the satellite trucks," said Commonwealth's Attorney Tom Smith. "I called it 'Camp No-J' because the only thing missing was O.J. himself."

Rogers was big news throughout Kentucky, the Cincinnati area and other cities up and down the I-75 corridor from Ohio to Florida. The afternoon *Richmond Register* had already gone to press when Rogers was captured around 3 p.m. on Monday, November 13. But this was a big story in the city of 62,000 — the biggest crime story in years — and the *Register* was not to be denied. On Tuesday it gave the story almost its entire front page. The main headline was succinct but the secondary banner was the most telling:

Accused serial killer
captured in county

Rogers wanted for
killings of redheads

Police and prosecutors in six states were jubilant that a serial killing suspect had been corralled. But if they thought it would be smooth sailing to the electric chair for this guy, they were mistaken.

They had a killer, but did they have a case? The real fight was just beginning.

20

RICHMOND, KENTUCKY • NOVEMBER 1995

Glen told his last employer he had earned $53,000 a year as a self-employed painter. On November 13, 1995, he signed an Order and Affidavit of Indigency, stating he was not employed, had no income or receivables and owned no real estate or tangible assets. "Plead Fifth Amendment when asked if he had any cash put back," pre-trial officer Joe King wrote on the order. Glen Rogers was taken to Madison Circuit Court, and charged with:

- Two counts of first-degree wanton endangerment, "by unlawfully driving an automobile at an extremely high rate of speed during an attempt to elude police officers," among other things.
- Being a fugitive from another state.
- Receiving stolen property.

Under search warrant and guarded at all times, the 1993 white Ford Festiva was hauled to the Central Forensic Laboratory in Frankfort, where technicians took latent prints and photographed the vehicle and some of its contents. They collected loose hair, fibers and blood from the driver's side door, the seats, the floor mat.

Meanwhile, Detective Skip Benton began sifting through a treasure trove of trash from the car and compiled an exhaustive list: every beer can with its batch number, "pair extremely dirty white socks,"

Swank magazine, fourteen coat hangers, a pair of bloodied tennis shoes, cigarette butts and their brand names, lottery tickets, business cards, scraps of paper with phone numbers, a stolen Social Security card, hundreds of items. There was a Jimmy Buffett tape, "Songs You Know By Heart" and "Hank Williams' Greatest Hits," 25-cent tokens from Ameristar Casino in Vicksburg, Mississippi, a Brandon-East Tampa telephone directory, an unopened letter to Tina Cribbs, all kinds of food, coins, writing material, and on and on and on. Benton was careful to note the inventory of Exhibit 67 as one knotted "Petro Shopping Center" trash bag containing: four empty "Budweiser" beer cans, all #2665H66 45; one napkin, "Thirstbuster" logo; one plastic wrapper, "Oscar Meyer" brand; one "Hot Pockets" wrapper, #EST7721 5151E2 10; and several white napkins. The inventory filled eleven typewritten pages.

Technicians photocopied every piece of currency and every scrap of paper from Rogers' wallet. They found check-cashing cards, one for Glen Rogers, one for James Peters, both with Glen's photo. They found earnings statements where Rogers had used an alias and phony Social Security number. Among the soiled clothes and potato chip crumbs and cigarette butts and other debris were disguise props Rogers had picked up along the way: auto license tags from Mississippi and Tennessee. The Tennessee tag was on the car; the legitimate Florida tag was in the hatchback.

The next day, November 14, technicians came after Glen with needles, combs and scissors. They collected head, facial and pubic hair and the clothes he wore when captured. They took oral swabs and five tubes of blood. They took an inventory of his body, noting the tattoo on his upper arm of a lady holding a glass and "DEBi" tattooed on his right hand, one letter to a finger.

All of this was important, but none more so than a key to room 119 of the Tampa 8 Motel tucked into a pair of Rogers' underwear. And they also found a pair of bloodied jeans shorts with DNA matching both Glen Rogers and Tina Marie Cribbs.

Within days, state crime lab authorities realized they could use help and called on the FBI. It wasn't that they couldn't do the job — prosecutors in Florida would praise their work — but Glen Rogers had become a national subject. The FBI could coordinate evidence gathering and act as an information clearing house for the many police jurisdictions who were pursuing him as a possible suspect in their unsolved murders.

There was plenty of evidence to study: one unopened pack of GPC cigarettes bought in Kentucky, a size medium T-shirt with Florida State University logo, a "Little Mermaid" brand comforter, a navy duffel bag, bow tie, some newspaper and direct-mail advertisements, a pair of size $9^{1/2}$ Dunlop shoes, a pair of Wrangler blue jeans shorts, blood from the driver's side door of the Ford Festiva, a pair of Fruit of the Loom sweat pants, a black-striped shirt, one pair of footie socks and a black tank top, vacuum sweepings from the car and samples of Glen's handwriting.

At first, police thought Glen was a stranger to their area, until they began poking into his past. Actually Glen had left quite a mark on East-Central Kentucky. He was especially well known in Clark County, between Richmond and Lexington. His earliest recorded local arrest was July 25, 1987, when he was charged in Madison County with drunk driving. In Clark County, he did ten days for contempt of court in 1993, twenty days for marijuana possession, and thirty days plus a fine for second-degree strong-arm assault. Other charges — nonpayment of fines and public intoxication — were pending. A 1993 charge of receiving a stolen vehicle had been dismissed.

Not long after Glen settled into the jail for his winter-long stay, Ernie Lewis came into the picture.

The first thing that Glen Rogers liked about Ernie was that Ernie opposed the death penalty under all circumstances, regardless of what heinous acts his client may have performed. That could be helpful, because Glen faced possible death penalties in four states.

Erwin W. Lewis, the assistant public advocate, flew into action immediately, launching of blizzard of motions and stalling actions in Madison Circuit Court. First he moved for discovery, to obtain police reports, policy statements on the use of force and the conduct of high-speed chases, WCPO-TV's video tape of the capture and arrest, a transcript of the defendant's oral statements ("Just me and you at the jail," Glen shouted repeatedly at a Cincinnati television reporter, who asked Rogers if he had killed those women, and the reporter never did learn if that was a challenge to fight or an invitation for an interview), and anything else of use to the defense.

Madison Circuit Judge William Clouse denied bail and set trial for February 6, 1996. Lewis got the case continued and then set out to show that his client was incompetent to stand trial. In January he filed a lengthy motion on Rogers' mental state that would become the foundation of Glen's defense. Lewis put forth these facts:

In November 1987, Rogers was beaten in the head with clubs and taken to the emergency room. (Later it was alleged that Rogers said he took Dilantin, for which he had no known condition, and doctors prescribed more without further investigation.)

On April 27, 1991, he was hit in the head with a pool cue, suffering a fracture of his eye socket and skull and intracranial bleeding.

On July 23, 1991, he was hit in the head with a tire iron that bruised his skull near his left eye. In 1993 he suffered head injury in a car wreck, and he has been involved in other auto accidents over the years.

He suffers a history of blackouts.

As a child, Glen put himself to sleep nightly by banging his head on the wall.

His father was an alcoholic. Glen began drinking at age 12.

While in prison in Ohio in 1988, he was diagnosed with porphyria, an inherited enzyme disorder that often results in seizures, psychosis, organic brain syndrome and hallucinations. His heavy drinking further aggravated this condition.

Lewis asked for medical and psychiatric exams. He said additionally that:

Glen Roger's history is full of bizarre and volatile behavior, usually associated with being severely drunk. In 1981 Rogers was charged with aggravated menacing after holding police at bay for four hours. In 1986 he tore up his furniture, threw it into the back yard and burned it, resulting in a charge of "inducing panic." In 1991 he used a blowtorch on a police officer attempting to enter Rogers' house. In 1994 he was charged with burning his girlfriend's apartment.

As a child, one of Glen's brothers injected him with "speed" (the street name for methamphetamine). He also ate paint and wet the bed until age 12.

In records from the Butler County jail from April 15, 1991, Rogers was noted to have had blackouts, including one for four days. Jail records of June 21, 1991, noted Rogers to be "somewhat paranoid."

The same record reported Rogers to be "quite nervous and shaky" and said "he feels he gets out of control and things happen to him."

On September 8, 1991, a physician attempted to have Rogers involuntarily committed after he took twenty-five Motrin and injected alcohol into his veins.

Two weeks later, Kentucky Governor Paul Patton announced a deal. Glen Rogers would be extradited to Florida. Under an agreement with Florida Governor Lawton Chiles, if Florida failed to get a death sentence, Glen would be dispatched to California. If Kentucky charged Glen with the murder of Mark Peters prior to extradition, he would stay in Kentucky. The gist of the agreement was that Glen would be passed around in order and everyone who wanted a crack at him would get it, sooner or later.

Just about everybody agreed with this arrangement — everybody but Erwin W. Lewis. Ernie Lewis faced a rocky road ahead, and he knew it. Hired by the taxpayers to defend Glen Rogers, he set out on a personal mission to keep his client in Kentucky and out of the electric chair.

His strategy was simple: deny and delay.

"We've been given no evidence that he killed anyone," Lewis said of his new client. Over the next five months Lewis tempered his denials with legal maneuvers. "Florida is a very efficient killing machine," he said. He believed extradition to Florida would be tantamount to a death sentence. He employed the usual tactics, buying time while he crafted a longer-term strategy: motions for continuance, motions for discovery to force the prosecution to reveal its evidence, motions for psychiatric and medical evaluations.

If Lewis had any illusions about the moral fiber of his client he did not reveal them. His best hope was to persuade the court that Rogers was either not fit to stand trial or was not responsible for his behavior. This he based on Glen's extensive medical history that was replete with pathology. Lewis was most interested in the brain injuries — head trauma caused by the pool cue and the tire iron.

"One of the things that is interesting about Glen is that several pathologies converged," Lewis explained. There was the rotten childhood, the violent combination of alcoholism and porphyria disease, the blackouts, and of course, the head injuries.

Indicted for the first-degree felonies of wanton endangerment of a police officer and criminal mischief, Rogers was arraigned via closed-circuit television hookup from the jail on November 21, 1995. Kentucky Circuit Judge William T. Jennings set trial for February 5, 1996. On January 23, Lewis filed a motion for continuance, and at the same time sought funds to hire expert witnesses.

Florida invited Glen Rogers to Tampa, but Glen declined. He preferred to stay in the relative comfort of the Madison Detention Center, in a state with no murder charge against him. In Kentucky he faced only three, what he considered minor, felonies: two counts of wanton endangerment and one count of criminal mischief resulting from the chase. He could handle that. One to five years in the Kentucky State Prison for each count of wanton endangerment, and he would be free to roam again. He felt immune from Kentucky charges for the murder of Mark Peters, for it was unlikely that anyone could prove where Peters was killed, or even that he was dead and not just missing. Without a place of death or a positively identified body, there could be no probable cause, Glen figured.

Certainly Glen's future outside of Kentucky held no happy thoughts for him. Mississippi and Louisiana each had a first-degree murder charge, Mississippi with the aggravating circumstance of simultaneous robbery that could warrant the death penalty. Florida had two aggravating circumstances, robbery and auto theft, and was eager to give him a seat in "Old Sparky," its unpredictable, occasionally flammable electric chair built by prison inmates in 1923. Old Sparky earned its reputation: After flames shot from the head of Pedro Medina in a 1997 execution, Attorney General Bob Butterworth had some advice for would-be killers: Florida's electric chair doesn't work very well. Maybe it's best you commit your murders somewhere else.

California had a good case because, unlike all the others, it had an eyewitness to the murder. Lea Purwin-D'Agostino was disappointed that California would not get him first, but she and her troops would wait, if not patiently, for the eventual extradition.

California did not have the "special circumstance" necessary for a death penalty case. Under a point of law not well understood by laymen, the murder of Sandra Gallagher was not a capital case in California because she was already dead when Glen Rogers set her truck on fire and threw her body into it. Therefore, the arson was unrelated to the murder. With no other felonies connected to the murder, the best California could get was life in prison. On the other hand, conviction of murder in another state would constitute a "special circumstance" and thus grounds for a death sentence. Florida or California: Neither was an inviting prospect for Glen Rogers.

21

LOUISVILLE • JANUARY 1996

The warring parties went to their corners to map strategy. Ernie Lewis worked furiously from his Richmond office. Meanwhile, lawmen decided it was time to convene a high-level conference, to sort out what they had, where they were going, and who would get the first shot at trying Glen Rogers. Politics and egos clashed. Rogers was hot property. Nobody understood the perils — and the opportunities — better than Gil Garcetti, the district attorney for Los Angeles County. He would watch this one closely.

Under the watchful eye of a uniformed guard, the police van rolled through the security gate and stopped at Lea Purwin-D'Agostino's front door. Spiffied up in sport coats and ties, the van's three occupants — Angel Lopez, Mike Coblentz and Steve Fisk — were most official-looking, though neighbors up and about at this early hour would not recognize them as detectives from the Los Angeles Police Department. The nosy ones might have wondered if Lea was getting hauled off to the hoosegow. She was new to the neighborhood. They didn't know her.

They loaded her luggage and then headed off, their immediate destination the L.A. International Airport and then three hours east, into snow-packed and biting cold Louisville.

A similar scene was playing out in Tampa, where Karen Cox and Randy Bell were preparing to board a plane. Others were getting ready to drive from Jackson, Mississippi. Another group departed from Bossier City, Louisiana.

Lea Purwin-D'Agostino had trained for this moment — it was her kind of battle, her kind of arena. In an earlier life, after emigrating from her native Israel, she operated a disco and managed a theatrical agency. To get her law degree at the University of West L.A. in Culver City, she fought her way through four years of night school, making the dean's list while working in public relations and marketing, as a social club hostess and at anything else that came along. She liked to come at defendants with both barrels, even when one would suffice. The object is to win, she explained, so why not uncork the whole arsenal? She could be feisty, argumentive and annoying. She swaggered around courtrooms like she owned them. Always bedecked in tasteful jewelry, her raven black hair tied back in a bun, she stood only a shade above five feet but her presence in a room was never unnoticed. Doors opened for her.

She acquired the "Dragon Lady" handle from one of her more celebrated victims, Muharem Kurbegovic, the Alphabet Bomber, who blew up three people and injured thirty-six with a bomb he planted at LAX in 1974. It was one of her big, high-profile early wins, coming just three years out of law school. Muharem and Lea, it was agreed, didn't much care for each other.

Lea liked to mix it up both in and outside the courtroom, and she was not always discreet about her choice of targets. In a public act that lacked even a scintilla of subtlety, she encouraged the city attorney to run against her boss, District Attorney Gil Garcetti. Garcetti needed a way to retrieve his political image from the toilet, get his smiling, victorious face back on television and Page One of the *Los Angeles Times*. He was desperate for a high-profile, big-league win to help fog over the still too-recent O.J. Simpson and Menendez brothers public relations disasters. What he did not need was a lippy underling leading the charge up San Juan Hill on the sure-win Rogers case. D'Agostino not only had thrown gasoline on the election fire, she was known to have political ambitions of her own and was frequently mentioned as Garcetti's next election opponent. He picked her to lead the prosecution team on this one anyway.

She was accustomed to the bright lights, the roar of the grease paint, the smell of the crowd. She had put away some doozies in her nineteen years on the job, and was respected, though not always adored, by those she met in the trenches. Her first major loss under the national glare was the "Twilight Zone" trial, in which she failed to win convictions of five people charged in the movie-set deaths of actor Vic Morrow and two Vietnamese children. It was a bruiser, but the two defense attorneys she battled supported her selection as leader of the Rogers prosecution team.

"The D.A.'s office is usually fearful of assigning high-profile cases to anyone with political ambitions," criminal defense attorney Harland Braud, a frequent Dragon Lady opponent, told the *Los Angeles Times*. "They usually assign such a case to a non-entity. And Lea is not a non-entity."

D'Agostino came to Louisville from another world, a land of glitz and glamour where some of the nation's goofiest murder defendants could attract the attention of Hollywood and become instant, albeit notorious celebrities. But this was Kentucky, a slow-paced world of leisurely deliberation, far from the bright lights of Hollywood. It would be interesting to see how she meshed with the Howdy, ma'am Southern prosecutors and hayseeds from the Kentucky State Police. Elegant sophistication and down-home practicality. The Dragon Lady and Detective Stephens. Rodeo Drive meets Yard Sale Alley.

They gathered, finally, in a Louisville hotel meeting room to map the campaign against Glen Edward Rogers. Their hosts were FBI agents from the Child Abduction/Serial Killer Unit at Quantico, Virginia, the Evidence Response Team, the Violent Criminal Apprehension Program and the Rapid Start Unit. The FBI was making something abundantly clear: It was not fooling around.

There was no doubt about where California stood on this case, either. First to file extradition papers, armed with DNA analysis, exhaustive, police work, its trial preparation nearly complete, its strategy in place, California came to Louisville and expected to leave with orders to take Glen Rogers out West and do a number on him.

At least that's what Lea Purwin-D'Agostino hoped for. Garcetti was uneasy about her perch atop the highly public case. So long as California made noise about wanting Rogers but did not actually get him, Garcetti could let the charade unfold without risking a confrontation. Garcetti figured all along that Glen would first go to Florida where the gears of justice could grind up a year or better. California's theatrics would play well to the L.A. television audience (and voters), and that's all that really mattered. He could deal with this renegade later.

For two days, January 10 and 11, they thrashed it out. First they needed to dispense with the media detachment hunkered down outside the meeting room. They chose a spokesman, invited everyone in for pictures and a statement, then ran the press off and began working in private. Prosecutors and detectives from each jurisdiction spoke in turn. They looked at Glen's background, the facts of each case, the evidence, the climate for a death penalty case in each state. They debated amongst themselves: Who has the best chance of sending Glen Rogers to the death house? Kentucky's attorney general, Ben Chandler, took part in the discussions, and he would make the recommendation to Gov. Patton on where and whether to extradite. Glen was his prisoner. He would have to be persuaded.

They had five murders from which to choose. There was Mark Peters, the first known one, but Kentucky was adamant that there was insufficient evidence to charge anyone. That left the four women: Sandra Gallagher in Van Nuys, Linda Price in Jackson, Tina Cribbs in Tampa and Andy Sutton in Bossier City. They had to pick one but they knew there was lots of synergy among them: all were killed up-close and personal, three by stabbing, one by strangulation. Two were dumped into bathtubs, one left on a punctured waterbed. The killer had tried to clean up two of the scenes and left feces in two of the toilets. The killings underscored Glen's rage, his hatred of women. Hatred of his mother, too, probably.

Eventually everyone came to understand that the only practical choices were California and Florida. Louisiana, though well prepared with carefully drafted supporting documents, didn't have a certain death penalty case; Mississippi's was good but not airtight, and it was in no hurry to spend money needlessly.

Following opening remarks by the FBI agents, D'Agostino presented California's case. First she had to dispel the popular notion, fueled by the televised O.J. Simpson circus, that California takes forever to put on a murder trial.

She reminded them that California law calls for sixty days from arraignment to trial. Assuming one or two defense delays, D'Agostino predicted Rogers could be brought to trial in four months. Six weeks of trial and he's off to Florida, where prosecutors could talk all they wanted about his status as a convicted killer. Getting a death sentence in Florida would be no more difficult than shooting a fat, slow pig in a pen.

"It's important we work as a team to ensure that the individual who committed these crimes receives the ultimate sentence possible," she reminded her cohorts. Although California did not have the "special circumstances" necessary for a death penalty case, she made the case for California anyway.

"A first-degree conviction in any other jurisdiction would help Florida," she said, "and I believe we can provide that underpinning. We are ready to proceed."

LAPD investigators had taken the Rogers case seriously from the beginning, even before he was tagged with the serial killer label. For the meeting they produced a report that contained every fact known to them: names, motive, the homicide follow-up report, witnesses, evidence. It was a sophisticated, professional job that showed serious intent. D'Agostino said this was common practice, and she sought to erase the ugly caricature developed during the O.J. Simpson and Rodney King ordeals of a bumbling, violent and racist police force.

D'Agostino realized she was walking a fine line. She wanted Rogers, wanted him badly, knew deep down that she could get a conviction. At the same time, she had to acknowledge that the objective was results, not personal political gain. As such the talks were congenial, friendly. They may have pitched a particular viewpoint but all were on the same page.

But they faced a dilemma and they knew it. California or Florida, both routes contained risks, land mines that could derail the best of cases.

Anything could happen in California. Twelve jurors, each with his own goofy view of how the law should work, could look at Glen's pathetic childhood, buy the defense line on brain damage, figure if O.J. Simpson can get off why shouldn't a white man, ignore the evidence and acquit. Or they could convict on second-degree murder, hardly a mandate for Florida to follow.

Karen Cox, who initially thought she wouldn't be ready for trial, had changed her mind by the time she got to Louisville. At first she thought a conviction in California would ease the way for a death sentence in Florida. Normally you can talk about prior felony convictions. If Florida went first, there was a chance the jury would not hear about any of the charges in other states. They might see Rogers as some poor, unfortunate, brain-damaged drifter who lost his temper in the heat of passion. They might return a verdict of less than first-degree murder. They might find him insane. Or an appeals court might even find him unfit to stand trial. Anything could and was likely to go wrong.

Now Cox was ready. She had the victim's and the suspect's DNA all over his jeans. She had his fingerprints on the "Do Not Disturb" sign. She had his signature on the motel registration card. He had Tina Marie Cribb's car. Her body was found in his motel room. Let's see him talk his way out of this one.

The risks were real. If Florida got him and failed to deliver the ultimate sentence, ominous clouds would gather around the case and taint the efforts elsewhere. Everybody understood that. Glen Rogers could be sent to the death chamber, or he could get an easy ride to the nut house, frustrating the pursuit of justice elsewhere. Worse, he might get just five years for auto theft and walk free again. The decision was critically important. It was also not theirs to make.

It was up to the attorney general and the governor of Kentucky.

The Kentucky State Police went on record: Send him to California. They have the best case and they are ready to go.

LAPD wanted him. Lea Purwin-D'Agostino wanted him. So did Karen Cox. Two days of meetings, and it was time to go home, and wait.

They had plenty of time to think, all of them, on the way home. Cox did her job, gave it her best. It was up to someone else now to decide on the next move. She didn't take it personally that the Kentucky State Police, who captured Rogers, recommended that he first go to California. She presented her case and would be ready to try it whenever Glen became available.

Winging over the Western Plains, Lea Purwin-D'Agostino contemplated the task before her. She was confident she would get the leadoff spot and was excited about her role in this saga. She was a pro, this is what she did, put away society's dregs. Once again, she had been called upon to do a job. And yet she knew ominous potholes lay ahead. It is so easy for killers to duck the death chamber, this she knew well from her two decades on the front lines. Innocent little mistakes — hers, witnesses', the judge's — could queer the whole deal, make her look like an oaf and turn loose a killer. What about the DNA, the fingerprints? There was no murder weapon, and the only eyewitness was unreliable and, coincidentally, in jail. Anything could happen. Anything.

22

RICHMOND, KENTUCKY • WINTER 1995-96

During his confinement Rogers cooperated with his jailers and treated them respectfully. It was his Southern ways. He got in trouble once in December for making hootch out of rotting fruit he and other inmates hoarded. The penalty was loss of commissary and telephone rights. Rogers was remorseful: He wanted to call his mother on Christmas. On appeal, Jailer Ron Devere relented.

"I was filled with the Christmas spirit," Devere explained.

It wasn't Devere's only soft spot. Though inmates are not allowed to have outside food or chewing tobacco, Devere let them smoke.

"The jailer tried to quit and couldn't," Beulah Phelps, Devere's administrative assistant, explained, "so he said he wasn't going to take that away from them."

Glen said, "Please," and called his jailers "Sir," and didn't ask for special favors. He understood that the way to make jail life easiest was to follow a simple credo: Play along, get along. "Dangerousness is situational," explained FBI serial crimes profiler John Douglas in *Mindhunter.* "Model prisoners often kill again when released."

"He never made any requests," Beulah Phelps said. "We have a lot who are kind of spoiled — they ask for things that are out of line — but he never did."

As expected, the relationship between Rogers and Tom Smith, the commonwealth's attorney in Richmond since 1981, did not get off to a chummy start. On the night of Glen's arrest, Smith drove to Post 7 headquarters along winding roads lit by the moon to immediately prepare the complaints and arrest warrants for wanton endangerment. Troopers pointed him out to Rogers as "the one who will be prosecuting you in this jurisdiction." It was an introduction, though it lacked the formality of a handshake and country charm of a how-do-you-do.

"I wasn't his favorite person," Smith said. "My first encounter with Mr. Rogers, my debut in Mr. Rogers' Neighborhood, was at the State Police post. He tried to stare me down and kind of swelled up a little. I asked him things like 'What are you doing here? Where have you been?' It was not a social call. Then in court I'd see him in the hallway, or on occasion he would try to stare me down — look ugly at me. I was the man basically trying to get him on his first step toward the electric chair."

It wasn't long after his capture that Rogers decided he needed some attention. He placed a collect call to *Richmond Register* reporter Todd Blevins. Blevins had given his business card to a female admirer of Rogers who visited him in jail. Blevins asked him, "Did you kill those women?"

"No, I've never killed anyone," Rogers answered.

Meanwhile, police and the commonwealth's attorney's office were mired in logistical problems. Requests about Rogers were coming from everywhere, among them agencies in Augusta, Maine; Michigan; Canada; Versailles, Kentucky; and departments in Virginia and Florida. Police agencies were looking for shreds of information that might tie Rogers to their unsolved murders. They wanted samples of hair, blood, fiber,

DNA and clothes. Callers burned out the jailer's fax machine.

"If everyone who requested a blood sample had gotten one," Tom Smith observed, "he wouldn't have any blood left."

Though the Ford Festiva had been removed to the state crime lab in Frankfort, Post 7 and Smith's office were getting the requests. The prosecutor's office staff of one, who handles perhaps twenty-five telephone calls on a busy day, was buried by up to 100 in the days following the arrest.

"From a logistics standpoint," Smith explained, "you've got evidence from at least four homicides that needs to be processed. You've got to process his clothes, you've got to get hair samples from him, you've got to get blood samples from him. We've got our own cases to handle. We can't be handling four out-of-state cases plus investigating untold however many requests that were coming in. So we really ended up in a logistics crunch. How are we going to process this evidence? At this point the FBI volunteered to take the evidence, process it, hold it, and appear at the various trials."

At the Madison County Detention Center, Glen's life was routine and predictable. Activities unfolded at the same hour of each day: wakeup, breakfast, lunch, dinner, lights out.

Prisoners were allowed one twenty-minute visit per week. These were not cozy gatherings with picnic lunches and the chance to touch and hug. Always under watch, visitor and inmate sit in booths separated by glass and converse by telephone.

Though the Rogers family was not close-knit, visits quickly became a family affair. Three days after his capture, on November 16, Glen received his first visitors. There were seven of them including his mother Edna, sister Sue Rogers, brother Gary Wayne Rogers, and Aunt Lillian Rucker.

The only family member missing from this sad parade from Ohio was Clay Rogers, and he was missing for a reason. His brother hated him. Clay was the one who dropped the dime on Glen, who told authorities that Glen was most likely the killer of Mark Peters and then led them to Peters' remains. Hamilton relatives returned often. Each time, television crews were waiting.

"The family, they were very nice," Beulah Phelps said. "They seemed a little embarrassed when they first came in. They were not real talkative out here. After a while, they would all smile and we would wave at each other."

Between visits Glen could stay occupied just reading his mail. Most of it was from female admirers and groupies, former girlfriend Maria Gyore, and a girl from nearby Berea with the air of a coalminer's daughter who pretended to be a relative. She visited and wrote constantly, falsely logging in at the jail as a "step-niece."

Glen liked to write letters — it was something to do, at least — and he answered many of the hundreds of letters he received. Among them were nine letters from his mother. He did not answer any of those.

The System — reporters, police, prosecutors — called Glen Rogers a serial killer, though he had been charged with only one murder. It didn't matter. The label, once applied, stuck like a playground nickname.

The serial killer identity propelled Rogers to national prominence and gave him instant access to news media, much to the consternation of his defenders. From jail he began calling reporters collect, and they eagerly accepted. Glen showed his taste for celebrity status during his November 21 arraignment in Madison Circuit Court. The scene was straight out of the Charles Manson story, *Helter Skelter,* and its drama was not lost on Associated Press writer Charles Wolf: "Inside

Judge William Jennings' courtroom, Rogers blew a kiss to a woman in the front row of the spectator section. As he left, he gave her a clenched fist salute. The woman, who appeared to be near tears, refused to identify herself to reporters before putting on sunglasses and hurrying from the courthouse."

At first Glen bragged about his exploits, one time claiming he had killed seventy women. Later he thought better of this tactic and became a bit less cocky. He called a reporter in Hamilton to state that, "I'm not allowed to say anything about any of these women," though he did allow that, "I've traveled in bars all over the world . . . I've probably met millions of women." From then on he denied he had ever killed anyone.

The letters poured in, sometimes twenty a day, from hangers-on wanting to bask in the glow of his notoriety and women wanting a piece of his heart.

Everyone, it seemed, wanted in on the action, and Ernie Lewis used the occasion to bemoan Glen's mistreatment and this miscarriage of justice. He said his client was in "a very vulnerable state of mind" because he was kept in an isolation cell, badgered by police from Ohio who insisted on interviewing him against his will and without counsel present. He stood at Glen's door like a mother hen.

"Some of the media have been writing very personal letters to him saying we will tell your story, we will not hurt you," Lewis complained. "But anything Rogers said would, in fact, hurt him. And of course he's in a position where he doesn't know any better. I've made an effort to keep him from talking to anyone about this. He's continuing to make calls to the media. If I could stop him, I would have."

In time, though, Glen started to get knocked around like a badminton shuttlecock.

By early spring of 1996, Florida authorities were growing impatient. They didn't like it that Glen was sitting in a Kentucky jail 800 miles away. They wanted him in Tampa to face charges for the robbery and murder of Tina Marie Cribbs. The real fight was just beginning. The drama escalated on Tuesday, April 30, when Gov. Patton signed the extradition order. Its timing, however, caught Ernie Lewis by surprise, and he had little time to respond.

The order came down at 3:30 p.m., an hour and a half before closing time in Frankfort, forty-five miles from Richmond. He knew the order was coming, but not when. It appeared from nowhere, at the end of the business day. Lewis was in a bind. He had to write the appeal and get it to the Supreme Court by 5 p.m. to protect his client. Assured that nothing would happen before the court opened at 8 o'clock the next morning, Lewis sent the appeal by overnight mail.

Figuring an appeal sent by telefax would not constitute a legal filing, Lewis took the chance that mailing it would, and that the postmark would establish the legal time of appeal. What Lewis did not know was the attorney general's dramatic side deal with Tampa police:

"If you can get him before 8 a.m. tomorrow, you can have him."

23

I haven't killed anybody. And if I did, I could certainly tell you about it.

— Glen Rogers, interviewed at Post 7

BEATTYVILLE, KENTUCKY • MARCH 11, 1996

The dog's name was Bingo and he came with the dozen or so people to the Rogers family farm near Beattyville for what authorities hoped would be the second and last sweep of this land. They were looking for evidence of buried bodies and searchers would not come away disappointed. There were troops from the Kentucky Army National Guard and an FBI team. On the first day it was slow-going. Searchers walked shoulder-to-shoulder and criss-crossed the property.

The FBI team concentrated its efforts around the house. Others looked for soft areas or depressions where digging might have occurred. Bingo, the dog owned by Sergeant Fred Davidson, was given free rein. Bingo followed his nose but found nothing, and as darkness closed in, the search was terminated. But not all returned home to a hot meal and the comfort of bed. The National Guardsmen stayed behind. The search had only just begun.

The following morning, the officers returned to the site. Three men headed for the cliffs above the ramshackle house where two years before Mark Peters' remains were found scattered across the floor and into the woods. They found nothing up above. In the old homestead on a slight ridge just below the cabin, Captain Owens, Courtney and Sergeant Ray sifted through the debris and dirt. Bingo again cruised the scene, nose down and curious. Hours passed with no tangible results.

Above the crumbled old house, where only a stone chimney and caved-in roof remain of what was once a habitable hunting shanty, men moved in line, shoulder-to-shoulder. They walked slowly and used rakes to remove the top layer of foliage. After searching for more than twelve hours on two days, they finally made a discovery. Within the ruins of the debris at the lower site, an investigator found a bone shortly after 1 p.m. An hour later, four more bones were found inside the upper cabin — the one that still stood — and underneath the floor. Hours more would pass in painstaking search before investigators made a stunning discovery shortly before 5 p.m. A T-shirt was found in the debris. The front of the shirt had lettering that read "Kentucky Shows." Det. McIntosh looked under the shirt tag, and there a name was printed: Glen. As darkness fell, the search was halted and again the guardsmen set up camp for the night.

The following day, McIntosh returned and at 10 a.m. Trooper Wright took one last bone from the cabin. The search of the Rogers farm ended shortly after noon and investigators returned to Richmond with their booty: two magazines, a blanket, seven envelopes containing bone fragments, two envelopes containing hair, a box of ash and debris from a pair of fireplace pits, the T-shirt and a white pair of Nordstrom XL 18-20 boys' briefs. The Kentucky State Police Crime Laboratory would analyze the material, and a handful of men would not soon forget this campout.

It would take two months for the report to get back from the forensic laboratory examination. Barbara P.

Wheeler and Linda Winkle reviewed the trace evidence from the scene and reached a couple of conclusions. The bones were human. Emily Anne Craig, a forensic anthropologist, determined from the weathering of the bones that they most likely belonged to the same individual. DNA analysis was recommended but was never carried out.

The Nordstran briefs were blood stained but the blood was too degraded for its origin to be determined. If the briefs had been brought two years before, after the first search, the results would have assuredly been different. The most staggering finding was yet to come. Mrs. Wheeler, who studied the original bones found on the site, analyzed the fireplace pit debris. There was melted polystyrene, sections of paraffin and strands of fiberglass. But the most stunning revelation was yet to come.

Two portions of debris from two separate fire pits on the Rogers farm contained evidence of a human body. One sample of ash held a Caucasian head hair fragment. Another exhibit contained a clump of deteriorated Caucasian head hair and even more head hair fragments. The finding was dramatic because the only other body found on the scene, that of Mark Peters, was not burned but left to rot in the Kentucky sun, fodder for varmints and dogs.

The results of the fireplace pit analysis was chilling. Brother Clay was right, again. This hillside was Glen Rogers' killing field. Investigators filed a report about the finding but never followed up. The fireplace ash proved that Glen — or somebody — had killed before.

24

Anything else, Miss Cox, for Dr. Mayer? Anything for a headache? Anything further on the motion?
— Judge Allen, hearing pre-trial arguments

TAMPA • MAY 1, 1996

Around 10 p.m., two Tampa Police Department pilots fired up the PD's single-engine Cessna 210 at Tampa International Airport. Extradition orders in hand, Hillsborough County sheriff's deputy Ryan Balseiro climbed aboard, accompanied by Tampa Det. Randy Bell. Balseiro was the official emissary, the one to whom, according to protocol, Rogers would be handed over by the Commonwealth of Kentucky. Balseiro was relieved to learn that Bell would be his travelling companion. Bell was the lead detective on this case, and Balseiro, a warrants section deputy and dive-team instructor, had never heard of Glen Rogers until his sergeant asked him what plans he had for the evening. Glen might get talkative and start mumbling, telling details that would mean nothing to Balseiro.

The mission was super secret. The deal between Kentucky Governor Patton and Florida Governor Chiles was specific: Get him out of the Madison Detention Center and clear Kentucky airspace by 8 a.m. — the very hour the Kentucky Supreme Court would open and consider Ernie Lewis' extradition appeal — and you can have him. Otherwise, he stays. Balseiro didn't tell anyone of his mission, not his roommate, not his girlfriend, not his mother. "I'm busy," he told them. "I'll be gone for a day."

The little plane winged its way through the darkness, cruising below 10,000 feet at 180 knots, northbound to Lexington. There was enough fuel for a nonstop flight. The race was on.

Bleary-eyed from the all-night flight but ready for action, they landed around 4 a.m. and were greeted by the attorney general himself, Ben Chandler. Halfway down the twenty-two-mile trek to Richmond on I-75, they were picked up by high-ranking brass from the Kentucky State Police and escorted to the jailhouse. They had plenty of time according to the clock, but nothing could be left to chance. It was tension time. They had to get him out of there lest Ernie Lewis came up with some dark-of-the-night plan to throw a wrench into their machine.

At 6 a.m. they pulled Glen from his cell. Only Balseiro was allowed into the holding cell near the transfer door. He brought along a change of clothes: an orange jail jumpsuit, faded blue windbreaker, white socks and sandals, and he didn't look forward to letting Glen know he would have to get naked for a strip search. Glen had been a resident here five months, and anything could be hiding down there in his pants. Balseiro was surprised when Glen co-operated fully. Glen didn't say much, just went along with the program.

Balseiro presented his credentials and signed countless forms. Then he offered Glen some friendly advice.

"I don't know anything about this case," the 29-year-old deputy explained, an air of compassion in his voice. "But I have orders to bring you back to Florida, and I have to operate under the assumption that these charges against you are true, even if they aren't. If you try to do anything, I must act accordingly." Glen knew the drill. He knew how to get along when someone else was in charge.

It wasn't that Glen could have done much, barring blind luck. Shackled at the ankles and waist, he was no match, at 180 pounds of flab fueled by five months of high-fat, low-energy jail food, against the younger Balseiro, 225 pounds at 6-1, Marine-fit with a close-cropped haircut to match and a 9-mm revolver at his side, beefy Randy Bell his backup.

At the Lexington airport, Glen became agitated when some of the Kentucky State troopers posed for pictures next to Glen while their compatriots fired away. They knew a celebrity when they saw one. Balseiro stepped in, apologized to Glen for the gaffe and advised him to get used to it. Det. Bell, a good 250 pounds or so, shoehorned himself into the rear seat (really a luggage compartment) of the Cessna. Balseiro shackled Glen into the starboard side of the middle seat, then took his own on port, his pistol on his left side, safe from danger. As the morning sun peeked over the Appalachian foothills, the captain shoved the throttle forward, and five men with vastly different agenda lifted off, headed south to Florida. Ernie Lewis made a fateful decision and lost. Ernie Lewis had been snookered.

25

TAMPA • WINTER-SPRING 1996-1997

During months of pre-trial activity while they prepared his defense, Rogers' lawyers waged war simultaneously on two fronts: They tried to convince the court that he was mentally unfit to stand trial, and they tried to convince Glen to keep his mouth shut. They failed on both counts.

By the time he got to trial in April 1997, he wasn't Glen Rogers the charmer anymore. In news reports he was always "Accused serial killer Glen Rogers."

In a pre-trial motion, Nick Sinardi said his client had been so smeared in the press that he could not possibly get a fair trial. "The problem with Mr. Rogers is not the facts," Sinardi argued, "but the accusations that Mr. Rogers is a serial killer. We're going to be hard pressed to pick a jury of twelve or fourteen." He complained about "extra-judicial statements" and asked the judge to extend her months-long gag order to trial witnesses.

Prosecutor Karen Cox countered that the loosest lips belonged to Glen Rogers himself. "The person making the extra-judicial statements in this case is the defendant," she said. "Mr. Rogers gets on the phone constantly and promotes his agenda."

"Fine," Sinardi shot back. "Then extend the order to the defendant." He would take any help he could get.

From the defense table, uninvited, Glen decided to join the fray. "Your honor, I have not made one phone call to no news media," he said. His attorneys and the bailiffs swarmed around him to forestall further damage, but Glen wasn't finished. "Well, I haven't," he added.

It was the only time Glen spoke at the proceedings. One statement, one act of perjury. The judge ignored it.

Because of the gag order, reporters had few good sources of information. The judge wasn't talking, attorneys weren't talking, and the police were talking only reluctantly and not revealing much. They hid behind the judge's gag order that they all welcomed. It was a convenient way to keep reporters from pestering them.

Whether Glen's lawyers believed he was truly mentally ill was not the issue. Certainly they wanted to convince the judge that Glen was incapable of defending himself. And if they couldn't convince the judge, they wanted to plant enough doubt to establish grounds for appeal later on. Insanity might be his only hope for acquittal. This was just one firefight among many waged during months of pre-trail battling, and theirs was a familiar strategy: Our guy didn't do it, but if he did, he was mentally ill and therefore unfit to stand trial.

When it came time to put on this act for a jury, the phrase "serial killer" would be avoided. The lawyers would play it as if Glen was charged with only one murder, a single event in an otherwise mysterious life the jurors would learn almost nothing about. Rogers would be tried in Florida only for the murder of Tina Cribbs, and Judge Allen ruled inadmissible any mention of the other murders of which he stood accused.

It wasn't that "serial killer" lacked accuracy. Though Glen was being tried for only one murder, few other than his own mother made any serious claim that he had not killed others. When police around the country got onto Glen's trail in late 1995 they were desperate to catch him, for not one of them believed Glen would stop killing if he remained free. *They* considered him a serial killer, and they knew the definition well: one who kills and kills again and keeps on killing until caught. Whatever had sparked this spree, there was no reason to believe it would miraculously stop on its own.

Whether or not Glen was a serial killer, there was no disputing the diagnosis of psychopath. Doctors who examined him observed the psychopath's attributes: They found him to be not well educated but of average intelligence; at least when sober, he is rational and calm; insincere, without remorse and having poor judgment; unable to love, has no long-term goals, has poor insight and abuses alcohol.

For the psychopathic killer, the issue is control. The look of fear, the indescribable terror in the victim's face, that's what they're after, that's what turns them on and makes them unable to stop. It is the ultimate act of control: to take the victim's life, or spare it.

What Glen's examiners would never learn was whether murder was his primary motive or a necessary task in order to remove the witness.

Ritual often is part of the killer's *modus operandi.* An unnamed killer described this in criminologist Eric W. Hickey's- book, *Serial Murderers and Their Victims:*

". . .It always involved stripping the victim, forcing them to strip themselves, cutting them, making them believe that they were going to be set free if they co-operated, tying them down and then the real viciousness started. The victim's terror and the fact I could cause it to rise at will . . .their pain didn't register. All I could relate to was the ritual and the sounds. All this was proof to me that, I'm in control, I am playing the star role here, this person is nothing but a prop.

I'm growing and they're becoming smaller. Once both the violence and the sexual aspect were completed, then that was it. That was the end of an episode."

The evidence suggested that Rogers acted not according to a planned ritual but spontaneously, when something set him off. But investigators would never know for certain. Rogers never talked about it.

A rotten childhood and a dysfunctional family are the two ingredients that always seem to be in the background of the serial killers. Some collect souvenirs of their escapades. Glen was one of these. Though he often stole in order to raise operating cash, he held onto scads of trinkets, as evidenced by the inventory of the car he was driving when caught.

"That tells you he is fantasizing," said criminologist Terry Danner, who followed the Rogers case. "Those souvenirs are ways of triggering those fantasies. They stimulate the fantasies and allow the person to get off by reliving the fantasy."

Along with souvenirs, there were signature acts and symbolism in the Rogers saga, or at least the appearance of them; feces in the toilets where two of the victims were killed, their bodies dumped in bathtubs; large knives used in the stabbings, and similar stab wounds in three of the victims; and the occasional use of arson.

There is a psychiatric belief that arson sometimes has a deep-seated sexual meaning. Even if Rogers didn't have sex in the usual sense with all of his victims, he could have gotten sexual pleasure from the way he treated them.

Leaving feces in the toilet and dumping the bodies in the bathtub may be seen as the ultimate insult, a message that the victim is nothing but garbage not even worthy of proper disposal. With Rogers, it could mean more, though those who examined him have never said.

The feces may just be a territorial marking. “Particularly the crazies will defecate on the victim, or around the victim,” forensic psychiatrist Robert G. Kirkland said. Rogers didn’t do that, and he also did not rape the two victims (Cribbs and Price) where the feces were left.

“His sex may be shitting in your purse,” Dr. Kirkland observed.

In Courtroom 13, the only thing that mattered to Judge Diana M. Allen was the opinions of expert witnesses who testified.

Psychiatrist Michael Maher wanted to treat Rogers with drugs designed to improve his memory and thus his ability to aid in his own defense. A minor brouhaha broke out during a pre-trial hearing when the state’s psychiatrist refused to allow Glen any medications unless she examined him, and Rogers refused. Judge Allen had allowed the medication to be prescribed, and Dr. Maher said Glen would not be much help without it. The state’s psychiatrist stood firm and prevailed.

“Let me get this straight with the attorneys here,” a frustrated Judge Allen fumed on the Friday before the trial began. “I’m not going to sit up here and order any doctor to prescribe medications. I’m not a doctor. The order I entered was sent to the jail, and I can’t get it past the jailhouse door. So that’s the end of that motion. Next motion.”

Prosecutor Cox argued that Glen was indeed competent to stand trial. “The experts may say he is psychotic, but there is no question that he’s competent,” she said, and the judge agreed.

“I don’t know of any case that says we have to treat defendants until they are not psychotic before they go to trial,” Judge Allen said. “Competent, yes.” And she found him competent.

It was a chancy move, if on firm ground. Early in

the pre-trail phase, Glen's attorneys sought to have a Positron Emission Tomography, a PET scan, performed to determine if there was loss of brain function from his many head injuries. The state objected on grounds of cost, said to be $14,000 for the procedure, its interpretation, and transportation with maximum security, including lead and trail vehicles, from Tampa to Jacksonville, 194 miles away.

"Rogers," Cox argued, "is probably the most dangerous person we have in the county. It is very apparent he has a history of violence, particularly toward police. He poses a real flight risk and a real safety risk."

Judge Allen denied the motion and took the chance of an appeal on grounds of judicial error. She denied the PET scan but allowed a locally administered Magnetic Resonance Imaging scan (MRI) that could reveal brain damage but not loss of brain function. The differentiation was critical: Defense attorneys were hopeful that a recent Florida Supreme Court ruling in a Palm Bay murder case could allow Rogers to duck the death penalty.

Johnny Hoskins, convicted and sentenced to death for the rape and murder of an 80-year-old neighbor in 1992, should have been given the PET scan but was denied it. The examination would have allowed a neuropsychologist to determine the amount of purported brain damage, his attorneys have argued. The state Supreme Court did not overturn the conviction but did order the psychologist to determine if his conclusions would have been different with results of the scan. Psychotics are said to represent about ten percent of serial killers. The rest are psychopaths, antisocial types who know full well what they are doing but have no remorse, take no responsibility for their actions, and don't care about the past or future. But the defense team's only hope was to show its client was not responsible for his acts.

"He suffers from a chronic, ambulatory psychotic disturbance that appears to be. . .a byproduct of a series of brain injuries, and that it has had a significant impact on all his thinking, his perceptions and his judgment for many years," said Robert M. Berland, a psychologist who testified for the defense. "He is a chronic drug and alcohol abuser, and there is evidence of brain injury which has had an influence on him both in terms of his mental illness and his general functioning."

Dr. Berland did not use the term insane — insanity is a legal term, not a medical one — but that is what he was implying. Glen, he said, suffered from perceptual disturbance: hallucinations.

"When he's alone in a room he hears grieving. That's mostly when he's locked up — that's a greater stress for mentally ill people, so it brings out symptoms that might not be there otherwise." Dating from early childhood, "He hears music playing with no source. When he takes certain drugs he hears voices warning him of things or commanding him to do things, since at least age eight. He sees shadows moving in a semi-dark setting. When he checks, there's nothing there (even when not influenced by drugs or alcohol). He feels things crawling on his skin with nothing there, not just a tickle. He feels movement across the skin. Some of the delusions he admitted to is he believes nearby groups of people are talking about him as he walks past them. He believes he's being followed.

"He has what. . .I would call a manic disturbance. He's always extreme high energy and as he put it, going ninety miles an hour, and poor sleep patterns and trying to drink himself to sleep, and pressure to be doing something all the time, inability to sit still for as long as he can remember. Then he has episodes of intensified mania. . .where he is nearly or completely sleepless for several days in a row. These episodes began in his early twenties. They are usually two days in length. In those episodes he would drink all night and be unable to drink himself to sleep, an average of once a week over the ensuing years."

The significance of all this, Dr. Berland explained, is panoramic: These maladies affect all of his behavior. "Not to say he goes through his daily life with the voices telling him what to do. That's clearly not what we're talking about here. But his generally paranoid perceptions of other people's intentions around him, his sense of excessive vulnerability, all have an influence. His pressured interior, his manic disturbance, make him more likely to act on whatever bizarre or disturbed or even aggressive impulses that he has." Glen's problems are biological, the psychologist argued.

In his examination, Dr. Berland found seven incidents that could have contributed to Glen's brain damage. The first occurred at birth. Glen was born five weeks premature.

The placenta presented before Glen himself following a difficult labor, and he was delivered by emergency caesarean-section. "The medical records show rapid, shallow respirations at birth," Dr. Berland said. "He was placed on oxygen therapy for thirty-one hours after birth. And they noted in the medical record that old blood was passed when the membrane ruptured, suggesting that something had happened during the pregnancy over and above whatever problems he appeared to be having at the time of birth." Whether Edna Rogers suffered some kind of injury during pregnancy, she has never revealed.

Dr. Berland was not certain that Glen's troubled delivery contributed to his mental illness. He was more certain about the pool cues and tire irons that found their way to Glen's skull during bar fights.

"He was apparently in a fight in a bar, which he does not remember. He was attacked with a pool cue and was seen in the emergency room on April 27, 1991 (at age 28), with a series of significant structural injuries that were discovered in CT scans. They show right frontal and right temporal parietal contusions or hemorrhages. There's a fracture in the superior right orbit. There's a fracture in the anterior maxillary sinus. So he has fractured bones in his face, around his eyes and nose."

Glen's reward for this incident was blurred vision, severe headaches, vertigo, excessive fatigue, memory loss and changes in his mental status — a shorter fuse. Another time, he took a lug wrench to the face and came away with a concussion and broken nose. The end result of all this activity, Dr. Berland said, was paranoia. If anyone during these long months of motions and trial offered any insight — not an excuse but perhaps an explanation — of his behavior, Dr. Berland was offering it here.

"And one of the things paranoids do is perceive danger or mistreatment in things that you and I wouldn't pay attention to," he said. They launch a preemptive strike: "They are going to protect themselves before they can get hurt. And anger is the way. That's the chronic emotion that most paranoids experience. They're just angry all the time for no apparent reasonable reason."

Samantha Gallagher's mother Jan Baxter and Kathy Carroll, Linda Price's sister, had both asked the same question and neither ever got an answer: What did those women do that was so offensive to Rogers that he had to kill them? Glen never did say. Perhaps now there could be insight — not understanding, not sympathy, only insight. It would bring no joy, perhaps not even closure, but it was something.

26

I can hardly wait.

— Judge Allen, reacting to Rogers' motion to fire his attorneys and represent himself

TAMPA

Though Courtroom 13 awaited an important trial on April 28, 1997, Judge Diana M. Allen first faced the daily chore of clearing her docket.

Usually it's controlled bedlam in the felony courts of the Hillsborough County Courthouse. Each morning handcuffed defendants are paraded in for hearings and pleadings, a dozen or more in each court. Accused murderers, rapists, drug salesmen and a scattering of women and budding apprentices, line up along the wall on benches or in the jury box. Fresh-faced but harried young public defenders work their way down the line practicing law assembly-line style, furiously taking notes on yellow pads, assessing the chances of clients they've never met, quickly advising some to take a deal and be on with it. ("I can get you a year in state prison. It's probably the best you'll get.") People constantly scurry in and out of the courtroom. Across the bar, the gallery is filled with family, non-jailed defendants and their lawyers, and *everybody* is talking, while teams of prosecutors and defense counsel huddle near the bench, negotiating. The judge looked on in befuddled amusement.

The April 28 docket was short in deference to the main act, the State of Florida v. Glen Edward Rogers.

Off the back hallway in a holding cell, Rogers changed into a new business suit and white shirt (a gift from his brother Claude) and was shackled and cuffed for the twenty-foot walk to the courtroom. At 9:12 he entered through a rear door, took a seat between his lawyers and began writing on a yellow pad while the judge and lawyers went over lists of instructions and procedures.

At 9:51, fifty prospective jurors filed in through another rear door and filled the jury box and right side of the spectator section.

Judge Allen made introductions as if this were an audition for a play, which in a sense it was. This is Linda Collier, the court reporter. Here is Linda Versa, the deputy court clerk. This is Jack Laughlin, the chief bailiff. Here are Karen Cox and Lyann Goudie, the prosecutors. This is the defense team, Nick Sinardi and Robert Fraser. And this, of course, is Mr. Rogers, the defendant. All stood. Mr. Rogers, the star of this show, nodded politely.

In the galley, families of the principals quickly established their turf on the front row. It was like a wedding, defendant's family on the left, victim's on the right.

Most in the jury pool, unfamiliar with the aura of a major criminal trial, listened closely, intense and curious, as Judge Allen read the three-count indictment and reminded them this is not evidence, only an accusation: that on December 13, 1995, grand jurors determined there is reason to believe that around the fifth day of November, 1995, Glen Rogers did kill Tina Marie Cribbs in a premeditated manner, stabbed her with a deadly weapon, robbed her of her purse and its contents, car keys and jewelry "with the intent to deprive her of these items," and her automobile. And so, a few days shy of eighteen months following Tina Marie's murder, the State of Florida finally got to face off against the accused.

Attorneys on both sides played to the jury pool, careful not to insult, always respectful. Theatrical skill was a trade qualification: They had studied the seating charts during late-night strategy sessions and could address many of the prospects by name. They wanted to come across as human, not as the stereotyped characters many of these people had known only from television dramas.

Nick Sinardi knew the stage directions well. Forty-eight, a former assistant state's attorney, well over six feet with an imposing figure, polished demeanor and, dark, elegant Italian features, he commanded respect. Slowly walking over to his client's chair, he rested his hand on Glen Rogers' left shoulder and addressed the jury pool: "Does everyone understand that there is no burden on Mr. Rogers to do anything but sit here?" And then he asked them not to be swayed by the very theatrics he was performing: "Neither Miss Goudie nor Miss Cox nor Mr. Fraser nor I is on trial," he said. "Glen Rogers is on trial."

The youngest prospect was Dawn Stewart, who looked like she had come directly from her classes at high school. She wore a U.S. Marine jacket and carried a backpack. She wore glasses and parted her reddish-blond hair in the middle — a look that caught the defendant's eye. Single, employed and living with her parents, she was witnessing the inside workings of justice for the first time.

"I heard that he might be a serial killer and that jury selection was Monday," Dawn said when prosecutors asked what she knew about the case. "I heard about it on an advertisement for the news."

Anything else? Lyann Goudie asked. "No ma'am."

Did she know what "serial killer" means? "To kill more than three people." Could she set this knowledge aside when weighing the arguments? "Yes."

The day before, on Sunday, both the *St. Petersburg Times* and *Tampa Tribune* carried prominent front-page stories on the trial.

"Did you read anything Sunday?" Sinardi wondered.

"No, sir. I only read the comics."

Dawn Stewart was about to get an important lesson in American government. When the final cut came at the end of Tuesday, she would sit on this jury of twelve.

Many tried to weasel out; some succeeded; others had legitimate commitments or distracting preoccupations. "I am a teacher. I can't be away from my students that long," a woman whined. Vickie Chachere, a *Tampa Tribune* reporter, found this amusing, if pathetic. "I hope she's not a civics teacher," she whispered.

Others picked up the scent. A school secretary said she's simply indispensable. Likewise for the principal of the Jewish high school. (The jury would include two teachers, however.)

Mr. Hudson was reflective. Had he heard of this case? "Yes ma'am. I think everybody in the city had to have been (exposed). I think I could (be objective), but I'm not sure. There's been a lot of publicity."

Did he have an opinion? Yes he did. Would it affect his judgment? "I'm afraid it would. It would take a lot to overturn it."

What is that opinion, Sinardi asked. "My opinion is he is guilty." Hudson was excused for cause. Others were excused for various reasons — some had been crime victims; one man did six months for drunk driving, and his two sons were tried for manslaughter in a bar fight.

Mr. Loftus' wife was having a bone marrow transplant. Miss Cobb had plans for a family trip. One man recently had a biopsy and was concerned he might have prostate cancer. Mr. Singleton, a longshoreman, would lose income. His luck worsened; that afternoon a tornado swirled through his neighborhood, and the next morning his truck was stolen. Mr. Rose broke the tension with his plea to the court.

"I'm to be married Saturday and we have a honeymoon trip planned next week," he said.

"Where are you getting married?" Judge Allen asked.

"At the Church of God in North Tampa," Rose replied.

"You have plans to leave town after that?"

Rose, grinning, had a ready reply: "We sure do."

Excused by acclamation.

One woman was sympathetic. "The fact that the way he was apprehended — dragged to the car handcuffed. I felt sorry for the person he was. . . I'm a little bit shaken because when I walked through the door. . ."

"You recognized him?" Sinardi said.

"Yes. It was just too bad."

The perfect candidate, Sinardi knew, a bleeding heart who could hang the jury and delay Glen's appointment with Old Sparky. Justice delayed is justice denied, and Nick Sinardi's client wasn't here looking for justice — he was here looking to stay alive.

Sinardi also knew he had a better chance of getting his own law partner on the jury than this woman.

Timothy Des Marais, a first officer for Southwest Airlines, had important plans: "My only daughter is graduating from college this weekend," he explained. "I went through great sacrifice to get this three-day period, and I sure would like to enjoy this time with my family. We have friends and relations coming in from out of town."

During a break with the jury pool absent, Sinardi

objected to Goudie's use of the term "people" instead of "the state." "It's the State of Florida trying Mr. Rogers, not the people of the state of Florida," he lectured.

"It's improper, and we vehemently oppose it," added co-counsel Bob Fraser.

The sparring continued; Goudie finally gave up.

"OK, I'll cease and desist," Goudie said. "Because I don't want Mr. Fraser's vehemence."

Jury selection staggered into Tuesday. Pre-trial publicity had been extensive, and some prospects didn't like having reporters around and were especially uncomfortable with the pool cameras (one television, one newspaper). One prospect, fuzzy in his understanding of the constitutional right to public trial, asked, "Do the media have to be here?" (Where are the civics teachers when they are really needed?)

Some had an opinion about Rogers' guilt and could not weigh the evidence fairly. And still others, because of physical or mental impairments, were simply not suited for jury duty. Fearing depletion, Allen summoned twenty more prospects.

To serve, jurors must be willing to impose the death penalty if warranted, even if it conflicts with their personal views. Some weren't sure of their own feelings.

Mrs. Chin, an older black woman, had no such ambivalence. "I am extremely uncomfortable with it," she said. "I honestly say I cannot do it. I'm opposed to the death penalty." Another perfect defense juror. She and eight others of like mind were excused.

And so were most of the others.

But not Timothy Des Marais. Fifty, a former fighter pilot who commanded thirty-five fliers at McDill Air Force Base in Tampa just before his retirement, he had worn a madras sport shirt on the first day of jury selection for what he assumed would be a one-day obligation. On this second day of selection, Tuesday, he wore a tie. Duty called.

He got one last chance to duck, and he declined it.

"After hearing some of the stories in this courtroom from the other potential jurors, my story is trivial," he told the court.

"I did not want to serve," he said several weeks after the trial. "I knew it was going to last a long while. On the other hand, I felt it was my duty to serve if selected."

For nearly two days lawyers questioned the prospective jurors, individually and as a group, trying to flush out subtle biases in order to make the tricky call of who would serve their side best. Does anyone have guns at home for security? (several did). Does anyone belong to the National Rifle Association? (none did). Is anyone the relative of a crime victim? (a few were). Questioning ended at 2:58 p.m., and it was time to begin making the final picks. One by one undesirable prospects were eliminated, some by preemptory challenge, some struck for cause. Fraser challenged the prosecution's dismissal of Juror Number 37 as racist (she's black). He couldn't see the need to dismiss her, "other than a wishy-washy attitude toward the death penalty, which most of them have. We move for an inquiry."

"She had a blank stare," Goudie answered. "She said 'until proven innocent.' She said emphatically she could not support the death penalty. It's the same reason we strike Mr. Burton, who's a white male."

"This is a pretext for racial discrimination," Fraser countered, "because African-American people are known to be much less inclined to impose the death penalty."

One prospect simply didn't like jury duty. Another just didn't like lawyers. One had wondered, "If the defendant admits guilt, why should we have to feed him?" Mr. Smith said the system was too slow. Mrs. Bruce agreed. One by one the undesirable prospects were eliminated.

It had been a long day. Earlier, just before court convened at 9 a.m., Frank Taylor, Jr., a courthouse police officer, was standing outside the holding cells, and overheard this exchange between Rogers and two other inmates:

"Yo, yo, Glen, have they picked your jury yet?"

"They'll never get a jury," he called across the hall. "I'm too famous."

At 4:06 p.m., seven women, five men and two alternates were seated and sworn in. Number 47, the last picked, the one who had wrangled three days off to attend his daughter's graduation, was Lieutenant Colonel Timothy Des Marais, USAF retired. Unaware of the pivotal role he was about to play, he only knew that duty had called.

27

TAMPA • MAY 1997

Nick Sinardi had a problem with Bob Stephens and the other Kentucky State Troopers who testified at the trial. He tried to portray them as inept bumpkins, and they simply wouldn't cooperate.

It was deceiving at first. Boyish-looking Sgt. Joey Barnes, tall and lean with close-cropped hair, spiffied up in jacket and tie, smiled as he took the stand, said good morning to the judge in his aw-shucks Kentucky drawl, then nodded, still smiling, to the jury. The same with Detectives Stephens, Skip Denton and Floyd McIntosh. They were polite and friendly; they seemed eager to please. It was a long way from the hills of Kentucky to the city on historic Tampa Bay with its harbor, the lively night life in Ybor City, the big airport, the big league sports. They enjoyed the sights, enjoyed the change of scenery, the break from the routine. Only Ron Devere, the elected jailer in Richmond, where Rogers spent five months following his capture, didn't enjoy the flight. In fact he refused to fly under any circumstances and made the fourteen-hour drive alone. Sinardi wanted to make them look like bumbling fools the way they chased and captured his client. He had video tape to illustrate: officers approaching from both sides of the car, a local cop dropping his gun, and each side tugging in opposite directions trying to get Rogers out of the car. The only problem was, Glen, his hands resting on the steering wheel (He understood well the rules of engagement), was strapped in by his seat belt and couldn't move.

Sinardi hoped to show that police over-reacted and indeed had no reason even to be chasing Rogers. Under direct examination by prosecutor Karen Cox, Stephens had an answer:

"He ran several cars off the road. He ran a school bus full of kids off the road." With that, Sinardi objected, and the courtroom drama escalated.

"I object," said a clearly audible voice across the bar, and all eyes turned to the front row of the spectator section.

"I'm sorry," the woman said in a quieter voice under the piercing glare of Judge Allen. "I'm Edna Rogers, his mother."

"If you're going to remain in the courtroom you're going to stay quiet," Judge Allen barked.

"I'm sorry," Edna replied.

"You'll be removed from this courtroom and you will stay out until the end of this trial," Allen said, ignoring Edna's response. "I don't care about your apology. Do you understand it?"

When the courtroom regained its composure, Cox argued that Stephens' answer "was evidence of flight to show the extreme measures this man will take to avoid law enforcement."

Allen wondered how far Cox intended to take this argument. What's next, she asked, "somebody pushing a baby stroller across the road?"

Sinardi wouldn't leave the seat belt caper alone, so ludicrous he found it.

"You had some difficulty removing Mr. Rogers because he still had his seat belt buckled?" Sinardi asked. "You tried to pull him out of the vehicle while his seat belt was on?" Sinardi hoped to show that Rogers did not resist arrest, and in fact was stunned after having been forced to crash-land in a culvert.

"The only resistance," he continued, "was because of law enforcement's failure to unbuckle the seat belt."

Sinardi's only hope was to distract the jury by showing the chase and capture as a farcical circus act conducted by hapless buffoons.

"Once it was determined that it would be easier to remove him with the seat belt off," Sinardi said, the sarcasm diffused by his polite tone, "you were able to get him out, right?"

The state troopers weathered the snide treatment with good nature, obviously veterans of the witness stand. They must have all had the same coaching, the way they looked earnestly at the questioner, then turned slightly toward the jury to answer. When they finished, they looked back to the examiner, ready for the next question. They were pros, and the defense could not shake them. The frustration would dog Nick Sinardi till trial's end.

Theft was a staple of Rogers' modus operandi, but was theft his principal motive or just a sideline, an afterthought?

When it was time to move on, Rogers usually took something with him. Often it was operating assets: cash or jewelry, an automobile, anything of value he might pawn or use. He also liked to collect mementos of his busy life as a drifter. In police interviews, Glen had a horrible memory. He professed to not remember where he had been the day before, the name of the woman he had briefly lived with and then ripped off on his way out of town, how many victims he had racked up in his life on the road. One day he said he had killed fifty-five women. Other days it was sixty, then seventy. The next day it was zero; Glen Rogers didn't kill anyone. Perhaps the mementos, a scrapbook of the mayhem and hurt he had caused along the way, would someday refresh his memory.

When it was time to defend Rogers for the murder of Tina Cribbs, Sinardi knew there were some established, incontrovertible facts that would be pointless, even ludicrous to deny.

"Hey, my client is a thief," he told jurors. "He left in her car without her consent. It is consistent with Mr. Rogers taking Tina Marie Cribbs' car, leaving on November 6, 1995, consistent with Mr. Rogers being a thief. He comes back, can't find her. He says she's not here, I'm out of here." Translation: Give him five years for auto theft. He's served two; he'll be out in three more.

Sinardi even allowed the possibility that Glen stole Tina's purse and wallet, though he stopped short of conceding this as fact. "Glen Rogers may be a thief," he said. "Maybe he did take it. Maybe he found it in the car and threw it away."

In fact Rogers did throw the purse and wallet away, at a rest stop near Tallahassee the morning of November 6, 1995.

The purse contained a checkbook, a Florida driver's license and a Social Security card, all in the name of Tina Marie Cribbs. Rogers kept the $283 in cash from her paycheck.

He kept other items as well. On the final leg of his long journey, Glen left Bossier City on his flight to Beattyville, Kentucky. At the Fast Cash Pawn Shop in Lake City, Tennessee, he disposed of Tina's jewelry: two black-stone sapphire rings surrounded by diamonds; a mother's ring with a lattice band design and three stones; and a women's Aegean gold watch with a bracelet band and twenty-eight diamonds around the face. Glen Rogers supported himself through active trading on the street market. And, Glen's own wallet contained a paper trail that allowed investigators to construct a picture of his travels. In it they found a storehouse of identification documents, receipts and business cards, a treasure map of Rogers' dark past that stretched back several years.

There was a receipt from the Lake City pawn shop. He carried a slip of paper with Andy Sutton's name and telephone number (Rogers told Kentucky State Police he didn't remember her name), and two check-cashing cards with Glen's photo from Anykind Check Cashing Center. One was in Glen's name, the other in the name of James Peters.

An unsigned Social Security card was in the name of Rodney Maurice Whiteside Jr., brother of Linda Price's roommate. He carried business cards from: a Jackson car and boat repair business; the Jackson office of AMVETS; California Custom Painting, where he once was employed; and from Maintco Corp., a Burbank company that advertised "your property is our business." One card held the Social Security number, birth date and driver's license number of Maria Gyore, the California girlfriend who wrote to him daily during his Kentucky incarceration.

He carried his chauffeur's license from Jackson and had telephone numbers for unidentified acquaintances Jessie, Michael and Leroy and for the Sportsman Bar and Sun 'n Sand Motel Lounge. He had Billie Lee's number in Shreveport, a phone number for someone in New York state and a number for Uncle Denny in Florida. In case he got confused over his true identity, Rogers carried a tattered copy of his birth certificate, issued September 12, 1994, by the registrar of vital statistics at the Hamilton City Health Department.

Some things police never retrieved, including Linda Price's antique machete that had once belonged to her grandfather. It was taken from her apartment and was the presumed weapon in her murder. Everywhere Glen Rogers went, it seemed, something turned up missing. And in many of those places, someone turned up dead.

28

COURTROOM 13, TAMPA, MAY 1, 1997

Carolyn Wingate's body was rigid. It was impossible to keep her frail, thin hands from shaking, her body language defying her determination to look strong and under control. She took the witness stand and locked herself into a fixed stare straight ahead, careful not to glance to the right, toward the defense table. She caught only a glimpse of Rogers, but that was enough to rattle her. Carolyn Wingate was intimidated and she knew it. She could feel the heat of his piercing stare as if it were a laser beam burning a hole right through her head. This was the man who broke bread at her dinner table. This was the man who murdered her daughter. Just now she would give anything to be back home in Jackson, or anywhere but here.

She was nervous, too, because she was under court order not to talk about her daughter's murder, not show any emotion, not break down in tears at the mention of her daughter's name. Judge Allen, fearing grounds for appeal, had ruled inadmissible any evidence of crimes for which Rogers had not been convicted. Rogers had not even been charged for the killing of Linda Price. Had she blurted out anything about Linda's death, a mistrial would likely follow. Carolyn knew that. Karen Cox knew it, as did the judge, the defense table, every reporter and almost everyone in the room. The only ones who didn't know that were the jurors.

This was to be the prosecution's closer.

All Carolyn Wingate had to do was identify the black Shey watch Glen Rogers wore in that picture with his arm around her daughter. If she could put that watch on Glen Rogers the jury would have no choice but to accept that he was the one who murdered Tina Maria Cribbs. That very watch with the broken wristband was the one carelessly left behind, under her body in the bathtub in room 119 of the Tampa 8 Inn.

"No!" she blurted out when Karen Cox asked her if that was the one. Silence enveloped courtroom 13. This was not the answer Cox expected, not the one they had rehearsed.

For a moment, the defense thought it had detected a ray of hope. Reasonable doubt, that's all Glen's defenders needed. Slide through this quagmire and acquittal was no longer an absurd fantasy. But Carolyn Wingate didn't make two trips down here from Jackson to be jerked around by those who would exonerate her daughter's killer. She was stronger than that. Carolyn Wingate regained her composure, changed her mind and said yes, that is the watch Glen Rogers wore when he dated Linda Price.

Afterwards, she explained: "I don't think the watchband threw me off as much as he did because I tried not to look at him, but when I went to say yes — and those eyes. It was a fear I can't explain. It was just terrible, the feeling I had, and I knew the influence he had on these women who fell in love with him, because it was like he was taking control or something. When I wanted to say yes, I said no, because he scared me. I said no, but I knew it was the watch. No doubt in my mind, as much as I've seen it."

The press, eager for excitement, played Wingate's lapse as a major gaffe ("Watch stumbles murder case," the *St. Petersburg Times* blared the next day). Cox wasn't bothered by it.

"To the media it was the biggest thing in the world," she reflected. "You're not going to tell me Carolyn Wingate is lying. She's the sweetest thing in the world. It made good copy, but I don't think it was a big deal." Time would tell, and the time was drawing near.

On the afternoon of Tuesday, May 6, 1997, the seventh day of trial, testimony was complete. Following some motions the next morning, Karen Cox began her closing arguments at 1:22 p.m. A new mother, the wife of a fellow assistant state's attorney, Cox was making her last appearance in Hillsborough Circuit Court. Months earlier she had accepted a position as a federal prosecutor but delayed the move because she intended to finish what she had begun. She wanted this trial and this conviction.

Through round eyeglasses and a round face with sometimes disheveled hair that belied her sense of organization, she stood and faced the jury. Karen Cox was not an orator, that much was apparent. She did not speak with a voice trained to deliver deep resonance, nor did she flail around the courtroom unleashing dramatic bursts of theatrics. She stood matter-of-factly, calmly, her voice rather high and ordinary, and yet as she and her teammate Lyann Goudie had done throughout the trial, she spoke passionately but never in anger. If she was out to get somebody, it did not show. However personally committed to this particular cause she may have felt — she was deeply sympathetic towards Mary Dicke and Carolyn Wingate — she approached it as another duty not unlike those that came before, not unlike those that would come tomorrow.

Cox wasted no time getting to the point.

Tina Marie Cribbs, she told jurors, "died a horrifying, agonizing death. It wasn't enough for this man to plunge a knife eight and a half inches into her. That wasn't enough for this man. He twisted the knife. This is how she died." Pointing to the defendant, she reiterated: "This is what he did to her.

"There's no reasonable doubt that Tina Cribbs wasn't just stripped of her life. Rings were stripped from her fingers. The heart-shaped watch. Her car keys. Her wallet. And so it's a felony murder as well."

One by one, Cox moved through the points and counterpoints of the trial, attempting to pre-empt any explanations she thought Nick Sinardi would offer in his own closing arguments.

The defense had revealed that strange hair — someone else's hair — was found in the sink of room 119 of the Tampa 8 Motel, meaning that someone else, not Glen Rogers, could have killed Tina Cribbs. Reasonable doubt. She had to erase any notion of reasonable doubt.

It would not be so unusual, she said, for places like the Tampa 8 and its next-door neighbor, the Tropicana, to have leftover hair from some previous guest.

She made one reference to the Tampa 8 as "a dump." As for the strange hair, "What will it show, that the Tampa 8 and Tropicana are the hotels of choice for criminals? What does that prove? The only way you could stay there is that they are economical. We are talking about run-down places to stay. We're not talking about the Ritz Carlton or the Don Cesar."

Cox spoke for twenty minutes. She finished with a compelling statement that would be difficult for the jury to ignore and the defense to refute: "Tina Marie Cribbs was found in a locked motel room. Tina Marie Cribbs was found in a motel room that was registered to only one person, Glen Rogers. He paid for an additional night so he could have a long time to distance himself from her. The key was found on him. There is no reasonable doubt whatsoever that this here is the man that killed Tina Marie Cribbs."

And then Nick Sinardi took the stage, his task monumental at best. About all he could do was pick at technicalities, pointing out inconsistencies and faults in the prosecution's logic.

Mary Dicke, he argued, "could not testify as to whether her daughter had on any jewelry that Sunday in the Showtown Bar. No jewelry was found at any time in the possession of Glen Rogers — none, zero, zilch."

He said the prosecution failed to prove a motive. He said no witness could place Tina Cribbs and Glen Rogers at the Tampa 8 Motel together, though he acknowledged their presence there. He pointed out that Glen made no attempt to conceal his identity.

"They'd been drinking, clearly," Sinardi said. "The purpose of Ms. Cribbs and Mr. Rogers returning to the Tampa 8 was for more drinking beer and (to) have conversation. They were returning there to have sex. Let's face it."

He said the state could not prove its theory that Tina died sometime between 7:30 and 10 p.m. that Sunday night. He wanted the jury to believe that Glen left the motel in Tina's car long before she was murdered. He hammered away at his principal defense: There simply was no direct evidence to convict his client of murder. Everything was circumstantial, he argued, and it wasn't enough.

"I told you before, I'll tell you again. Glen Rogers is a thief, not a murderer," Sinardi argued. Conviction, he pleaded, would be nothing more than a rush to judgment.

Nick Sinardi faced a monumental hurdle. He had played the best hand he could with the cards he'd been dealt. A shred of doubt, that's all he needed to save his client from the death house.

In her rebuttal, Cox was curious. "If he was just a thief, why did he take such extreme measures to avoid being caught?" she asked. "Mr. Sinardi likes to paint the Kentucky State Police as Keystone Kops. Frankly, they did a fantastic job in this case."

And then Cox delivered her final line:

"I know you will know, as we all know, that Mr. Rogers is a cold-blooded killer."

The guilt phase of Glen Rogers' trial ended at 5:22 p.m.

Counsel on both sides had played every card. For Nick Sinardi, it was another accused killer he hoped to save from the electric chair, guilty or not. For Karen Cox and Lyann Goudie, it was the climax of a real-life drama that began eight months earlier in that Louisville hotel room, and soon they would know if their decision to fight for first rights was the right one.

Reputations, if not whole careers, were on the line.

Four years of college, three years of law school, the pencil-chewing ordeal of preparing for and taking the bar exam, years in the trenches honing the skill of putting away the accused or saving them from punishment. That's what these lawyers had behind them. And now it was up to twelve average citizens plucked off the street, people with no training in the law or understanding of its subtle workings and often screwy twists of logic, people with who-knows-what personal biases, to decide the fate of the guest of honor, Glen Edward Rogers.

Excused without sequester, the jury began deliberations the next morning.

The first order of business was to elect a foreman. Timothy Des Marais, the reluctant participant who had never served on a civilian jury, broke the ice with a joking comment, wondering where the foreman's manual was kept. But everyone understood this was no joking matter. There were no instructions from the bench on how to proceed, no advice on picking a leader and moving forward with deliberations. Twelve strangers were huddled in a room with instructions to decide the fate of an accused killer. No training, no experience, no feel for nuances of the law and the rules of evidence or knowing when the barristers were making profound legal arguments or just blowing smoke. They had to decide, based solely on what they had heard inside that courtroom, whether or not Glen Rogers killed Tina Marie Cribbs. They had been unable to interject, to ask questions or demand clarification or challenge ridiculous pronouncements. Des Marais, former squadron commander, leader of men, led the discussion and asked who wanted to be foreman. Nobody came forward. He didn't seek the job and when it came time to vote, he cast the only vote for someone else. All the others voted for him, and Tim Des Marais assumed command of the Glen Rogers jury. He would lead this jury to consensus. Duty had called.

Presumably, the jury acted only on words spoken inside these walls. It was put on the record that its members were ignorant of the Glen Rogers saga. Some had heard about it or made forgettable glances at newspaper articles, but jurors arrived without any known prejudice. Presumably they hadn't heard about the murders in California, Louisiana, Mississippi, Kentucky and who knows where else. Maybe they didn't recall the words of one of their own during jury selection when Dawn Stewart said the only thing she knew about Glen Rogers was that he had been called a serial killer. Nobody was supposed to hear the words "serial killer," but there was no control over a jury prospect's innocent offerings. Maybe it wouldn't become an appeal issue. But then maybe it would. They didn't know about Mark Peters and the family farm Clay Rogers described as Glen's favorite dumping ground for bodies. They didn't know Glen once met police at the door with a blowtorch and almost burned the house down. They didn't know about the bar fights, drinking binges, threats, thefts, reform school, beatings administered to girlfriends, the prison sentence. Had they known these things it is unlikely he could have gotten a fair trial. Glen Rogers was tried in Tampa for the murder of Tina Marie Cribbs and nothing more.

He wasn't tried for being a bad-ass who nearly tore apart the taxi office where he once worked, or for beating up his mother, or for breaking into houses when he was a kid, or for causing mayhem at school, or anything else on a long, long rap sheet. He wasn't tried for stabbing Linda Price and dumping her body in a bathtub. The jury didn't know anything about these events, alleged and known; it only heard evidence about the murder of Tina Marie Cribbs. It was up to them to decide if Glen Rogers committed it, stole her belongings and took her car. For all they knew, he could have been a choir boy prior to November 5, 1995. Only the events of that day mattered.

They would, it was assumed, arrive at their decision dispassionately, not swayed by Glen's tragic past, not by the brain damage inflicted when some unhappy bar patron took a pool cue to his temple, not about the other alleged murders.

Twelve jurors, who wanted nothing to do with these proceedings when called, got down to work. If we have to be here, they reasoned, we might as well do it right.

"This is the way I think we should proceed," Des Marais told his partners. "If anybody has a better idea, jump in."

The first hour was free-wheeling discussion.

"Let's just go around the room, let's talk about what you think, what are your feelings right now," Des Marais suggested. After two hours, all agreed to a secret ballot.

Five guilty, two not guilty and five not sure. There was work to do.

There was doubt, not only about murder, but about robbery as well. Defense counsel Sinardi conceded in trial "My client is a thief" when he acknowledged that Rogers took Tina Cribbs' car. That would not have been an issue had Rogers been acquit-ted of murder. But murder during the commission of another felony would qualify for the death penalty.

"One of the jurors had a real heartburn with, did he in fact commit the crime to rob her?" Des Marais said. It was a key point. Sinardi had his own case of heartburn over this during pre-trial maneuvering: She was already dead when Glen took the car. It wasn't robbery; you can't rob a dead person. Sinardi and penalty-phase defense counsel Bob Fraser faced a dilemma from which there was no escape. At the same time they were trying to win acquittal for murder, they had to anticipate conviction and try to save Rogers from the electric chair. The argument was something like a perpetual motion machine: Our client didn't kill her, but if he did, he didn't rob her because she was already dead when he took her car. To rob, you have to threaten the victim with harm if he doesn't hand over the goods. She faced no such threat.

"That's what this guy was having problems with," Des Marais said. "To me, it didn't make sense. So I was having a hard time remaining civil and logical. Because everyone else didn't have a problem with it. And we spent more than an inordinate amount of time discussing this, because he did not want to sign off on that indictment. And I go, what's your point?

"He was getting wrapped around the axle over semantics. We finally got that resolved, but he said okay, I will sign off on this but I want you to know I still have trouble with it."

The defense had got wrapped around the same axle and lost.

And still there was a holdout. One way or the other, the vote had to be 12-0. Anything else would hang the jury, create a mistrial and the process would start all over.

Overcome with tediousness, they took a break. When they returned, Des Marais tried to pull it together.

"What aren't you sure about?" he asked. One by one they went through the major points, hauling evidence out of boxes, laying stuff on the long table, reviewing testimony. As he sought consensus, Des Marais fought to maintain control. Groups of two or three conducted side discussions, going off on tangents. Two jurors were studying a document; others were discussing something else. It was beginning to have the decorum of a high school homeroom.

"What are you guys doing?" Des Marais finally asked in desperation. "We're talking about something else over here." Curiosity had driven the jury into subcommittees with no cohesion.

Six hours into deliberations and a lone female juror, one of the teachers, stood fast against conviction. Des Marais asked again, what was someone unsure about, what part of the evidence doesn't make sense?

Officially, he was not trying to convince them how to vote, though he had long since determined that Glen was guilty on all counts. Second-degree murder never came up as an option.

Des Marais made it clear that just because he was the foreman did not mean his opinion counted for any more than anyone else's. "I have one vote like the rest of you," he told them. "But I felt it incumbent to keep bringing them back to the issues when they were going off in goofball tangents."

The pilot-foreman remained focused, disciplined.

"So sometimes that was a little frustrating," he said, "because the people who were going off on tangents were the ones who weren't sure, and I think they were just groping for something to cling onto, that would justify their belief, and that's only natural, I think. So I felt it was my job to bring them back to reality and say, I think you are looking at the wrong things here when this evidence was presented that I think clearly points towards, for example, his guilt. Well slowly, two hours in the discussion, we take another ballot.

"I said does everybody feel like we're ready to go for another ballot? Yeah I think so. It was always a unanimous thing. If somebody said no, I'm not ready, okay fine. Let's take a break and we'll come back in and discuss whatever. The second ballot, again the numbers could be off one or two. It was like eight guilty, four not sure. At least we've gotten rid of the not-guilties. Okay, let's talk some more. What is it you're not sure of? So another couple of hours of discussion. Then, take another ballot. And we got down to eleven and one. One still not sure. And now it's getting to the point where, if we don't come up with a decision we're probably going to be sequestered in a hotel, because we'd already been told to bring our bags in. So we brought our clothes in, and I don't want to spend a night in a hotel. And I'm going, look sports fans, you know I spend enough time in hotels. So I said, 'not sure is not an option here. Okay, it's either guilty or not guilty."

Still, the teacher was not convinced. Des Marais kept working.

"Some of her reasoning seemed to me to be a little faulty, so I said, talk to me again about what it is you're not sure about. Her logic, faulty logic is what I guess I would say, is that A didn't lead to B and B didn't lead to C. It was like A went to D, came back around and D led to C, and, it wasn't A equals B equals C, and therefore, equals D. That was not the process that her mind was going through. So we spent another hour, I guess, discussing that and going over some more evidence, and talking about it, and everybody inputting. This isn't just me now."

In time, the teacher came around.

And then there was the uneasy matter of Carolyn Wingate's testimony. It didn't seem to fit. Finally, someone asked a simple question: Carolyn Wingate's daughter was the girlfriend. Why didn't *she* testify? The jurors looked around at each other and shrugged, but nobody said anything. They didn't need to. The answer was obvious. The watch was critical.

Des Marais sought to reassure his partners that their votes were arrived at by logic and not by pressure.

"All right now," he told them, "for all the people who originally voted not guilty or not sure, this is pretty serious. Does everyone feel beyond a reasonable doubt if you had to put your name down, sign your name to a piece of paper, convicting this guy of first-degree murder, that you can go home tonight, look in the mirror, and feel good about it?"

Quickly he scanned their faces for clues, but he knew that only a secret vote would tell the truth. And yet he was confident a consensus was close at hand.

In the end, twelve would have to agree, even if that meant swaying the eleven in favor of conviction over to the acquit side. It had happened countless times before in jury rooms. A dozen would be on the verge of a decision only to teeter at the brink, retreat, think it over some more, listen to the passionate lone argument for the other side. Gradually, reluctantly at first, they would accept the logic of one who would become a hero for justice. There was more debate and more ballots. Nothing was certain except that complete solidarity was needed: convict or acquit. Or else give up as a hung jury. For a time, opinions swelled and ebbed like the rolling sea. Eventually, all converged around a single belief, though some would leave this room today believing more in their decision than others.

When the ballots were counted, for the first time twelve had voted in unison all three counts. Six hours after they began, Des Marais took the form to the bailiff and rang the bell. The jury had its verdict.

Reporters, family, lawyers keeping vigil back in their offices, spectators — they all scrambled like fighter pilots when the courtroom buzzer blurted its double ring, signaling that a verdict had been reached. The courtroom filled instantly, tensions rising with each tick of the clock. At 5:45 Lyann Goudie approached Mary Dicke's party in the right front row and warned them: "No matter what the verdict is, there's no outburst in this courtroom. That will make the judge mad."

Nick Sinardi entered at 5:50, Judge Allen a minute or so later.

As he had for every session of this trial, Glen stood inside an entryway in back of the courtroom while bailiffs removed his shackles. He entered the courtroom and gave the customary wave of his left hand to his family. Then he looked at his mother. Edna leaned forward in her pew, gripping her hands tightly with tissue. The jury entered at 5:54.

All eyes were on the jurors' eyes, searching for clues. It is said that jurors won't look directly at a defendant they've just convicted, nor will they smile. They stood without expression, even Tim Des Marais, whose poker face did not betray the emotions he felt after working so hard to bring in a verdict. It was impossible to tell.

The crescendo everybody had anticipated for so many months was about to come down.

Judge Allen repeated Goudie's warning to all: "There will be no displays of approval or disapproval of the jury's verdict in this case. If you cannot abide by that order, I invite you to leave the courtroom now."

Deputy Clerk Linda Versa read the verdict: guilty of first-degree murder, guilty of robbery with a deadly weapon, guilty of auto theft.

In three minutes it was over.

Judge Allen excused the jury at 5:57 p.m. Then she turned to Glen Rogers, standing before her flanked by Sinardi and Fraser, and affirmed the guilty verdict. What most had suspected was now official. Glen was fingerprinted and escorted from the room.

Claude Rogers met reporters outside. He was disappointed, but he not surprised at the verdict.

"I think the jury has been under a tremendous amount of pressure," he said. "I think they tried to take their time to go over all the evidence, although it wasn't really that long a period. I'd rather see them take another day.

"But I think it was just a foregone conclusion when they were seated what the verdict was, and they were just waiting for the prosecutor maybe to point out something that would lead them in the direction of a guilty verdict. They weren't really looking for evidence, just maybe some confirmation of their own opinion.

"With all the pre-publicity and the tag of being a serial killer, when you have that much pressure on you and you hold the trial in the community where the murder took place, it's very, very hard to assume that any other verdict would be given.

"I would still hope that my brother is not guilty. The jury made its decision. It's just hard to believe that your own brother would be a serial killer."

29

TAMPA • MAY 8, 1997

It was, of course, not over, though many believed it was over the day Kentucky State Troopers pulled Glen from Tina Cribbs' car in that ditch in Waco. There remained the serious matter of punishment. And here the stakes were even higher. For if the jury were moved by the testimony about Glen's childhood, his brain damage, his alcoholism, the touching moments of his life when he brooded over his children because their mother was incapacitated by drugs, the kindness he showed Lillian Rucker, it might recommend life imprisonment without parole, and Judge Allen would have to show compelling legal reasons for ignoring a jury's recommendation. The gamble would have failed; California, waiting in the wings for its shot at Glen, would not have a death sentence as part of Glen's history to support its argument for capital punishment. There was reason for the tension in the air.

Thus began the penalty phase of the State of Florida v. Glen Edward Rogers.

First there was more testimony. For the first time jurors got to hear things about Glen, brought out in months of pre-trial hearings, that had been shielded from them in trial.

There was testimony about a conviction in California, though Los Angeles Police Detective Kevin Becker's account was thrown out when the court learned the crime was a misdemeanor and not a felony and thus inadmissible. Could this become grounds for appeal, since the jury heard about something it should not have?

On the defense side, Claude Rogers painted a pathetic picture of life on Park Avenue in Hamilton, Ohio, one he described as devoid of outward signs of affection or love.

Claude sought to show another side of Glen, that of loving father to his two children. He wanted to present Glen in a human light in contrast to the animal he had been portrayed.

"Glen mostly cared for the children," he said. "He'd be out trying to make money," while their mother contributed little, "never cooked for them, never changed their diapers. . .They were with him night and day. You'd always see the dishes stacked up."

In the fight for his brother's life, Claude was not without humor.

"They threw the dirty laundry down the cellar. When you run out you go to the thrift store and buy more," he explained. "The joke around there was, when the cellar got full, you moved."

One thing Claude could not explain away was his mother's abrupt flight from Tampa on the morning she was supposed to testify on Glen's behalf.

"Somewhere between here and Ohio," he testified. He did not pretend to know why his mother suddenly bolted. "One day she was afraid. The next day she didn't have anything to wear. The next day she didn't want to say anything to hurt Glen. I got the feeling she didn't really understand. I don't know why she isn't here."

Fraser's witnesses included the psychiatrist and psychologist who examined Glen, and a couple of character witnesses. One was Sgt. Tom Kilgour, who grew up with the Rogers kids and had known the family for about twenty-five years. As a street-level drug informant, "Glen did a pretty good job for us," Kilgour said. "We didn't have any problems with Glen when he worked for us." Another was his former cab company boss, Doug Courteny, who revealed that Glen "showed up on time and was well dressed" and produced high fares because "People liked him, liked being around him. He even worked on his days off." Courteny said Glen generated lots of "personals," taxi driver lingo for specific requests for him as their driver. Glen even drove the special education car for children and handicapped adults.

Courteny's testimony was not wholly effective. On cross-examination he acknowledged that on two occasions Glen flew into an alcohol-induced rage in the dispatcher's office, "belligerent, threatening, starting to get very violent when I got there."

When it came time to close, Karen Cox wanted jurors to remember not the tragedy of Glen Rogers' childhood but the tragedy of the loss of Tina Cribbs.

"Just as Glen Rogers is a human being," she said, "so was Tina Marie Cribbs. Just to show you the unique loss, the life this man chose to extinguish. . ." and she presented the very real, human side of the woman most in this courtroom had never met. Tina, she said, "had a very hard life, a woman who had to work for everything she had. She tried to educate herself," but badly in need of dental work, she felt constrained, perhaps embarrassed. And so, Tina Cribbs toiled away at two low-pay jobs, supporting herself and her children, "which she did with a smile on her face," and despite this rigorous life, "always had time for somebody else's problems.

"We have all lost because of the death of this responsible person," Cox continued. "Her children are split up, and one of her sons may never be the same."

And then Karen Cox talked about duty.

"The thing about duty is that it's always difficult," she said. Her voice falling to a softer, quieter pitch now, she talked about her late father, a physician and commander in the Naval Reserve whose terminal brain tumor should have kept him from serving overseas in the Gulf War but who insisted on going anyway. He had to go, he had told his daughter the prosecutor, because it was his duty. It was no unplanned coincidence that Karen Cox recounted this anecdote to this jury or that she looked directly into the eyes of jury foreman Timothy Des Marais, fighter pilot, military man, when she delivered these final lines.

"It is without any pleasure that I stand here and ask for the ultimate punishment," she concluded. "Justice can be harsh and demanding, but there is no room for compassion. May you have the courage and moral strength to do what is right."

Bob Fraser, former newspaper reporter, is an intense man who confronted the stress with an immediate reach for his cigarette pack during breaks. His only concern was his client, and accordingly he had nothing to discuss with his former colleagues. He knew he would follow a tough act. His only hope — and he had used this strategy defending other capital cases — was to show the death penalty as a barbaric response that only would prolong the slaughter.

"We're not talking about whether he is fit to walk among us," Fraser began. "You have already decided that he is not. . ."

"What the state wants to do is cook him. They want you to destroy the mind and body of one of God's creations. That's what the state wants you to be a party to."

Fraser tried to shift some of the blame to Edna. "We never got to meet the other half of the gene pool because his mother took off," he said. "Most of us have parents who love us. Cut the family out of the equation and what do you have? His mother could not be bothered to say anything good about her son. It's an instinct to protect your offspring. She doesn't have it."

He referred to a letter Clay Rogers had written long ago to Glen warning him not to admit to crimes they had committed together or to implicate Clay. "Don't talk about those 200 breaking-and-enterings," he quoted Clay. "Don't rat me out. I'm nineteen. I'm going to prison."

So, Fraser asked, "Where are the parents? Well, Dad was drunk and using Mom for a punching bag."

His words flowed evenly and had time to sink in, for Bob Fraser knew how to talk at a reporter's note-taking speed.

"He's crazy, brain damaged. Look at the medical records. He's spent half of his life getting hit in the head. I'm not surprised he's here.

"We'll never truly know what happened between this unfortunate woman and this unfortunate man in that motel room," Fraser continued. As passionate as Karen Cox before him, he implored jurors to send his client to prison for the rest of his life, a place, he reminded them, where "every other inmate is just like him. They're not all as sick as he is, but they're all criminals. It's a little version of Hell on Earth."

A sick man should not go to the electric chair, and Fraser left no doubt in anyone's mind where he stood on this issue.

"If you don't follow the law," he told jurors, "then all you are is a well-dressed, orderly lynch mob."

It was a fingernails-on-the-blackboard zinger that caused an obvious stir in the courtroom.

"The death of Ms. Cribbs is tragic, there's no doubt about that," he continued, and then he returned to those awful events of November 5, 1995 that began in the Showtown U.S.A. Lounge. "He shows up at the bar with stale beer on his breath, it's noon and he's drinking. I don't know the precise definition of alcoholism, but I think we can all agree this fits it. Sure he was kicked out of school in ninth grade for threatening a teacher or something similarly stupid. Where was Mums then? The same place she is today and yesterday. Not here."

He paused. Then Bob Fraser looked at the jurors intently and uttered what would become the very theme of the Glen Rogers story:

Nobody ever did anything about it.

The oldest of seven children, Claude was the first to escape the chaos of the Rogers household when he was drafted in 1970 and left for the relative comfort of the Army. After service, when Glen was ten, Claude settled in Southern California, interrupted by a temporary move back to Hamilton in the early 1980s. ("California is about as far from Ohio as I could get," he explained.) Remarried following the death of his first wife from cancer, he has no children, fearful, he explained, that old demons from the Rogers gene pool might surface in his own offspring.

A few days before the trial began Claude arrived from California and met his mother Edna, brother Gary and his wife, and his aunt, Lillian Rucker. He had not seen his mother for nearly eleven years.

The others would say little.

"My deepest sympathy goes out to Linda Price's relatives who are here. I did hear the Price family say they would like to see my brother put to death. It's a tragic situation." He then argued against the death penalty. The other states where Glen is suspected of murder should try him in order to bring closure to the victims' families, he explained.

"For the state of Florida to seek the death penalty in this case is immoral, unjust and unfair to those family members," he said. "My brother has had a tragic childhood. There are things about my brother that the press and the public will never know about. My family is very closed-mouthed."

And then he extended an olive branch to reporters:

"I did not mean to be rude or obnoxious. There are things I possibly could have said (during the trial) that could have been damaging."

In a quieter moment, away from the television cameras and reporters, Claude Rogers reflected on a lifetime of events that led, inevitably, he believes, to his brother's trial for murder.

"I love my brother," he said. "I'm not ashamed of who he is, but I'm not necessarily proud of what he has done, either."

Through two tedious days of jury selection, more than six days of testimony and nearly two days of deliberation, Claude Rogers stood by, the loyal brother and son, providing stability most in this family had never before experienced.

In his direct examination of Claude, Bob Fraser wasted no false praise on Edna Rogers or Claude Rogers, Sr. He talked about the instincts most parents have, instincts of protection and nurture. He said Edna Rogers did not have those instincts. He said the senior Mr. Rogers was an alcoholic who abused his wife and children, who saved his sternest discipline for those who interrupted his nap while overlooking such indiscretions as breaking and entering. The dysfunction of this family, Fraser concluded, was complete.

On the stand, Claude gave his take on his mother.

"In our family there's lip service to love and affection," he explained. "There's an outward appearance. As an example of outward appearance, my mom, by all social standards, she would have been here. Well she got here. It was a pain for her to be here. Not because of my brother, it was an inconvenience, in my opinion."

"Mr. Fraser was relating the truth," Claude said following his testimony. "In essence our family — I've got five brothers and a sister — we're geographically separated and socially and emotionally separated. We are a product of the same genes. All the individuals in my family are out for self-preservation. That is my opinion, but I think if you look at some of the things they have done, you would understand that. An example, my sister is selling stories to *Hard Copy*. My brother Clay is trying to sell stories to rag magazines. My mother afraid to get up on that stand because she didn't think she would look good. Every day there was a new reason why. People afraid that someone where they work might find out that they are related to Glen Rogers. That type of stuff."

And then Claude Rogers began talking about the growing-up years in Hamilton, Ohio.

His father, since deceased, toiled as a pump operator for Champion Paper Mills but lost his job to alcoholism after sixteen years. Forced onto welfare and out of their home, Claude Sr., Edna and the seven children moved to a house on Park Avenue, where the rent was fifty-five dollars a month, and lived there twenty years. The house, a two-story frame structure badly in need of repair, stood out as an eyesore in this otherwise fashionable west side neighborhood. Lacking even basic amenities, it escaped condemnation by local housing inspectors because they felt sorry for the family.

Just as juvenile authorities overlooked Glen's behavior, building authorities looked the other way at code violations and let the landlord avoid even basic upkeep.

"Well they kept trying to," Claude remembered, "and then my dad at the time, he's excellent with his hands — carpentry, brick laying and all of this stuff — would try, but he had no money. So he truly couldn't fix it up."

The house looked like something from a movie set, past due for an appointment with the bulldozer. It was shabby both inside and out, and had it not been for the bicycles and toys strewn about the yard, would have appeared abandoned. Its most comical trait, were it not so sad, was its posture, listing as it did a good fifteen degrees to the side. In some ways this was just another source of ridicule for the Rogers children. In other ways it was a pathetic symbol of the turmoil that churned inside those tragic walls, a household out of balance, out of control.

Sue, the only Rogers daughter among six sons, ran away from home and married at age 14. The boys pretty much set their own agendas, coming and going as they pleased. Claude Rogers Sr. kicked around picking up work where he could find it, but failed to hang on to steady employment. The family survived on public assistance.

"Glen was born in that house on Park Avenue. It was a two-story, wood-frame, gray-shingled house, two bedrooms upstairs. As you got into the house, the front living room was pretty sad. It had linoleum, the walls were all cracked. All the windows in the house were broken, and they had real thick plastic over the front of them, no air conditioning. We had one space heater in the living room. Then you went through a center room and then the kitchen, then the bathroom to the left. You went upstairs and there was a small rear bedroom and a larger, what I guess you'd have to call a master bedroom. One little space heater upstairs. As the home got worse and worse over the years, the floors rotted out. The crawl space was so low that the cross members had sagged down and eventually rotted out.

"Now the front of the house, the living room, the floor was always pretty stable there. But again, all the walls were cracked, all the windows were out. You got through the center room, it sagged a little bit more and the floors started rotting there. But it was in the kitchen and bathroom that the floors truly were rotted out. I mean everything just sat on the ground. You actually had to walk through dirt to go to the bathroom.

"When wintertime came, the two little space heaters didn't heat it very well. The bathroom itself was not heated, and it had one of those old claw-legged bathtubs. Everything always leaked there, and that probably helped rot out the floors, too. There was always ice in there. There'd be an inch of ice in the bathtub in the wintertime. You could see your breath when you walked in there, and I can remember that as far as towels to dry with, we basically had dish towels. You know how you'd have a worn-out dish towel. That was our bath towels. You'd turn the water on — you'd get it as hot as you could. Steam would be coming up out of the tub. You undressed and ran in as quick as you could because you were freezing. And then as soon as you got through you were freezing. I mean you couldn't dry off you were so cold. And you were throwing on anything you could to keep warm.

"As far as the bedrooms upstairs, everybody slept in the master bedroom. The little back bedroom, there was a bed in there. And it became a storage or junk room. So when you slept in there — no one wanted to sleep in there — but when you slept in there, you were surrounded by stuff stacked up all over. You had to crawl through a tunnel to get to the bed.

"The space heater was in the main bedroom. The other room had no heat in it. . .We had two beds in the main bedroom, and out of two beds, you had five boys to sleep in them. So there happened to be a mattress in the other room. . .And that also had two little windows, and when the guys wanted to sneak out at night, they could open that window and sneak across the roof of the kitchen and drop off and keep on going."

To qualify for welfare, Claude Sr. was required to work full time for the county. In exchange, the family got a voucher for rent and a monthly distribution of surplus government commodities.

"You had to work for your welfare. I'm not saying my father was a drunk, lazy person. He was an alcoholic, he was very mean. But he always tried to work, always. I mean that it wasn't that he hung around the house. Do not misunderstand me. But with that said, you would have to go down once a month and it began about seven o'clock in the morning. You'd stand there and start lining up. But if I recall they didn't open the doors until about eight or nine. So you would have to get there early unless you wanted to stand there all day. Literally this was a barn on the edge of town that was turned into a warehouse. What they had stored there, if I recall right, there were number ten cans of peanut butter, five-pound blocks of cheese. We had a big enough family, we qualified for two blocks of cheese. We got ten pounds of cheese to last the month.

"I think we got about a pound of butter. I think we got a ten-pound bag of rice, maybe it was five pounds. But it was a big bag of rice. Pinto beans, soup beans, whatever you want to call them. Flour and cornmeal, because I can remember my mom making the cornbread. When she made cornbread, she fried it in the skillet.

"If you didn't get there early — the line was literally wrapped around the block several times, and I don't mean just ten people in line. There were hundreds."

The process seemed to take forever.

"That's just how the system worked. . .You just stood there and waited. I'll criticize government agencies. It's real simple. They get paid whether they work fast or work slowly. It was utter contempt for the people out in line. In other words they seemed to have no respect for anybody in line. . .The trick was getting there early. You knew that if you were at the end when five o'clock came, they locked the doors. It didn't matter that everybody didn't get their food. You had to come back the next day. Whether it's wintertime, whether it's summertime, whether it's raining — they didn't cancel it because of bad weather. You stood out there. And then, standing out there, you've got all the neighbors and traffic going by, seeing who's standing in the welfare line."

It's the indignity of being on public display, he said.

"Does that make someone a killer? No. But that's part of the package of who you are.

"They didn't give you stuff to keep yourself clean. There was no shampoo, there was no soap, no laundry detergent. There was no toothbrush, no cigarettes, no nothing. And you did not have the ability to buy them, because they didn't give you money. For the rent, they gave you a voucher. What happens is, the first of the month, you've got a landlord, there's no check, it's late, (and) you couldn't even get your food or your voucher for your rent if, for some reason, they messed the time card up. If you worked four weeks during the month, you worked your forty, sometimes fifty hours a week, and one day you were legitimately sick, you'd have to go prove it, or you wouldn't get your check. They'd hold your check up for a couple of weeks. So in the meantime, you're wondering where do I eat, I can't get commodities, the guy's going to throw me out of the house. What's going on? They could have made an error on the time card because these were just guys out on the field kind of supervising, cleaning parks or buildings. Had the guy in charge marked his card incorrectly, you'd have to go down and argue and beg.

"You're screwed. It doesn't matter. And I guarantee you my father showed up for work every morning, did his job very, very well. In fact they put him in charge of stuff. They even sent him to school, drafting school.

And he aced that, got a degree, not a college degree but some sort of certificate from the courthouse.

". . .And my mom, she took in ironing for twenty-five cents a basket-load, and she would work a long time. So that was a good thing . . .It was to buy cigarettes and makeup. But we did manage to get our clothes clean."

As the family eked out its existence in the house that continued its decline into squalor, the father continued to drink and abuse Edna.

"He'd broken her nose on several occasions," Claude testified. "He would start breaking things in the house. My father had a fascination with pistols. He usually would strap on a pistol and proceed out the door and shoot up the neighborhood."

Meanwhile, Mother was in charge of discipline. Her weapon of choice was a switch or broom handle, or anything within reach.

"She would put you in a corner and dare you to make a sound. She would stand you in the corner at seven in the morning and make you stay there till five, six, seven. If you had to use the bathroom and couldn't hold it, you'd wet your pants. Then she'd take you into the bathroom and wash out your clothes and make you stand there in the corner naked."

He may not have made a connection, but in his testimony Claude noted that Glen wet the bed until the age of twelve.

Low-grade criminal behavior — what Claude called normal events — did not bring forth their mother's wrath. If the boys would break into places, "that didn't seem to draw much punishment from my parents," Claude testified. "It was overlooked." Serious punishment was saved for more serious infractions in her eyes, like disturbing their father's nap.

In the Rogers household, meals were as spotty and unpredictable as the rest of family life. Claude doesn't remember his mother as much of a cook or homemaker.

"She may have cooked something and as you passed through you ate it," he testified, listing TV dinners as frequent fare.

Fraser had put Claude on the stand as a character witness, hoping to wring some sympathy from the jury. The effort was futile, but Fraser, recognized in the Tampa Bay area as one of the best in defending against the death penalty, gave a perfectly-scripted, well-rehearsed performance.

Fraser: Was there ever any loving in your family, hugging?

Rogers: No, we never did. There was never any outside sign of affection in our family.

Fraser: Did your parents ever read to you?

Rogers: Never.

Fraser: Did you ever go to church together?

Rogers: Never.

Fraser: Did your family ever eat together at the dining room table?

Rogers: Never.

On cross-examination, Assistant State's Attorney Lyann Goudie tried to unravel the image of Claude Rogers, loving brother. She reminded the jury that Claude couldn't remember the name of one of Glen's two children or whether the child was a boy or girl.

"I can say I have never had a lot of contact with any of my family," Claude admitted.

"In the last five years prior to his arrest, you didn't have any contact with your brother, did you?" Goudie asked.

"I didn't know where my brother was, and he didn't know where I was," Claude replied.

And yet through it all, Claude tried to hold things together and make the best of a tragic, pathetic situation. He praised his brother Gary, the only other

Rogers sibling to attend the trial.

Speaking of Gary, the silent one who smiled politely and said hello but little else these two weeks, Claude said, “My brother stands by his other brother. I can’t speak for any of the other brothers.”

Like Claude, Gary was a stable family member, holding the same job in Hamilton for about eighteen years. Yet the trip to Tampa was a financial burden for him. The trip, Claude explained, was “a family project only by the fact that had it not been for contributions by others, then no one would have come. That would have been a reason not to come. Listen to what I’m saying very carefully here. It wasn’t necessarily that they couldn’t afford it. It would have been an excuse not to come.”

Outside the courtroom, Claude hedged when asked a direct question about his brother and Tina Marie Cribbs. Did Glen kill her, and did he admit it to him? “I know my brother killed her. But I am not comfortable saying whether he told me,” Claude said.

In the end, it was childless Claude Rogers who displayed the parental instincts lacking in his mother and father. When the verdict was read, Edna had left the courtroom sobbing. Claude, who could offer little evidence of a loving relationship with his mother, nonetheless bolted from the courtroom and ran interference for her, asking the press to leave her alone and direct their fire at him instead. He stood by his brother in a hopeless situation, explaining that “I would hope anybody’s brother would do that. . .It’s something that you just have to do.”

30

TAMPA • MAY 9, 1997

Tim Des Marais knew that Friday, May 9, would challenge the previous day for toughness. Glen Rogers was a convicted killer. Now it was time to recommend his punishment. A unanimous vote wasn't necessary, and that alone would relieve some of the pressure on all of them. But if he could get it, Des Marais wanted unanimity, one way or the other. He knew at least four, maybe five, opposed capital punishment. Others would fight for it.

Regardless of their personal beliefs, jurors had taken an oath to follow the law. That meant recommending death if death were appropriate.

And yet the anti-death arguments surfaced. A juror who voted guilty on the first ballot argued against on grounds that making Glen spend the rest of his days in prison would be the worse punishment. A couple of jurors were adamant, at first, against death for personal, religious or philosophic reasons.

"You've got to put aside those personal feelings about the justice system and the way people on death row are handled, and the way the appeal system works," Des Marais lectured the jury. "That is the wrong reason for voting the way you are voting."

Des Marais reminded his teammates of Judge Allen's pronouncement: The issue was not whether Rogers was mentally ill; he might very well be; the issue was whether he was competent to stand trial, and she had decreed that he was. That Glen sat there seemingly oblivious to the goings-on was not their concern. Maybe his brain damage was so advanced that he could not understand the proceedings; maybe he was smugly confident that none of this mattered because of Florida's system of endless appeals. His mental state? Grounds for appeal, maybe. But that was not for them to ponder on this day in this room. That was somebody else's problem.

They had three choices and three times in preliminary ballots they split between death, life in prison without parole, and not sure. For most, it was a gut-wrenching experience, one they did not enjoy. A vote for death would follow them the rest of their lives. Ditto for anything less.

The weight of the decision was heavy on all of them. There was a lot of crying inside that jury room.

Shortly after lunch, the dozen who sat in judgment returned with their sentencing recommendation. When the buzzer rang twice at 1:04 p.m., Courtroom 13 filled quickly. Judge Allen arrived at 1:30. In the front row, Claude Rogers took the left aisle seat, Mary Dicke the right.

Glen stood before the bench surrounded by his attorneys and by Det. Randy Bell and four bailiffs. His reaction to the verdict was the same expressionless gaze he'd had throughout the proceedings. Maybe he expected it; maybe he didn't even hear what was said, maybe it was like Claude had theorized, that it was like Glen was watching a movie, unaware that this was *him* they were talking about: The jury recommends by a vote of twelve to zero that the defendant be sentenced to death for the murder of Tina Maria Cribbs. In two minutes it was over. Judge Allen released the jury at 1:32.

Mary Dicke glared at Rogers but as usual, Glen

did not make eye contact with her. Juror Nancy Thoreaux looked toward the gallery, the first time, probably, that any in the box paid much attention to those who had witnessed the events unfold. Juror Bandy Dickerson dabbed her face with a tissue. Lyann Goudie hugged Detective Bell.

The prosecutors and the victims' families heard what they had come to hear. But there was no joy over this trial or this verdict that Glen Rogers had purposefully taken the life of another and now must suffer the consequences of his actions.

Outside the courthouse on a warm, sunny day, Mary Dicke paused briefly for the cameras and microphones. She still mourned for her lost child, and in her heart remembered the stuff of her daughter's life: growing up in New York state, the play dolls and the spring dresses, the carefree bike rides and getting ready for school, and many years later all those mornings together over coffee.

"On behalf of my child, my family and our friends," she said, "we're going to try to put together the pieces of whatever is left of our lives, and we'll go on." Then she left the Hillsborough County Courthouse for the last time and disappeared into the warm spring afternoon.

Meanwhile, bailiffs tried to sneak the jurors out through a rear door of the courthouse. Reporters and television cameras found them anyway, but most were not eager to talk. Tim Des Marais did not speak to reporters and turned down several interview requests. It was an emotional time, he explained. There was some crying. So, twelve people who had just agreed that Glen Rogers should die in the electric chair, people who had come to know each other well during the past two weeks, said their good-byes, unlikely to cross each other's paths again. They had been prevented from talking to reporters during the trial, and most saw no reason to change things now.

In her office, Karen Cox could finally let out the breath she'd been holding for ten days. She had learned never to let the highs take her too high or the lows too low. For this was just a job — a damned important one, for sure — a place to go every morning to make a living, and she never let it get in the way of her prosecutor husband and three children. Still, this was a victory, one to be savored. Winning was so much more satisfying than losing, as much as anything for the absence of that sinking feeling in the stomach that anyone who's lost a close election understands very well. She was smiling and relaxed as she reflected on her dramatic appeal to the jury, the one about duty and her terminally ill father's insistence on reporting for duty in wartime, an appeal she aimed like a laser right into the very soul of Timothy Des Marais, fighter pilot and jury foreman.

"That was a nice touch, don't you think? I thought that was pretty good," Cox said, not with smugness or arrogance, not with conceit or haughtiness. It was time to enjoy the moment, that's all. After this was all over, she would move on to the U.S. Attorney's office, where she would work at the same furious pace, getting ready for the next show. Right now, it was time for celebration, controlled and measured, but celebration nonetheless.

Her appeal to duty would bring far more scrutiny to the case than she could ever imagine.

A few weeks later when Des Marais finally agreed to an interview, he vented his feelings: "I think they saw that given the preponderance of the evidence, the aggravating circumstances of the death that they already agreed he was guilty of, and the fact that the defense didn't really put up any valid mitigating circumstances that we saw but, yeah the childhood, all this other stuff that says hey, this guy was predisposed to being just an awful person. Well, I'm sorry. Claude lived in that house. Clay lived in that house. You have to say, okay, it's a shame that this young man had a shitty childhood. But a lot of people had shitty childhoods who didn't go out and kill people."

For most of those who came here there was relief. For Glen Rogers, whose blank stare did not waver even as he heard the reading of the verdict this day, it was the last time he would wear the grey business suit with the sparkling white shirt and the black loafers his brother had bought for the occasion. Back into his orange jail jumpsuit, white socks and sandals, chained and cuffed for the six-block ride back to the Morgan Street Jail, he would return to Courtroom 13 only one more time, for sentencing.

By mid-afternoon all the players and all the observers had scattered to their respective corners, Glen to his cell, jurors to the welcome anonymity of their homes, Judge Allen to the privacy of her chambers, Claude to his motel room — where he would hole up for the weekend in order to see Glen on visiting day — the camp followers to the macabre trappings of their respective liars, Mary Dicke's supporters to the warmth and safety of the Showtown USA Lounge. It was time for the healing to begin.

Later that night Mary Dicke, refreshed and ready to celebrate a bittersweet victory, re-appeared at the Showtown to a hero's welcome.

After a night of drinking and dancing with a live country band, everyone gathered around the dance floor as Mary took the microphone. "We've won," she proclaimed. "And he'll never forget Gibtown." It was a parting shot at the man who sat across the courtroom bar during two weeks of trial and would not look at her, a man who now was on his way to death row.

On this night, Mary Dicke danced and laughed. She was among family.

"This night," wrote Barbara Boyer in the *Tampa Tribune*, "Dicke danced and laughed. Her 'family' bought her flowers and drinks. As midnight neared, she placed a yellow rose and a shot of tequila at the stool where Tina once sat with her."

As she did this, Mary Dicke remembered the lines a reporter had sung for her two nights earlier during the Showtown's karaoke session, a Beatles' song written by Paul McCartney and John Lennon and one of Tina Marie's favorites:

". . .And when the broken-hearted people
Living in the world agree
There will be an answer, Let it Be. . ."

After one delay because the defense team staged a futile eleventh-hour attempt to establish an alibi, Judge Diana M. Allen set July 11, 1997, for sentencing. It was time to settle the accounts on Glen Rogers.

They stood before the judge in a semi-circle: Detective Bell on the left, then Claude Rogers, Nick Sinardi, Glen Rogers, Robert Fraser and two bailiffs, with Chief Bailiff Jack Laughlin directly behind them in the secondary. What Allen was about to read would surprise no one:

"The Defendant, Glen Edward Rogers, was tried before this Court on April 28, 1997, through May 7, 1997. The jury found the Defendant guilty on May 7, 1997, as charged in the Indictment of Murder in the First Degree, Robbery with a Deadly Weapon, and Grand Theft Motor Vehicle. . .On May 9, 1997, the jury returned a twelve-to-zero recommendation that the Defendant be sentenced to death. . ."

First Judge Allen noted that the capital felony of

murder occurred while the defendant simultaneously robbed the victim and stole her automobile, an aggravating circumstance she said "was proved beyond a reasonable doubt."

Then she concluded that among the aggravating circumstances of his crime, the murder "was especially heinous, atrocious, or cruel: Tina Marie Cribbs died as a result of two fatal stab wounds inflicted while she was conscious. . .At some point during the attack on Ms. Cribbs, she struggled for her life evidenced by blunt impact injuries to her torso and a laceration to her left wrist indicative of a defensive wound. All this took place in the small confines of a motel bathroom with little, if any, chance to escape, where Ms. Cribbs would have been face to face with her killer and his weapon of choice, a knife with a blade at least nine and one-half inches long. Ms. Cribbs was conscious at least long enough to realize her lifeblood was flowing down the bathtub drain and that she could not escape. This aggravating circumstance was proved beyond a reasonable doubt," the judge concluded.

She next turned to the mitigating factors, beginning with Glen's diminished capacity to appreciate the effect of his actions:

She acknowledged defense testimony that Glen is psychotic, is brain damaged from trauma and suffers from the physiological disease porphyria. She noted that these conditions, along with chronic alcohol abuse "may have substantially impaired the Defendant's capacity to conform his conduct to the requirements of law." To this factor she gave "some weight."

Next, she agreed that Glen had "a childhood deprived of love, affection or moral guidance. The testimony," she said, "established that the Defendant's father was an alcoholic who physically abused the Defendant's mother in the presence of the Defendant and his siblings. The evidence further established that the Defendant was introduced to controlled substances at a young age by an older brother and that the same older brother encouraged the Defendant to participate in numerous burglaries as a child."

To this "lack of moral upbringing devoid of good family values" she gave "slight weight."

She next referred to Glen's work history, including testimony from his former boss that he was a reliable and well-liked taxi driver. And she noted that at one time he was solely responsible for the care of his two sons. To these factors she gave "slight weight."

Not leaving any appeal-grounds stone unturned, she even acknowledged that Glen was friendly in the Showtown USA when he bought rounds of drinks with "no indication that this was done with any motive other than generosity." But she gave this factor "little weight."

On the basis of these pronouncements, everybody in the courtroom knew what was coming next.

"The Court has very carefully considered and weighed the aggravating and mitigating circumstances found to exist in this case, being ever mindful that human life is at stake. The Court finds that the aggravating circumstances present in this case outweigh the mitigating circumstances present. The Court further finds that the contemporaneous conviction of a capital felony is a valid, sufficient reason to depart upward on the sentencing guidelines for the non-capital crimes."

And then, here it came:

"Accordingly, it is ordered and adjudged that the Defendant, Glen Edward Rogers, is hereby sentenced to death for the murder of Tina Marie Cribbs."

Next Judge Allen sentenced Rogers to life imprisonment for robbery with a deadly weapon, and five years for automobile theft.

"The Defendant is hereby committed to the custody of the Department of Corrections of the State of Florida for execution of these sentences as provided by law," she ordered in conclusion. "May God have mercy on your soul."

Actually, Judge Allen wasn't finished. She had more for Glen. First she gave him credit for 607 days already served in jail. Then she hit him with fines: Fifty dollars to the Crimes Compensation Trust Fund. Three dollars in court costs. Two hundred dollars to the Local Government Criminal Justice Trust Fund. Three dollars to the Teen Court programs. Three dollars to the Juvenile Assessment Center.

Glen's reaction to all this was the same he'd had throughout the long months of hearings and trial: He stood expressionless, giving no indication that he even understood what was going on. Silent Bob Fraser, who during this entire ordeal had confined his words to the courtroom, finally paused to answer reporters.

"He understands it," Fraser said, still inside the bar, holding his briefcase and eager to leave. "Whether he appreciates it is another question. He looks normal, takes notes and talks to us. But he has a deceptive appearance. When you sit down and really talk to him, you realize he doesn't think the way we think. Even as a layman, when you sit down and talk to him for an hour you realize he's different. . .You notice when he walks he kind of shuffles, like a kid. He's like a big dumb kid."

Still, Fraser explained, "He's got his emotive side. He's not catatonic."

In Bossier City as in other places where Glen brought heartache, there was predictable relief.

"My sister can finally rest in peace," Mary Shook told the *Shreveport Times*. Though there would be no trial in Louisiana — the charge would have been second-degree murder and not worth the expense in the local prosecutor's opinion — Andy Sutton's sister accepted the Florida outcome as closure. "I'll go sit beside her grave and tell her it's over. It's finally over. She can rest now, and I can say goodbye and let go. I've been waiting for this day for a long, long time."

The buzzards began circling above Glen Rogers' head even before he got back into his cell.

Not five minutes after court adjourned, Claude Rogers held a press conference on the courthouse steps to announce he was trying to put together a movie deal. He failed to mention that earlier he had berated his sister Sue for trying to sell her version of events to tabloid television. The young groupies who attended the trial said they were planning to make a film documentary because, as one loyal follower of perhaps nineteen had lectured reporters, "There's more to this story than you people realize."

A female admirer was there gathering material for her Glen Rogers web page, a report on Glen's life that was light on details and thin on accuracy. She did have a letter from Glen in which he proclaimed, after he was sent to death row, "It ain't over till the fat lady in the bathtub sings Ha Ha!" and a recipe from Glen's "Evil-Ass Cookbook" for human stew, whose ingredients are "10 fingers, deboned; 10 toes, deboned; 2 kidneys, cubed; 50 tears for flavor; 1 cup of spit for seasoning; 1/2 cup of blood, virgin; 2 teaspoons of lung mucus and 1 teaspoon of female sweat." And Clay Rogers, who sold his story to *Inside Edition,* tried his hand at writing his own book, a piece of work that Aunt Lillian Rucker, upon reading the first ten pages, described as "trash, illiterate and unreadable." Glen Rogers might be on his way to the death chamber, but friends and family were not about to let business opportunities pass them by.

At first Glen was eager to talk to reporters, calling them from jail to deny his guilt, though never offering anything new or substantive. Once his trial began, he steadfastly refused to be interviewed by the legitimate press. His attorneys and his mother were equally silent. Even when Clay got himself interviewed on *Inside Edition* to trash his family and accuse Glen of committing murder, mother Edna, Glen and his two trial attorneys had nothing to say in response.

Though he would not talk to journalists, Glen did welcome overtures from the pseudo-celebrities of television. One, a woman from ABC television, visited him on death row in Florida and infuriated Glen because she had her own agenda and wasn't interested in his. "He wanted to get it out about the injustice of his trial," Lillian Rucker explained. It never came up in the interview. "Claude set this up, and Glen thought he was getting help."

Glen was not sitting around doing nothing, however. He signed his name on index cards, offered in the *Crime and Criminals* catalogue for thirty dollars. As Paul Wilborn wrote in the *St. Petersburg Times*, "His autographs are featured alongside letters from migrant murderer Juan Corona, a 'video poster' of Florida serial killer Aileen Wuornos and original pencil drawings by death row inmate Jack Trawick." Rogers found a market for his hair, too, and smuggled out locks of it for sale to admirers.

31

HAMILTON , OHIO • PRESENT DAY

Mark Peters is buried beneath a flat bronze memorial in St. Mary's Cemetery on Pleasant Avenue. It is a simple memorial along a gravel cemetery road on the edge of town near a school. The gruesome saga of the Glen Rogers killing spree began with Peters' death and could have ended there, too, if only police in Ohio and Kentucky had acted quickly to catch this man's killer. And they could have done something. They could have done plenty.

The remains that police collected from that hillside near Beattyville ended up here in this cemetery, though Kentucky authorities waited three months to identify the remains as Peters.' There was plenty of evidence to make that determination earlier and to tie Peters' death to Rogers. But nobody acted. The interest was not there to solve this crime, to commit court and prosecutorial time and taxpayer dollars to the case. Rogers was free to roam and kill again.

The first and most telling clue that identified the man on the hillside came from the pocket of a striped shirt buried under the debris of the hillside shanty where the search party found the skeletal remains. Inside the front pocket, authorities came upon a pack of cigarettes, and inside it, unbeknownst to Mark Peters' attacker, was a calling card of sorts, a fingerprint linked to this man's last day: a stub for a drawing at a V.F.W. post in Hamilton. The $2 raffle ticket was signed "MCP" in quaking handwriting and listed Peters' phone number and address at 304 Fairview. On the back of the ticket were the bell, whistle and gong: the words "Grandfather Clock."

Detective Nugent followed the trail of that ticket from the Van Heusen shirt pocket to a friend of Peters who remembered selling him the ticket. For Nugent, that was good enough; he had found Mark Peters. The ticket bore his initials and phone number. What more could anybody want? But it was not good enough for Kentucky authorities, who still carry the case as an unsolved death.

"We didn't have enough to charge Glen," Det. Bob Stephens explained. "We were ninety-five percent sure it was Mark Peters, but the coroner's office would not identify him as Mark Peters." (Eventually the coroner did identify Peters' remains.)

Authorities didn't rely just on a lottery ticket for identification. They authorized a review, then ignored it, too. Elizabeth A. Murray, a forensic anthropologist and assistant professor of biology at the College of Mount St. Joseph, was commissioned by Kentucky to perform a case study on the remains. Police collected what the dogs left behind — canine teeth punctures were prevalent — and David Jones of the Kentucky State Medical Examiner's Office brought the remains to Dr. Murray's Ohio riverside office on January 13, 1994. She analyzed the bones for age, wear and tear, sex and race, and came to a near-immediate conclusion: a white man who was older than sixty, wore dentures, was likely in jawbone pain and arthritic. To do more, she needed X-rays. Hamilton police contacted medical authorities in Colerain Township, Ohio, where Peters sought relief for his back pain, and in February 1994, Hamilton Detective Rick Simpson shipped Peters' chest X-rays from April 1992 and January 1993.

Hamilton police did not exactly cough up the X-rays to the Kentucky State Police, however. Instead they sent the material directly to Dr. Murray, filling in Kentucky authorities only later when investigators demanded to know about the X-rays.

Hamilton police had no use for the way this investigation had been handled. Hamilton had been on the hillside from the beginning, had, in fact, led local police to the body. "Screwed-up investigation from the get-go," Nugent concluded when asked about the Beattyville crime scene. "I wasn't pleased about it but there wasn't anything I could do. They wouldn't listen to us. I mean, their examiner came and turned a box over and sat on it to go through the bones! People were walking everywhere through the scene. We went back to the car and waited." It was the worst handling of a murder scene he'd ever seen in 150 murder cases, he said.

About a month after receiving the bones, Dr. Murray issued her report. The body was Mark Peters. She compared the X-rays with several bony elements from three areas of the body: the jaw, the fifth cervical vertebra and the left clavicle or collarbone.

Citing points of bone flare, tubercles, protuberances, arthritis, crests, facets and miscellaneous indentations, she found no less than eight areas of airtight consistency between the bones and X-rays and determined that there was nothing that would cause a pathologist to believe that the remains were of anyone but Mark Peters: a white male over sixty who was five-foot-eight with gray hair about four inches long who had severe osteophytosis.

Kentucky authorities promptly ignored the report. Lee County Attorney Thomas Hall held to the position that Kentucky could not prosecute for two reasons: the inability to establish the place of Mark Peters' death, and the inability to positively identify the body.

In Ohio, Butler County's prosecutor, the late John Holcomb, chose not to prosecute. And so, the Peters report went into a file and the file drawer was closed. Once again, Rogers had slipped from the law's grasp.

Kentucky authories, also, apparently, had an eyewitness. According to investigative records, Beattyville Police Chief Danny Townsend, his wife and her sister were headed home from dinner in Richmond shortly after dark on October 18 when they came upon a woman walking along the highway near Yellow Rock Road. She was clearly distracted, perhaps a little tipsy and she seemed to gaze off into the night. While they spoke, a report came over Townsend's radio of an automobile accident and possible post-wreck skirmish out on Highway 52 near the Phillips place a few hours earlier on the evening of October 17. The woman was hurrying to get away when the chief found her and told her to get into his car. At the accident scene with Townsend out of earshot, the woman spoke to the chief's passengers.

"They killed that old man," she told them. "They killed that old man."

Because nobody was dead at the scene and no old man was missing in Lee County or anywhere else within twenty miles of this country crossroads, police ignored her comments, though the chief soon learned that she was wanted on other charges. He locked her up for the night.

When McIntosh learned about the wandering woman and her chilling backseat comments, it was months later. He learned, too, that the car was gray, the color of Mark Peters' car. But there had been no point in filling out reports at the time of the accident. Fellows drive cars into ditches all the time on a Saturday night. By late January, when McIntosh had finally caught up with the woman, her story had changed.

Blame for events in 1994 does not fall solely on

Kentucky and Ohio authorities. In Los Angeles, police repeatedly ignored pleas from James Peters to do something about the man who was impersonating him: a man he suspected was Glen Rogers. His pleas were ignored, lost in the bureaucracy of an overloaded California criminal justice system.

In September 1995, the law finally caught up with Glen Rogers. Hamilton police received a call from a Van Nuys detective. Rogers' girlfriend, Maria Gyore, became suspicious when she found James Peters' driver's license, Social Security card and other identification in Glen's wallet. She had filed an assault complaint against him at the Van Nuys police station. Rogers, already on probation for the knife assault in the apartment building, pleaded no contest. He had been sentenced to six months in jail but only served forty-two days, according to the *Los Angeles Times.* With the jail on full, Van Nuys Municipal Court Commissioner Rebecca Omens gave Rogers the usual two-day holiday for misdemeanor spousal battery and ordered him to a domestic violence course. It spared him thirty months in the L.A. County Jail.

But for a while, California had him. Did Hamilton police want to come to California to talk to Rogers? That call from Los Angeles to Hamilton triggered immediate action from Nugent and Kilgour. They found cheap lodging in California and discounted airline tickets. The trip might prove fruitless, for Rogers was a hardened criminal who knew the rules of law well. Still, they were hopeful. Perhaps it would lead to a confession. After all, Glen had been an informant numerous times for Kilgour. Perhaps he would open up this time. Nugent, too, believed the trip would have been worthwhile even though Kentucky authorities never declared the Peters case a homicide.

The detectives got a shocker: Though their bags were packed and there was more than enough reason to fly west, Hamilton Police Chief Simon Fluckiger refused to sign off on the trip. He didn't want to pay the bill. Kilgour and Nugent were beyond disappointed, particularly Kilgour, who had worked with Rogers years before when he was a drug snitch. Kilgour had another reason for disappointment. Rogers had called him two years before. Knowing he was wanted for questioning about the Peters death, Rogers seemed ready to talk.

"I told him, 'Glen, I need to talk to you,' " Kilgour said, but not over the phone. Rogers had to come down to the station. Rogers, knowing that a personal appearance might result in the sudden loss of his freedom, instead wanted to talk about hypothetical situations. Suppose, he said, that he just dropped off Peters that night and something happened. No murder. Peters just died. Kilgour was non-committal and again said they had to talk. Rogers hung up. He was gone, off again to California, a new ID in his pocket. When he resurfaced years later in a familiar way, as an arson suspect in a domestic violence case, Kilgour was ready to interview. "I knew Glen really well," Kilgour said. "I thought at the time that he would have talked to me. Who knows what he might have said? Maybe he would have told me that he pushed Peters. That he got into a fight with him. That it caused Peters to die."

Kilgour believed that while they were unlikely to get a murder confession, they might have gotten a manslaughter charge out of the trip. Nugent wanted to go simply because he wanted this guy. Years later, the decision not to pursue Rogers still haunts him. An arrest would have saved lives.

"What can they do to me? I'm ready to retire. We should have gone. We were all ready to go. If Mark Peters was the daddy of a rich man, somebody who was important, we would have gone." The trip was cancelled because the city got cheap, Nugent said, and that is one of the most troubling aspects of the whole

Rogers case. “If you can’t pay the freight, then you oughta get out of the business,” he said four years later. “You never know what you’re going to get unless you go there and find out.”

Hamilton City Manager Hal Shepherd said he was not consulted about whether the city was willing to finance the trip. Had he been asked, what would have been his response? Shepherd would not comment directly. He did, however, point out that when he was an assistant city manager and the city was seeking information about a toxic dump called Chem-Dyne, an EPA Superfund waste site, he authorized trips to San Diego by two detectives. “And that wasn’t a murder case,” he said.

Fluckiger, who has since retired, never would talk in detail about the decision to walk away when Rogers was in custody. “Why didn’t Beattyville go?” he said when asked about the decision to scuttle the trip. “Where was the body (found)? I really don’t have anything to say about it.”

Ohio was not alone in sitting on the Peters case — Kentucky played the same game but in the end decided not to fly west for an eye-to-eye interview. “We talked about it,” Det. Stephens said. “At that point it was (Ohio’s) call as to whether they should go out to California to interview Glen Rogers. The body had been turned over to them, the curtain, all the evidence.”

Yet the remains were found in Kentucky, making it Kentucky’s case to solve, whether the murder was committed there or elsewhere. Tom Smith, the commonwealth’s attorney who would have prosecuted Rogers had he been tried for his flight to avoid prosecution, said it was unfair to say Kentucky botched the Mark Peters case. “The general theory of investigation is that you don’t approach a suspect until you have all the facts in hand, so you know how to question him,” he said.

Not long after the discovery of Peters' remains on the hillside Bob Smith, publisher and editor of the *Three Forks Tradition*, had a telling lunch with Tom Smith and Det. McIntosh. McIntosh, Smith said, "kind of made it known he wasn't real happy with the press, I guess because we called it a murder. He said they have never ruled it a murder, and they still haven't to this day. I said, 'Floyd, they found his bones strapped to a chair. If this wasn't a murder, then it was the damnedest case of suicide I've ever seen."

All this time, Rogers must have been amazed at his luck, his wild-eyed ability to sneer at the system with astonishing frequency. Had authorities issued an arrest warrant in 1994, there would have been plenty of chances to nab him. FBI records indicate that Rogers was stopped in routine patrol checks in Kentucky in January, February and March of 1994. Because Rogers was not wanted he was allowed to go free. He apparently returned to the farm on November 9, 1994, a Monday morning, when a state trooper pulled him over, then again let him go. It was about the time that Carol Branham, a red-headed woman who ran with a biker crowd, disappeared from her home in nearby Winchester and has never been found. (Rogers has never been linked to her disappearance.)

Rogers was in many ways a creature of the criminal justice system. He was a paid drug informant, one of the best in Southwest Ohio. He learned the ways of law from the lawmen themselves. Today they say they wanted justice to be served. But they were handcuffed. Nobody in the local prosecutor's office wanted anything to do with the Peters case.

"I know the family. They are real good people. I really wanted this one," Kilgour said. Kilgour knows Rogers better than most. He received another telephone call from Glen only weeks before he was captured. Unlike most detectives, Kilgour lists his home telephone number in the directory, and Glen rang him up at home. Kilgour again told him that they had to talk in person, not over the phone. Glen said he was coming back to Hamilton and that he would look up Kilgour when he returned. It was as close to a confession as Glen would come. It would also be the last time they talked. “The only thing I can figure is something snapped,” Kilgour said.

His former partner, Nugent, moved on to other homicides, other crimes and is now retired. He does not care about labels. Serial killer? Spree killer? Nugent has his own ideas: “I just think he was a mean son-of-a-bitch.”

Joan Burkart will never forgive authorities for what she sees as substantial and repeated lapses. Had Hamilton police gone west they might have interviewed Rogers and charged him. Had L.A. police moved on the Peters ID complaint, Rogers might have been locked up. Had California judges created jail space for a knife-wielding wife beater, Rogers would never have been able to ramble and nobody would have been hurt on his last coast-to-coast rampage. Had anybody done anything about Rogers, incalculable tragedy would never have visited four — and perhaps more — families. “People say you can’t predict the future,” Burkart said, “and that may be true. But by not going to California when they had a chance, didn’t they create a future? If they’d have gone, those women would be alive today.”

32

HAMILTON, OHIO • PRESENT DAY

Months later, long after the courtroom drama was over and the appeals had begun to wind through Florida courts, a middle-aged man stood on the side porch of his house and remembered what he could of Mark Peters. What first came to mind was a simple red wagon, the wagon the man's daughter once had, now long gone, given away to another child, another family grateful for a hand-me-down. Mark Peters had found the old Radio Flyer at a flea market and thought of the curious girl across the way. He took it home and fixed it up. All it needed was a coat of paint and a little work, nothing that Peters couldn't handle. Micaela Bailey used it for a time, too, to drag her dolls and toys past Peters' corner house on the sidewalks of Lindenwald in a clatter of hope and youth. Neighbor Dennis Bailey remembered that wagon four years to the day after Peters' disappearance, and when his thoughts turned back to that summer, that sinister season when malice came to call, the Mark Peters he fondly remembers is the "crazy old guy," a tag spoken with a nod of endearment to a town putterer. On this day, fall brings a chill to the porch steps and chases summer into memory. Peters, too, is back in time and the wagon thought of less and less. Streets change, people change, the times change.

And Bailey, too, remembered Glen Rogers, the

strange guy who came to live in the Peters household, an unnerving man who wore t-shirts and blue jeans and seemed to lurk about the neighborhood during his time there. Glen was a forgettable fellow except for that aura about him. Bailey right away pegged him as somebody who sponged, who spent his nights in bars and his days asleep, just another young ex-con with a bad attitude and something grim about him.

"Anybody about my age, living off other people, well, he was the leech type," Bailey said. Bailey, too, has his own thoughts on that last bloody road dog run. Rogers, he said, was as dangerous as a man could be. "It was like Rogers wasn't afraid of death and when you have a person who's not afraid, it's hard to tell what that person will do. They're out of control. They're on their own. They're unpredictable because there's no fear.

"You can get a long way with no fear," he said. "Police are trained to know fear but if a person has no fear, the cop, he won't see it. And that's, I guess, what makes them dangerous. People with no fear — you never know about them."

Relief came finally to those with roles in this tragic drama, but it was not a satisfying feeling. They knew it wasn't over. In fact they knew that many miles lay ahead on the long road to justice. There would be appeals, perhaps a reversal of the conviction, more trials in other cities and more plane tickets and more hotel rooms, more anguish and more waiting.

Michael Hunter, awaiting execution in California's gas chamber, speaks of this in his tome *"Living on Death Row":*

The process of appealing a death verdict "has been much more like a lazy baseball season. Lots of games are played, many of them go into extra innings, and even if you lose a game, no one panics, no one dies, you move on and play another game in a new park before new umpires/judges and the season loafs on and on and on."

Nobody knows how may serial killers run free in America. Former FBI profiler and author John E. Douglas estimates that between thirty-five and fifty serial killers leave several hundred dead people in their wake each year.

For those touched by Glen Rogers, the saga will never end. If he's not out there somewhere, in a prison cell, reading mail from female admirers, ever smirking at his morbid celebrity, then the memory of him will always be present, right next to the beloved pictures of the departed on all those family room walls: a road dog of death who one day came to call and took away something precious, someone who can never be replaced, someone who will never be forgotten.

- end -

Epilogue

Although the Florida trial had concluded, Rogers was not finished with the U.S. criminal justice system. In the summer of 1999, he was extradited to California to face capital murder charges for killing Sandra Gallagher four years before. During the trial, his defense attorney attempted to prove that Istvan Kele was the killer. After all, Kele already had one murder under his belt. In 1972, he was convicted of pumping six shots into the head of an elderly security guard during a bank robbery. At the time of Gallagher's murder, he was allegedly working with Rogers in a bad check scam.

The California jury was unmoved — despite hearing testimony from Rogers' mother about his brutal childhood and father and even from Rogers himself, who took the stand in his own defense to say that he had no idea how Gallagher died but that he had nothing to do with it. Rogers told the jury that after he returned from the Van Nuys bar with Gallagher, he passed out and when he woke up, Gallagher was gone. That's all he knew, said the now-trim and polite defendant. The jury would have none of it and found Rogers guilty of second degree murder and recommended that Rogers be put to death. Judge Jacqueline Conner upheld the verdict two weeks later.

Though now facing two murder convictions, Rogers still had hope. His appeal of the Florida case that spring picked up momentum when the Florida Supreme Court decided that prosecutors cannot talk to juries about duty. The high court had reversed a conviction and ordered a new trial in the case of Walter Ruiz, a murderer who was hired to kill Rolando Landrian, a Tampa grocer. During the penalty phase Prosecutor Karen Cox should not have told the jury about her father, the court found. She should not have spoken of his fatal fight with cancer and his decision to serve his country in the Desert Storm war despite his illness, a decision that took him away from his family in his last days, a decision he made because he believed in duty. The high court determined that Cox's comments were "egregious and inexcusable."

Cox had used the same argument with success in the guilt phase of Rogers' trial. The Ruiz case created a modest furor among the pundits. *South Florida Sun Sentinel* editorial writers lamented prosecutors who "stoop to misconduct" to get convictions. Cox no longer had a professional stake in the finding. She had left the state criminal justice system long before the editorial was penned to become an assistant U.S. attorney in Tampa.

Despite the two murder convictions pending against her client, Rogers' new Florida public defender, the sixth public defender in three years assigned to protect Roger's rights, vowed to use the Ruiz decision to overturn her client's death sentence.

The Ruiz decree became a moot point in June 2002 when the U.S. Supreme Court ruled by a vote of 7-2 that death sentence procedures in a number of states, including Florida, may violate a defendant's Sixth Amendment right. The court found that responsibility for the ultimate punishment should not be shared between a judge and jury. Attorneys for Miami killer Linroy Bottoson took cheer in the ruling and insisted that because Florida juries can only recommend the death sentence — a recommendation that can also be over-turned by the presiding judge — the Florida criminal justice system was fatally flawed. As the legal debate played out on the national stage, many Florida death row inmates received a reprieve of sorts. Experts estimated that cases involving 800 inmates in nine states were affected by the high court finding.

On October 24, 2002, the Florida Supreme Court upheld the state's death penalty. At the time of this printing the issue awaits likely review by the U.S. Supreme Court.

By mid-2002, Florida housed 371 inmates on death row. A killer from Ohio named Glen Rogers was one of them.

Timeline

1962

July 15 - Glen Rogers is born in Hamilton, Ohio

1988

Jan. 19 - Rogers begins serving his first adult prison sentence.

1993

Oct. 17 - Mark Peters is last seen alive.

1994

Jan. 10 - Peters' remains are found at the Rogers family cabin.

1995

Sept. 29 - Sandra Gallagher is murdered in Van Nuys, Cal.

Oct. 2 - Rogers arrives in Jackson, Miss.

Oct. 6 - Linda Price meets Rogers, and they move in together.

Nov. 3 - Price's body is discovered in her apartment.
Rogers meets Andy sutton in a Bossier City bar, says he will return after a quick trip to Florida.

Nov. 4 - Rogers arrives in Tampa via bus from Louisiana.

Nov. 5 - Tina Marie Cribbs is murdered in Tampa.

Nov. 7 - Rogers returns to Bossier City. Tina Cribbs's body is discovered in a Tampa motel room.

Nov. 8 - Andy Jiles Sutton is murdered at her home in Bossier City.

Nov. 9 - Rogers flees Bossier City, heads for Kentucky.

Nov. 12 - Rogers arrives in Beattyville, Ky.

Nov. 13 - Rogers flees Beattyville and is captured near Richmond.

Nov. 21 - Rogers is arraigned on charges of wanton endangerment of a police officer and criminal mischief.

1996

April 30 - Gov. Patton signs extradition order.

May 1 - Tampa police grab Rogers from the Richmond jail and take him to Florida.

1997

April 28 - Jury selection begins in Hillsborough Circuit Court.

May 1 - Carolyn Wingate identifies the Shey watch.

May 7 - Jury finds Rogers guilty of murder, auto theft and armed robbery.

May 9 - Jury recommends death sentence

July 11 - Judge Allen sentences Rogers to death.

1999

June 22 - Rogers is convicted of murdering Sandra Gallagher, Los Angeles Superior Court

July 16 - Rogers is sentenced to death, Los Angeles Superior Court.

Where they are today

Diana S. Allen, Florida Trial Judge - Died of natural causes, July 2000.

Joey Barnes, KSP - Administrative Sergeant, Post 7.

Randy Bell, Tampa PD - Killed in line of duty, May 8, 1998.

Skip Benton, KSP - Retired Oct. 31, 1998.

Ricky Childers, Tampa PD - Killed in line of duty, May 8, 1998.

Mike Coblentz - Supervisor of Detectives, LAPD. Headed the investigation that led to Rogers' conviction and death sentence in California

Karen Cox - Assistant U.S. Attorney for Southern District of Fla., Tampa.

Lea Purwin D'Agostino - Deputy District Attorney, Los Angeles County. Was unsuccessful candidate for City Attorney.

Timothy Des Marais - Retired from flying on medical disability but still employed by Southwest Airlines.

Simon Fluckiger, Hamilton PD chief - Retired June 1998. Now works for the Butler County prosecutor.

Lyann Goudie - Attorney with Cohen, Jayson & Foster in Tampa.

John Holcomb, Butler County Prosecutor. Died of natural causes, July 2000.

Thomas Kilgour, Hamilton PD public information officer.

Charles E. Lee, Jr., Jackson PD - Promoted to sergeant, Internal Affairs.

Floyd McIntosh, KSP - Retired Sept. 1, 1997.

George McNamara, Tampa PD - Promoted to captain, March 3, 2002.

James Nugent, Hamilton PD - Retired Dec. 16, 2000. Now an investigator for the Butler County prosecutor.

Glen Edward Rogers - On Death Row at Florida State Prison, Starke.

Robert Stephens, KSP - Retired July 31, 2002.

Carolyn Wingate - A former widow, now Carolyn Evans, she is married and living in Richland, Miss.

Additional Notes

Photo credits: Back cover photo of Stephen Combs by Doug Seibert, Esquire Photographers. Photo of John Eckberg by Dick Swaim.

The authors wish to thank the following individuals for their contributions of expert background information: Special Agent John Evans, (retired); Deputy Chief Jimmy Houston, Jackson P.D.; Robert G. Kirkland, M.D., Mary Randall, R.N., and Donald R. Reed, M.D.

Endnotes

Some quotes from pages 55-56 in chapter 8 were first published by *Cosmopolitan* Magazine.

In Chapter 17, the source of some of the history of Beattyville is *Kentucky: Land of Contrasts,* by Thomas D. Clark.

Judge Allen's quotation on page 186 was reported by Sue Carlton in the *St. Petersburg Times,* July 9, 1996.